THE LEAVE-TAKERS

FLYOVER FICTION

Series editor: Ron Hansen

THE LEAVE-TAKERS

A NOVEL

Steven Wingate

University of Nebraska Press
Lincoln

FX : 04-21

Epigraph is from "Because Everybody Looked So Friendly I Ran"
by Kenneth Patchen, in *We Meet*, © 1946 by Kenneth Patchen.
Reprinted by permission of New Directions Publishing Corp.

An earlier version of chapter 1 was published in
Salamander 18, no. 2 (Summer 2013).

Library of Congress Cataloging-in-Publication Data
Names: Wingate, Steven, author. | Hansen, Ron, 1947–, editor.
Title: The leave-takers: a novel / Steven
Wingate; series editor, Ron Hansen.
Description: Lincoln: University of Nebraska
Press, [2021] | Series: Flyover fiction
Identifiers: LCCN 2020029267
ISBN 9781496225023 (paperback)
ISBN 9781496226433 (epub)
ISBN 9781496226440 (mobi)
ISBN 9781496226457 (pdf)
Subjects: GSAFD: Love stories.
Classification: LCC PS3623.I6623 L43 2021 | DDC 813/.6—dc23
LC record available at https://lccn.loc.gov/2020029267

Set in Whitman by Laura Buis.
Designed by N. Putens.

Oh, the kind of angel I'm on the side of

Won't ever try to hide from the terrible responsibilities of love!

—Kenneth Patchen, "Because Everybody Looked So Friendly I Ran"

ACKNOWLEDGMENTS

Thanks to the artists who've mentored me, especially Stan Brakhage, Robert Olen Butler, Ken Jacobs, Steve Katz, Elizabeth Kostova, Margot Livesey, and Phil Solomon.

Thanks to those who've supported me with their friendship, even from afar, especially Ernesto Acevedo-Muñoz, JoAnn Borys, Evan and Robin Cantor, Jeremiah Chamberlin, Neil Connelly, Patrick Hicks, Adrian Koesters, Robert Garner McBrearty, Christine Stewart, Jörg and Andrea Waltje, Don and Evelyne Yannacito, and Rolf Yngve.

Thanks to Jonis Agee, Chip Cheek, Kent Meyers, Paula Saunders, and Robert Vivian for their support of this novel.

Thanks to the University of Nebraska Press for helping the world meet this book, especially Laura Buis, Elizabeth Gratch, Courtney Ochsner, N. Putens, Rosemary Sekora, Sara Springsteen, and Anna Weir.

Thanks to South Dakota State University, especially the English Department, for the home it has given me on the Great Plains.

Thanks to Irving M. Weinberg, my seventh grade music teacher, who taught me that it's better to practice fifteen minutes a day than to practice three hours on a Saturday afternoon.

Thanks to Rick Haugen, Lisa Myhre, Casey DeJesus, and Jordan Eaton at Bronze Age Art Casting in Sioux Falls for the wax, the clay, the iron, the bronze, and to Tuck Langland, whose book *From Clay to Bronze* made me want to make things with my hands.

Acknowledgments

Thanks to Susan Davis Warren for the maamoul.

Thanks to Karol and Agnes, even through the hard times.

Thanks to my family, especially my brother Tom, my wife Jennifer, and our miracle babies Lucas and Landon, without whom life would feel empty.

THE LEAVE-TAKERS

PART 1

Citizens of the Lost and Found

1

Cherry-Red Fender

For a truck pushing fifty, it ran damn fine. A 1971 Dodge Power Wagon crew cab—Camper Special, 383 V-8—painted a custom purple with chrome wheels and a steel front bumper ready to ram anything that pissed it off. Inside, a swirly amber ball embossed with a map of Earth sat atop the gearshift. From the rearview mirror hung a rabbit's foot dyed lime green, and on the crew bench in back sat a man with greasy dark-blond hair down to his bare nipples and a waxy face that hadn't felt the sun in months. A drunk, you might think at first glance. A junkie, if you knew better. He stared at the open hood before him, feeling the engine rumble. The truck sat idling at Kroeplinaq Truck Plaza outside Blunt, South Dakota, where US 83 merges with US 14 until Pierre, and outside the window big tufts of snow that looked lost from their mother storm floated through a streak of sunlight.

Beneath the hood another man—taller and sharper in the face, his light chestnut hair in a frayed ponytail—set his elbows down near the radiator and cried in the biting December wind instead of checking the transmission fluid like he was pretending to do. It was the song, the damn song, making him remember the hole inside himself he could never fill. He let the sobbing last its allotted minute and slammed the hood shut without bothering to dry his eyes. Then he opened the driver's side door, threw off his tan canvas Carhartt coat, and tried to stare the other man down.

"You still dead?" he asked.

"What do *you* think?" said the man on the crew bench, his voice thick with the sharp vowels of Boston. He stuck his tongue out, pretended to choke, then lolled his head sideways. "That song freak you out, poor baby?"

"Yeah, it was the song."

The figment in back was Daniel Nassedrine, who had died one year ago that night—the twelfth of December—from a heroin overdose in Hot Springs, South Dakota. The man staring at him, Jacob Nassedrine, was Daniel's elder brother by two years and refused to forgive himself for a moment living longer. Jacob cranked the heat and the stereo, vowing to get through the song this time. It was the Allman Brothers' "Ain't Wastin' Time No More," which the Nassedrine boys had played together on their last shared night on Earth. Merging onto 14, Jacob looked in the rearview mirror and caught Daniel playing air guitar, leaning over the neck and closing his left eye tight for the high notes.

"You dumbass," he told Daniel when the song ended. "Why'd you pick December 12 to off yourself, of all the fucking days? Just to jerk my chain?"

"Save the lectures for when you die, Big Bro. Unless you think you never will."

"I'll die, Runt. Just not by my own damn hand."

"You're sure about that?"

"Yeah. Now fuck off and let me drive."

* * *

Their visit a year ago had started better than the previous one. Daniel didn't cancel halfway through Jacob's five-hour cross-state drive to their rendezvous point at the Evans Plunge in Hot Springs. He'd been coherent on the phone that morning and even told a joke about a hen and a box of matches that Jacob desperately wished to remember.

It didn't seem like a suicidal day for Daniel. Jacob had nursed him through a few of those and thought he could smell them coming.

"Saved your spot," Daniel had said as he watched his brother approach, and he patted the water beside him. Jacob stepped into the lukewarm pool at two in the afternoon and took his customary spot on the wall opposite the lifeguard. The water was only 87°, nothing like a hot spring at all, but if you stayed in it long enough, your muscles eventually let go. They hugged, which turned into an arm wrestling match that Jacob (as usual) won, then raced to see who could get farthest across the swimming pool in a single breath. Then they took turns swinging on the rings that ran across the width of the pool, counting each one off until they dropped into the water. Daniel managed to get across twice and lost his grip on the next ring, which meant that he (as usual) won.

They'd played those games since their first time at Evans Plunge eighteen years ago, on the day their great uncle Ed brought them out to Hot Springs the weekend after they arrived from Boston. They were freshly orphaned then, placeless in the world, and uncle Ed wanted to show them some fun. Evans Plunge remained their designated place of fun, their refuge from the world's evil forces, and they didn't see any reason not to keep playing those games as grown men. When their bodies wore out, their mouths spoke, as they always did on December 12, of the event that turned them into orphans and gave the date its somber weight. This was their first Deathiversary Day without Uncle Ed and Aunt Paula—their first truly rudderless one.

"Remember Mom made us those sandwiches?" Daniel asked. He floated on his back, his wild beard almost as wide as his shoulders. "With extra meat 'cause she didn't think Dad was showing up for supper?"

"Yeah," Jacob said. He floated beside his brother, his hair surrounding his skull like a mane. "Turkey, wasn't it?"

"Nah, it was darker than that. Roast beef."

By the time Jacob agreed it was roast beef, they were deep inside December 12 and its imperfect memories. Mom jumped every time the phone rang and slumped her shoulders when it wasn't Dad on the line. Who made the very last call she picked up? A cop? Jacob had been fourteen, old enough to guess. Daniel was twelve, just a kid who wanted to hug his daddy and know he was safe.

After supper Mom sent them down the street to the Mancini house for a sleepover, armed with twenty bucks for Mrs. Mancini's trouble. They played video games with her sons, Vince and Johnny, and fell asleep on a fold-out couch in the basement listening to a hockey game on the radio. Sometime that night Michael Paul Nassedrine (aka Paulie) had come home and engaged in an altercation over money and another woman with his wife, Grace, who stabbed him with an eight-inch kitchen knife. Paulie disarmed her, strangled her to death, then attempted to hang himself on the back porch of their third-floor apartment.

When this failed, Paulie got into his 1978 AMC Pacer carrying the rope he'd tried to hang himself with. He drove up Dorchester Avenue to Columbia Road and skirted the edge of Boston Harbor, at some point stopping long enough to tie his wrists to the steering wheel with eleven knots. He gathered speed and crashed his Pacer through a previously weakened guardrail and into the water. He'd untied three of those eleven knots, said the police report that Jacob saw a decade after the fact, by the time he drowned. The stab wounds on his arms and belly, if left unattended, would eventually have killed him on their own.

So, December 12 was a hard day for the Nassedrine boys. A day of wariness, of checking in with each other to make sure they weren't going down the same road as Paulie. Or, if they felt like they were, to try pulling each other off it.

"What's easier for you to think about?" Daniel had asked on his last living day. "Him strangling her or him trying to dig those knots loose in the water?"

"How the hell am I supposed to answer that? Neither."

"If you were gonna die and you could know the truth about only one of them, which would it be? I mean *your* hands knowing how *his* hands felt."

Jacob stared at the water and then at his own hands, which he felt sure would never hurt a woman.

"Take your time, Jakey," Daniel told him. "I got all night."

* * *

When the Nassedrine boys had enough of the water, they climbed down the banks of Fall River and followed it to a clump of trees beneath the WELCOME HISTORIC HOT SPRINGS sign and the businesses on River Street. There they got stoned with Daniel's first pot pipe: flat, thumb-sized, made of stone, and kept for convenience in his right boot. Those newfangled vape pens, Daniel believed, were for loser pussies ashamed of their habit. Jacob, though he'd smoked his share of pot and done more than his share of prescription pharmaceuticals, was in Daniel's eyes a lightweight. But on Deathiversary Day, Jacob let himself get righteously stoned. They smoked three bowls of high-grade stuff that Daniel's landlord had snuck in from Colorado, watching the river and feeling the sun set behind them over Hot Brook Canyon.

"Hey, Saint," Daniel said, tapping out his pipe and sticking it back in his boot. He shivered and pulled up the collar of his ratty Carhartt coat, a hand-me-down from Jacob. "Thanks for not being a saint tonight."

"Sainthood's overrated," Jacob said, pulling up his own collar. It was 35°, downright balmy for December in South Dakota, but the temperature would plummet with the sun. Jacob got so stoned that if he closed his eyes too long, his chest felt like millions of tiny fish trying to bust through an aquarium wall. He tried not to blink and stared at Fall River trickling by. A tiny river, barely deserving of the name even when the spring thaw came, and now only a trickle that would soon freeze over.

"How are you doing?" Jacob asked. "The big picture, I mean."

"Oh, geez." Daniel rolled his eyes. "It's that time already? When Big Bro acts like *I'm* the only one in trouble? How's life back at the house?"

"Fine." The house, across the state outside Clark, was a sticking point for them. Ed and Rhonda had no kids of their own, and when they died the previous February—she first, he two weeks later—Jacob and Daniel jointly inherited the house. Jacob had already been living there six months, hanging around as they finished dying, and he cajoled Daniel into moving in once they were gone. That had been a disaster, mostly because of the heroin, and Daniel had gone back to Hot Springs after six weeks. He'd hedged his bets and hadn't even given up his apartment.

"Find some woman to trick into moving in with you yet?" asked Daniel.

"I don't want to talk about the house." There had been a woman, but she worked out about as well as Daniel. Soon the sun was gone, and the pot made their saliva feel thick, so they followed the river around its bend and climbed up to River Street, where they walked arm in arm and stepped on each other's stoned feet.

"Here's a place you can crash tonight," Daniel said as they walked past the Flatiron Inn, a once run-down warehouse rebirthed as a boutique hotel. "You got the cash."

"Thanks, I've already got my accommodations. Generously provided by a generous benefactor."

That gave Daniel a big smile. The accommodations Jacob spoke of would be the ratty couch in Daniel's basement apartment on Happy Hollow Street. Before that came dinner at the Vault, where Daniel hated the politics but loved the burgers. It had a log cabin feel inside, with raw wood at the bar and dead animal heads on the walls. Daniel insisted on paying for dinner and told Jacob to pick any extras he wanted for his burger. He also insisted on buying them cosmopolitans and asked their waitress to add umbrellas.

"What's the occasion?" asked Jacob, but his brother only shrugged. Daniel was notoriously cheap, so Jacob should have taken his extravagance as a sign. But he missed it, as he missed all the other signs that night. When their waitress brought their cosmos, Daniel delighted in sniffing it and swishing it around in his mouth like wine. He had no idea what he was doing—he was a tequila guy if he drank at all—but enjoyed the pantomime.

"I think Mom would've liked cosmos if she'd married somebody classier," Daniel said. "C'mon, drink up."

Jacob raised his glass with a flourish and took a sip with his pinkie out. He indulged his brother's fantasies about who Mom might have been because Daniel was so young when he lost her. Jacob had already had wet dreams and been in fights over girls. He could grow a tough, bony turtle shell around himself and pretend convincingly that he was going to make it through life no matter what shit got dumped on him. Daniel couldn't build a shell at twelve. He was always missing a layer of skin until the drugs built it up for him.

"It's a fine cosmopolitan," Jacob announced. "Sweet. Sour. Urbane." He took a slug and put the drink down. "Do you think Dad would've liked cosmos too?"

"Nah, that fucker didn't have taste in anything. He'd take whatever booze or pussy came his way."

"Hey, that's our own flesh and blood you're talking about."

"Yeah," Daniel said. "Who killed our *other* flesh and blood. Why defend him?"

"Why attack him? Don't you think he's getting what he deserves down there?"

Jacob pointed at the floor—their shorthand gesture for Paulie's place in hell. They always took turns defending him and attacking him, depending on who needed to bitch more at the moment, and played their roles like actors locked in eternal rehearsal.

"It doesn't matter if he's getting what he deserves," Daniel said. "It's what he left behind that matters."

"Right. So you can either wallow in the shit he left behind, or you can wash it off your skin. Scrape it off if you have to."

"I got you stoned so you *wouldn't* lecture me, Big Bro. Drink your damn cosmo."

Daniel went to the bathroom and came back all smiles, bobbing his head to some imaginary music. He hadn't been gone long enough to shoot up, so maybe he'd popped some pills. But Daniel always said that pills—even the opiates Jacob liked—were for wimps too chicken for needles.

"I want to have a good time with my Big Bro." Daniel raised his glass and waited for Jacob to clink it. "Kiss all the old shit goodbye."

For a while they bullshitted about the future. Jacob's new sculptures, the commissions he lobbied for and very occasionally got. The Draconian budget he kept himself on so he could stay a starving artist and not give in to the hell of a day job. SurvivorsofMurderSuicide .com, the website he'd set up for people like them that Daniel said was utter bullshit and refused to participate in. Tammy Bund, Jacob's crush from junior year in high school, a woman he wouldn't mind shacking up with if she ever divorced that pissant Mitchell Gerd.

Daniel didn't have much to say beyond bland speculation about what he'd do for money come April, when his snowblowing jobs dried up and the lawn service jobs hadn't picked up yet. The bullshit didn't last without him holding up his end, and despite their intoxicants, the negative energy of Deathiversary Day wouldn't leave them alone. They wondered what Mom wore the night she died and whether she already had her hand on the knife when Dad walked into the kitchen. Wondered why she stabbed him with the eight-incher when she had a ten-incher in the block and how a bigger knife might have killed Paulie before he strangled her. What went through her mind while the man she loved choked off her air and how a throat feels with a hand clenching it ever tighter. What went through Dad's mind when he stopped on the shoulder of Columbia Road to tie himself to the steering wheel.

"You figure out your answer to my question yet?" Daniel asked. "Which thing you'd remember?"

"Yeah, digging the knots loose," said Jacob. "That's him, really *him*. When he strangled her, something else took over."

"It's *him*, man," Daniel snarled, instantly belligerent. He stood, pushing back his seat and making people stare. "The guy who strangled her is the same as the one digging the knots. If you don't know that, you don't know shit."

* * *

After three cosmos they walked to Happy Hollow Street, where Daniel's truck driver landlord was gone again. They wailed on their guitars until eleven, when Daniel uncharacteristically declared himself ready for bed. They smoked one last bowl and talked about the pieces of their father that had passed on to them and the pieces that hadn't. Anger and hate stuck to their bones, and whenever they got into a jam, their first instinct was to lie their way out of it. But neither had ever raised a hand to a woman. Never would.

"That's why we're single," Daniel said. "Don't want to take the chance."

"Speak for yourself," Jacob told him. "I take the chance all the time—they just run away when they find out what happened."

"Ever think of lying? They'll only figure it out if they're librarians who dig through old Boston papers."

"Nice try. I only date librarians."

They closed out the evening with a slow version of "Heading for the Light" by the Traveling Wilburys, and when they hugged good night, Daniel wouldn't let Jacob go.

Part 1

"You know what I love about my Big Bro?" Daniel said as he finally stepped into his bedroom. "My Big Bro never gives up. For nothing."

Daniel, smiling through the crack in the doorway, blew Jacob a kiss and closed the door. Jacob fell asleep on the couch with his guitar over his belly and woke at ten the next morning when two kids outside screamed at a runaway dog. Daniel didn't open his locked door—not to knocks, shouts, or pounding—and Jacob shouldered it open to find a corpse on the bed. Daniel wore his best jeans and boots, plus the only button-down shirt and sports jacket he owned. His grandmother's crucifix—an object that held no meaning to him on any day but December 12—lay between his right hand and his heart. His left hand, echoing the murderous hand of his father, grabbed his own throat.

"You *fuck!*" Jacob yelled as he stood over the body. There were four tiny plastic baggies on the floor. He clubbed Daniel's ribcage with the side of his fist so savagely that two ribs broke. "Why'd you have to chicken out on me, huh? Why *now?*"

* * *

Jacob dealt with the cops and arranged for his brother's cremation, then chucked or gave away everything in the basement except for a stray syringe and Daniel's guitar—a cherry-red Fender Telecaster, customized for some half-famous session guitarist whose name Jacob couldn't recall. The guy played with Three Dog Night and Bachman Turner Overdrive back in the day, and Daniel had landed it in a complicated drug deal. After he picked up Daniel's death clothes from the coroner, Jacob drove home, expecting his brother's ghost to live with him for keeps. It would work out better than last time because the house wasn't tainted by the possibility of failure since the worst possible failure had already happened.

Jacob rolled out the welcome mat for the ghost, vacuuming Daniel's under-insulated bedroom and turning the mattress, which he dressed with a set of Minnesota Vikings sheets that Rhonda had bought when the boys first arrived. He carefully dusted and rearranged his Shrine Room—Rhonda's former sewing room, where he kept his reliquary of the Nassedrine family dead. Photos, the feet of several rabbits, a broken ukulele and an even more broken clarinet, shoes and purses, and sheaves of drawings and photos. Everything Daniel would need to live in the past.

Despite Jacob's efforts, Daniel's ghost kept its distance. They'd hear each other puttering around the house but hang back, retreating until the threat of interaction blew over. Things changed in the depths of February, when Jacob started leaving Daniel's syringe on the kitchen table before going to bed. Then the ghost stayed around longer, let the living man come closer, and Jacob started to feel a presence in the Shrine Room between two and three each morning. He'd wake up and check for Daniel there, sometimes finding him transfixed by a single piece of memorabilia and not even noticing his Big Bro watching from the doorway. Other nights he'd head down to the kitchen to find his brother staring at the syringe on the table. But Daniel didn't say a word until the second week of March, when he appeared outside the house for the first time, and he knocked on the kitchen window in broad daylight.

"Just gimme some time," Daniel said, the way he always had whenever someone expressed concern over his bad habits.

"You're dead," Jacob replied. "You've got all the time in the universe."

"Just gimme some time," Daniel repeated. He vanished until April Fools' Day, when Jacob saw him stretching out his hamstrings by the twin black walnut trees. Back in high school he ran every day, even after the drugs started, and his state 400-meter record stood for nine years. He always started his runs against the easternmost tree and always wore the same outfit: ribbed yellow tank top, tight blue shorts with white piping, knee-high tube socks with red-and-green stripes. He looked like a walking advertisement for the year 1979. Daniel washed his clothes after every second run, and he wouldn't let anybody else touch them.

"Didn't think they made socks that long anymore," Jacob called from the other tree. "You want to borrow my iPod?"

"If you can't hear the music in your head, you don't deserve to run. Hey, you know where my headband went?"

"If I find it, I'll leave it for you. You can pick it up after your first lap."

Daniel saluted Jacob and started downhill on Chambrell Road, a line of dense gravel that snaked from their house—the highest point of elevation they could see, though that wasn't saying much in the flat half of South Dakota—toward County Road 46. His run brought him north to Mud Lake, where he turned around and took the hill of Chambrell Road as hard as he could. Then he'd loop around the house and do it again until his body gave out.

Jacob tried to run with him a few times but couldn't keep up. He was built for standing his ground, not running. As soon as Daniel's ghost took off, Jacob stepped into a stumpy, messy grain bin that Uncle Ed, a complete non-farmer, had repurposed as a storage shed. He flicked on the fluorescents and in fifteen seconds found Daniel's headband behind a dead snowblower, stuck in a gap between the rings of sheet metal.

How many years had it been in that crack, keeping out snow and rain? Colors had bled into it: silver from the metal, brown from the rust. Jacob stuffed a wad of duct tape into the gap instead, then putzed around rearranging things until he sensed his brother running up the hill. Then he stepped out of the grain bin toward the driveway, where Daniel would soon come by wiping sweat from his face with the back of his hand.

But no, he'd mistimed things. Daniel was either running slow or fast. Jacob stood by the easternmost black walnut tree, holding out a filthy headband until his arm got so tired it shook, and that's when he cried. How many fucking times did he have to cry for his brother? What would ever be enough? Jacob tried to make himself into a bronze statue, holding out that headband forever, but his arm finally gave out and he dropped the thing to the ground.

Daniel would find it when he ran by. Daniel, with those eagle eyes of his. He'd pick it up and put it on his head without even breaking stride.

* * *

For most of May, while the earth thawed, Daniel stayed away from the house. He never liked mud season, and death hadn't changed that. Once the wind and sun dried out the ground, Jacob found that his brother came more readily when he treated himself to a painkiller or two. Then they could enjoy the glorious stillness of an opiate haze together—perhaps on the equally glorious wraparound porch or on hammocks by the COCKLEBUR FARM archway sign that Jacob had welded junior year or on Adirondack chairs overlooking the hill full of noxious weeds that gave the quasi-farm its name.

There, in the opiate haze, they could chat without getting too serious—they absolutely avoided discussing the motivation behind Daniel's suicide, for instance. Jacob didn't like his pill jags to last more than ten days because then he started slouching and losing muscle, but once he stopped popping, Daniel stopped coming by. It was a quandary. Jacob went to look for him in Hot Springs a few times to see if his ghost felt more loquacious there. At Evans Plunge on Labor Day he saw Daniel buck naked by the big blue slide with a duck-shaped floatie ring covering his privates, and he laughed so much that management asked him to leave. On Halloween he drove out again and drank two cosmos at the Vault, but Daniel didn't come—probably because of the stubby-fingered woman at the bar who kept bitching about immigrants.

In November, Jacob didn't bother going to Hot Springs. Then came December 12, Daniel's first deathiversary, and Jacob cried over the Allman Brothers' "Ain't Wastin' Time No More" at Kroeplinaq Truck Plaza outside Blunt, South Dakota, where US 83 merges with US 14 until Pierre.

"That song freak you out, poor baby?" Daniel asked.

"Yeah, it was the song."

Jacob finished the drive to Hot Springs without further incident and parked overlooking Fall River. He walked resolutely into the lobby, ready to compete with Daniel's ghost in all their usual games. He didn't see any reason to deny himself their pleasures simply because his competitor no longer had a physical body. No one in the water would hear Daniel whooping every time he held his breath for longer, stayed on the swing rings longer, swam farther underwater.

Daniel always won everything but their arm wrestling competition—at least in life. Jacob wasn't sure how death would affect his brother's performance, especially on Deathiversary Day. Jacob got his swimsuit on and met Daniel's ghost in the lukewarm water, and with a glance they decided to skip the preliminaries and jump right to their ultimate competition. Each brother would grab hold of a swing ring at opposite sides of the pool and launch themselves toward the middle, taking in the biggest breath possible and seeing who could hold it longest at the bottom of the pool. Jacob took his usual place on the lifeguard side and stared Daniel down across the water, expecting him to talk trash. But Daniel's lips stayed eerily shut, as if he took the competition seriously this time.

"Ready?" called Daniel, and Jacob nodded. The lifeguard noticed, which almost pulled Jacob out of his spell. The brothers grabbed their swing rings, counted to three, and simultaneously hurled themselves into the air toward the center of the pool. Jacob made his body straight and tight, trying to get to the bottom faster so he could stay there longer. When he reached the bottom, Daniel was already waiting.

"You coming to my place tonight?" he asked Jacob.

"Huh? You don't have a place anymore."

"My *side*, I mean. The dead side." Daniel pretended he had a noose around his neck and pulled it straight up.

"Don't start asking me every December 12 if I want to off myself."

Daniel smirked and squatted on the pool floor, knowing he had Jacob beat. He'd always won this game because he never cared how close he came to dying, never had anything to protect, and he knew that his Big Bro loved the world too much to take any chances. But Jacob wasn't giving up easy this time. *There's one game I didn't chicken out on*, Jacob thought, releasing little bubbles of air until he didn't think he had any left in him. *Staying alive.* He let out a burst of old, stagnant air that had been at the bottom of his lungs for who knows how long and launched himself toward the surface with those lungs emptier than they'd ever been.

Daniel never came up. He was simply gone—not at the bottom of the pool, not by the bend in Fall River getting stoned, not at the Vault eating a burger and sipping a cosmopolitan. Not at the kitchen window back at their lonely, windblown house outside Clark, not stretching out by the black walnut trees before a run. Just gone, as gone as he ever would be. Reduced to an absence, a nothingness. A void Jacob thought of every time he saw a road sign with no lettering, a clear sheet of plastic, a blank sheet of paper.

Gone, this nothing. Gone, this no-thing, to its predestined spot in no-thing-ness, precisely where it was meant to rest.

2

Laynie and the Dream of Dogs

TO: William Jackman, Hôtelier Extraordinaire
FROM: The Polka-Dot Kid

Dear Dad—

Remember right after Mom died we drove to Joshua Tree because somebody told you it was in bloom, and we ended up being a week early? On the way we stopped for donuts at the Winchell's in Victorville, and you bought me the first cup of coffee I ever had all to myself. I'm not sure if I'm in the same booth, but I remember looking out the window that day at the trucks coming on and off the interstate. They're still here, rumbling my feet and leaving diesel grit on my tongue.

Laynie Jackman tapped her pen against the notebook and smoothed the long silk sleeve of her black mourning dress. The phone in her woven straw bag from Kenya—her mother's last gift, fifteen years earlier—vibrated once again, but she ignored it. She didn't like her letter's tone: too formal, bludgeoned into artificiality by a too-neat cursive. She flipped to the end of her notebook and wrote in her usual scrawl.

P.S.: I was just about to say that being at Winchell's makes me think of Mom, but it's probably terrible karma to tell one dead person a lie about another. Being at Winchell's makes me think of you, who's still a real and solid person to me, while Mom is totally abstract by now. Is it terrible to think about dead people that way? Comparing them, when they're all equally dead? Anyway, please say hello to mom for me.

Laynie thickened the first *m* of her last *mom* to make it look more like a capital, then reached into the Kenya bag for a small ziplock baggie tucked beneath the veiled black hat she'd worn for the funeral. She opened it with one hand and, without looking, fished out half a Vicodin. But people go to jail for driving on Vicodin. People die. She put it back and fished out half a Xanax instead. Laynie just needed a pill to feel like she could handle her own emotions, which sloshed inside her like the water in a wave machine that someone turned to MAX and forgot to turn off. She lifted the pill to her lips and popped it dry so deftly that any observer would have thought she was merely scratching her lip. The short, dark man at the counter—Indonesian? Malaysian?—glanced at her again, unaccustomed to clientele in black silk mourning dresses.

"Just relax," her mother's voice said. "Let the pill sink in." Laynie didn't trust that imaginary voice anymore because she could make it give her anything she wanted: bland reassurances about her spectacularly unsuccessful art career, vile diatribes against her poor self-motivation, condescending quibbles over her choice of shampoo. She decided that the imaginary mother was right, sipped her too-cold coffee, and closed her eyes a moment. She remembered running into her father at the Lucky's in LA's Los Feliz neighborhood— right after her fiancé, Martin, died—as he bought food for a surprise picnic. Running into him on the Santa Monica Mall, where he was shopping for a Christmas gift that she'd just purchased for herself: a "Zen" alarm clock, which got her out of bed with tones that grew less gentle the longer she resisted waking.

When Laynie opened her eyes, she saw the counter man staring again: at her Medusa hair, at her funeral dress, at her notebook. Maybe he saw the shadow of the Lebanese great-grandmother who showed up in her eyebrows and lower lip when she felt feral or bewildered. Maybe he saw her cusp-of-thirty desperation to achieve a permanent identity or her perpetual grasping for ropes that could knot her to the earth—ropes she wriggled out of habitually. Her misguided feistiness, her unused talents, her lifelong refusal to add herself up for fear that she might be disappointed in the sum. Her stubborn insistence on knowing nothing in life so intimately as the art of taking leave of the dead.

Maybe he could see it all, this man. Laynie got up and walked to the counter, jiggling the coffee cup in front of her.

"Would you mind topping this off? Or microwaving it? I let it get cold."

The man nodded and poured Laynie a fresh cup. He looked her age, still young enough to work two or three jobs without keeling over, and he looked like a father: steadfast, ready to defend what he believed in, hard to knock over. His ring finger had a pale indentation that showed the world, even with the ring itself somewhere else, how married he was. When he handed her the coffee, he found two dollar bills on the counter, and Laynie waited for him to acknowledge them with a nod. She turned back to her booth, picked up the pen, and tried unsuccessfully to blow a stray curl from her eye before tucking it behind her ear with a finger.

I've been thinking about Mom a lot lately, and it bothers me that I can't remember how the two of you got along—I can never remember the little things, like which side of Mom's waist you liked to put your arm around. I can cramp my brain up trying to see the way she moved, but it's always some movie actress playing her. Not even a good one, just some hack copying the half-remembered gestures we showed her. I see things about myself that I know don't come from you—my nose, my fingers, my laugh, the way I go quiet over nothing sometimes—and try to put together a mother from that. I ought to have a shrine for her, I ought to light candles and say prayers for her three times a day. But I just don't feel like it, Dad, and it makes me worry that I won't feel like it for you someday either. That's when you start feeling *really* dead to me, as dead as somebody who died five thousand years ago.

Suddenly Laynie smelled everything all at once—the coffee in her cup, the mothballiness of her dress, the sticky-sweet donuts all around her—and wondered if she had a brain tumor like Mom had. That was the one aspect of her mother she occasionally did remember in visceral detail: the olfactory hallucinations in the middle of the night, with Mom poking her head out the back door and sniffing the air like a detective. Laynie gripped her pen and licked its tip like her mother used to.

We only had one really good cry about her, remember? It was on our way back from taking pictures at Joshua Tree with Mom's old camera, when we got stuck in traffic on the 10 in West Covina. I wanted to go to a photo shop and get our film developed fast so I could frame that picture of you standing on one leg like a cactus and put it on Mom's grave with some flowers. But on the exit ramp you started crying, saying "I can't do it!" and banging your head against the steering wheel.

I was a different person after that day. I felt scared of you in a way I'd never been before, but I don't know why. And I'm not going to figure it out at the Winchell's in Victorville either, so . . .

Over and out,

L

Laynie reached into her bag again, promising herself to leave behind the first thing of her father's that she touched. She pulled out a long-lost tube of ochre paint, then a clamshell of ancient birth control pills from her loan-heavy days at the San Francisco Art Institute. Useless! A stupid thing for a woman who was almost completely infertile to hang onto. A woman whose slippery, treacherous womb must have had a terrible reputation among the embryos of the world. Finally, she pulled out her father's cordless electric shaver, opened up its head, and sprinkled flecks of his beard hair on the floor as if sprinkling his ashes. Then she closed it up and hid it by her hip, where it rested on the vinyl booth seat as she left the Winchell's in Victorville, presumably forever.

But the counter man looked at her, then at the booth seat, then back at her. Had he caught her dumping those tiny flecks of bristle on the floor? Did they do that all the time where he came from, and did that explain his smile?

"Is a nice day, yes?" he said.

"Beautiful." Laynie stood with the door open for a moment, unable to place his accent any more than his skin. "Thank you, I had a wonderful time."

The man didn't say anything back. He just gave her an even deeper smile, as if to say *Don't give up, keep trying and you'll get it someday.* As if to say *Life's hard on everyone, and your happiness corresponds exactly to how nobly you bear your burdens.*

Or something like that. Laynie aped his smile and held it until she stepped out of the Winchell's and into the heat shimmer of the day, which made a truck down the road look like a mirage. But how could that be in December? Heat shimmer doesn't happen in wintertime, not even in the desert. She stood there like she didn't know where to go and didn't have a car to take her there. The truck got closer and closer, and she glued herself to the sidewalk until it rumbled past her, roaring through every bone she could name.

There must have been some culture on Earth, Laynie believed, that dealt with the possessions of the dead in her fashion. A tribe in which the still-living hauled them from place to place, leaving an object behind wherever they felt that some stranger might pick it up and love it anew. Some otherwise extinct culture that she alone, thanks to a fortuitous accident of genetics, represented in the modern world.

If no one had died on her, then she would never have known about this phantom gene she carried. But her mother died when she was fourteen, bringing about her first mourning drive (albeit delayed by three years, until she got her license). Laynie drove from LA to the north rim of the Grand Canyon, where a pregnant Evelyne Jackman had once tossed a silver 1943 penny into the chasm to ensure good luck for the fetus inside her—a miracle baby that the doctors, for reasons the child herself never learned, doubted would ever be born. Laynie, that miracle child in the flesh, tossed in her mother's gold fleur-de-lis necklace.

It was liberating. A gift to the world. Laynie didn't know she was addicted to this behavior until she was twenty-five and the small hobby plane of her fiancé—a budding hospital administrator named Martin Kaell—crashed on a runway at the Salton Sea Airport. A week later Laynie left his four hundred–plus collection of CDs in restaurants, gas stations, pet shops, etc., as she drove to the crash site. She saved his ten favorite vinyl albums for the finale: a delicately balanced pyramid overlooking the spot of his death, which she doused with lighter fluid but couldn't bring herself to set aflame. Someone could use them, she thought. Someone could love them.

Now, with her father dead, the ritual had grown enormous. As Laynie wandered east toward his birthplace in Flushing, Queens, she had an entire trunk and passenger seat full of his possessions that all needed distribution. She felt keenly aware that this mourning drive should logically be her last since she had no remaining family left. Had her ancestors been more enthusiastic about reproduction, or had she herself been keener on falling in love and/or keeping her friends, then she would have had other people to mourn and would have felt less pressure to perform the ritual drive for William Jackman quite so perfectly. But with no one left to do a drive for, she bore the emotional weight of every object she carried, from the stapler engraved with his signature to the folding leather bookends he bought at a garage sale. If she left them all behind with love and charity, then she would earn the right to never do another mourning drive again.

So her logic went, at least. By the time Laynie reached the edge of Las Vegas, her back—made wonky for life when she got thrown off an unfamiliar horse in college—hurt so badly that she could barely twist or lean. She needed that Vicodin for real, and she needed a place to enjoy it. A mom-and-pop place, preferably, with cigarette burns by the sink and blankets that didn't match the curtains. Anything but the big chains her father used to consult for. She found a room eight miles west of the city, right next to an all-night slot machine parlor. WAGON WHEEL MOTOR LODGE, said the pale blue neon sign. REST YOUR HEAD. Laynie insisted, as always, on a top-floor room facing the parking lot, from which she could peek through the curtains and watch people coming and going. Every motel had its own kind of client, as if only certain breeds of people were drawn by its particular magnetism. The Wagon Wheel apparently pulled in blocky, thick-limbed folk who yelled at each other constantly and only turned their heads aside to spit.

"Look but don't judge," Laynie heard her father say. She and Dad used to watch the world from hotel windows when she accompanied him on business trips after Mom died, and she tried to follow his advice as she observed the quotidian dramas in the parking lot below. She popped two Vicodins, took a shower that might have been five minutes long or fifty, and curled up on the bed with her sketchpad open to a new page. Nothing more than *Dear Dad* came out of her pen. Laynie pressed her forehead against the wet ink, then stepped into the bathroom to see the mark it had left. She wiped the steam off the mirror, expecting to read the answer to the deepest question of her life but finding only an incomprehensible smudge on her skin.

"Well there's your answer," she muttered. Laynie went to the window again, peeking through the curtains at her fellow customers, whose lives, filled with the joys of family strife, she could not comprehend. She saw the wagon wheel above the lobby, ten feet high and edged with flashing multicolored bulbs that didn't all work. In a far corner of the lot sat a forlorn gray horse trailer full of used car tires that reminded Laynie of her weekends all through high school, riding gymkhana at a ranch in Sun Valley. By sixteen she was already the best rider in the club, calling signals and riding flank to keep the new kids in line. She won every single barrel race she rode, and everybody loved to watch her bob and weave with that thick, black hair snaking out from underneath her helmet. People believed in her then, thought she could win every time she put her feet in the stirrups.

Where did that Laynie go? The scrappy one she used to love? Before she could answer herself, the phone rang. It was Maura Bast, her father's tennis pro live-in lover and the executor of his will, who'd been calling all afternoon.

"I'm not dead," Laynie said. She always felt like a teenager with Maura, who—though barely a decade older—had been her potential stepmother for three years. Maura now had the tough job of making sure Laynie was off drugs before she could access more than a trickle of Dad's money. "You can stop worrying."

Maura licked her lips. "You could have told someone you were leaving."

"Well, I thought people might figure it out. After I left, you know?"

"You're not the only one this is hard on, Laynie."

"Look, Maura, you know me. Go ahead and tell me not to go on a binge if that's what you need to do."

"Okay. Don't go on a binge, please. Where are you?"

"A motel outside Vegas. I'll call you when I get someplace or when I turn around. Don't worry so much about me. Let Rob do the heavy worrying."

"I'll tell people you got overwhelmed," Maura said. "But if you don't call me once a week, I'm giving Rob your new number."

Rob Givins was a hotel business friend of her father, a young widower with a daughter who'd been trying to scoop Laynie up since the day she finished art school. They had nothing in common except shared grief and family trauma, but that didn't stop Rob from adoring her. It didn't stop Laynie from accepting that adoration either, on those occasions when she felt she deserved it. But marrying Rob Givins? Impossible. He'd freak out if he ever saw a tenth of the darkness inside her.

After she and Maura hung up, Laynie resisted the temptation to turn on the TV and instead lay spread-eagled on her bed, focusing on the Vicodins as they suffused her bloodstream. Tiny luminescent bubbles of light, pale yellow with a hint of green, materialized in her extremities and reproduced tenfold, twentyfold, on their way through the veins that led to her heart. When they reached their destination, they gathered into a single mass and burst into her arteries, suffusing her with little balls of calm.

Pathetic, she knew, though it beat the other kinds of pathetic she could have let herself become. It beat suicide, alcoholism, the rotten-toothed stupor of meth, the rank desperation of promiscuity, the squelched cry of giving up on art to achieve some tentative normalcy. The Vicodins would soon make her feel indomitable, capable of handling anything. Five dead fathers? Ten dead fiancés? Twenty dead strangers dropping at her feet? No sweat. She reached for her notebook and pen.

TO: William Jackman, Hall of Fame Dad
FROM: His Loving Daughter Laynie

Dear Dad—

Lately you've been making me think we've got it all backward. Life is the boring part with all the repetition, and death is when you get to laugh. When you're dead you float around in this endless, perfectly warm pool watching the movie of your life unfold, and you understand it all—why things happened when they did, why you didn't get what you thought you wanted at point A or B or C. It's an infinite movie because there's infinite things you didn't notice or understand while you were alive. Like the way your aunt's smile made you feel or how playing baseball one day with that neighbor kid gave him a way to stay out of trouble for the rest of his life. Every second you lived can take ten years to understand if you have the time—and when you're dead, you have all the time in the universe, so understanding every second is what you do. Eventually, your life starts to feel like this One-Minute Miracle that you couldn't possibly have loved enough while you were living it. But by then you're so caught up in eternity that you forget you even had your minute at all, and that's when you really start to disappear.

Part of me says to hang onto you as tight as I can so you'll *never* disappear. Then part of me says I should forget you as soon as possible because everybody disappears eventually and it's wrong for me to try keeping you past your time.

I don't want to be stuck feeling this way forever. Please resolve.

Still smiling like when I was 9,

* * *

In the morning Laynie woke up soaked in sweat, dreaming of a tree in a dumpy suburban neighborhood with dogs hanging upside down by their feet from its branches. At first she thought they were growing there like coconuts, ready to swell and ripen and fall, but then she noticed that most of them had shriveled down to skeletons. They weren't falling off the tree at all but instead becoming its twigs and branches. Some still had fur on their heads and necks. Their eyes widened and their ears perked up when Laynie stared at them.

Then she saw a new dog, with all its fur and flesh still on it, and she realized that the dogs had been hung in the tree as punishment. A scraggly man in the yard, raking leaves behind a chain-link fence, looked up at her and grumbled incomprehensibly as she passed. Laynie ignored him and walked down the sidewalk backward, trying to hold the eyes of the dogs who had been in the tree the longest. They all stared back as if they knew her and didn't seem bothered by their predicament. Even the newest dog, who had probably been strung up by the man with the rake moments before she walked by, accepted his fate.

Laynie leaped to the bathroom, scrubbed the previous night's ink smudge from her forehead, and flopped back down on the bed. As soon as she closed her eyes again, the rest of her dream flooded back. She appeared on the front page of a newspaper, standing outside the revolving doors of the Hotel Monteleone in New Orleans like a cross between Jackie Onassis and a terrorist. She wore a gray trench coat open at the throat to reveal a stunning black-and-gold silk scarf, black boots up to her knees, tortoiseshell sunglasses, and hand grenades hanging from a magenta patent leather belt. Her hair was even thicker than in real life, matted and unkempt from her time underground.

In the dream she'd been crisscrossing the country for months, leaving mementos behind for her father in every room she took—fancy rooms, cheap rooms, it didn't matter. She wrote his initials (W.C.J.) in Band-Aids underneath a sink at an Econo-Lodge in Poughkeepsie, New York. Left a postcard of an Italian hillside, blanketed by white horses like she used to love to ride, stuck between the pages of a phone book at the Catalina on Miami's South Beach. Left a lipstick-kissed Polaroid of herself wearing a blue 1950s-style dress in a bottom dresser drawer at the Sky Vue Motel in Mobile, Alabama. Every front desk clerk in America kept an eye out for her, but she slipped under their radar in Madison, Wichita, Billings, Tacoma. At the height of her rebellion, she took out a full-page ad in the *New York Times*, which featured a color photo of herself in her regalia above this simple text:

I AM THE DAUGHTER OF WILLIAM JACKMAN,
HOTÊLIER EXTRAORDINAIRE,
AND I WILL NOT CEASE MY CAMPAIGN
UNTIL I HAVE STAMPED OUT ALL INJUSTICE.

Laynie had only been to the Hotel Monteleone once—with Dad for a conference just after Mom died—and barely remembered it. So she took half a muscle relaxant to fall back to sleep and dream of how it looked inside: whirly dark carpets, chandeliers, brass luggage carts, bellhops in shiny black hats. She kept waking up to jot down details in her sketchbook before falling asleep again, and the front desk clerk at the Wagon Wheel called twice to remind her that she'd missed the 11:00 a.m. checkout deadline.

After both calls Laynie fell back to sleep immediately, wondering what to leave behind for Dad. She didn't want to leave anything that had *truly* been his—the Wagon Wheel wasn't special enough for that. But the Monteleone dream compelled her to leave something, and she contemplated what during many brief snippets of sleep until someone banged on her door at noon.

"Five minutes!" she told whoever it was. "I won't even take a shower."

"I'll be back," a woman barked. As soon as Laynie heard that voice, she knew exactly what to do. She took a dollar bill out of her wallet and wrote THIS IS FOR MY FATHER on the thin top margin, then folded it down and stuffed it into the heater grate. Sure, it created a fire hazard. But if the management didn't clean the heater grates every once in awhile, then the fire would be nobody's fault but theirs.

* * *

In a Mesquite, Nevada, gas station refrigerator, Laynie left behind Dad's empty passport wallet—an old butterscotch leather thing that he carried with him all the time, as if perpetually ready to jet away. During the twenty-mile stretch that Interstate 15 went through Arizona, she gave away the last letter he'd read in his life: a lavender thank-you note from a small-chain client in Wisconsin, to whom he'd given twelve hours of consultation for the price of six. Laynie put the note in a roll of toilet paper at the Littlefield rest stop, imagining the woman whose lap it would fall into. One more person would know her father's name. One more person would ask, "Who *is* this William Jackman?" Would say, "What a wonderful man he must be!"

By the time she crossed into Utah, Laynie was in the mood to jettison all of her father's belongings as quickly as possible. In St. George she threw his driver's license out the window and regretted it immediately. What if someone stole his identity and went on a crime spree? Or bought thousands of dollars worth of tacky junk and saddled her with the bill? She got out to search for the license, but the earth had already swallowed it up. She sped through Zion National Park and threw his four favorite opera CDs out the window while she drove past a big red arch. Dad had never liked opera until after Mom died, and Laynie considered his sudden love of it a morose affectation.

"Opera killed you!" she shouted to another arch, and the arch shouted it back.

Laynie stopped awhile in Capitol Reef National Park, where the deer walked within twenty feet of her. In one hand she held the tie that Dad had picked out on the morning he died: purple silk highlighted with the slightest flecks of gold and black. It sat waiting for him at the edge of the kitchen counter, and if the aneurysm had come three minutes later, she would have found him dead wearing it loose on his neck, with his top button waiting to be fastened when he parked at his office.

She lifted rocks until she found one heavy enough for her taste, then placed the tie underneath it. A fawn, still small enough for Laynie to tackle, stopped munching on its food awhile to stare at her. *I'll never have a fawn*, Laynie told herself. *Even if I turn into a deer, I'll still never have a fawn.*

"A little gift for somebody," she told it, reaching out an empty, beckoning palm that had always worked on horses. "You'd do it too, if you could."

The fawn refused to come nearer, but it kept staring at her as she headed back to her little green Honda. That stupid fawn knew the truth about her as well as she did: that her task in life—her purpose, even—was to transport the leavings of the freshly dead into the hands of those who would love them next. She was a master trader in the seeds of the unknown. She was a ferrywoman between two realms, as important to the fabric of the world as that old Greek Chiron, who ferried the dead across the river from life to death but never brought them back.

Laynie ferried not with a boat but with wheels. She ferried not on water but on asphalt. And she refused to stop ferrying the possessions of the dead—tie clasps, bracelets, statues, flasks—until she drove her last mile on Earth and someone else leaped in to do the ferrying for her.

3

In Hot Water

Laynie enjoyed the thermal pools in Glenwood Springs, Colorado, so much that she decided to make the rest of her leave-taking drive a hot springs festival. The spa had a huge 90° swimming pool with diving boards plus a smaller therapy pool, 104° with bubbling massage chairs that she fed with quarters until closing time. She left her father's monogrammed snakeskin wallet in a locker and his portable hole puncher at the front lobby desk. That night she got a room at the Hotel Colorado, making sure to stay on its supposedly haunted third floor, but no ghosts came to visit.

"I'm not a ghost?" said her mother, sitting on the bed as her daughter watched cooking shows with the sound off. Evelyne wore a thick gold bathrobe with cheesy scarlet piping. People acquired new clothes in the afterlife, apparently.

"Ghosts are dead people you don't know," Laynie said. "You're family."

Evelyne gave a simper—a very specific smile that said *You're completely wrong, but have it your way*—and her outfit changed. For a single resplendent moment she looked like Greta Garbo, wearing a tux and top hat and leaning forward as provocatively as a lion tamer. As Laynie departed her room at the Hotel Colorado in the morning, she left her father's miniature screwdriver set and a tin box of buttons and thread, which she'd only seen him use once: while sewing up a ripped red dress she wanted to wear to a gymkhana awards ceremony.

She soaked in the therapy pool until she almost passed out, enjoying a ten-minute snow shower that prickled her warm, open face, then ate an enormous salad and kept driving east. That afternoon she made it to Idaho Springs, where she enjoyed being naked in the women-only vapor cave. She slathered herself with fine sediment at Club Mud and sat next to a fan, letting the mud dry on her skin until it looked like cracked August earth. In the locker room she left an autographed copy of Annie Proulx's *The Shipping News*, which neither she nor her father had read, and in the lobby she left a black felt box containing an assortment of unmatched cufflinks.

Where to next? A web search revealed several hot springs elsewhere in Colorado but none any farther east. Thermopolis in Wyoming looked delightful, as did Saratoga, but both were far off her route. She found the city of Hot Springs, South Dakota, established 1890, and pointed her car there without much research. Laynie rolled down Interstate 70 and plunged into the maelstrom of Denver traffic, testing to see how well two days in hot water had strengthened her sense of calm, and managed to get half an hour north on Interstate 25 before her back screamed with stiffness.

She stayed strong and avoided her pills, instead stretching out by the trees at a Kum & Go station while she watched traffic roll by on Highway 66. Her phone said it was five more hours to Hot Springs, and Laynie wasn't sure she could handle that without a pill. As she stretched out her permanently tight left hamstring, she doubted the wisdom of entering South Dakota at all. A man lived there—or at least had sent a message through mutual friends that he was moving back there—who'd once meant everything to her and by all rights still should have. If Laynie went through South Dakota, she'd have to drive past him to continue toward Queens. She couldn't trust herself to avoid looking him up because, in her freshly orphaned state, she just might trade her unused freedom for the comfort of someone who could understand her mourning.

It would be a good test of her will, at least. Laynie crossed the Colorado-Wyoming border, waving goodbye to legal marijuana and hello to gas stations that doubled as gun shops. She chugged water at the Chugwater rest stop, leaving behind the blue silk Hawaiian shirt with gold vines that her father wore to pool parties. She had excellent truck stop chili in Orin and a good conversation with a trucker from Ohio named Jerry, though she lied to him for no reason and said that she went surfing three times a week back in LA.

In the women's bathroom she left a dark-brown wooden nutcracker shaped like a Polynesian princess, then headed east on US 18 toward Hot Springs, asking forgiveness for her surfing lie from a God she believed in only 5 percent of the time. As she headed away from the interstate and its veneer of civilization, Laynie's conception of space and scale shifted. She was no longer a car compared to other cars but a car compared to endlessness—sky and land as far as she could see in every direction.

It wasn't a bad thing to experience, this endlessness, because her father was dead, and death was endless too. Laynie passed a few misshapen shacks with their backs turned to the road and imagined heavy, languorous blonde women inside each, reclining on their naked sides like ancient Romans while they ate marzipan. She held her breath through Lost Springs, population four, then made a beeline for Keeline and looked for a man in Manville. In Lusk she cooked up sentences containing the word *lust*, then plopped in the town's name instead. *The hardest thing to control is your Lusk. The problem with people today is too much Lusk and not enough love.*

In celebration of lust she scattered a few old birth control pills in the bathroom at Rough 'n Refined, an unexpected coffee shop that almost made her cry with gratitude. Laynie had a dirty chai and a Cobb salad, plus a chocolate red velvet espresso bean frappé for the road. At the Mule Creek Junction rest area, where she had to stop because of all that caffeine, she left a palm-sized leather notebook that her father wrote Spanish words and phrases in whenever he tried to learn the language—which, strangely, were also the times when he tried to quit drinking coffee. Once the zigzaggy highway brought her into South Dakota, the land got rockier and started rising, and after Edgemont she climbed up a canyon and coasted down into a valley, where something—corn, from the looks of what lay scattered on the overturned soil—had been harvested in the fall.

Next came Hot Springs, where Laynie imagined something like the vapor caves of Idaho Springs. Relaxation called to her brittle, dehydrated muscles as she rolled up River Road to Evans Plunge Mineral Springs, and she finished the dregs of her frappé as she parked in the lot next to a perfectly restored—but nonetheless filthy with dust—purple Dodge truck that was the coolest car in the lot by a mile. She paid her entrance fee and went to the women's locker room with her bathing suit still wet from Idaho Springs, wondering which paternal memento from her Kenya bag to leave behind when she left.

The 87° water was, after the heat of Glenwood Springs and Idaho Springs, disappointing, and Laynie chastised herself for not bothering to read the Evans Plunge website more closely. But this water, more than the others, resembled the water she'd imagined in her most recent letter to her father: the perfectly warm place where the dead floated as they looked back on the one-minute miracle of their lives. Laynie sank into the water neck deep and watched clips of her own miracle-baby life play against her closed eyelids, and she didn't notice the man surfacing ten feet to her left and inspecting her profile. He slipped back underwater and circled behind her, and when he resurfaced, Laynie felt his touch before his hand landed on her shoulder.

"Can I help you, miss?" said the man who had once meant everything to her, the man she'd pondered as she crossed the South Dakota border. Jacob Nassedrine, six feet three, with his chestnut hair freed from its ponytail and his eyebrows as bushy as a Scotsman's. With his cleft chin like John Travolta and nose like some French actor and the light in his eyes even more muted than it had been when she knew him in LA. She whirled to face him.

"No fucking way," Laynie told him. "What are you doing here?"

"I live here."

"*Here?* In Hot Springs?" She heard the panic in her voice. If he lived here and she couldn't resist him, she could be stuck in Hot Springs for the rest of her life.

"No, East River. Other side of the state. I'm here for Deathiversary Day."

"Your mom and dad, right?"

"Yeah, plus my brother, Daniel. Just last year."

"Ah, shit." What else was there to say? "Are your aunt and uncle—?"

"They're gone too." Jacob stared momentarily at a wall, then shook his head back to attention. "What the hell are *you* doing here?"

"Just doing a drive."

Jacob knew what the word *drive* meant to her. "For who?"

"My dad had an aneurysm last week."

"No fucking way." Jacob punched the water. "What the fuck is wrong with us, Lane?"

"You really want me to answer that?"

Jacob smiled hopelessly, showing the dimples she loved, and fell backward into the water to pretend to be dead awhile. Laynie tried to imagine herself in the endless pool that dead people got to float in, but there was way too much splashing and echo. Dead people would be far more sedate than the folks at Evans Plunge.

"Run from that man before you lose everything!" said her dead mother's voice. Laynie's equally dead father replied with, "You've got nothing to lose, Sweets. Take your time." So she stood in the water, at once fully unmoving and fully unmovable, and watched the man who was all but legally her husband rise to the surface again.

4

That's My Face

Laynie and Jacob had met four years earlier, during a spring gallery opening at the Barnsdall Arts Center in Los Feliz, where they both had work in a group show. Four of Laynie's six-foot-square acrylic-on-plastic micro-landscapes, depicting enlarged and finely detailed surfaces of rocks, sand, wood, and human skin, hung across the hall from Jacob's life-sized cast aluminum human figures with clay heads. His piece showed a father, mother, and two children seated at the edges of chairs, their backs erect and heads turned sideways as if facing an intruder. He'd fired the heads in an anagama, a Japanese wood-burning kiln that takes three days to do its work, and their alternately shiny and ashy gray surfaces were streaked or splotched with brown, silver, gold, and jet-black.

Laynie recognized the anagama firing right away but was less drawn to its patterns than to the shape of the mother's face: as feral and foxlike as her own, with the same wild mess of hair and a mouth that looked as ready to bite you as to kiss you. Laynie tried to stop staring at Jacob's sculpture, particularly when she saw people clustering around her own work, but gravitated inexorably toward the mother. She got so brave as to smell the surface of her face, and for a moment their noses touched.

"Can I help you, miss?" said a voice behind her. She turned to see a big, bearded, ponytailed man standing a foot away in a suit jacket so tight he couldn't button it.

"That's my face," Laynie told him, pointing at the anagama mother. "Do we know each other from somewhere?"

The man shook his head. He'd been staring at her tawny, sinewy back for a solid two minutes, asking himself that same question.

"I want to buy it." Laynie straightened her spine, which brought her not quite up to the man's throat. "I'll pay whatever."

"It's commission, sorry." He had an accent—East Coast somewhere.

"Don't you have a mold of her?" Laynie flipped her Medusa hair—usually a sure heartwarmer for strangers—then stood with her face beside the anagama mother's. "Isn't it weird how she looks exactly like me but we've never met?"

"We should talk." The man pulled a business card out of his jacket, checked to see if the person it came from held any significance in his life, and crossed out the printed side with a thick, decisive X. On the back he wrote his own name and number. "I'm Jacob, by the way."

"Laynie Jackman. The big acrylics over there." She pointed.

"I'll check 'em out," Jacob said. They shook hands and avoided each other for the rest of the evening. Jacob checked out Laynie's micro-landscapes while she visited the bathroom, putting his nose almost to the glass to make sure her brushstrokes had as much integrity from up close as they did from arm's length. Later on, a couple oozing money chatted Jacob up at the drinks table and distracted him long enough for Laynie to caress the anagama mother's face. She closed her eyes and leaned forward to kiss it but stopped when three overdressed art snobs clucked their tongues at her.

"I know you," she told the face after both the snobs and the momentary inspiration to kiss it had passed. "You'll be mine. Watch me." But it wasn't clear—neither to Laynie Jackman nor to the listening universe—whether she meant to possess the sculpture, or the man who made the sculpture, or her very own self.

* * *

Whatever else Jacob could say about Laynie—that she seemed lost in her own world, pushy, manipulative, and too tightly wound—he could never call her insubstantial. She phoned the next morning to try buying his sculpture again, even asking for the number of the person who'd commissioned it so she could buy it from them.

"It's a lot of money," Jacob told her. "Maybe more than you've got."

"Let's see about that." She had no money at all but plenty of new-found bravado.

"If you just want the face, I'll do one for you. Brand-new."

"But you did it before you met me. That's the magic—that's why I need it."

"*Need?*" asked Jacob.

Laynie groaned. "Let me come see you, okay? I don't like phones, I like people."

That wasn't strictly true, but Jacob didn't know her well enough yet to question her. He gave her directions to his home and studio, a reclaimed locker factory deep in the bowels of downtown LA that he shared with five other bronze guys, and told her to stop by any time. He even gave her the keypad combination to get through the security gate—quite necessary in his part of town—and an hour later he saw a little green Honda pulling through on the makeshift security monitor. Jacob went to the loading dock and found Laynie in paint-smeared jeans, orange sandals, and a slinky black-and-gold paisley blouse that he loved instantly.

"Welcome to Smeltville," Jacob said. Then he walked her down the grimy green hallway to the main floor and gave her a tour. He introduced Laynie to his roommates, two of whom had hit on her at the Barnsdall, and showed her his current project: a series of small, mummy-like bronzes based on Cycladic Greek figurines from the sixth century BC, which he hammered with stamps and ridged with files until they looked like scarified Polynesian gods.

Laynie soaked everything in with eyes big enough to drive a truck through. She tried out the stamps and files, asked the melting temperature of various metals, felt how warm lead got when you hammered it. When she plunged both hands into a barrel of aluminum shavings and took two long, deep whiffs of the metal, Jacob knew he had to marry her. He showed her the equipment on the foundry floor and explained the lost wax method of casting, let her hold the tongs and crucibles, and put goggles on her so she could have a go at the sandblaster. By the time he dared her to smell a jar of his patina, he'd already figured out what their kids would look like.

"I know what liver of sulphur smells like," she said. "You go first."

The tour ended on Smeltville's roomy but spartan second floor, which consisted of six egalitarian bedrooms, a locker room–style bathroom with thrift store showerheads, and a makeshift kitchen with exposed plastic pipes. The common room featured a magnificent walnut meeting table rescued from storage, its surface cluttered with Plasticine models and sketches of potential installations. Laynie nodded along while Jacob talked about his ambitions for the Smeltville gang, and she seized the conversation as soon as he stopped to catch his breath.

"So, about that face." She folded her hands together on the table.

"What do you need it so bad for? Are you so vain nobody else can have it?"

"That's not even close." Laynie stared at him, then past him, then fell silent. Jacob examined her every feature, loving the animal confusion in her eyes and the wounds that showed so clearly on her face. Wounds he recognized without knowing their source. Wounds he knew how to soothe or make worse.

"Well why, then?" he asked. "Spit it out."

"Do you want a real answer or a bullshit answer? Because I can give you a bullshit answer right now."

"You didn't drive to this dump to feed me bullshit, did you?"

"Do you get mail here?" Laynie settled back into the space, back into their conversation. "I might need to write it down."

"Sure, we get mail." Jacob wrote his address on the back of a mediocre sketch, then handed it to her. "Don't send me a check or anything."

"No, it's bigger than that. I have to go now, please."

"Let me drive you out of the neighborhood. Lots of freaks down here."

Jacob's Chevy van led her Honda back toward the civilized part of downtown, and when things felt safe enough, he pulled a U-turn. Laynie gave him a dainty little finger wave accompanied by a huge, gap-toothed smile that made Jacob laugh—a full laugh that flushed and rounded his entire face. When he got home, he glowed with such perfect contentment that none of his roommates dared talk to him. Less than two hours later, one of them saw Laynie driving through the security gate again.

"Hey Jake-a-rooni," he called out. "Your girlfriend's back."

By the time Jacob got to the loading dock, Laynie had driven off. He saw an envelope on his van's dashboard and sat behind the wheel to read the letter inside.

Jacob:

Your question about why I need to *have* that sculpture, instead of simply being satisfied with its existence like I probably should be, wasn't the mystery that made me leave. The mystery is why I didn't have the courage to simply come out and tell you the truth, and that's what I had to go home and figure out. So here's a stab, at least.

I've lost a lot of things in this life, mostly people I've loved, and because of that I lose track of who I am a lot. If I had that sculpture, then I'd have something three-dimensional I could look at whenever I forgot who I was. Not that there's anything wrong with losing track of yourself—that's why we do art, right? You forget who you are and find yourself again, and you feel all shiny and new. But I have a hard time finding my way back to myself sometimes, and seeing your sculpture in front of me would remind me who I am when I don't have any other way to know. Can I live without it? Yes. Do I need it more than anybody else on Earth? Absolutely.

Am I making sense? I don't actually know what I'm saying anymore. This may just be a very complicated way of saying that I want to see you again. You knew my face, Jacob. You touched it with your fingertips before you ever met me. If life has any meaning at all, that fact has to mean *something*.

Surprise me,

Jacob tracked down Laynie's address in Los Feliz via the gallery director at the Barnsdall, shaved off his scraggy beard, showered, and headed over that night at sundown. She lived in a large, bee-hiveish apartment complex terraced into a hill that faced the woods of Griffith Park, and when no one responded to his knocks, Jacob sat against her door to wait. She arrived half an hour later carrying two Trader Joe's grocery bags, one of which she handed to him as she fished for her keys.

"About time," she said. "I almost gave up on you." On the other side of her door was a studio not much bigger than his bedroom at Smeltville. It had a fold-out futon at the far end, but that was it for furniture. Easels, half-painted sheets of thick plastic, and a four-foot-high auto mechanic's toolbox full of art supplies took up the rest of her space. A slide projector, aimed at one of the easels, sat on a rickety stand. Jacob followed Laynie into a tiny kitchen that featured an oven without a door.

"Not what you expected, huh?" She took the grocery bag from his hand, ripped open a giant bar of dark chocolate inside it, and gave him two squares. "You thought I was rich, didn't you?"

"Wouldn't you, if I talked about buying your stuff the way you did?"

"Oh, I probably just wanted to get you into my lair." She slid her groceries into her cupboards and set off a mousetrap by mistake.

"So, who died on you?" Jacob asked as he reset it for her.

"My mom, when I was fourteen. How old were you when yours died?"

"Is it that obvious?"

"You've got those orphan eyes."

"Fourteen, same as you. Both of them at once." He swallowed and corrected himself. "Almost at once."

"I lost a fiancé, too, five months ago. You should know that."

Laynie gave him another piece of chocolate, and they talked about their dead, cursed and fretted over their dead. Then they unfolded Laynie's futon and hugged each other wordlessly, nuzzling but not kissing. They confessed how hard it was to love people when all they could think about was how they'd feel when those people died on them.

"That's why you scare the crap out of me," Jacob said.

"Yeah, well." Laynie blew her nose. "It's a lot easier for me to stick my head in the sand too."

They spent the night together, fully clothed in each other's arms, and kissed goodbye in the morning like a married couple starting their busy workdays.

"Want to come live with me?" Jacob asked on his way out the door.

"Sure," Laynie said back without hesitation. "But let me torture myself about it awhile. It's sort of my routine."

* * *

Laynie went on a three-day pill binge, then flushed her stash down the toilet and pronounced herself clean enough for love. She made a quite theatrical entrance at Smeltville while Jacob helped with a bronze pour, striding up and French kissing him in front of everybody, and by the time the pour was finished, she'd hauled her suitcases up to Jacob's room and settled into his bed. Jacob showered before he went to her, but his skin still smelled like metal.

"Who's that god who married Venus?" she asked when they finished claiming each other. "Patron saint of blacksmiths, something like that?"

"Vulcan. But don't say we're Venus and Vulcan 'cause she cheated on him right and left."

"That is *not* happening," Laynie assured him, and she kept her word. Jacob carved out a studio space for her on the unused third floor of Smeltville, scraping down its birdshit-encrusted floors and replacing its smashed windows. Laynie cleaned its closets, painted its walls blue and orange, and painted an abstract fresco in her private bathroom. Halfway through the cleanup she found a tinfoil ball, squirreled away in the deepest corner of a closet, with six pills inside it. She recognized all of them: three Xanax, two Vicodins, one OxyContin.

"What's this?" she shouted above the roar of Jacob's floor sander, walking toward him with the foil ball in her palm.

"They're mine." He turned his face away. "I've got a problem sometimes."

"Hey." Laynie put her face where he was looking, but he turned away again.

"It's not every day, just when I'm—"

"Jacob." She grabbed his chin and made him look at her. "I know what these are. I've had every one."

He looked away again, so Laynie popped them all into her mouth at once. Jacob pried her jaw open and stuck his fingers in her mouth. She spit them onto the floor, and they stomped them to dust together, closing ranks against their newfound common enemy. That night they started a six-week raw food cleanse that ended when one of Jacob's roommates asked if Laynie was pregnant, at which point they started drinking red wine and smoking dope like everybody else to squelch all rumors of reproduction. But in their bedroom it was a different story.

"You're ovulating?" he asked that night, getting ready to come inside her.

"Don't get my hopes up, please. Just come like you mean it."

Jacob knew by then that Laynie had a malformed uterus— discovered during an MRI before one of her college back surgeries and probably inherited from her mother—that gave her a 3 percent chance of carrying a child to term in her lifetime. Any baby she had would be a miracle baby, just like her, and she didn't want birth control to reduce her chances any further. Yes, she'd practiced unsafe sex, but only with the two men she deemed marriageable. Her college boyfriend, Phil. Her dead fiancé, Martin, who'd never officially gotten her pregnant, though there was one time her period came six days late.

Jacob knew all this, and he approached impregnation with the single-mindedness of an assassin. He tracked her cycle on his calendar, and when Laynie was most receptive, he got her on all fours and came inside her from behind—a strategy suggested by a painter friend with five kids.

"I don't like your math," Jacob said once they collapsed to the mattress that night. "You keep saying 3 percent, but it seems like it's a 50 percent chance every time. Either you get pregnant or you don't."

"I get the 3 percent from doctors. I didn't make it up."

"Screw the doctors. I say it's 50-50."

Laynie let the charm of Jacob's belief suffuse her lungs and her blood, and all summer she bloomed. She filled out, found a better gallery, and sold enough paintings to quit her part-time job at a coffeehouse—though not quite enough to quit her part-time job at a frame shop. She showered less and enjoyed her own scents more. She liked pouncing on Jacob in one of Smeltville's many crannies and humping him on the sly while his roommates were within earshot. She sang along to radio songs she didn't really know and occasionally made fabulous stews or salads for everyone out of leftovers. Three of Jacob's roommates, just from being around her, picked up girlfriends.

Laynie's father, who had her over for dinner every Wednesday night, noticed the change. He insisted on meeting the man behind her smile, and Laynie brought Jacob over one Wednesday. The two men clicked instantly since Jacob hailed from Boston and Bill from Queens. Jacob gave Bill one of his scarified faux-Cycladic figures, and Bill gave Jacob a smooth, voluptuous marble woman who looked like she could have been Henry Moore's take on the Venus of Willendorf.

"You carved this?" Jacob asked. Laynie had never told him that her father made anything or even intimated that he cared about art at all.

"Before Lane was born, yeah. College and a little after."

"I know some marble guys if you ever want to—"

"That's the old days," Bill shrugged. "Family first, you know? Speaking of which, I haven't seen my girl smile this big since before her mom died, so keep on doing what you're doing. Deal?"

* * *

In September they had the first of three consecutive brushes with pregnancy, and Jacob started bandying about baby names once Laynie's period was four days late. Sam, Oliver, Jeanette, Eliza, Patrick, Annika.

"Three percent," she reminded him. "Let's not get too crazy."

"Fuck the 3 percent. Let's just promise not to name 'em after dead people. No Michaels, no Graces." Daniel wasn't dead yet and thus not on the prohibited list.

"Deal. No Martins or Evelynes."

They went camping on the beach near Oxnard and spent a perfect night together, letting the moon turn into the face of their someday child. At four in the morning Laynie got her worst cramps ever, and their wave of expectation crashed into a sullen, heavy-limbed dejection. The specter of reproduction then retreated until October, when she was six days late.

"We should get engaged," Jacob suggested. "Might help the bambino stick."

"That's superstitious bullshit," Laynie snapped back. "Plus, I'm not ready to have a fiancé, I told you that fifty times. You'll just die on me."

"Then marry me now so we'll never have to be engaged. One of the guys I do pours for is a Wesleyan priest—he can do it."

"You'll just be stuck with a wife who loses all her babies. And Wesleyans have ministers, not priests."

Laynie holed up in her studio to wait for her period alone, without Jacob and his baby names torturing her. She let him do all that fantasizing on his own while she sat around looking at her empty easels and watching pigeons bicker by her windows. She searched the nooks and crannies of every closet for more tinfoil balls because she might need one when her period came. When she lost another baby, when she had to mourn again. She could feel it coming, the stabs in her belly and the doubt in her mouth.

"The worst pain of all," her mother's voice said. "Unbearable."

"You're chickening out on your whole life," her better self said. "This is your life—this is what you're supposed to feel. So feel it, dammit!"

"Feel it!" her mother agreed. "Don't hide, no matter how bad it hurts!"

"Feel it!" repeated Laynie's better self. "And if the pain's hard enough, maybe God will give you a baby someday."

It was one of those 5 percent moments when Laynie believed in God. Pain did that to her. She found one of Jacob's tinfoil balls with three Percocets in it and sat rocking on her futon at two thirty in the morning, squeezing that ball while the cramps came.

"I'm feeling it, all right?" she told God. "So now I want my fucking baby."

By sunrise Laynie had squeezed the ball so hard that she could see, through the foil, the 10-235 imprinted on each pill. But she didn't take a single one. Didn't even unwrap the ball. Cured for sure. Done with pills for good. *For good!!!* The feeling of never having to take pills again was a better painkiller than any pill could ever be. But when Jacob came in with two Tylenol 3s, the kind with codeine, she scooped them greedily off of his palm with her lips.

"I lost another one. But I found this." She handed him the foil ball. He flushed it down the toilet and sat next to her on the futon.

"You didn't *lose* anything. It just happened."

"You're *so* new at this." She let her weight fall onto him for a moment, then sat back up. "Thanks for checking up on me. But you should go."

"Why, so you can be miserable alone?"

"You can't share *everything* of mine, Jakey. Not this."

Ten days later Jacob coaxed her out for dinner with her father, who poured two glasses of brandy while a still-sullen Laynie retreated to her old room above the garage and looked for a Gauguin book she claimed to have misplaced.

"She's pretty fragile today, isn't she?" Bill asked.

"No shit." Jacob downed the brandy like a shot. "I've been thinking it might be different if I married her."

"She's pretty skittish about that." Bill sipped his brandy once, then slugged the rest down. "Look, she was so ready to get married last year it hurt, but when Martin died, she sank like a stone. If she ever says yes, you have to be careful she's not asking you to finish off something Martin started. You have to know it's really you."

"How can I tell?"

"Hell if I know. I'm just her dad, I haven't seen inside her head since she her mom died. Nobody has."

They almost broke up on the drive back to Smeltville that night, but Jacob said all the right things. Laynie slept in his bed, let him caress her, let him come inside her. They didn't make love again all month, but in November, Laynie's period was six days late again. Jacob got down on one knee and proposed to her, claiming that two late periods might be a coincidence but three was clearly a sign from God. Jacob believed in God sometimes too, when things got bad enough. Maybe 2 percent of the time.

"If we have a baby, then I'll marry you," Laynie said. "I told you that already."

"I'm in," Jacob told her.

"You have no idea what you're in for." She kissed him on both cheeks.

"Doesn't matter. I'm brave."

"Brave's not far from stupid. Be careful."

* * *

Laynie couldn't stand being around Jacob's constant hope and expectation—around his eyes that seemed to ask, "Still pregnant?" every time they met hers—so she holed up at her father's house and watered the plants while he was out of town. On day ten Jacob drove out to Glendale with a peace offering of Trader Joe's chocolate, dried dragon fruit slices, and a pink pregnancy test wand.

"My head's gonna explode," he said when she met him at the front door. "Do the test, hon, I can't take this shit anymore."

"It doesn't mean I'm marrying you."

"I know. Can I come in?" He watched Laynie walk solemnly to the half-bathroom off the kitchen and slam the door. Jacob sat on a stool—the very same stool on which William Jackman would be eating breakfast four years later when the aneurysm hit him—and poked through the *LA Times* on the counter. Three minutes later Laynie came out and slapped the wand down next to him with her hand covering it.

"I don't want you asking me again," she said. "Let's get hitched today, before I change my mind."

She lifted up her hand. Two red stripes, the brightest she'd ever managed.

"I already did the paperwork on the computer," Jacob told her. "We just have to pick up the license, then Victor can marry us. He's on standby."

They drafted vows in their respective vehicles at traffic lights on the way to the Los Angeles County courthouse branch where the 405 met the 105, then refined them while waiting together in line. That evening they walked through the doors of Smeltville arm in arm to find that Jacob's roommates had put up streamers and bought a cake. Immediately after the ceremony, Victor ran off to a church event and left the wedding license—signed by him but not by the bride and groom—on a workbench.

The roommates left the newlyweds alone for the night, and they pretended that Smeltville was a geodesic dome up in Laurel Canyon. One they'd repaint and refurnish and redecorate, one they'd fill with enough children to make up for all those Laynie had lost. After they made love and called each other "Mr." and "Mrs." for the first time, Jacob remembered what Bill had told him in October.

"So you really wanted to marry *me*, right?" he asked Laynie casually, almost offhandedly, as they pretended to squabble over the bedsheets. "Or am I just finishing off something Martin started?"

Then everything broke at once.

"*What?* Did you just say what I think you said?"

All of it, broken. The spell, the glue of grief that bound them together. The will to get clean. All of it, irrevocably. Laynie threw her clothes on and left with nothing. Jacob could have defended himself by saying that her very own father had fed him those words, but he refused to pin the blame on anyone else. Laynie grabbed the wedding license on her way out, tore it into the thinnest strips she could manage, sculpted it into a nest, and burned it in the parking lot of a dumpy motel near the airport. She holed up there until day fourteen, then bled so furiously that she thought she was dying and started to call 911.

What if I die in this crappy motel? she wondered when she put the phone back in its cradle. *Lose my baby and bleed to death. Wouldn't that fit?*

"You need to relax," said her faux-mother's voice. "Take a little something for it. Don't worry about being perfect all the time."

The baby, Laynie's better half thought but didn't say. *The poor baby. Almost made it this time.* Once she got mobile, Laynie had her oil changed and drove aimlessly for three days between Los Angeles and the north rim of the Grand Canyon, working up the courage to heave her pregnancy test wand over the same cliff edge where her mother once threw a silver 1943 penny and where she once threw a gold fleur-de-lis necklace. Everyone in the park seemed determined to linger on that spot, and Laynie leaned against the guardrail for twenty minutes with the test wand in her jeans pocket.

To the never-ending stream of tourists she must have looked like a woman about to jump. Which she probably was, she had to admit. Finally, Laynie got a moment alone, though she had to act quickly because she heard more people coming. She held up the wand and whirled it around 360 degrees as if the two red stripes were the eyes of her latest dead embryo.

"See that, kiddo?" she said. "Your grandma's down there, some- where. Sort of." Laynie kissed the wand and held it briefly to her forehead. She reconsidered hurling it off the cliff before her but instead left it at the edge of the concrete walkway.

There a child might accidentally kick it off into the canyon, she thought. Or even a good stiff wind.

5

The Upturning

They caught up with each other's superficial details, declared how scared of each other they were, and followed Jacob's reenactment of his last night with Daniel as best they could. A walk down to the river, though without the pot this time, then burgers and cosmos at the Vault, followed by a visit to the house on Happy Hollow Street and a peek through the window of the room where Daniel had died. Laynie didn't think much of the cosmos, though she admitted that the dirty looks she fielded at the Vault impaired her judgment.

"They're pretty anti-California here." Jacob pointed at her Kenya bag. "They see something like that, it tips them off that we're libtards."

"Does that go for where you live too? For *East River*?"

"Picking up on the lingo already, huh?" He grabbed a pen from his pocket, turned over a paper place mat, and drew a rectangle with a crooked diagonal line bisecting it. "West River, East River, Missouri River." He pointed at each element. "Left side's like Wyoming, right side's like Iowa."

"You didn't answer my question. Do they hate Californians?"

Their burgers came at that exact moment, and the scrunched-up face of their waitress gave Laynie her answer. Jacob drew a map to his house while they ate, marking HERE and THERE and various highway numbers. He added 1 CHAMBRELL ROAD and COCKLEBUR

FARM and a few directional notes, then slid it across to Laynie. She folded it into quarters and tucked it into her Kenya bag.

"Isn't that a bit presumptuous?" she asked. "Thinking I'll just show up?"

"You've done it before."

"I'm predictable, is that what you're saying?" Laynie downed her cosmo in a flash. "Mademoiselle!" she called as their waitress passed. "Uno mas cosmo, por favor."

Jacob gave a big laugh. "Oh, they're going to hate you as much as they hate me."

"You're *so* convinced I'm moving in with you."

"You've got nobody, and I'm your somebody." He cocked his head and gave her a TV newscaster's smile. "You'll stew about it a few days, then realize it's meant to be."

"What happens then, Mr. Fortune-Teller?"

"We make our last stand together and try to become real human beings who don't bullshit ourselves."

"That sounds *so* romantic," Laynie said, and they clammed up. She stared at his face and saw how much more broken he was now than he'd been in LA, how diminished. Less of a self in ways he knew and in ways he didn't. Jacob must have seen the same things in her. How could he not? How could *anybody* not?

"Where are you sleeping tonight?" Jacob asked after supper as they walked arm in arm back to the Evans Plunge parking lot.

"Do you think I'm telling you? You'd say 'C'mon Lane, don't forget we're married,' and you'd try getting into my pants."

"Would you change your mind if I told you I'm sleeping in my truck?"

"No." She stopped on the sidewalk. "You're sleeping in your truck in December?"

Jacob shrugged "I've got a pad and a sleeping bag that goes to twenty below. But I wouldn't turn down an invitation if you're feeling charitable."

"Standing my ground," Laynie told him with a smile that bared her incisors. "Otherwise, I'm just a fly in your web."

They got to her car and stood by the driver's side door. Jacob looked through her window at her father's stuff on the front passenger seat. "What's your favorite thing of his you left behind so far?"

"A bottle of cologne in a gas station fridge in Wyoming. Worth more than some of the guns they were selling. You'd probably keep it if it was your dad's."

"You bet your ass. Use it every Deathiversary Day till it ran out."

Laynie tried to laugh, but it came out like a squelched dog bark. "You know who else I did a drive for?"

"The last baby we didn't have, right?" Jacob waited for her to nod. "Did you pick any names for it?"

"A couple. You?"

"Roscoe or Bertha. Just joke names. I think it was a boy, though."

"Me too," said Laynie. "I picked Jeffrey James."

"Everybody'd call him Jesse James, you know."

"Stop. I'll cry, and you'll feel guilty all night."

Jacob nodded, and when Laynie didn't meet his eye, he reached for her hand instead. He held it for three seconds, then patted his hood. "Did you know this thing was mine when you parked next to it?"

"No clue at all. But it's super-rad." Laynie started blowing Jacob a kiss but pulled it back and waved instead while sliding into her Honda. *Of course you're going to his house*, she told herself. *It's just a question of how fast and how much dignity you want to keep.* It was a knowable formula, this ratio of dignity to waiting time, but she didn't know if there was a big enough chalkboard in the universe for even Einstein to figure it out on.

* * *

Laynie hadn't actually found a place to sleep yet but saw a vacancy sign just down the street and pounced on it. Americas Best Value Inn, with faux–log cabins that looked out over Fall River. Once settled in, she briefly inspected Jacob's map, finding the route he described ridiculously circuitous and marked with phrases like PRAIRIE DOGS and LEFT AT DEAD ROADHOUSE.

Too complex. Too many unnameable emotions dotting the roadway. Laynie folded up the map and tried writing a letter to her mother about Jacob, but Mom wouldn't understand the attraction between them at all. She wouldn't like him, period—too blue-collar, didn't even go to college. Laynie considered taking a pill but felt the presence of Daniel Nassedrine, who was spiritually—if not quite legally—her late brother-in-law and therefore entitled to a leave-taking drive if she could only amass enough of his stuff.

"None of that bullshit, Sis," Daniel told her, stumbling around the motel room and high on heroin. Laynie had never even seen a picture of Daniel, so her imagination was free to turn him into anything. She turned him into a potbellied cowboy, with spurred boots and a body like a drug-bloated Elvis Presley. He wore a Levi's jean jacket and had an enormous bald spot like a man in his fifties.

"That's not you," she told him, and he laughed. Laynie had a great night's sleep and rewarded herself with a corned beef hash breakfast at the Daily Bread Café, followed by a large coffee with two espresso shots from Mornin' Sunshine Coffee. Then she followed Fall River down her old friend US 18, past pine tree–covered ridges like the backs of dinosaurs that might wake from their slumber any moment. Jacob's map said LEFT AT 79, and she stopped for gas at the turn, setting a small black metal Scottish terrier atop her pump because she hadn't left anything in Hot Springs. She wasn't done with that town, she suspected. Jacob would drag her there again next Death-iversary Day, if she lasted that long.

Laynie passed north through Buffalo Gap (population 128), after which she tossed a ceramic cat encrusted with fake jewels into the almost dry bed of Beaver Creek. For the next three miles she had the divided two-lane highway to herself, though it didn't feel quite as mystical as when she first left the interstate. When a pickup came the other way, she exchanged waves with its driver, grateful not to be alone. Jacob's directions took her through the dirt road town of Fairburn (population 85) for no reason whatsoever before spitting her back onto SD 79. Was Jacob trying to show her the kind of town he lived in? She opened her window and spat out dusty saliva, unafraid that it would hit another car because there were no other cars. Laynie tried to throw a steak knife with a fake pearl handle out her passenger side window into Battle Creek, but her aim was bad, and it landed on the shoulder. The town of Hermosa, which she drove through of her own volition, had mostly dirt roads but a paved Main Street, and from there she decided to break free of Jacob's directions and bushwhack her own way to the next landmark on his map.

BADLANDS, he'd written. DON'T MISS.

He must have wanted the landscape to change her before he saw her again, softening her up to the general emptiness of South Dakota so she wouldn't freak out at the specific emptiness of the place he lived—COCKLEBUR FARM, whatever *cocklebur* was. She gassed up and asked the clerk whether they'd gotten any snow lately. She'd driven on dirt roads before, especially during her horsey days, but snowy dirt was another thing—especially forty miles of it.

"Nothing sticks anymore!" the woman said almost angrily. She had the sallow skin of a longtime smoker. "Last year it was January before anything stuck."

Laynie had seen the movie *Fargo*, which had entirely shaped her perception of the Dakotas, and didn't quite believe in a December here without snow. She took screen shots of her map app in case she lost her signal and followed Main Street, which turned into SD 40, and the expected banks of snow did not materialize. She found no sign of moisture in the dry, stunted ground that surrounded her, not even behind rocks where the sun didn't shine. Laynie turned north on Spring Creek Cutoff, which was dirt, and rumbled over it at various speeds until settling at thirty-eight, where the pitch of her tires on the road matched the pitch of the buzzing in her head. Then she could let the emptiness of the road call to the emptiness in her, and these twin chasms felt perfectly balanced.

She could drive for hours in this perfect state, she figured, but the rumbling eventually made her back feel tweaky, and her bushwhacking adventure turned into a personal endurance race. Laynie held her breath and rolled down her window to toss out an LA Dodgers baseball cap that her father had bought but never worn—he retained his childhood loyalty to the New York Mets—and she wondered what the rancher who found the cap would think when he picked it up.

Damn Californians, probably. A lone cow stared at her, its eyes asking, "What on earth are you doing here?" and Laynie parked a moment to get out and stretch her back. She stared back at the cow and thought of what to give it. A tie, much like the one she'd left with the fawn back in Utah, seemed most logical, so she tied it to the barbed wire fence and let it twist in the wind. She spent over an hour on dirt roads, growing more familiar with her own emptiness than she wanted to be until she became terrified of dying alone. Laynie knew that this fear, in itself, would lead her crawling to Jacob. It was barely even a debate in her mind, and her cells had already decided.

Finally, she reached asphalt again on SD 44, and she stopped illegally on a bridge to drop a box of keys—one from each car her father had ever owned—into the Cheyenne River. The next town, Scenic, was almost a ghost town, and looked like a set for a 1950s movie about how the West was lost. Bare wood storefronts, tin shacks, a cow skull–festooned sign for Longhorn Saloon that said INDIANS ALLOWED.

Laynie gassed up again just to use the restroom and left behind a shoehorn made of what she hoped wasn't ivory. Then it was back to dirt: Sage Creek Road, which wound through ancient limestone and meticulous farms and into Badlands National Park, which looked unspectacular at first. Dry, scrubby earth and rock that crumbled into pale dirt—not much different than what she'd seen on the way in. But then she saw a horde of too-distant bison and a clutch of pronghorns, and the landscape grew more extraterrestrial: spires and striations in red and pink and white, knuckles of rock folded in on each other.

A dozen histories of earth, each one pressed into sedimentary rock millions of years ago and buckled up again by other histories, asserting themselves and declaring themselves equally true. Laynie felt tiny, which was simultaneously freeing and dangerous. Being a speck in an endless sea made her own problems infinitesimal, which meant she didn't need to fret over her failures or run to the shelter of pills. On the other hand, being a speck meant she might as well disappear. She couldn't do that in the touristy Badlands, but twenty miles back on Spring Creek Road—where that cow might still be waiting, like some new kind of sphinx, for her to ask it three questions—she could have let herself be sucked into the navel of the world and absorbed into whichever layer of its crumbled histories would take her.

Laynie stopped at every pullout and overlook, half to feel the beauty of the world and half to stretch her back. At Sage Creek Basin she ran into a park ranger who noticed her Honda's lack of an entrance tag, which she promised to obtain. On her way to the pay station she stopped at Roberts Prairie Dog Town and watched the animals stand alertly and bark at each other, wondering whether Jacob would bark along with them if she did it first.

The Jacob of their first time around certainly would have. He had humor then, and verve. With today's Jacob, so beaten down by Daniel's death, she couldn't be sure. He seemed shrunken, less full of himself (which was good) but less full of hope (not so good). In truth he would be exactly as much of a fixer-upper as she was herself. The wind blew through Laynie's insufficient coat, and she moved on to Hay Butte Overlook, where the upjutting gray-tan rocks went on and on and seemed like people to her, silently congregating and waiting for something. What? The same thing she waited for, which didn't have a name. The same thing the mountain goats waited for, standing at weirdly canted angles on the rock like they'd been glued onto it.

The goats didn't care if what they waited for didn't have a name, Laynie reasoned. Why should she? Seeking names was an inevitable part of her human inheritance, a glitch in one of those histories periodically upturned by the earth and lifted to the surface, only to erode with time. Whatever name she found for the thing she waited for would be similarly upturned and replaced, so why bother with names at all? Laynie got off the dirt and welcomed the asphalt of SD 240, then dutifully paid her park entry fee. As the ranger processed her credit card, Laynie dropped a plush keychain in the shape of a pug beneath the booth's window.

"Thank you!" she called too loudly, then she drove off searching for the kindly ranger so she could show him her pass. She never found him, but at Yellow Mounds Overlook she parked next to a trio of immaculately maintained Harleys. The mounds had plenty of green and red streaks in addition to the yellow—all those pasts, all those upturned attempts to name the inexplicable! Laynie didn't know she was crying until one of the Harley guys, all leather and goatee, tapped on her window.

"You okay, miss?" he called.

Laynie rolled down the window. "My dad died, that's all."

"Well, that's no little thing." The phrase made him seem southern, though he didn't sound it. He pointed at the yellow hill to their right. "Climb up there, it's worth it. You can almost see forever."

"Thanks," Laynie told him. "I already can."

6

The Well

Jacob loved the big white house known as 1 Chambrell Road, with its ramshackle nooks and its wonky skin that let in too much air each winter, but he hated where it sat. Sure, it was perched on the highest hill for dozens of miles—the *only* hill for dozens of miles, to be honest—but it was in South Dakota, a place he'd never taken to, despite a total of six years living there, and in fact generally loathed on principle. He had no home in Boston anymore, and he'd given up the makeshift one he'd clawed out in LA, so if he ever wanted a home in the world, he'd have to reconcile himself to the tiny patch of South Dakota he owned, five miles south of the thousand-citizen megalopolis known as Clark.

Being stuck in South Dakota galled Jacob every day, though he knew his hatred was unreasonable, pathological, and incompatible with the smallest shred of happiness. He wasn't a member of a community but an exile from that community who happened to still live near it—a bit like his wheat-farming ex-Hutterite neighbor, whose name he didn't know, who'd left the Silver Lake colony nearby but never integrated with the "English" around him. Jacob had plenty of logical reasons to avoid the people of Clark since he'd never been anything to them but some East Coast kid whose father was a murderer. In the twelve years he was gone, from eighteen to thirty, he'd had plenty of time to recalibrate his relationship to the place if he wanted to. But he'd arrived in South Dakota because his parents died, and he'd come back because his aunt and uncle were dying, and he didn't have the strength to leave because his brother died. He knew it was nonsensical, but he blamed South Dakota for all the death he'd seen. Even Daniel, who'd had more reasons to hate the state than Jacob did, had come to terms with it long before he died. His ghost never said a bad thing about the place.

"You really think she's coming?" that ghost asked from his old bedroom doorway as Jacob put fresh sheets on the bed. "A flake like her?"

"Don't call her a flake," Jacob said back, aloud.

"Why not, Big Bro? You called her that a hundred times, easy."

"New rules. Let me love somebody, dammit."

Daniel lifted his hands in surrender and disappeared. Jacob searched the bedroom for tinfoil balls of pills because things would never get off the ground if Laynie found them. Finding the stash balls would be hard because he'd gone ninety-six days without a single pill, so his spidey sense for their location was deactivated. When he felt The Void, it could lead him to hidden tinfoil balls with alarming speed. Then he'd go on a jag, taking what he could find and accumulating a bit more, and when he hit his ten-day limit, he'd stash the leftovers in tinfoil balls until next time.

It was survival instinct at its finest, though Jacob knew it was his addiction that wanted to survive and not actually himself. But was he really, truly, an addict? Not by Daniel's standards. If his brother was a major league baseball player, Jacob was a kid playing stickball in a parking lot. How could he be an addict if he stayed clean for months at a time? Seven months and two days after Daniel died, in fact. He had a pill problem, sure, that he could admit. But an addict? Not a chance. And he sure in hell didn't consider himself a victim of America's opioid epidemic because opioids accounted for barely half of his cumulative pill intake. He took muscle relaxants, tranquilizers, antianxiety meds. He wasn't some trailer trash kid who'd sell his mother for whatever cheap opiate was at hand.

Jacob heard Daniel's ghost laughing at him from the Shrine Room, and the ensuing anger helped his search for pills. He got under the bed to pull back loose molding and found a stash ball in a hole in the drywall. Two and a half Skelaxins, his favorite muscle relaxant. He flushed them down the toilet before he could pop them and went back into Laynie's room—yes, he was stupid for calling it that already, but the place had to be hers before he could truly clean it out. Jacob checked the other baseboards and found another tinfoil ball at the very back of the closet, hidden underneath a loose corner of carpet. He didn't even check to see what they were, and when he went to flush them, he heard the kitchen door open and close downstairs.

"That you, Lovetrain?" he called toward the sound.

"Expecting somebody else?" came the reply. Lyle Mott, known to all as Lovetrain, was a twentysomething from Portland, Oregon, who'd met Jacob through SurvivorsofMurderSuicide.com and moved to South Dakota for a fresh start. Lovetrain professionalized the site in exchange for a couch to surf on while his tricky housing situation in Aberdeen, where he'd finally started college, rebalanced itself between semesters. He was only alive, he liked to say, because he was smoking dope in his treehouse when his father came home with the gun and shot his mother, sister, and self. Part of him, he admitted, would never come down from that treehouse.

Jacob trotted down the stairs and found Lovetrain eating salami slices over the kitchen sink. He wore a blue suit jacket that got canceled out by his seedy goatee.

"Got a gig?" Jacob asked him. "You're looking fancy."

"A couple more maybes. How'd it go up in the mountains?"

"Eh, met a girl. Gotta kick you out."

"Moving that fast, huh?" said Lovetrain. "No sweat, I got my next move all set up. Giving me any details?"

"Nope, long story. Any good chatter on SMS?"

"Simeon and Alicia getting into it again." Lovetrain finished the salami and threw its baggie in the trash. "Hey, can I grab some of your peanut butter or something? I'm just here to tank up and get back out on the job hunt."

"Sure. Doesn't make sense for you to stock up if you're going back to Aberdeen."

"Especially if you're kicking me out for a girl. Sure you don't want to tell me more?"

"Loooooooooong story," Jacob said, laughing. Staying to watch Lovetrain raid his fridge would just make the poor guy feel guilty, so he retreated upstairs to the Shrine Room. It had looked pretty dingy back when it was Rhonda's mazelike sewing room, and Jacob congratulated himself for lining its walls with solid oak shelves that paid suitable respect to the mementos of his dead family. Daniel had two shelves to himself, loosely arrayed because he'd thrown away so much stuff the second time he lived in the house. All that remained were repair receipts for a truck he'd crashed into a tree at age thirteen, a felt cowboy hat he'd stolen from Wall Drug, an arrowhead he'd found at Custer State Park his first summer in South Dakota. A *Boy Scout Handbook* he'd defaced with drawings of oversized genitalia in thick black marker. The running shoes he'd worn the day he set the state 400-meter record.

Jacob kept a few more of Daniel's things in the basement—his guitar, death clothes, and syringe—because they were too sacred for daily viewing. On the next shelves over sat the few mementos Jacob still possessed of his parents. A black-and-white wedding photo of Grace and Paulie cutting the cake, Mom's big purple sunglasses, a check for twenty bucks made out to Dad that he signed but never cashed. An eight-by-ten-inch family portrait from Sears that everybody hated. A ratty army coat with a name tag reading NASSEDRING that had been corrected with a black marker. A badly decomposed alligator skin purse that Mom had bought at a yard sale and tried to sew back to life.

He wondered if the alligator purse had been in the kitchen as a silent witness when Grace grabbed the kitchen knife—the eight-incher instead of the ten-incher, for reasons unknown—and thrust it into her husband's abdomen. Jacob knew that he was no more capable of leaving that moment behind than Lovetrain was capable of coming down from his treehouse. He was stuck in its prison forever, constantly worrying that he'd succumb to the same violent curse that made him an orphan. Having Laynie in the house—a wife, just as Grace Nassedrine had been a wife—would mean he'd have to be even more vigilant, more aware of every buried shred of violence within himself, and the stress of it would bring that violence closer to the surface if it didn't kill him outright. Any woman could see the crazy in his eyes. The only reason Laynie ever latched onto him was because she had plenty of crazy in her own. Jacob picked up the alligator purse, ran his fingers along its sewn-up seams, and placed it silently back on the shelf.

"Am I like my father?" he remembered asking Uncle Ed on his deathbed. "Am I stuck turning into what he was?"

"You're not stuck with who *anybody* was," Ed told him. "Find a girl who makes you laugh easy and dump everything else overboard. Just dump it. Forever."

* * *

At five o'clock that afternoon Jacob's best friend, Ryan Donatelli—aka Don-o, a short, squarish teddy bear of a man with the bristliest beard in human history—strapped his sleeping eighteen-month-old son, Richard, into a baby carrier and got ready for the half-mile walk to his mailbox. Like Jacob, he lived on the last remaining unsold patch of a once-spacious farm. His was an hour north of Jacob's, outside of Groton, where he had all the space he needed to make sculptures out of hammered metal in a semi-soundproofed barn. Before he could leave his kitchen, the landline rang. Its incoming call display read JACOB NAS.

"So you survived the annual pity party, huh?" Donatelli said, his Boston accent blaring. The two men had grown up six blocks apart in blue-collar Dorchester, though they hadn't known each other then because Donatelli was five years older. Now they couldn't escape each other if they tried: Donatelli's wife, Chrissy, was Jacob's high school girlfriend, and Jacob was Richard's unofficial godfather. They brought out the Boston in each other, which alone was enough to keep them jabbering on the phone almost daily. They got together in person whenever possible, especially when the stultifying conformity of the northern Great Plains made them miss the East Coast grind of one abrasive personality against another.

"Yeah, Don-o," Jacob droned. "I survived it. You doing anything right now?"

"Getting ready to go hit my mailbox. You?"

"Nothing. Hey, you still got any of that fancy Irish shit I left up there?"

"Uh-oh." Don-o checked his fridge. "What happened?"

"I met the license burner in Hot Springs."

"Ho-ly shit." Don-o felt Richard stirring and bounced him up and down in the carrier as he pulled a Kilkenny Irish Cream Ale from his fridge. The nitrogen widget let out a satisfying sigh, and Don-o poured the beer out into a ceremonial pilsner glass from his and Chrissy's wedding. He listened as Jacob popped his own can and poured the beer into a matching glass. "Who's the lucky lady we're toasting?"

"To Alania Simone Jackman," Jacob said, raising his glass. "Goes by Laynie."

"Cheers." Don-o lifted his own. "So where is she?"

"Hell if I know, man. I gave her a map—we'll see what happens."

"Want to do a throw for her?"

"Got your fancy coins right in my hand." Jacob jangled three coins next to his phone so Don-o could hear them.

"Okay, make a wish," Don-o told him, even though they both knew that making a wish before throwing your coins wasn't part of any recognizably Taoist *I Ching* practice. But it was part of Don-o's personalized divination ritual, which Jacob had come to know and love. Jacob had stumbled onto the *I Ching* first, picking up a book from a fellow anagama guy back in LA, but Don-o morphed it into his own thing. He had eight books of interpretation and a collection of authentic Chinese coins. When Daniel died, Don-o gave a set to Jacob: smooth green bronze ones from the late 1600s, about the size of a nickel and with square holes through the center.

They were a nice gift from a de facto older brother. Jacob closed his eyes and wished for Laynie to show up as soon as possible, then for a real marriage that she couldn't weasel out of on a technicality. And a couple of babies if it wouldn't kill her to have them. He shook the coins in his fist and blew on them like dice, then skittered them across his kitchen table six times. Jacob called out each result, and Don-o jotted them down on a sticky pad while his son fell back to sleep in his carrier.

"It's *Ching*," Don-o pronounced after the sixth throw. "The Well, or The Source. '*The town may change shape, but the source of its water always stays the same.*' That means a couple different things."

"Lemme guess," Jacob droned. "One of them's about Laynie."

"Bingo. Your soulmate's your Well. There's one person, one *kind* of person, who you're always drawing your strength from no matter what kind of situation you're in. I'm one of those, she's one of those. Follow me?"

"Keep yapping."

"Getting *Ching* means you have a chance to connect yourself to the deep, basic truths of human life, which you've kinda got your head up your ass about." Don-o closed his eyes a moment, remembering a line of interpretation. "'*In your personal relations, try to focus on the universal biological and spiritual truths that bring people together, instead of on short-term individual goals.*' Which means you should settle down with the woman you love instead of chasing tail."

"I don't chase tail."

"With an ass like yours, who needs to?" Don-o laughed and took a gulp of beer.

"I'm flipping you the bird right now," Jacob said, though he didn't actually do it. "So, is she coming or what? What does the Tao say?"

"Oh." Don-o furrowed his brow as he crumpled up the sticky pad and threw it away. "I thought you wanted to know about you guys' future. You know she's coming, bud. You don't have to ask the Tao that."

After they finished their long-distance beer, Jacob scrubbed the kitchen and bathrooms, hoping it would drive the nervous energy out of him. It wasn't enough, so he put on a hat and gloves and went out to his Destruction Shack: a decrepit and tilting former outhouse, older than any building on the property, which he'd been trying to destroy with lacrosse balls since he first got to South Dakota. After he got into a fight at school, Ed pulled an old wooden lacrosse stick from the 1940s out of a cranny in the barn and bought Jacob a dozen balls.

"Go knock that fucker down," Uncle Ed used to say whenever Jacob got too belligerent or sulky. He developed an incredible shot from all the practice, but nobody else he knew even had a lacrosse stick. He'd broken a few boards back then, but when he came back to Clark as a grown man, he started making real progress on bringing the outhouse to the ground. More muscle, more anger. Jacob dumped the dozen balls on the ground—he'd never lost one for more than a day—and went to work on a board he'd been trying to split for months.

Whap! Jacob rifled a ball at that board from twelve feet, and when the rebound came out too fast for him to catch, he scooped up another ball. *Whap!* He daydreamed of different circumstances—discovering his talent for lacrosse back in Boston instead, where people actually played the game, and getting a full-ride scholarship to Syracuse or Duke. His parents would be alive then, and Daniel too, and after college was over, they'd watch him score five or six goals a game playing Major League Lacrosse for the Boston Cannons.

Whap! But that was somebody else's life. It took a whole bucket to split the board, and although that gave Jacob some satisfaction, it didn't bring the Destruction Shack any closer to falling down. Its framework stubbornly remained at the same angle against the earth it had maintained for decades. For all he knew, his constant battering only gave it more resilience. Jacob wished he felt that way about himself as he chased down his rebounds, scooping up the farthest ball and then cradling through the rest like they were defenders trying to poke check him. *Whap!*

It was a strange way to stay in shape, but his body felt fierce and wiry. Would Laynie find the habit weird or get it right away? Jacob put the stick and balls away and headed inside, firing up the laptop on his living room coffee table to catch up on the threads at SurvivorsofMurderSuicide.com. Laynie would have a lot bigger problem with sms than with his Destruction Shack, he figured, and in his head he could hear her logic.

"Don't you have enough problems of your own?" she'd ask him, and she'd be right. But Jacob needed people to talk to who understood the shit he'd swum through, and the fine citizens of Clark, South Dakota, didn't. Nor did he really want them to—they'd known what his father did before he even set foot there and judged him from the moment he arrived. A murderer's kid, that's all Clark would ever let him be. And sms was a chore too. Most days he didn't give a shit about what his fellow survivors had to say about depression and mourning and manufactured memory, and today especially he didn't want to read Simeon and Alicia's exchange on the difference between murder-suicides and regular ol' murderers. But they were his people, a lot more so than the ones in Clark who watched him grow up and didn't lift a finger to make him want to stay.

Quite a few of the SMS regulars—Janet Crain, Burke Levin, Frank Fuller, Kevin Ardnoy—had messaged him asking how the Glenwood Springs trip went, so he felt an obligation to post something about it. Everything he tried felt insincere: the forced smiles on his attempted videos, the false good cheer of his too-controlled sentences. He tried to think up decent things to say about his brother's deathiversary and about maintaining healthy relationships with the dead, but instead kept imagining Laynie giving him an ultimatum about SMS.

"It's them or me," she'd say, leaning against the doorway while he scrolled through the message boards. But she wasn't here, so Jacob checked the murder-suicide versus murderer thread that Frank Fuller had started after reading about a quadruple murder in Ohio. A guy had shot his ex-wife and three kids, then turned himself in. Why didn't he shoot himself after all that? Didn't it seem like the logical thing to do? A few people piped in, but then it turned into a brawl between Simeon Gartner and Alicia Cantrell, who lived forty miles apart in Illinois but said they'd never met. Jacob resisted the urge to suggest that they start fucking each other as therapy and in fact stayed out of the thread entirely.

SIMEON: Of course nobody can logically say who should kill himself (or herself, sorry ladies) and who shouldn't. We're talking murder here. No logic applies. We're talking people who can't even remember that killing is wrong. How can you expect them to turn around after they've killed a bunch of people and say "Oh, I've done something terribly wrong, why don't I off myself now?"

A-LEASH-A: Do you think that the human moral code just goes away permanently when somebody kills somebody else? Sure, it's gone during the act—otherwise the act wouldn't happen. We all know that. We've all LIVED that. But look at the guy's picture from right after he turned himself in. He KNOWS he did the wrong thing. The only decent reason for him to NOT pull the trigger on himself is to make sure that he stays alive to experience the most humiliating suffering he can possibly imagine. Plus a little more, for killing a baby.

On and on it went, through fifty-seven exchanges, until Frank locked it. Not the nastiest flame-up Jacob had ever seen on SMS but top five. It surprised Jacob because Simeon—corporate asshole and male chauvinist pig though he was—usually kept everybody laughing with his borderline obscene jokes. Alicia, sweet as pie, sent out her latest "one pot wonder" recipe every Sunday. Jacob went back to cleaning the house, though the flame war stirred the old sediment of fear and worry inside him.

Look at the guy's picture from right after he turned himself in—that was the line that did it. Jacob kept imagining his father driving to the police station instead of to Boston Harbor and tried reconstructing the look on his face that said *I've done something terribly wrong.* It woke up the hollow in his chest that he'd nicknamed The Void, which vibrated supernaturally fast and filled him with a panic that only a pill could ease. Every sound felt like it could turn into a train whistle or a human scream. Around every corner a woman's strangled body could fall breathlessly to the ground, and a man bleeding from a knife wound to the gut could lurch forward, looking for a rope to hang himself with.

Jacob's whole body shook as he gathered stray laundry hanging on the backs of chairs and threw it into his washing machine. Stacks of unopened mail piled by his front door got separated into junk and non-junk. Kitchen gadgets got sorted until he put his hands on what The Void was looking for: his Temptation Bottle, always left in plain sight to remind Jacob that he wasn't an actual addict, that he didn't have a real drug problem like Daniel had. To remind himself that he had control and could always walk away.

Two beige Percodan tablets, one bright yellow Nembutal capsule, and five white generic Vicodin tablets. For the past ninety-six days it had lived in a spice rack by his microwave. Jacob could walk by his Temptation Bottle fifty times a day without caring what was inside, and when he was clean, it reinforced his cleanness like a good luck charm. But when The Void caught him and the time came to get unclean, he knew exactly where to start his jag.

It was a perfectly ordered system, though Daniel always said it was for pussies. With Laynie coming, Jacob needed a less obvious place where he could still walk by some pills to test himself without anybody else seeing them. He lifted the Temptation Bottle high in the air and almost hurled it at the kitchen floor, though he knew he'd just pick up the stray pills and find another bottle for them. He'd hunt down every last one on his hands and knees, and the image of Mom and Dad clutched together in violence against their kitchen counter in Dorchester would fill his head and he'd pop one. More than one.

No, he couldn't be on a jag when the woman he loved—the woman he should rightly call his wife—showed up and decided whether to stay with him or not. Impossible. As Jacob fought off The Void, which grew inside him and crowded out his inner organs, a new hiding place suggested itself. In the mudroom by the back door stood an old chest of drawers full of household tools, and the bottom one was chock full of screws and nuts and bolts and hooks—some in jars or pill bottles and some loose, their sharp edges dangerous to soft, unwary hands.

The drawer was so full that Jacob could barely pull it out. He dug a spot for the Temptation Bottle at the back right corner and shoved it in, then smoothed the small chunks of metal over so that no one, not even himself, would think he'd buried a damn thing.

1

Places to Hide

After a night in another log cabin motel, Laynie saw snow coming and followed Jacob's directions. US 14 stairstepped her up to Pierre, where the saw the state capitol dome and tried to throw her father's tie tack spy camera into the Missouri River from the crest of the bridge. It landed on the pavement, waiting to be crushed.

Once she crossed into East River, the soil looked darker and the land grew flatter. In Huron, which smelled like a turkey plant, she left U.S. highways for state highways. SD 37 North took her to SD 28 East, and the bare horizon called to her from every direction. Through her windshield, through her side windows, in her rearview mirror. Emptiness let Laynie know that it would be in constant communication with her, reminding her of infinity and giving her the tools to make her inner world as spacious as her outer one. Those horizons were occasionally broken by clumps of buildings that sometimes called themselves towns, sometimes didn't. Silos of all sizes, most of them dusty gray or chromed silver but a few old brick ones too, were more common than homes. Cadres of birds flew south for winter, and raptors hovered in the wind to watch for prey below.

Laynie expected tumbleweed because the only frame of reference she had for this kind of emptiness was westerns, or more honestly TV commercials cashing in on western tropes. But this was farm country, not cowboy country. It was Laura Ingalls Wilder country, *Little House on the Prairie* country, and she kicked herself for calling those books and the TV show hokey without ever reading or watching them. Her karmic retribution for her urban snob insults would be getting stuck here forever, wearing a calico prairie bonnet and spinning flax in some dimly lit sod dugout. Breaking ice with her fists on a frozen lake and carrying it in pails that hung from a pole on her shoulder.

She laughed at herself for not even having an educated fantasy about a part of the country she'd never imagined but was now about to call her safe harbor. Laynie saw kids on ATVs, racing along the edges of ditches in nothing but camo hoodies even though her dashboard said the outside temperature was 27°, and wondered if Jacob and his brother had been like that. Wondered if her kids—if she ever managed to have them—would be like that. How did it feel to grow up in this emptiness, to let it shape you? Laynie queried the signs she passed, looking for clues.

DOUGS HOTEL

FAMILY FARMS, NOT HOG FACTORIES

ROBS BAR

FRIENDLY NEIGHBORHOOD DONKEY FARM!

JULIES RESTAURANT

She'd gotten away from corporate America, that's for sure. She pictured Julie's Restaurant as just a step above coming over to Julie's house for dinner—menus and swinging doors between dining room and kitchen but otherwise the same. That's what happened when there weren't enough people around to sustain an organic salad bar or even a McDonald's. People *had* to be able to eat at each other's houses because you never knew who'd have to go out in a blizzard to fetch your favorite calf or who'd need you to bring their pig to the vet.

She knew zero about living here, but it had to be better than how she lived in LA. Didn't it? Somehow? More sincere? Every interaction back home had been commodified, every smile calculated.

To survive on the Great Plains she'd have to be more bare, like the horizon. There weren't enough buildings to hide behind for people to be false like they were in LA, not enough institutions that could prop you up just because you said you belonged to them. Oh sure, there would be churches and Lions Clubs and what have you, but nothing like the interlocking yet highly differentiated micro-tribes of LA. Nothing like the *One of us versus one of them* turf wars that poisoned every human situation.

Laynie scanned the fields around her for another cow to stare at, but everything was yucky brown dirt. Some of it turned over after growing season, some of it left alone to revel in its plant debris. If she lived here, would she need to know why farmers chose to clear their land or not? Would she not be taken seriously if she couldn't tell one brand of tractor tire from another by the shape of their tracks? It would be exhausting to live that way, like being dropped into a language you've never heard. Jacob wouldn't be much help. He'd hardly said a thing about South Dakota during their first go-round, and if you asked him where he was from, he'd say Boston.

This place she was escaping to had always been the place he escaped *from*. How would it ever work? She could drive past his place and try her luck elsewhere, but what better thing than Jacob had her luck ever brought her? The closer Laynie got to the COCKLEBUR FARM mark on his map, the more inevitable staying with Jacob felt to her. She kept picturing other versions of herself, bundled up to twice her size to survive the weather, lurking around every silo and barn she passed. Carrying a bucket of corn to the pigs. Hanging out clothes to dry, though that seemed absurd in the wintry wind. Pushing a reluctant sheep up a ramp and into the bed of a truck that would lead it to the slaughter.

Why so may animals in her fantasies? Laynie tried to shake them and instead focused on agricultural equipment, from gigantic sprinklers lurking in the fields to decrepit, comblike objects as wide as the highway that lay unused by the sides of ditches. She reached the point on Jacob's map that said LEFT AT DEAD ROADHOUSE and slowed to examine the ugly brown building with its windows boarded up and shot-out BUDWEISER signs on three sides. One sign called it RAY'S TAVERN and another CORNER BAR, but neither identity had stuck. Would her own new identity stick, whatever it chose to be?

For reasons secret to herself, she thought of her father. Laynie hadn't given away a single thing of his all day, so she pulled into the parking lot of the dead roadhouse and reached for the pile on her passenger seat. She found a flat-bottomed glass globe with a purple Siamese fighting fish inside it, possibly real and possibly an expert fake. A relic of his own childhood that he'd never talked about once. She set it down on the roadhouse's top concrete stair for some adventurous child to find, then got back into her little green Honda to follow the last direction on Jacob's map: TURN LEFT AFTER ANTELOPE LAKE.

Laynie caught a glimpse of water ahead of her, with the slightest skin of ice along one edge, then turned at a mailbox and a sign that said Chambrell Road. A nice name, a road she could live on. It sounded French, though an extra *e* at the end would make it more so. The gravel road switchbacked up a hill, and at points a big white house at the top revealed itself before shyly hiding from view. A final climb led her to two square columns of brick holding up a metal archway—aluminum, it looked like—with letters spelling COCKLEBUR FARM affixed to two curved bars.

One of Jacob's early metal projects, she guessed, and she was right. The house was two stories high, with a magnificent covered wrap-around porch on the first floor and a smaller one on the second, which Laynie knew that Jacob would want to make love on at every opportunity. The place looked well cared for, which she expected, because Jacob knew how to put a pleasant surface on even the most rickety skeleton. He could keep up appearances just as well as the

South Dakota people he'd always chastised for doing it. The driveway led her around back, where patterns on the gravel suggested Jacob's preferred parking spot. She took it without compunction. Farther on was a huge red barn, and behind her were three stumpy metal silos—though Jacob would later tell her to call them grain bins—and an ancient-looking outhouse.

A workable mess, Laynie concluded, like her and like him. But too empty. It needed a garden—actually several gardens—to live up to the word *Farm* in its name. She got out and surveyed the land, wishing she knew how much of it made up an acre. It didn't look farmable except immediately around the house. The hill she'd just driven up couldn't be tilled, and on the three other sides it descended steeply to the fence lines of someone else's dormant farm. Dried weeds littered the bottom half of the hillside all around, surrounding the house like a moat.

Cocklebur, maybe? It seemed to be the only thing that grew there. Laynie looked at the sign and laughed at the joke and figured she'd be just fine here. A farm for weeds was a perfect place for a workable mess like her to thrive. She locked her car, then unlocked it, then headed up the well-worn steps of the wraparound porch. There was a great rocking chair by the back door that she promised herself to sit on at the first opportunity, even if it meant wearing three coats.

Inside was a cluttered mudroom where she hung her blue wool coat with black embroidered horses on an empty peg. Jacob had a dozen pairs of boots and shoes strewn around, summer mixed up with winter, and she arranged them in a neat row according to the season. That way Jacob would know, the second he walked into his house, that inviting Laynie Jackman in meant letting yourself be organized. A heavy-looking chest of drawers had its bottom one slightly open—chock full of screws and nuts and bolts and hooks—and she squatted down to close it after trying unsuccessfully with her feet.

Next came a good-sized, open kitchen with a too-old fridge and vinyl flooring that peeled at the seams. Laynie walked past the white table where Daniel's syringe had sat not too long ago, then exited into a strange, cramped space where the stairs to the second floor led up to a too-broad landing. She shimmied past that into a living room full of sculptures and books, then collapsed on an L-shaped blue sofa that bore not a single sign of Lovetrain's former occupancy. It pulled her into its embrace, told her that she'd never leave a single object of her father's here, and whisked her into sleep.

* * *

Two minutes before Laynie pulled onto Chambrell Road, Jacob had rolled out of it to go visit Elizabeth Medgefield, an eighty-six-year-old widow and stroke victim who lived halfway between him and Clark. He was her third-string caregiver, filling in occasionally and getting paid under the table by her asshole software executive son in San Jose. Jacob did what the nursing service wouldn't: buying Medge groceries, taking out her garbage, helping her channel-surf, and—for each visit's finale—singing and playing guitar. He'd pull the ottoman close to her wheelchair so she could feel the notes vibrating out of the cheap acoustic he kept at her house.

"How about some Dylan?" Jacob suggested. Medge, who could only communicate in grunts and gestures due to multiple small strokes, didn't argue. He strummed out "I Dreamed I Saw Saint Augustine" and sang it pure and wistful. Medge never recognized his Dylan or Van Morrison tunes, but she smiled when he played jangly TV commercial ditties from the 1970s. The Ken-L Ration song ("My dog's better than your dog / My dog's better than yours!") always won her over. When Jacob finished, he'd kiss her on the lips, wiping his mouth with his wrist so that her sour, metallic taste wouldn't linger.

If he was in the middle of a jag or even contemplating one, he might slip into his pocket a pill or two that he'd pilfered from her bathroom medicine cabinet. Medge had three-month prescriptions for Percocet, Vicodin, and Demerol, among others, and never missed the few he took. Today Jacob felt too full of hope to steal anything, but he tempted himself by throwing open the medicine cabinet and staring down its contents.

"I got my wife," he told the bottles. "Who the fuck needs you?"

He gently shut the cabinet and drove home to find Laynie's car parked in his spot, then opened his own back door as quietly as a burglar and went about his day. He fixed himself a grilled cheese sandwich and a can of tomato soup, and when he sat down to eat it, Daniel's ghost stared at him from across the kitchen table.

"She's waiting for you," Daniel said. "Wonder if she's got any clothes on."

"Shove it," Jacob whispered. Daniel kept raising his eyebrows and winking, so Jacob went to eat alone in the barn. Daniel had never liked the barn in life because it meant work, and he rarely visited in death either. Jacob pulled off the thick canvas tarps over his foundry gear because he wanted Laynie to think he'd been making something instead of grappling with the worst creative rut of his life. He'd poured only a single bronze since Daniel died, a bust of some dead agricultural magnate who'd gotten a new building at South Dakota State University named after him, and hadn't touched his tools since he delivered the commission in June. Jacob spent more time figuring out how long he could live off the proceeds than he did making any more art. He uncovered his clay bench too, though he hadn't done much with that either. All he had to show for the last year were a set of six eyeless clay masks, modeled vaguely on the Japanese Noh style, that he'd bisque fired but considered lifeless. They were technically ready for the anagama, but they didn't deserve it. You don't spend three days on an anagama firing simply because you need to feel productive. There has to be urgency. There has to be some change to the artist that the firing itself brought into being.

At least that was Jacob's theory. As he folded and stacked his tarps, the barn door slid creakily open, and Laynie stepped in, wearing her blue horse coat and one of his fake fur trapper hats even though it was barely cold. The hat looked fantastic on her, and he took it as proof that she belonged here.

"I smelled your cooking," Laynie said. She had a harder time closing the door than opening it, but so did everybody. They smiled but looked away immediately, which gave Laynie a chance to look around. The working half of the barn had a variety of wood flooring, no doubt cannibalized from other buildings, and the storage half was dirt. Between them rose a dangerous-looking wrought iron spiral staircase. Laynie hoped to recognize some of the equipment from Smeltville, but she didn't.

"What are you making?" Laynie asked.

"Not a damn thing." Jacob took a drink of his soup, and his honesty made it taste divine. "My brother died, and I ran out of shit to say. You've been there."

Laynie nodded, stepped over to him, and held out her hands for the soup bowl. She finished it, handed the bowl back, and walked to the staircase. When she ran her fingers on the handrail, she saw dust.

"What's this go to?" she asked Jacob.

"It's widow's walk, an old Boston thing. Where the sailors' wives went to check if their husbands were still lost at sea."

"Charming. Can I go up?"

"Knock yourself out," he said. "The middle's spooky where the weld is, but it holds. When you get to the door, just knock it with your shoulder."

Jacob held the staircase, sensing that Laynie didn't trust it, and watched her climb. There were actually two staircases welded together, and she took the second flight gingerly. At the top it got more stable thanks to tons of two-by-fours, and she shouldered open the door at the end of it. Then she crouched through the opening onto a cramped platform five feet square with rib-high iron railings. The space barely gave her enough room to pace in. The railing was high and thick enough so that a widow in denial of her husband's disappearance couldn't casually fall off and kill herself but would have to plan her jump. Laynie felt Jacob on the stairs and looked through the doorway to see his eyes at the level of her feet.

"Did you build this?" she asked.

"I helped my uncle. You like it?"

"I love it. Can I hang out and enjoy the view?"

"Just don't get too lost in any widow fantasies," Jacob said. "Anything you want from your car?"

"There's a suitcase in the trunk, thanks."

Laynie looked around at the property and saw that the house and barns were surrounded by armies of what had to be cocklebur. It looked dead and scraggly for the winter but would rise in spring to continue its encroachment. Would she stay long enough to watch it bloom and flower—to even see what it looked like—or be long gone by then? If she stayed, she'd want a studio, and she knew which of the stumpy gray silos she wanted to claim: the easternmost one, the least hemmed in, which she could watch the sunrise from if Jacob would cut her a window.

On the ground Jacob opened the back trunk of Laynie's Honda and inspected its contents. Beside her black suitcase sat three boxes full of her father's stuff—a plastic rhinoceros, a gold-plated orange, various loose pictures, an appointment book, two watches, a harmonica. One of the pictures showed Bill and Laynie standing next to a horse; she was fourteen or fifteen then, right after her mom died. Her dad looked about the same as Jacob remembered him but with widower-ish eyes that no doubt cried a lot.

"Hey, daddy Bill," Jacob told the picture, gently kissing both faces on it. "I won't fuck it up this time, don't worry."

* * *

As Laynie settled into the bedroom that had twice been Daniel Nasse-drine's, she had no idea of the place's history of hosting wayward souls or how perfectly she fit in with it. Many before her had slept in that spare bedroom and pondered the same burly, irascible issues that faced her, though most were navy men. The house had been built in 1920 by a World War I bombardier named Olin Darson, whose infirm parents had subdivided their farm in his absence to stay afloat. When his folks died five years later, Olin opened up the house to his fellow veterans, who'd come home to a different America than they'd left and hoped that the open skies of South Dakota would help them trade the label of *useless vet* for another one. Some became *plumber*. Some became *drunk*. Some became *fireman*. Some failed to achieve any identity at all and drifted farther west.

One of those who slept in the room bore the name Roland Astrin as well as the labels *sniper* and *one screw loose*. He liked the house so much that in 1927 he used his gambling winnings to buy it from Olin Darson, who took the money to Kansas City and disappeared from human history. Astrin impregnated a woman named Teresa Flint, who claimed to be a quarter-Portuguese but was actually half-Shoshone, and a week after the Wall Street crash of 1929, they welcomed a child named Rhonda into the world. They married a short time later, and the house continued to serve as a way station for the displaced. The family survived Prohibition and the Great Depression thanks to Roland's whiskey still.

In 1958 a Korean War U.S. Navy vet from Boston named Edward Hollins Nassedrine decided that he needed to get as far away from the ocean as possible before he became a navy lifer. He asked around and learned about the Astrin house through a fellow sailor's father, who'd stayed there twenty years earlier. The continental pole of inaccessibility in North America was actually five hours southwest, in Allen, South Dakota, but the house outside Clark was close enough for him.

When Ed Nassedrine called the number he'd been given, Rhonda Astrin—over for her weekly dinner with Mom and Dad—picked up the phone because Teresa was busy taking a ham out of the oven. Rhonda didn't have the heart to turn a vet down, and by the time her mother got to the phone, it was too late to stop Ed from coming. He hitchhiked out, stayed in the tiny spare bedroom on the second floor, and found a job as a welder. Four months later he proposed to Rhonda Astrin. They got married and tried valiantly but without success to have children, and eventually her parents died and left them the house.

Laynie didn't know any of this history, and Jacob only knew Ed's hitchhiking tale and the legend of Roland's still. When Jacob and Daniel arrived from Boston, freshly orphaned, Ed and Rhonda didn't want them to know the house's long history of giving shelter to the out-of-luck and the transitory. They wanted to exude stability—a specifically blue-collar stability based on frugality, continuous hard work, and not blowing off so much steam that the fire inside you went out. They never told the boys that the room used to have nicknames: Chambrell Road Lost and Found, Astrin Home for the Wayward, Stray Man Depot. They didn't know that dozens, if not hundreds, of people had fallen asleep in that room while their heads spun with uncertainty, doubt, hope, clandestine and sometimes illegal machinations, and the all-pervasive fear of failure.

Laynie didn't need to know that such restless emotions were embedded in the DNA of the room in order to feel their force. When the sinking sun hit the window, she unzipped her suitcase and stared at her things. Nothing she owned would help her survive a South Dakota winter. Nothing she *was* suggested survival either. Too small, too delicate, too birdlike. But she had to make it through because her old self wasn't exactly surviving in LA either. Her old self barely clung to life. Here she could drag it up from the ground, rebuild it, rehabilitate it.

Or could she? Laynie looked out the window and saw only the unfamiliar. Only a landscape that was part of other people's psyches. *If I can pick myself up here*, she reasoned, *I can pick myself up anywhere*.

"And if you can't?" her real voice asked. Then the light outside brightened—a physical reality caused by the angle of the sun, not some trick of perception—and Laynie brightened too. She pictured herself years later, long after meeting Jacob in Hot Springs had faded into memory, and knew that this instant would echo in her mind as the moment she truly moved in at Cocklebur Farm.

8

The Last Hexagram

While Laynie was communing with God / fate / the universe atop
the widow's walk, Jacob had called Don-o and arranged for a visit
from the Donatellis that very evening. Don-o proposed spaghetti
and red wine, and all Jacob had to provide was pasta and a kitchen.
It was completely dark by the time Don-o's gang arrived at six thirty,
so Laynie felt like it was already bedtime.

"Do people sleep a lot in the winter this far north?" she asked,
yawning. Even Richard Donatelli—aka Rico Suave, Little Richard,
Ricardo Montalban, Tricky Dick, or whatever else Don-o felt like
calling him—laughed at her.

"This isn't winter yet," said Chrissy. "But you make up for it in the
summer, when the sun's out till ten."

Don-o came across exactly as Jacob advertised: big-hearted, great
hugger, bristly, sarcastic. But Laynie had no idea what to make of
Chrissy, who seemed way too artsy and progressive for a fifth-
generation South Dakotan. She was dirty blonde and bony, taller
than her husband by two inches, and with her long face she looked
as laconic as the Marlboro Man. But she had a nose ring, liked Bernie
Sanders, and talked up a storm about her new business venture: the
Flat Earth Boutique up in Aberdeen.

"You'll need some clothes if you came here with just one suitcase,"
she told Laynie. While the men cooked, Chrissy breastfed Richie in

the living room and showed Laynie some eBay winter options on Jacob's laptop. On a budget of $90, Chrissy found her Boggs snow-boots, Smartwool thermals, a Marmot fleece, and a slightly overused North Face jacket.

"I can watch the bids for you," she told Laynie. "Unless you want me to pull the trigger right now."

"Is this a test to find out if I'm staying?" Laynie wanted to be as forthright as Chrissy, who'd be her instant best friend if she stuck around.

"If you want it to be." Chrissy switched her son from one nipple to the next. "If you're wondering how many details we know about you, the answer's a lot. You're pretty famous for burning a certain piece of paper with certain signatures on it."

"Well, you have to be famous for something."

"Not that we blame you. Jacob was *nothing* like being ready for marriage then."

"Is he now?" asked Laynie.

Chrissy thought about it. "He's more stable in some ways, less in others. Danny dying did something to him he hasn't figured out yet."

"You knew his brother?"

"If Clark Junior-Senior High had an election for most likely to die of a heroin overdose, Danny would get every vote. Jacob always thought he could save him."

"Jacob's like that," said Laynie.

"Which is why you scare us a bit. He always talked like he wanted to save you."

"Does it make it better or worse if I want to save him too?"

Chrissy put a finger to her lip. "Better, but just barely. We'll be watching you both for signs."

Signs of what, Laynie thought of asking, though she knew the answer was pills. "Anything else I should know?" she asked instead.

"Jacob and I dated senior year in high school. We were the artsy ones everybody hated. But you probably knew that."

Laynie hadn't. Meanwhile, back in the kitchen, the pasta cooked and the men's vegetarian sauce simmered. Jacob did a throw with Don-o's most ancient set of Chinese coins—though not his rarest.

"It's *Wei Chi*," Donatelli said when the final coins settled. "The last hexagram, R. L. Wing's real good on this one. '*There is grave danger in proceeding without caution immediately before the end. You must—*'"

"The end of what?"

"Shhh." Don-o closed his eyes to focus. "'*You must prepare yourself with wariness and reserve, for the coming situation will be unlike any you have ever experienced. Receiving this hexagram may suggest that you are not prepared to see clearly what must be done to take the final steps into your future. All aspects of life and human affairs must come to an end and begin anew. Awareness and acceptance of this cycle is the truth of human life. All else is an illusion as insubstantial as air. Do not become suspended in a meaningless midbreath.*' I think I got most of that right."

"Shit, Don-o. The end of what? Me and Laynie?"

"The end of *you*, pal. Of Jacob Nastydream, as you know him. '*In many ways this time will be nothing short of a rebirth.*'"

"Fuck rebirth." He covered Richard's ears. "I've been reborn so many times I don't even notice it anymore."

"Well, I can't help you there," said Donatelli as he dropped the coins into their pouch. "I'm still waiting for my first time, you know?"

* * *

The evening was by turns intimate and superficial, and it served its purpose perfectly. Laynie learned that Jacob had living, breathing friends, and the Donatellis learned that Laynie was more than a license burner with a malformed uterus. When they put Rico Suave on her lap, the boy didn't fling himself off screaming—a crucial test of her good-heartedness. They stayed until ten, when they popped their head outside and got worried about bad weather rolling in.

"I'm not sleeping in your bed just because I met your friends," Laynie told Jacob once the Donatellis left.

"Duh," said Jacob. "I made your bed already."

"Thanks, I noticed. That used to be your brother's room, didn't it?" She waited for him to nod. "Don't you think that's dangerous?"

Jacob settled against the wall. "Daniel never cared about saving himself. That's the difference between you."

"Does that make me easier to save?"

"Of course. It means you'll try saving me too. Did you talk to Chrissy?"

"Is she the world's foremost expert on your savior complex?" asked Laynie, and Jacob just laughed and went to his bedroom. Laynie set herself up in the guest bathroom between Daniel's bedroom and Jacob's, then shouted good night to him and silently counted out the pills in her Kenya bag. She got up to seventeen before reddening with embarrassment, then declared that this house would be where she made her final stand against pills. She couldn't flush them tonight, though. Jacob would sniff that out somehow.

Sleep came kindly and lasted until one in the morning, when a wind from the north came and shook the house almost as hard as an LA earthquake. But the South Dakota wind didn't undulate and roll away. It insisted, and it battered. It bullied into every space it could, forcing its way into cracks between jointed pieces of wood, between roof shingles, between lengths of siding. Then it made a high-pitched chiseling sound that had Laynie covering her ears. Other times it caught the whole house like a sail, making a *whoosh* like a sharp whip, and she pictured the whole thing lifting up into the sky like Dorothy's house in *The Wizard of Oz*. She panicked at her rattling window and checked the weather on her phone, expecting a tornado, but there wasn't even a note from the National Weather Service. Down the hallway Jacob snored as if it happened every day.

What if it did? Could she live like this? Laynie listened to the wind for an hour, feeling its cold move through the siding and the drywall and eventually through her flesh. She wanted to call Chrissy and have her buy those eBay clothes immediately, regardless of what the bids were. Something on the other side of the house crashed to the ground and skittered. From her window she saw a metal deck chair tumbling by on the ground, which had a thin layer of powdery snow. The chair stayed put as the wind relented momentarily, but like the Big Bad Wolf, it gathered itself and tried to blow the house down again, and the chair continued tumbling end over end.

She wished there were a tree out her window to gauge the power of the wind by. If Laynie stayed, she'd want such a tree as part of her bargain. But who was she kidding? If she stayed, she'd be moving down the hall to his bedroom. When a fresh blade of wind stabbed between the cracks in the windowpane and chilled Laynie's skin, she stepped back to bed and balled up with the blankets over her head.

Impossible to sleep. She heard another knock that seemed to come from the hallway and stepped out into it with the blanket over her shoulders, then checked out the small, square room across the hall. Jacob had glided by it on his house tour that afternoon with a comment about "old family junk," but as he closed its door, she'd seen beautiful oak shelves.

Laynie tiptoed down the hallway, turned the knob silently, and let herself in. She expected to see Jacob there, contemplating his family mementos, but the room was empty. She found a huge butterscotch leather lounger and settled into it, using her phone as a flashlight to survey the shelves.

The lounger was placed perfectly so that she could see nearly everything with a simple swivel of her head. The room was a museum of Nassedrine-hood: a framed photograph of a teenage Jacob playing tennis with a graying woman—Great-Aunt Rhonda, she guessed. A ukulele, a ratty alligator skin purse, a stack of neatly folded Hawaiian shirts, a glass clown holding an accordion. Her bowels shook at the sight of so much stuff that belonged to dead people. *Out! Out!* she wanted to shout, like some backwoods exorcist. She wanted to tell Jacob that if you hang onto dead people's stuff like that—or even worse, show it off in your home!—you guarantee disquiet for them *and* yourself. They'll always come back to their stuff, which is why you have to scatter it around and help them truly die.

The light from Laynie's phone kept finding a check on a clothespin recipe holder. She got up to fetch it, then sat back down in the lounger. It was from a man named Stan Guliemi of 24 Winter Street in Boston, written out to one Michael P. Nassedrine for $20 and dated December 11. The day before Jacob's family exploded. On the back she found the daddy longlegs signature of Jacob's father. It looked nothing like Jacob's own, which was tight and controlled. The same way Jacob was tight and controlled, unless he wasn't.

Down the hallway his bedroom door opened as if Laynie touching the check had set off an alarm. He had a real flashlight, and its beam caught the halo of Laynie's hair from the Shrine Room door.

"What are you doing here?" he asked. Calm, not violent. Nothing like his murderous father. Then Jacob saw the check in her hand. "Careful with that. It's fragile."

"Who's Stan Guliemi?"

"A guy around the corner. Locked his keys in his car, my dad helped him out. I don't want to hear any jokes about this stuff, Lane."

"I'm not making any." She kept her voice flat. No false moves or surprises.

"You've got your way to remember dead people, I've got mine. Okay?"

Jacob held out his hand, which shook as she handed him the check, and he solemnly clipped it back into its appropriate spot between the accordion clown and a chipped, unpainted plaster grizzly bear. He loomed over her for a moment and sat on the floor to let the electricity dissipate from his face and hands.

"I can't live here, Jacob," she said. "I know it's what you want, but I can't. This room feels like a morgue." Laynie spread her arms wide to gesture at the whole collection. "It smells like a morgue, and I'm sick of that smell."

"Then I'll burn it. Or I'll give it away like you, all over the place."

"That's *my* thing, I can't ask you to—"

"You don't *have* to ask me, Lane. If I need to get rid of this stuff for us to have half a chance, then it's an easy trade."

Laynie nodded, but she didn't like the terms of the deal. Jacob would find some way to hold it against her, to turn it into a hidden grudge that he trotted out during their most heated arguments. *You made me give up all I had left of my family!* His eyes roved over the shelves and hers followed, but they stopped on something Laynie hadn't noticed at first: the small marble woman that William Jackman had given Jacob in LA, back before the drama and the burned marriage license. Jacob followed her gaze to it, then stretched out to reach for it.

"This we keep." He picked up the woman and balanced her on his palm.

"No. My dad's dead. It should go."

Jacob shook his head, resolute. "If I ever have a kid, I want to be able to say, 'Your grandpa made this.' It stays, or you go."

He put the woman back in place, and Laynie relented, chewing over his words. If *I* ever have a kid, he'd said. Not *we*. By saying *I* instead, Jacob turned away from the idea of ever having a child with any other woman in the universe.

So sure, so definite. How the hell could she turn away from that?

PART 2

The Rise and Fall of a Private Bohemia

9

Wabasso, Sleepy Eye, and Points Beyond

Thirty hours later the Shrine Room's contents had been boxed up and arranged in rough order of significance in the covered bed of Jacob's Dodge. Laynie suggested that he put the most trivial objects toward the tailgate, since they'd be easiest to give up, and hide the more sentimentally valuable items deeper in.

"That way you can save the good stuff for when you really start liking it," she said, sliding her father's mementos in beside those of the dead Nassedrines. They watered the three sad houseplants, made coffee for the road, and climbed into the purple truck to begin their leave-taking adventure. It didn't start up until Jacob's third try.

"Can this thing make it to New York and back?" Laynie asked.

"Watch my coffee," Jacob told her. He revved the engine and zipped backward thirty feet over the snow-crusted ground. In one motion he jammed the steering wheel to the left, stepped on the clutch, and whipped the wheel to the right. The truck lurched heavily but stopped with its nose pointed 180 degrees from where it started. He slipped into first and headed casually down the driveway as Laynie whooped.

"That's what you call a Nassedrine U-turn." Jacob patted the dash-board. "I'll teach you how if you ever start using the name."

As they passed beneath the COCKLEBUR FARM sign, Laynie decided to love this place. Not to do her best, which implied failure, but to ferociously love it no matter what that cost her. She decided to be a life lover, one of those exuberant people who leaves smiles and better posture in their wake. On a hairpin turn she saw, at the bottom of the hill, a pile of enormous, pale silver tree trunks tumbled on the ground like a campfire abandoned by giants.

"What's that for?" she asked Jacob.

"When God wants to set the world on fire, he can start there. That's what Daniel used to say."

"He believed in God?"

"Believe, yes. Follow, no. People clear the land and forget about it. My aunt Rhonda said they were there her whole life." Jacob rolled by the tree trunks slowly so Laynie could get a good look, then turned left onto the asphalt of County Road 46. It was also called 424th Avenue, so they decided in LA fashion to christen it "the 424." They went past two little farms and an extremely decrepit barn, its wood bleached as silver as the tree trunks. Next came a cramped feedlot full of waiting-to-die cattle, which Jacob said she'd only get a whiff of when it was just about to snow. Then the road cut between two ice-skinned surfaces, and Laynie saw a post sticking out the water with an inexplicable old electrical box on it.

"This is Mud Lake," Jacob said. "Great for fishing bullheads, if that's your thing."

"It's not yours?"

"I haven't gone native yet. Not exactly a son of the prairies, you know."

She heard the venom in his voice and didn't like it. "Are there at least people you talk to here?"

"I'll talk to anybody, sure. But there's only a few of 'em I'd tell you're part Lebanese, let's put it that way."

"What would they do? Tell me to go back to my own country?"

"California's sort of its own country, isn't it?" They crossed County Road 54, and Jacob announced, "Voilà, we're now on South Smith Street in beautiful Clark." The houses weren't shabby at all, and some even looked new and custom-built. Soon sidewalks began, and they passed a church, and they came to something like a downtown. Another church, a bar, an auto parts store. Quaint but at the same time depressingly sedate. Jacob took a few turns and drove by his old school, more churches, a bait shop, a coffeehouse called Caffeine Paradise that Laynie liked the look of, and what he called the cleanest gas station on Earth. They headed east on US 212—which they of course nicknamed "the 212"—and within a few breaths were out in the winter-bare fields again.

"Cute town," Laynie said. "Population six hundred?"

"Don't sell us short, city slicker. A whole thousand."

"It's nice. I could stay awhile."

"Awhile, huh?" Jacob asked.

"Don't get offended. People say they'll stay *awhile* and never leave."

"Or people say they'll stay *awhile* and leave a month later."

"Is that what your brother did?"

Jacob nodded. He wanted to get rid of something immediately— ideally Daniel's *Boy Scout Handbook* with the scrawled genitalia—but asked the expert if they were far enough away from home.

"I wouldn't do it," Laynie said. "You don't give dead people's stuff to friends, and you don't leave it where you'll see it again. That's basic common sense."

* * *

They followed the 212 through Watertown, which Jacob called "the big city" even though it only boasted twenty-some thousand souls. It had a Target, a Walmart, a rec center with a swimming pool, and an Irish bar that specialized in pizza. Once they hit Minnesota, Jacob got tired of driving straight lines and stairstepped down on US 75 to State Highway 68, through Ghent and Marshall and Lucan, looking for a place to leave his first thing behind. Nothing called to him or Laynie until Wabasso, where he started thinking about his gas gauge and stopped at a Cenex. She took Jacob's credit card inside while he pumped gas, and when he joined her inside, he could tell she had a plan.

"What's up your sleeve?" he asked as they walked along an aisle of canned beans, corn, tuna, Spam, chili.

"Nothing at all." Then she slid something between two cans so stealthily that Jacob couldn't tell what it was or even exactly where she'd put it. Laynie grabbed a bag of cashews and headed for the pasty-faced teenage counter boy in triumph, as if she'd left behind a mystery no one would ever solve. Jacob lingered by a display of glowworms and chewing tobacco while she paid up.

"Where you from?" asked the counter boy.

"South Africa," Laynie replied in an atrocious accent. Back outside, Jacob refused to start the truck until she spilled her secret.

"It was a nail file, okay? We were on our way to a party where I was supposed to meet Martin, and it was right after Dad broke his ankle, so he couldn't drive. I was in heels, driving us up to this swanky house in Topanga Canyon, and he was filing his fingernails. I'd never seen him do it before in my life and never saw it again, so that was the world's one and only William Jackman memorial nail file."

"Do I have to pry it out of you every time you leave something? Aren't I your partner in crime here?"

"I've never done this with anybody before, Jakey. Give me a break." Then she blew a kiss toward the gas station. "Bye, Dad!"

"Bye!" called Jacob. He stairstepped down the backroads some more until they reached US 14 and the town of Sleepy Eye. Its golf club was asleep for the winter, but Laynie made him pull over. She fished out her father's golf cap left over from a breast cancer charity tournament, which he'd played in even though his wife had never had cancer. Cancer, brain tumor—did it matter? Not to William Jackman, whose white cap with a pink embroidered ribbon and crisscrossed black putters Laynie left at the clubhouse doorstep.

"That's all there is to it," she said as she hopped back into the truck, bursting with life as she celebrated death. Jacob got tired of driving, and Laynie didn't feel like taking the wheel just yet, so they started looking for places with great names to spend the night—in separate beds, at her insistence. Across the border in Iowa the town of Spillville sounded promising, but it didn't have a motel. They considered sleeping in the truck in the parking lot of St. Wenceslaus Catholic Church, but they only had one sleeping bag. In nearby Decorah they took a room at Zack's Motor Inn, around the corner from a Norwegian-American museum. Once they checked in, Jacob tried to get into the swing of things by leaving Daniel's record-setting running shoes underneath the sink. Laynie gave him a dour thumbs-down.

"Two basic rules. In hotels you can't leave anything until right before you're ready to check out."

"Why's that?"

She handed him Daniel's shoes but didn't answer. "And you can't start with the heavy stuff. You bring a whole bunch into the room the night before, and when you're ready to check out, it hits you what to leave."

Since she was the world's foremost expert on this practice, Jacob didn't argue. He pulled the most accessible box of relics out of his truck and set it by the television next to a box of Laynie's. He turned off the lights and crawled into his lonely twin bed, but the room felt too crowded for sleep—all the things he and Laynie wanted to say to each other but weren't brave enough to mouth, plus the voices of the dead Nassedrines and the dead Jackmans and the perfect fiancé Martin. The voices of the miscarried babies that couldn't be called dead because they'd never lived. Jacob listened to those voices until three in the morning, when he gave up on sleep and crawled into Laynie's bed.

"What the hell?" She got rid of him with a few kicks. "Don't blow it, okay?"

"I just wanted to show you I love you." Jacob retreated back to his own bed.

"You already showed me." Laynie mumbled into her pillow. "G'night sweetie. G'night darling."

At dawn somebody outside their window took five minutes to start a reluctant truck engine, which woke them both irrevocably. As they packed up to leave Zack's Motor Inn, Jacob realized—exactly as Laynie had predicted—what to leave behind. When he was a senior in high school, his brother, then a sophomore, had gotten into all sorts of trouble. Mooning his social studies teacher, defacing cars, blowing pot smoke through the principal's office window, etc. The cross-country coach wrote a note to Ed and Rhonda explaining that Daniel would lose his athletic eligibility if such behavior continued. The note ended:

> Although Jacob does make some effort to be a good influence on Daniel, I think he could make a lot stronger one. Jacob acts as if small, gentle reminders will be enough for Daniel, but I (as both his coach and teacher) feel that stronger measures are necessary. I'm not criticizing your discipline in the home. I'm sure you run a tight ship and demand a lot from these boys, and you're good people for taking them in after their tragedy. But Jacob is the boy Daniel looks up to most, and his biggest influence. If Jacob cares about his brother, as I'm sure he does, he'll put more effort into preventing further deterioration in Daniel's behavior and work habits. A little nudge here and there, at this point, isn't enough.

Jacob kissed the note and slipped it inside his pillowcase. Laynie exited the bathroom just in time to watch him stash it.

"Nice going," she told him. "I'm going to copy you." She rifled through her box for a Certificate of Appreciation given to her father by the University of California–Irvine Alumni Association, thanking him for the scholarship he helped set up so poor kids could study hotel management. Laynie showed him the paper and slid it inside her pillowcase.

"It's all about surprise," she explained. "Some random person finds it, and they think 'Who the hell is William Jackman? Who the hell is Daniel Nassedrine?' And that makes both of them smile, so we can smile too."

* * *

In Monona, Iowa, Laynie left her father's thick 14 karat gold bracelet in a tray full of machine screws at a farm supply store. In Wauzeka, Wisconsin, Jacob disobeyed Laynie's rule of priority and hurled Daniel's tied-together running shoes onto a set of power lines that gave light to a Lutheran church. He walked to his truck feeling exactly like Daniel—the scruffiness, the irresponsibility, the lust for freedom, everything.

At a bone-chilling turnout on the Wisconsin River near Easter Rock, Jacob left a pair of plastic water pistols—his red, Daniel's green—that had miraculously survived their journey from Boston among their unused Sunday clothes. He filled them with Gatorade and blasted a few squirts in Laynie's direction before setting them at the edge of a snow-covered picnic table. Meanwhile, Laynie buried an old silver saxophone mouthpiece under a mound of snow at her end. She'd found it by chance when she was eight, during a three-hour antique shopping spree with Dad while Mom was at the doctor for—

At the doctor for what? Laynie wondered, and the whole story of her life changed in a flash. Maybe Mom had been dying since she was eight, not twelve, as she'd always thought, and her parents had hidden the fact so well that it took her almost two decades to figure out the truth. The day they got the mouthpiece must have been the day Mom found out about the tumor or the day she started treatments. It had to be a meaningful day, or there would've been no reason on earth for Dad to spend three hours antiquing and come out with nothing but a part of an instrument that nobody in the family knew how to play. Laynie, lost in packing snow over the mouthpiece, grew weary at the prospect of rewriting her personal history once more.

"I'm freezing my ass off," she told Jacob, digging the mouthpiece out of the snow and pocketing it. "I'm out of here."

They followed the Wisconsin River and didn't stop again until they found August Derleth Park in Sauk City, which didn't look as cold as Easter Rock but turned out to be far worse thanks to the wind. On a bench by the river's edge, Laynie left the cufflinks she'd given her father for his fiftieth birthday: black and flat and square with a tiny diamond chip in each. She felt nervous because she couldn't be sure their finders would appreciate them and assuaged her fears by writing a note that she weighed down with a rock.

> These cufflinks are expensive and valuable—the diamonds are real. Don't just throw them away! They were my dad's and he doesn't need them anymore. Give them to a man you know who is kind-hearted and gentle. If you sell them, use the money to do something nice for someone. Don't be selfish with these cufflinks or the money you get from them, or the universe will be pissed at you *FOREVER!!!*

Jacob had already picked out something to leave behind in Sauk City, but he waited until they got back to the pavilion near the entrance to put it down: a little green ceramic box shaped like a turtle that Aunt Rhonda kept her pills in. Letting go of her turtle box, he thought, might signal the end of his on-and-off love affair with pills. Laynie was better than pills, anyway—Laynie and the children they'd have if he could only keep his shit together, only stay straight for the rest of his fucking life and never fuck up, not even once, not even for a minute.

Jacob felt like his chest was in a giant vise, and he wasn't sure he could hack being a saint forever. He took Laynie's pen and notebook to write a note of his own. The turtle box sat in his coat pocket with his left fist clenched protectively over it.

"Okay if I write a note?" he asked. "Or is there a 'one note at a time' rule?"

"One note at a time, let's say. What's going on?"

"Oh, nothing." Jacob set the turtle in front of Laynie and pushed it toward her. "My aunt Rhonda's pillbox."

"Pillbox, huh?" Laynie lifted off the top. Empty inside. "What was she into?"

"Fuck if I know." Jacob explained that Rhonda used to keep the turtle box on her bedside table with a stash inside it—her "night vitamins," she called them when Jacob and Daniel first moved in. When they started smoking pot, she hid the box under some musty sweaters in her armoire, and although Jacob had seen her go to it many times, he never stole a pill and never told Daniel about its new location. After her funeral Jacob pulled the box out from between the sweaters and showed it to Daniel, who cursed himself for not finding the stash years earlier. They'd split her last four pills: two Seconals, two Darvocets.

"If me and Daniel raided that pillbox when we were teenagers," he said, "then I wouldn't have the house right now. She never would've left it to us if I stole from her."

"Good thing you were a trustworthy boy, then."

"The question is if I'm a trustworthy man." His gloved hand found hers. "Look, Lane. What if one of us falls off the wagon? What'll you do if it's me?"

"Same thing you'll do if it's me, I hope. Fight like hell."

"But not chicken out, right? Not lie?"

Laynie shook her head and pushed the turtle back toward Jacob, then stood. She noticed a car approaching, and by mistake she caught a glimpse of its occupants—a stone-faced older couple, their mouths locked in disapproval of the modern world. One of her cardinal rules of leave-taking was to not be caught in the act, and Jacob understood that without having to be told. He stuffed the pillbox back into his pocket and waved gleefully at the old couple, who didn't wave back.

10

A Montezuma Goodbye

Rhonda's pillbox disappeared a few hours later in the men's room of a rib joint in Peru, Illinois, where Jacob left it atop a condom dispenser. In Peru they made love at a motel called Stan's Motor Plaza—in honor of Stan Guliemi, whose $20 check to Paulie Nassedrine got hidden in a stack of brochures advertising local tourist traps. The place had been inexplicably booked up, so they got stuck with a lumpy king-sized bed in a room with a malfunctioning heater. They sat fully clothed under the covers, drinking red wine and watching Chicago Blackhawks hockey with the sound off until Laynie drifted off into sleep. She got up to brush her teeth, and when she opened the bathroom door, she found Jacob standing naked in the doorway. His fingertips brushed her collarbone.

"Jakey," she said, the droop in her voice mildly pleading to be left alone. His hand went to her cheek, and he stroked it more softly than she thought he could. More humbly than she remembered from their first time around, when he was brash and wanted to fill the world with himself.

"Look," he told her. "I don't care if it turns out like last time—"

"Don't curse us like that."

"Even if it does." Jacob's hand shook as it slid from her cheek to her jaw, from her jaw to the nape of her neck.

"I hope you know what you're doing," Laynie mumbled. Then

Jacob found the spot she always loved him to touch: the hollow at the base of her skull. She felt too cold to take off her T-shirt and sweater, but she lifted them up partway so their bellies could touch. He sank into her slowly, wanting all the things they wished they could be for each other in LA but weren't brave enough for yet—weren't beaten up by life enough for yet—to flood inside them and fill their skins and lungs and vessels.

"I'm not holding back," Jacob said right before he came. "Say we'll try, Lane."

"We'll try." She closed her eyes and prayed to God—this qualified as a 5 percent moment—for Jacob's sperm to find an egg, for the ensuing embryo to stick to the lining of her womb. She didn't orgasm, not even close. But after he did, everything in her mind went blank like an old TV that got unplugged by mistake. All the static between her functioning emotional stations, all the maybe-ness of her life, all the fuzz and rolling bars simply ended, and Laynie rebooted to find the man she loved inside her where he belonged. The man who'd stay through fifty miscarriages if she let him. Laynie scratched Jacob's back hard enough to break his skin because love had to be made with the whole body, the whole orchestra of human feeling, or it wasn't love at all.

"Three percent," Laynie said when Jacob rolled off her. "Don't get your hopes up."

"Fifty-fifty chance," Jacob replied. "Don't drag your hopes in the mud."

* * *

When they left Stan's Motor Plaza the next morning, Laynie left her father's deck of Belgian pornographic playing cards from the 1920s, and Jacob left a live .38 caliber bullet that Daniel used to keep in his pocket. They blazed through Illinois and much of Indiana saying almost nothing, with Laynie resting her head against the window to feel the rumble of the road. She let Jacob have his silence, knowing that she'd need her own before too long. Sometimes he broke it to talk about his dad.

"One time he bitched me out for spending money on a Celtics hat," he said. "With my *own* money, stuff I earned cutting laws. He's grumbling down the stairs—drunk or on his way to get drunk, I was too young to tell. And he says 'Fuckin' kid. Nobody asked for you.' He didn't even know I could hear him. Or he knew and didn't give a shit."

"Did he ever hit you?" Laynie asked him.

"*He*? Try *they*." Jacob rolled down his window to cool off his tight face. "It wasn't punching. Mostly pushing and shoving. Daniel got it worse—he was always in trouble. And the people on SMS, pretty much *all* of them had it worse than both of us. Shit, Lane. I'm totally not ready to be a dad. And I thought I was four years ago."

He checked his mirror to make sure he was still himself, then pulled hard onto the shoulder and parked. They were on Hoagland Road in Boston Corner, Indiana, trying to get unlost and about to cross the Ohio border. "You drive, hon. Pick some music too."

Once they switched, he put his head against the window and closed his eyes, not caring where she took him. She was his escape hatch, and as weak and chickenshit as that sounded, he'd go wherever she drove him. Even if he ended up living through a miscarriage every month, it was better than living in the nowhere he'd boxed himself into. The no-thing-ness he'd built for protection but couldn't protect himself from.

* * *

In Defiance, Ohio, Jacob talked Laynie into breaking her rule about mom-and-pop motels and renting a honeymoon suite with a jacuzzi at a big chain hotel. They ate a room service dinner of scallops and asparagus so Jacob could feel extra spermy. He shaved with the complimentary kit in the bathroom while she waited in the hot water, eating the last of his scallops so she could feel extra spermy too. She swore she felt the pinch of ovulation the next morning and left her whole clamshell box of birth control pills in the bathroom. They had nothing to do with her father, but she could feel him smiling down on her gift nonetheless.

Welcome to your first day of true fertility! called an exaggerated two-dimensional William Jackman from behind a heavenly cloud. He had a crown, scepter, and fur cape, and his jaw came completely unhinged like someone in an old Monty Python animation. They spent the next night in Burning Well, Pennsylvania, and Christmas Eve in Roscoe, New York, where they toasted all their former embryos with sparkling water instead of wine. They wanted to be clean, clean, clean, just in case Laynie's dropping egg met a sperm it liked.

In Tranquility, New Jersey, they holed up at a bed and breakfast to plan their strategy. After Laynie made her last dropoff in Queens, they'd drive in whichever direction struck them, forbidden by rule from crossing their previous path. She constantly rearranged her five last mementos of her father on a coffee table, trying to iden-tify the Three Sacred Things that she'd keep forever. Jacob, in a fit of post-orgasmic honesty, confessed that he'd kept Daniel's guitar, syringe, and death clothes in the basement so Laynie wouldn't make him give them away. She graciously counted the death clothes as a single object, and this grace helped her choose her own Three Sacred Things:

1) the saxophone mouthpiece, made more magical now by her realization at Easter Rock;
2) the green lizard brooch that Dad had given Mom, which she'd worn the night she met Jacob at the Barnsdall Arts Center;
3) a strip of photo booth pictures taken at Santa Monica pier when she was three, in which she and her parents looked unimaginably bright faced and grateful for her existence.

Laynie left the runner-up object behind at the bed and breakfast: a red coffee mug with a picture of her grinning father, who held another red coffee mug with his grinning face on it. Looked at with the right tools, it might go on into infinity. Jacob left Aunt Rhonda's well-thumbed book on the Bermuda Triangle, which had been her most persistent obsession.

Five hours later, thanks to wrong turns and traffic jams, they arrived at Flushing Hospital Medical Center in Queens, where William Jackman had been born. Laynie stepped into the lobby, which was as close as security would let her get to the maternity ward. In her fingers she held a picture taken on her first birthday of Dad tossing her up into the air. She could see a sliver of blue between her yellow outfit and his hands, as if she might lose her gravity and float up into the sky.

"That's what happened, isn't it?" Laynie asked the picture as she circled the lobby, looking for the perfect place to leave it. "You let go of me, and I lost track of gravity." She kissed the picture, stuck it inside an issue of *People* magazine on a coffee table, and hurried away.

"Bye!" Laynie blew another kiss at the picture. A big, surly woman sitting on a couch thought the kiss was for her, and she glared back archly. Laynie waved at the woman, blew a second kiss that truly *was* for her, and dashed out to the loading zone, where Jacob sat idling to speed their escape.

"Did you lay your burden down?" he asked.

"Yep. Laid it right down. Your turn now."

Once they escaped Queens, they broke their rule forbidding major highways and took the Jersey Turnpike south, both of them hungry for the rush of high-speed driving. But it was eight o'clock at night before they got above thirty miles an hour, and they ended up sleeping at a chain motel in Perth Amboy. All they could taste in each other's mouths was exhaust fumes, and it killed their desire to make love. At five in the morning they blazed south through the rest of New Jersey, but once they hit Delaware, they returned to the backroads plan. Jacob left behind Daniel's favorite guitar pick in Jimtown, Delaware, because he'd mistakenly read the sign as *Jimitown* and thought of Hendrix. He liked the sound of Shaft Ox Corner, Maryland, so he dug a tiny hole by the side of the road and buried a shark's tooth that he'd bought for Daniel's thirteenth birthday.

Then he decided, for no particular reason, that they should head west again. In Stronghold, Maryland, Jacob threw the trophy that Daniel got for winning the nine-year-old division of Punt, Pass, and Kick into a lake. In Needmore, West Virginia, he threw the key to Daniel's basement in Hot Springs out the window and onto somebody's lawn. At a gas station in Torch, Ohio, he left a photograph of John Elway with a signature forged—quite expertly—by Uncle Ed. For reasons Jacob couldn't explain, losing that one made him testy. In bed that night, in Olive Branch, Ohio, he got sullen and barely touched Laynie.

"I can't go through with this shit," he said. His shoulders weren't hunched so much as squished down, as if he wanted to stifle his own heartbeat. "Every time I open up the back of that truck, I feel like puking."

"It's down to the hard stuff. Hard choices."

"I want three more things, okay? I've got to have a family picture—everybody's got a fucking family picture."

"So keep three more. I'd rather see you keep ten than get like this."

"Get like *this*?" Jacob growled. "Like *what*?" He propped himself up on his elbow, ready for a fight. He heard his father's voice resonating in his own, and he cried, and Laynie comforted him. Just like Grace Nassedrine, bless her strangled little throat, had no doubt comforted her Paulie many times.

* * *

In the light of day Jacob started getting rid of things again, and they both drove like maniacs because they wanted to get back to Cocklebur

Farm and restart their lives. Plus, they were running out of cash and room on their credit cards. The black-and-white photo of Jacob's parents cutting their wedding cake disappeared at a sub shop in Marengo, Indiana. The loathed family picture from Sears came to rest in a gas station bathroom in Olney, Illinois. The hood emblem from the 1958 Cadillac on which the Nassedrine boys learned body work with Uncle Ed found a new home, with another Cadillac of similar vintage, in Bolivar, Missouri. By the time they got to the Chatwin Motor Lodge in Montezuma, Kansas, at almost midnight on New Year's Eve, Jacob had only two things left to give away: his mother's tattered alligator purse and his father's misspelled army jacket.

"You can keep a couple extra things," Laynie suggested. "Or you could trade your mom's gator for the needle and your dad's coat for the death clothes."

"Stop. No jokes."

"That wasn't one."

Laynie stayed up half the night checking to see if Jacob slept at all. The coat and purse both hung from a rack across from his side of the bed—he'd insisted on breaking their habitual sleep position to have them more directly in his line of sight. Even in her dreams he kept his eyes glued on them, as if they'd start singing and dancing. At three in the morning the strap on the purse, unaccustomed to hanging, broke. Jacob shot out of bed, swore and sweated and trembled, and slept awhile in his truck. Laynie dressed and packed up just in case she heard his engine start and had to hustle out to keep from being stranded. At sunrise Jacob finally stepped back into the room.

"I need to be alone with them." He loomed in the doorway, fists balled as if ready to have it out with his mother and father once and for all.

"Fine," Laynie said, but only because she didn't want to seem like such a nobody that she couldn't make a peep. She strapped herself into the Dodge's passenger seat even though she had no idea how long she'd be waiting there. The motel room door slammed, but even through the windshield, she heard Jacob shouting.

"A dishonorable discharge!" he told the coat. "That's all you got from the army—no badges, no Purple Hearts, nothing. And *you*." Jacob kicked the alligator bag. "*You!*"

He kicked at the bag again, missing this time, then fell onto the bed and wept. That voice—that demeaning, accusing way of saying *You!*—had passed down to him from his father like some ancestral venereal disease of the soul. He begged God / fate / the universe to never let him use that voice on Laynie, to never put that kind of hatred into the world again, to extinguish it whenever he smelled it burning. When the tears stopped, he stared at the coat, with its moth-eaten lapels and its NASSEDRING in faded black letters, and tried to imagine his father's face popping up from inside the collar. But he barely remembered the man's breathing flesh. Every image he came up with looked like a bust in a wax museum.

Jacob buried his face in a pillow, pounded the mattress, and shouted a string of curses. He fell silent, holding his breath, and waited for his father's voice. Nothing. More curses into the pillow. And then:

"I'm tired," his father groaned. "Leave me the fuck alone, will you?"

Jacob held his breath and waited for more. He wondered whether the voice was a spontaneous memory from childhood or something he'd manufactured to get himself out of the room, but when it kept mumbling and swearing, he knew the answer didn't really matter. His father wouldn't mind being ceremonially forgotten, didn't have any attachment to the living anymore. In fact, he couldn't bring himself to care about anything but the path he was grinding into the bedrock of eternity as he relived his self-defeating, resentful time on Earth over and over. As he squandered his afterlife in vain attempts to gain justice, to get a fair shake from all the people who supposedly screwed him over. As he continuously replayed the grand act of violence and hate that scarred the boys who bore his name.

The scar ends with me, Jacob decided. *Whatever part of me I have to kill or cut off, I don't care.*

He closed his eyes and pictured himself in the shower, holding a knife like his mother had on the night everything happened. He didn't imagine cutting himself with it or stabbing anybody. He simply scraped its sharp edge against his skin—arms, legs, chest, belly, ass—until not a fleck of his father's memory remained on him. Then he set the imaginary knife down because everything had been scraped off and left behind. Jacob leaped up from the bed humming, blew a kiss at the alligator purse on the floor, and gently closed the motel room door behind him.

"The old Nassedrines are dead," he told Laynie as he hopped into the truck and fired it up. Then he tickled her just below the ribcage, where she'd felt her ovary pinching a week before. "Long live the new ones." She wasn't supposed to respond, and she didn't.

11

Rings

Their first stop back in South Dakota was the Clark city-county building, across the street from the police station, where they paid the Register of Deeds $40 in cash for a license they both signed and didn't immediately burn. A clerk of the court officially married them. Laynie stopped in at the County Treasurer's Office to trade in her California driver's license and car registration for South Dakota versions, then registered to vote at the County Auditor's Office. Just like that she became, in the eyes of the law, an official South Dakotan. Then they drove up to Aberdeen, bought each other pawn shop wedding rings, and ambushed Don-o and Chrissy at Chez Donatelli outside Groton.

"No fucking way!" shouted Chrissy when she saw the rings. Don-o hugged them both at once and couldn't talk for a solid minute.

"That's an accomplishment," Jacob told Laynie. "Getting this guy to shut his yap."

Don-o held up a hand, requesting silence. "All I can say is that you're now respectable adults, and I expect respectable adult things from you."

Then they ogled the rings. Jacob's was white gold with a knurled, Scandinavian-looking pattern on it. Laynie's looked a bit thick for her finger, but she couldn't stop staring at its seven little elliptically arranged diamonds. The men drank Kilkenny Irish Cream Ale, while Chrissy and Laynie, one breastfeeding and the other hoping she was pregnant, had a shot glass of white wine each. As Little Richard slept, they all wandered out to Don-o's barn, where he showed off the seven-foot-tall gong he'd just finished hammering from the hood of a 1934 International Harvester panel van. It looked magnificent hanging from the rafters.

"Painting it or leaving it raw?" asked Jacob.

"Raw!" Don-o shouted, as if the answer were obvious.

"Do I get to be the first one to bang this sucker?"

"Sure thing, married guy. Knuckles only, though."

Jacob rapped the metal, and it rang out—not the deep, calming sound he expected but a thin and unsettling one. He stepped back from the weird vibration.

"You look terrified," Don-o told him.

"That's the creepiest gong I ever heard," Jacob said, and Chrissy nodded.

"Don't listen to those fake Zen people who tell you gongs should always calm you down." Don-o held his ground. "As long as they call to something inside you, they're doing their job."

"Can I?" asked Laynie, and Don-o agreed on the condition that she let him do a throw for her. She closed her eyes and tried to tune herself to the metal, then rapped at it decisively. Did it call to anything inside her? To a blastocyst that might become an embryo, that might become a fetus, that might become a child?

Live! whispered the metal. *Live live live!* Laynie stood with her ear almost touching it, feeling the vibrations long after the others lost track of them. Then Don-o pulled a small silk bag out of his pocket, tapped Laynie on the shoulder, and dropped three coins into her palm.

"T'ang dynasty, year 841," he said, dusting off a workbench and inviting Laynie to sit with him.

"I'm supposed to make a wish before I roll these, right?" she asked. "Throw them, I mean?"

"Nah, not your first time. Just think about a question you need answered, something you're too scared to ask yourself. Probably *not* about making babies, though. I know you're kinda tense about that."

Laynie knew the right question, which had been growing inside her without words ever since her father orphaned her. Not whether she would ever get to be a mother, not whether she would be able to handle Jacob and his demons, not whether she'd survive if he died on her like everybody else seemed to. But something about peace and purposefulness, balance and dignity and the fluid, relinquishing ease that she'd never found in herself but knew *had* to be living somewhere beneath her crust of grief and mourning. She felt the question fill her to the brim and let the coins skitter across the workbench.

"Okay," Donatelli said nervously, as if her first toss had gotten her off to an ominous start. He scooped up the coins and handed them back, and Laynie tossed them five more times. Don-o stacked them up, set them down out of her reach, and breathed slowly with his eyes closed.

"Something you don't want to tell me?" Laynie asked him.

"Just lining up my words. It's *Fu*, the Returning Point. I'm gonna stitch a few interpretations together here, no single authority. '*You have split from your path, or are about to, and you're in danger of falling back on old, harmful ways of living in the world. You feel the need for instant progress that you must turn away from, because the next phase of your life can't be speeded up. You need to conserve your energy for the change that's coming, or you'll abandon the path you need to return to right now.*'" He opened his eyes. "Make sense?"

Laynie nodded. "I don't have to tell you what I was thinking, do I?"

"Hell no. Just sit with it and decide if you want to do another throw."

"Sure," she said too instantly for Don-o's taste. He covered up the coins and looked at her sideways a moment, mock-wary of her eagerness, then smiled and slid the coins over. "*Now* make a wish."

"Thanks, Don-o." She winked. It was a nice moment between them, a rapport that promised to grow. Laynie simultaneously wished that she'd never have to mourn Don-o's death and wondered which possessions of his she might leave behind if she ever had to. She closed her eyes tight and wished for children, though just one would do. Then the coins fell.

"It's *Ko*," Donatelli said casually after her sixth toss, dropping the coins back into their silk bag. "I get this one all the time. '*Revolution is necessary. No further progress can be made under the conditions you are now in.*' Heavy, huh?"

"Very."

"'*Through careful adherence to the Tao, you'll let yourself change gently when it's necessary, without striving for a perfection you can't achieve. If your motives are pure, you'll let change happen. Resisting it, or hurrying or being greedy, will lead you nowhere.*' Is that what you wanted to hear?"

"I guess." Laynie threw up her hands. "It's something to chew on, at least."

"That's the damn thing about the coins," Don-o said. "They're always right, but you can never figure out what they're right about till it's all said and done."

* * *

Laynie wanted to get to know Clark now that she was a proper citizen of East SoDakistan—a phrase she'd picked up from Chrissy—but the weather had other plans. It snowed for two days straight, and they got nine inches of it, the topmost two unseasonably heavy and lousy to drive on. Plowing the entirety of Chambrell Road was, according to Jacob, ridiculous except under exceptional circumstances. Ed and Rhonda used to wait for the snow to settle by baking pies, drinking whiskey, and watching TV, and he didn't see much reason to do more than that.

Watching TV was out because the house didn't have cable anymore. Laynie desperately wanted it when Jacob got lost for hours at a time in the threads at SurvivorsofMurderSuicide.com. He seemed satisfied to poke around in them, trading memes like a teenager. Laynie would almost have preferred the old Jacob, obsessing over the names of babies that might never get born, to this new one who spent so much time with virtual people connected to him only by membership in a specific kind of hell.

"You've got a wife now," she reminded him on the third evening of their snow-in. They'd already made love twice and were exhausted, but Laynie at least wanted to talk with a real human being. "Don't you want your wife to be happy?"

"I do. But I want my friends to be happy too." Jacob pointed at his computer. "Some of these people don't have any friends outside SMS. I kind of pulled them together, so it feels like I owe them something."

"Do *you* have friends outside SMS?"

"Look." He shut his computer and stood up. "You came here when I hate this place the most. Don't ask me to go out and do the damn 'community' bullshit dance."

"I didn't say anything about community," Laynie told him.

"I know. But I can smell where you're going. This is just the place I live. Don't ask me to pretend I like it."

Jacob tromped to the barn and left the house to Laynie, who smelled problems down the road herself. His loathing for the place made no sense at all, and she felt like she'd never get to the bottom of it because he'd never let her. That night, in a perfect homage to Ed and Rhonda, they poured each other whiskey and snuggled on the couch to watch Craig Ferguson and Trevor Noah on YouTube. In the morning the 424 was plowed, so Jacob threw all his sandbags into the bed of the Dodge and drove Laynie down Chambrell Road, nonchalantly navigating its twists as if he could have done it blindfolded. When Jacob reached the mailbox, she hopped out and opened it.

"Who's Denis Nasreddine?" she asked, holding up a thick, magazine-sized envelope. "14 rue Simoneau, Thetford Mines, Quebec?"

Jacob almost ripped it out of her hands. Laynie checked behind them to make sure they weren't blocking traffic—an LA habit she'd have to lose—as Jacob fumbled to open the envelope. He scanned the first sheet in a thick, binder-clipped sheaf, then held it out so they both could read it.

Dear Cousin Jacob:

You are probably surprised to hear this word, but we are fourth cousins. It took me many years to find you because of how the name was changed in America. I don't say much here because this must be big news to you, but I hope we will talk some time and you can help me fill out our family tree.

I hope this news is good for you. Take the time you need to write back. I am a history teacher and very patient.

Salut,
Denis

"Holy shit, you've got a family!" Laynie squeezed Jacob's arm.

"*We've* got," Jacob said, and they leafed through the papers. Apparently, *Nassedrine* was an Americanized corruption of *Nasreddine* that originated when one branch migrated from Quebec to Maine in 1902. The sheaf started with a North American family tree that included 116 Nasreddines (26 still living) and 12 Nassedrines (only Jacob still living, with Daniel erroneously listed as so). Next came a few speculative name origins. The generally accepted theory claimed that it derived from *Nasruddin*, a thirteenth-century Persian and/or Turkish Sufi master, perhaps mythical and perhaps not, "known for his satirical wit and nonsensical humor." According to an internet printout, the United Nations had declared 1996 as the International Nasruddin Year.

"Better not tell Don-o," said Laynie. "He'll ditch all his *I Ching* books and go Sufi on us in a second."

"Or he'd hassle me till I did. *C'mon, Jakey, it's your heritage! Embrace it!*"

Jacob laughed, which filled Laynie with a wave of relaxation that flowed out from a spot below her navel. Her husband wasn't an orphan! Okay, technically he was. But he wasn't alone in the world, which meant she wasn't either, and if that news didn't merit angels blaring on trumpets, she didn't know what did. Next in the sheaf came photocopies of family members, and except for Jacob's nose—which suddenly struck Laynie as quintessentially French Canadian—he looked like no one else in the bunch. They had jet-black hair and narrow, delicate features, while he had honey-brown hair and a face like an anvil. She found an old photo that looked like Jacob at first, but the resemblance evaporated when she held it near his face.

"My dad always said we were Italian," Jacob chuckled. "Do I look French Canadian to you?"

"What does a French Canadian even look like?"

"How about Persian?"

"Stop. I look *way* more Persian than you. You look like a Viking." Laynie thumbed through some maps and came to a closing note from Denis.

I hope you have enjoyed this, cousin Jacob. My translation has taken almost as long as putting together the pictures. We always make a family reunion at Christmas, and I hope you can come next year. We could make a collection to help you get here because everyone wants to see you. You are a long lost family member and so a small celebrity!

"Think you'd be ready for a drive by next Christmas?" Jacob asked Laynie. "I mean a drive to Quebec, not *your* kind of drive."

"Why not? We might even have another cousin for the family tree by then."

"That's the spirit. That's what I like to hear."

Laynie rubbed her belly, kissed Jacob on the cheek, and nestled against him to look at every name on that family tree. They liked how the old-fashioned French names sounded with Nassedrine, like Annabelle and Francine, Claude and Vincent. Gerard and Jean-Michel, Marielle and Beatrice.

* * *

Once they got to town, Laynie found a job. They stopped in at Caffeine Paradise and found a HELP WANTED sign, and the owner—Kade Brinks, a classmate of Jacob who'd barely acknowledged his existence but hadn't ostracized him either—explained that his barista had gone to work at an animal disease research lab down in Brookings. Laynie waited until she tasted her cappuccino before applying because she didn't want to serve people shitty coffee.

"Can you prove you know what you're doing?" Kade asked.

"Do you have a cloth napkin I could borrow?" Laynie replied. While he fetched one, she inspected the espresso machine. A black Gaggia with two double spouts—simple and familiar. She checked the pressure on the milk foamers and closed her eyes, touching everything with her fingertips to get the spacing right. Kade gave her a red cloth napkin that she turned into a blindfold, then watched her make him a cappuccino with a passable four-leaf clover in the foam.

"Well that settles that," Kade said, and Jacob left her at Caffeine Paradise to learn the ropes. He immediately felt like Laynie was trying to expose him—she'd make a bunch of friends and goad him into trying to make some too, only to learn just how badly he'd burned the bridges between him and the people of Clark. If she had a studio of her own, she might spend less time trying to prove she was a social butterfly, so Jacob walked over to Forslund Hardware and scoped out ways to put windows and insulation in the grain bin she liked. His go-to guy there, Braden Dennert, noticed the ring right away.

"What happened to you?" he asked. Braden was fiftyish and balding and barely came up to Jacob's nipple, and he had a neck beard that looked as bristly as Don-o's. He'd called twice to check in on Jacob after Daniel's suicide, which Jacob would never forget.

"Woman I used to know in LA." Jacob shrugged like he got married every day. "Kinda ran into her on the road."

"Better than running *over* her on the road. When's the party? Not every day a town loses its most eligible bachelor."

"I thought that was Ethan Sundvold."

"Ethan's not a bachelor," Braden said. "He's a bullshit artist who can't keep it in his pants."

Jacob laughed even though Ethan Sundvold galled the shit out of him. Clark's all-state quarterback and power forward had failed to crack a roster at multiple colleges in multiple sports before he dropped out to work on Daddy's farm. Yet he lorded it over Jacob, who'd *merely* sold sculptures to small museums and private collectors in six states and two Canadian provinces.

Fuck Clark, Jacob told himself after he got the window information he needed from Braden, and then he wandered around the store rehashing his endless internal bitch session about his adoptive non-home. Fuck all of South Dakota too. Prizing the jock, the farmer, the soldier, the northern equivalent of the good ol' boy. What were artists? Just dirty hippies, freeloaders who didn't know the meaning of *real* work. Meanwhile, the most stereotypical dumb jock in existence was the town hero.

Ridiculous. Jacob held Ethan Sundvold personally accountable for the way Clark's opinion of him shifted at the start of senior year. When he switched out of Metal Fabrication and took Art I instead, Ethan called him a faggot in front of everybody, even though he was dating Chrissy. Then after Halloween, Ethan started a rumor that Jacob bleached his pubes blond.

It was a fine burn, looking back on it. But back then it humiliated him, and he didn't have enough friends to fight back. Fifteen years later he could see his senior year troubles in a more sociological light. In switching from Metal Fabrication to Art, he'd made it impossible for Clark to contextualize him. Nobody had called him a faggot when he called himself *welder*, but everybody did when he declared himself *sculptor* and started dating Chrissy Sanheim, Clark's only emo girl, who was always drawing in her artsy-fartsy notebook with her stupid colored pencils.

"It's almost twenty fucking years," Jacob muttered to himself as he wandered through Forslund's, looking for things that could make Laynie happy there. Make *himself* happy there, to be honest. His place in South Dakota had always felt provisional, dependent on him blending in and not sticking out—a deeply Scandinavian thing, which made sense because he was surrounded by Scandinavians. He might have blended in if he'd stayed *welder*, maybe even put down something like roots and let the South Dakota soil nourish him. He might have even become like the people born here, who question the soil they grew up on as much as fish question their water.

Becoming *welder* had been his big chance to blend in, and if he'd embraced it wholeheartedly enough, it might have replaced the label *murderer's son*. But he and Daniel weren't born there, and neither was Uncle Ed, and that made his margin of error razor-thin. Only Rhonda tied them to the place, and since everybody figured she was part Indian, she didn't count for as much as a Swede, a Norwegian, a German, or a Dane.

Daniel had it easier in some ways, since he'd always been *fuckup* and never confused anyone by daring to claim another label. In the paint section of Forslund's, Jacob crossed paths with Lyle Gudbranson, a kid who'd turned on him senior year and now pretended not to know him, even though they were close enough to touch. Jacob wandered among the paints, wondering what colors Laynie might like, until he was standing next to Kristen Berggruen—the woman who'd lived with him for two weeks after Daniel left the house. She'd made him buy new pillows and sheets, then disappeared without even a note or a phone call. At least she looked at him in Forslund's, though it was just to give him a half-hearted uptick of the left side of her face. Not even a damn word, and then she was gone.

Act like you fucking know me, he wanted to tell Kristen. *Make me feel like I'm not a ghost, for old times' sake.*

Then he thought *Fuck this place.* Then he thought *No, Jakey, don't do this to yourself, don't do this to your wife. This is your place now.* Then he thought *If this is your place now, you're going to die.*

* * *

All this didn't mean that Jacob hated Clark every second of the day. For South Dakota—and especially for repressed, straitlaced East River—the town had more than its share of pizzazz. Ken Bell's parade of Ford LTDs west of town on the 212 announced that Clark gave a shit about what you thought of it and wanted you to find it quirky and cute. It had an identity, which Jacob appreciated every time he drove through other towns that lacked one.

And Clark had given him, in a weird backhanded way, the opportunity to escape it. The summer before senior year he got the sculpting bug after he'd discovered, while helping Uncle Ed clean out the workshop of a deceased fellow welder down in Hayti, a McEnglevan Speedy-Melt B30 furnace. Worth thousands, Ed declared, if you could find anybody to buy it. It weighed so much it almost wrecked the hoist they used to get it on the trailer. Aunt Rhonda was pissed because it meant Ed would spend the summer in the barn with Jacob when he should've been doing other things around the house, but that just made him more stubborn.

"It'll keep that boy off whatever shit his brother's on," Ed told her. "And don't start saying it's not my house when I keep it standing and pay all the damn bills for it."

The summer unfolded exactly as Rhonda feared. Jacob collected scrap aluminum wherever he could and bought C. W. Ammen's *The Complete Book of Sand Casting*, reading it like nothing else before. Ed spent hours helping him build frames and figure out formulas for sand molds that would hold up to hot metal, and after five weeks he produced his first sculpture: a cast of Rhonda's hands, which he filed and burnished until they looked like her own. She showed them to a friend in Watertown who was a potter, who showed them to a friend in Brookings who taught sculpture, who showed them to a sculptor in Sioux Falls named Brad Dingman. Brad saw promise and agreed to let Jacob observe a bronze pour coming up the next weekend, provided he was willing to sleep on the floor and pay for his own food.

Jacob had no idea at the time, but if an older version of himself had known whose pour he'd be observing, he would've shit his pants. Nolan Tinsley, an LA sculptor who had bronzes in Boston's Museum of Contemporary Art and the Art Institute of Chicago, was an hour south in Sioux City, Iowa, for the summer because his wife's mother was dying. The foundry he'd planned to work with there treated him with less respect than he demanded, and Brad Dingman offered him that respect. So, Nolan worked in Sioux Falls instead, and during Jacob's visit he planned to pour two busts of his dying mother-in-law, plus an abstract.

Brad told Jacob how lost wax casting worked as he set up the pour with Nolan, showing him pieces in various states of completion. Nolan was tight-lipped around his young observer, but he warmed up when Brad explained that Jacob built his own molds at seventeen. Eventually, he wanted to look at Aunt Rhonda's hands.

"Good start," Nolan said. "But the knuckles are too far apart for a woman's."

Then they put in the ingots. They gave Jacob a face mask and gloves and a leather apron, and they let him feel the heft of the crucible before doing the actual pour themselves. The older men left Jacob to sleep on the foundry floor while the mold cooled overnight, and there he wondered what it took to become a Rodin or even a Nolan Tinsley. He looked at every piece of equipment, felt it and smelled it and hefted it if he could. In the morning Brad and Nolan came back and knocked the plaster off the molds to reveal the raw, still-warm bronze beneath. The abstract looked like a legless giraffe trying to make a pretzel out of its neck.

"What would you do with it if it was yours, Mr. Jacob?" Nolan asked.

"I'd make it really rough up here," Jacob said, waving his hand around what felt like a shoulder, "and really smooth down here." He waved his other hand over what felt like a rump.

"Hmm." Tinsley nodded, stepped back, and shared a long look with Brad. Two hours later he left, and half an hour after that Rhonda came by to pick Jacob up.

"Do you know who you were working with?" asked Brad as they said goodbye.

"Sort of," said Jacob. When Brad explained, he let out a long, slow "Whoa."

"You're not kidding, *whoa*. Even more whoa is what he said about you."

"About me?"

"He said if you're ever in LA, look him up and he'll put you to work."

Boom! Jacob felt a wall thunder to the ground inside him, a barrier between who he was and who he might be. He was going to get the fuck out of Clark, South Dakota, go to LA, and work for a famous sculptor until he became one himself. Three days after high school graduation he got on a Greyhound with Nolan Tinsley's phone number and $250 in his pocket from Ed and Rhonda.

He didn't care about leaving Clark, but he felt like shit for leaving Daniel behind. Their last look through the window as the Greyhound pulled away stabbed him in the brain every week. He was leaving his brother to stand alone against the rest of Clark Junior-Senior High School, who knew a *fuckup* when they saw one and never let Daniel forget it.

That was the year his brother started dying, Jacob told himself as he lingered lost in the paint section at Forslund's. Would it have happened if he'd stayed *welder*? Stayed who they told him he could be instead of giving them the finger and becoming who they said he couldn't? Jacob thought he'd never come back to Clark except to visit. Never thought that, as a defeated and despairing man of thirty who fucked up everything he touched, including the almost marriage to the only woman he'd ever loved, he'd have nowhere else to go.

He got done with his window-shopping and headed back to Caffeine Paradise, where his wife waved and shouted "Howdy, mister!"

There was nobody else in the shop, not even Kade. Jacob could've said anything in the world, but he couldn't speak at all and instead fell to his knees, sobbing.

"Quebec!" Jacob said when she ran over to him, running her hands over his head and letting him squeeze her so tightly by the waist that she almost fell over. "Holy shit, I'm from fucking Quebec!"

12

Magic Wands

Jacob spent the least cold days of January turning the grain bin where he'd found Daniel's headband into Laynie's studio. Braden at Forslund's scored him three curved windows, and he cut holes for them, reinforcing the metal walls so they wouldn't buckle in the wind. Once he squared the openings and put up encapsulated insulation, he brought Laynie over for an inspection. She loved it, and she planned to cover the insulation with the funkiest fabric she could find.

"It'll be like a yurt," she said. "I always wanted to paint in a yurt."

"Funny. I always wanted to make love in a yurt."

"Mr. Predictable." Laynie wrote the number 6 in the dust on the floor with her toe. "Guess what that number means."

"How many days late your period is," Jacob said instantly. "Don't think I'm not checking. I just learned to keep my mouth shut about it."

Laynie smiled, shivered, and went inside. Not even the used wool long underwear Chrissy bought her on eBay could keep her warm. She made a pot of tea, and when Jacob came in because he couldn't feel his fingertips, she poured him a mug.

"Need anything at the Target in Aquatown?" she asked him. She renamed Watertown the way Don-o renamed Richard. Aguatown. Wassertown. H_2Otown. "I could use a solo jailbreak."

Jacob said nothing, mostly because the windows broke his bank and he didn't want to spend a penny. Laynie borrowed his truck and felt like a badass behind the wheel until the first hairpin turn down Chambrell Road, after which she drove like a little old lady with macular degeneration. At Target she bought half a dozen pregnancy test kits, enough for a whole gang of women as desperate as she was, and drove home imagining Jacob's expression when they saw the result together. He was four years older than the last time they saw stripes, four years less naive, and he might finally understand the hell that his ridiculous hopefulness put her through. She came back to find him in the living room, mindlessly scrolling through SurvivorsofMurderSuicide.com again. She figured their marriage would come down to *Me or your damn website* sooner or later but didn't want that time to be now.

"I want to do this with you," Laynie said, dumping out her entire bag full of test wands next to his laptop.

"Do you want me in the room when you pee on it, or what?" he asked.

"You make it sound so romantic."

Jacob logged out of SMS but stayed on the blue sofa, stacking the test wand boxes into several cunning shapes. When Laynie called him, he hovered in the doorway and watched the red stripes appear in its window. Undeniable. Irrefutable. Husband and wife stood still, as if a cobra had slithered between them.

"Don't jump for joy," Laynie told him.

"Wasn't planning on it."

"And don't ask me to jump either."

Jacob kept his joy-jumping secret. He imagined it was July instead of January and pictured himself outside, leaping high enough in the sunny air to click his heels three times. He turned the wand face down and then back again as if he didn't trust the first result. The stripes stubbornly refused to change, and Laynie stubbornly refused to smile.

"In a movie we'd be hugging each other, you know," he told her. "Then we'd cut to a sex montage."

"Are you saying I'm not joyful enough?"

"I'm saying *we* look like we're scared to be happy."

"Well, lead the way, Jacob. Just don't be cheesy about it."

"I'm scared to smile, 'cause even *that* might be too cheesy for you." He flashed her a TV commercial smile until she gave him a real one, then rested her head on his chest and let him hug her.

"We'll get through this," she said.

"You sound like somebody who doesn't think she'll be pregnant for long."

"That's who you married." Laynie took her test wand, bundled up, and headed out to her quasi-yurt. She sat on a cinder block in the middle feeling like she'd just been forced into a life-or-death challenge. Stay pregnant this time or your life will fall apart like a junky old tractor. Stay pregnant this time or your brand-new marriage will end and you'll wander the horizon with no reason.

A horrible mind trap. No wonder babies flung themselves off her uterine wall! Laynie inspected the insulation, which Jacob had meticulously duct-taped along the seams so fibers wouldn't haunt her paintings or her lungs. She inspected the curved windows that must have cost Jacob a fortune and wondered how they'd hold up against the South Dakota wind, and the wind read her mind. It came softly at first, enveloping her someday-studio in a caress that became a squeeze that became a choke. A gust hit, and she listened for air chiseling through the grain bin's metal skin but heard nothing. Jacob had sealed it tight—his caulking gun lay in the dirt floor as evidence. The gusts grew stronger and knocked over a ladder Jacob had left outside, but she still didn't feel wind on her skin.

Laynie tried to imagine herself painting in that space, but it needed more than insulation to complete it. White fake fur on the walls, plus a gleaming white floor? There, that did the trick. She saw herself pregnant, sitting in white pants on a white stool with her legs wide and her heavy belly settling evenly between them. The image didn't last long enough for her to see what she was painting. Then she watched a trickle of blood emerge at the crotch of her pants, the thick blood of another lost baby, and the only thing that could make the scene white again was a little white pill between her fingertips.

An OxyContin. She saw an OP on one side, then an 80 on the other. Definitely genuine. The pill leaped up toward her waiting mouth, but the scene cut away before it reached her lips. Laynie stood up, kicked the cinderblock, and walked back to the house ready for the wind to topple her over like it had toppled the ladder. That's what she deserved for failing to imagine herself staying clean in this new world of hers, in this new workspace her husband made for her.

There was no perfect thought to end her train of calamity on, no profound or clever phrase that could throw her off it. All she could say was *We will win! We will win!* But what winning meant, exactly, escaped her as easily as happiness did.

* * *

On day sixteen of Laynie's lateness, after the blastocyst had officially become an embryo and attached itself more or less securely to her uterine wall, Jacob found himself in the middle of another flame war on SMS. Lovetrain went at it with Maurice Markley from Arkansas about whether getting stoned was an acceptable coping mechanism, which told Jacob that Lovetrain must have been smoking like a chimney. When Lovetrain told Maurice—a sweet-as-pie guy—that he was going into his treehouse to smoke himself to death, Jacob made a pilgrimage to Aberdeen.

He was the one who kept people from falling apart, after all. Daniel for a while, until he failed, and Laynie now in his place. The SMS gang, with all its infighting and despair. People living sad, insular little lives, just like him. A good day meant not wallowing in self-pity. Oh, and not killing themselves. Jacob knocked on Lovetrain's apartment door, and indeed, the place reeked of pot smoke.

"Just hand it over," he said, wishing he'd been that direct and authoritative with his own brother. Lovetrain stepped back to his camping pad on the living room floor and produced a small baggie from beneath his pillow.

"I paid good money for that," he told Jacob, who flushed the pot and sat on the floor.

"What the fuck's wrong, Train?"

"I heard a guy yelling at his kid, and I just imploded. The kid dropped a fucking soda, and his dad's on him like he dropped the Mona Lisa or something. I felt like I was covered in eggshells that'd break if I moved a muscle, and I flashbacked to how still I kept in the treehouse when my dad was yelling for me. *Move and you die,* you know? I went up in the treehouse, and now I can't get down."

They talked about other triggers, and other times they'd gotten through those triggers, until they agreed that the first thirty seconds were the most crucial. Hang on for the first thirty seconds, then for the first minute, then for the first two minutes, and usually something else in life comes along to keep you from turning into a twitching ball of fear. Lovetrain eventually pulled himself out of the muck, and Jacob left feeling like he'd done his good deed for the day. But how many people would he have to keep together to make up for letting Daniel fall apart? Ten? Fifty? A hundred?

There might never be enough. As he drove to the Flat Earth Boutique to visit Chrissy, Jacob pondered what it would take to let his savior complex go. Awareness was supposedly half the battle, but he'd been aware of it since long before Daniel died, and that only helped him refine the complex. He walked into Chrissy's store hoping to find the place bustling so he could have a superficial, see-you-later conversation with her. But she was all alone, opening her eBay shipments and calling the people who'd ordered them. One was a tan canvas Carhartt coat—a miniature version of Jacob's—that Don-o had insisted on buying for Laynie.

"Our gift," Chrissy said. "To congratulate her for making it to six weeks."

"If she loses the baby, she'll think you cursed her," Jacob said back. "Make her buy it from you. Please."

"She's that touchy, huh?"

"That touchy." Then Jacob disemburdened himself in front of Chrissy the way Lovetrain had done in front of him. While she listened, she made him try on a shiny purple shirt that made him look like a sixties guitar hero, especially only buttoned up halfway, and he bought it because Chrissy said it would make Laynie happy.

"You sound pretty sure of that," Jacob said. "Why?"

"Because it'll make her laugh, and she'll think you're still sane because she'll see your sense of humor."

"Is my sense of humor gone?"

"As gone as the fireflies, Jakey. It's like you're the one who's pregnant and whipping yourself for losing babies. Gotta snap out of it."

Meanwhile, at Caffeine Paradise, Laynie was having a stroke of luck. Offensive tackle Chad Willhart, a native son of Clark and recent second-round draft choice of the NFL's Cincinnati Bengals, stopped by for a coffee, and it just so happened that Mike Ruhwedel, a photographer for the *Clark County Courier*, was there to capture it. Laynie, who looked dainty next to Jacob, looked positively miniature next to a six-foot-six lineman over three hundred pounds. At one point he picked her up with one arm while his other hand raised a cup of coffee. Laynie clinked her cup to his, and Mike said the shot was Pulitzer worthy. He all but guaranteed that it would be on the cover of not only Saturday's *Courier* but tomorrow afternoon's *Watertown Public Opinion*.

"Ten percent of your extra income next week should be plenty enough thanks for me," Mike said, though he settled for Laynie's promise of free coffee for a month. When Chad Willhart left, Laynie felt elated. She felt like she *belonged* in South Dakota, Jacob's unreasonable hatred of the place be damned. It was possible for her to have an actual niche in this ecosystem, however small it was, that other people could recognize. Sure, she was just a barista. But a barista on the front page of a newspaper being lifted up by a pro football player becomes something more than *just* a barista, right? She becomes somebody with one tiny Little Engine That Could, which just might root her in her new place. And with no roots of her own in LA except her dead father's house that she might never be drug-free enough to inherit, even the most tenuous roots mattered.

The next few customers were treated to the most ebullient Laynie ever. She radiated, she shone. But even in the midst of that, she felt something slipping in her belly, and past experience shouted *miscarriage*. When things slowed down, she put the BE RIGHT BACK! sign on the counter and retreated to the bathroom with a pregnancy test wand, ready for the bad news. But the red stripes showed up, as stubborn as her this time, and she didn't know what to think or do.

* * *

That evening Laynie tried out the lingo of her new home—"Oofta" and "You betcha" and "Don'tcha know?"—that she'd picked up at the coffee shop. Jacob got such a kick out of it that he stopped hating South Dakota long enough to talk with her about paint colors for the house. If they ever worked up the cash, of course, which meant that Jacob had to sell some sculptures because he wasn't going to take some stupid day job and give the people who'd refused to let him be *sculptor* the satisfaction of watching him throw away his dreams.

In the morning they got a chance for a little cash because Jacob got a call from Medge's second-string caregiver asking him to cover for her indefinitely, starting immediately. Since he'd already committed to driving up to Aberdeen and moving Lovetrain in with roommates who didn't smoke pot, he gave Laynie the keys to Medge's house and relayed instructions over the phone while he drove north. Laynie had a glimmer of resentment—a momentary vision of herself working three shit jobs while Jacob tried to save everybody on that damn website—but she promised herself this was a one-time deal.

When she arrived, the old lady looked dead in her wheelchair: head lolled over, dry spittle at the side of her mouth, no sign of breathing. To avoid looking at Medge's possibly dead body, Laynie neatened up in the kitchen. She grabbed a handful of Frosted Mini-Wheats and soaked a few in milk for Medge to gum, as Jacob had instructed, and hoped this good deed wouldn't backfire terribly. What if little Marielle or Jean-Michel in her womb got exposed to death too soon and decided to die as well? She emptied Medge's trash and double bagged it for Jacob's trip to whatever dumpster he put their trash in—its location still a secret—then checked out the pills in Medge's medicine cabinet, which Jacob had warned her about over the phone.

This warning, she knew, was both a test and a helpful hint to keep her clean. Telling her about it risked sending her on a jag, but *not* telling risked blindsiding her with temptation. Laynie flung open the cabinet door and stared at the rows of pill bottles, some quite tempting. She focused on the Valium because it was so 1950s, something her grandmothers might have used. She counted out the Valiums (twenty-nine), then the Vicodins (thirty-three), then the Demerols (sixteen), and Percocets (fifty-one!). All of them had come in prescriptions of sixty, which meant Jacob might have already pilfered dozens. She could track the pill counts on her phone to keep tabs on him, but that didn't sound too trusting. A scribbled note in her wallet would do, revised whenever she raided the stash herself.

Laynie liked to believe that she and her husband trusted each other, but when it came to pills of any kind, they had less than zero. That mistrust radiated through the rest of their lives. Most couples about to have a baby act ecstatic about it, holding hands and making a nest for their child. She and Jacob barely touched each other, and she'd forbidden any discussion of turning the former Shrine Room into a nursery until the baby was actually born. Hardly a model for successful parenting preparation. But did she even deserve to be a mother as long as she was a pill popper? When she was no better than a junkie on the street in some people's eyes, including her own occasionally?

The Valium bottle rested in her hands, unopened, when she snapped out of her dark reverie. Then Medge yelled, "Yow!" or, "How!" and Laynie left the bathroom to check on her. A non-corpse, definitely. The shawl had come off her shoulder, and she struggled to get it back on, but she settled once Laynie pulled it into place. Her head lolled over again, to the other side this time, which meant the nurse would find a second line of dried drool on her chin. Medge would need a diaper change too, which wasn't in Laynie's job description. No, she was getting paid to clean up the house and keep the old lady company, and that's what she did. Laynie picked up Jacob's cheap guitar and sat on an ottoman next to Medge, strumming out the only four chords she knew.

"I'm going to play you a song, okay?" The chords sounded awful, but it sounded much better when she simply pressed her index finger down between the frets. She strummed randomly and sang fake lyrics for the theme song to *The Beverly Hillbillies* that her father made up for her.

Tell you a story 'bout a girl named Laynie.
Take away her toys and she screams like a baby.

She couldn't remember the rest. But she could imagine that she'd actually taken a Valium and that it was kicking in. Coursing through her vessels, coiling around her clenched muscles, bringing her back to herself. Out of the stratosphere, down from her worries. Her limbs started to loosen, and she could handle anything. A dead old lady, a dead husband, a dead self. Laynie closed her eyes and saw letters swirling around her head, then waited for them to become words and sentences. They did, but they were nonsense. *Thuku ambidisha gorety pmpak. Arinwa pkolnit heqbast, tutulna u tutulnaqop.* They led her nowhere. She didn't even know how to pronounce them.

"How about I tell you a story?" Laynie slowed and gentled her strumming. "I'll tell you about the last thing I said to my fiancé before he died. Not Jacob—he was never my fiancé, we just got married a couple times. I had a fiancé back in LA, though. Martin. We had a date set and everything."

She plucked each string, highest to lowest, then strummed again.

"He felt like flying and went to the airport—this was the last time I saw him. He was dressed sloppy, which wasn't like him, and I said he'd look great flying in a tux. He said, 'I can't wait to come home and see the woman who's going to be my wife.' So I said, 'I'm already your wife now, aren't I? Sort of?' And Martin said, 'You'll always be my wife, Laynie J.' Then we kissed and smiled at each other, and we never saw each other again because he crashed his plane landing it, and they had to use dental records to get a positive ID even though he's the only one who ever flew that plane. That's sad, isn't it, Medge? Nod your head."

Laynie nodded her own instead. "But you know what I thought when Martin drove off and I blew him a kiss goodbye? I was think-ing, 'I won't always be your wife, because I've still got four months to chicken out on you. And what if that plane crashes and you die?' Sometimes I think God heard me and said, '*Right you are, Laynie Jackman!*' and crashed Martin's plane just to prove some point to me. How'd you like to live with that over your head, Medge? Think you'd be a pill-popping piece of shit if you had that hanging over your head?"

She raked her fingernails over the strings as fast as she could. Even that didn't get Medge to budge, and Laynie really wanted to see her move. If she couldn't get Medge to react somehow, then she was no more present in the world than a ghost. And a ghost couldn't have a baby. A ghost didn't deserve a baby. She started strumming with her fingers high up on the neck.

"Did I ever tell you I had a pony, Medge?" Laynie asked. "Like a regular little cowgirl. I had a pony when I was nine—half of one, anyway, I shared it with another girl—and I rode it in a parade way up in Aptos, California." She slid her fingers closer to the guitar's body, ramping up the tone and tension.

"So, I'm nine years old in Aptos, riding a pony in the July Fourth parade because my dad's friend has a daughter riding in the July Fourth parade. We're next to each other, looking cute and having a great little time. But then this girl ahead of us, her pony gets spooked by some guy waving a red bandana, and her pony takes off and busts through everybody. Ponies are small, but try stopping one. Ever try stopping a pony, Medge?"

Laynie stared at Medge and got nothing back but a vague, omnidirectional smile. She raised the chord again. "I didn't think so. Anyway, the pony runs like hell through a field and stumbles on something, falls down and lands on this girl. A doctor comes running, and an ambulance comes, and it turns out the girl's paralyzed from the waist down for the rest of her life. So, my mom and dad freak out, and they sell my half of the pony, and little Laynie never gets to ride one again. I guess they were scared about her dying or getting hurt, which is too bad because she really loved riding that pony. That's a sad story, isn't it? Nod your head."

Laynie nodded and got Medge to nod with her. Then she took her fingers off the neck and slowed her strumming to sound as dolorous as possible.

"But it gets sadder, Medge. Five years later Laynie's fourteen and doesn't have a mother anymore, and Dad asks her what she wants to do most in the world. 'I want to ride horses again,' Laynie says. 'Remember how I used to love that pony?' Dad thinks about it awhile, rubs his jaw like he used to, and says, 'Okay, Sweetie. Riding horses it is.' Well, Laynie just thinks Dad's saying yes so she won't feel so bad about his daughter losing Mom. But there's another way to look at it that little Laynie won't understand until Dad's dead too, and it goes like this.

"Once upon a time her parents used to be so scared of her dying, so scared of anything bad happening to her, that they took away her pony so she wouldn't get hurt. But once Mom got taken away, Dad knew he couldn't protect his little girl anymore. He couldn't keep his wife from dying, and he figures he can't keep his little girl from dying either. So why not give her what she loves, even if it can kill her?"

Laynie stopped abruptly, rang out a few jangly, aggressive chords that finally made Medge lift her head in panic, then went back to a gentle, aimless strum.

"So, he let her go. He gave up on trying to protect her, and he told himself, 'If she dies, she dies. I can't lose much more, and she can't lose much more.' So, he let her start riding horses again because they had nothing left to lose except each other. Now isn't that a sad, beautiful story, Medge? Nod your head."

13

February

On the last evening of January, when Laynie finally stopped counting in days and declared herself seven and a half weeks pregnant, Jacob announced that February was his least favorite month. With a guaranteed week of the temperature never rising above 5°F, the cold would keep him cooped up inside and cause weird bangs in the house when old metal parts contracted. The sun would hang in the sky longer than in January, true—a whopping ten hours now—but the cumulative darkness since November would negate that. The wind would try breaking into the house as relentlessly as a computer virus. With all these struggles, the temptation of pills would hit him hard.

"Does that mean I should keep an extra eye out for tinfoil balls every February?" Laynie asked him.

"Maybe." He scrubbed the kitchen sink so he wouldn't have to look at her.

"Seeing people can make it easier." She hadn't tried to get him out on the town in a week, but now it seemed like she *had* to. "When I meet people at the coffee shop, I say I'm your wife, and they say 'Oh sure, I know Jacob.' But I never hear you talking about them."

"There's reasons for that. You married the town black sheep."

"There's got to be a blacker sheep than you."

"There was. Daniel. When he died, I took over." Jacob reached into a seldom-used Boston Bruins mug to see if it had a stash ball inside it. Nothing doing. "Please don't turn this into a lecture on how I have to blend in here. You've barely been here a month."

"I worry I'm living with a recluse. With a—a self-imposed pariah!"

Jacob smiled, took the phone into the living room, and dialed Doug and Karen Hatten to ask if they wanted to meet his wife. They were older and nowhere near as close friends as Don-o and Chrissy, but they'd show Laynie he was no pariah and get her off his back. The Hattens had met in the Peace Corps thirty-some years ago and were the most accepting people in Clark. A bit too Jesus-y for Jacob's taste, but they put their money where their mouths were and didn't judge. Yes, they absolutely wanted to meet his wife.

"Remember I said there were only two people you could tell you're part Lebanese?" he said when he came back to the kitchen. "We're going to their house tonight."

The Hattens, both in their midsixties, lived on the north side of Clark in a perfectly square house near United Methodist Church, where they were heavily involved. Both had been teachers in town, though never to the Nassedrine boys. Doug was as tall as Jacob but stoop shouldered, and he had a full thatch of pure white hair. He wore khakis and a frayed blue sweater and looked perpetually caught off guard. Karen came up to her husband's chin and had a yellow-gray braid down to her waist, with eyes slightly too far apart. She wore a down jacket inside and pressed her right index finger against her lower lip whenever she tried to think of something to say. They'd met in 1977, when Zimbabwe was still Rhodesia, and organized mission trips there every spring.

Their house was a mishmash of African knickknacks—wooden masks, swaths of cloth so colorful they deserved the frames around them, woven baskets—and embroidered Bible quotes like WHATEVER YOUR TASK, WORK HEARTILY, AS SERVING THE LORD AND NOT MEN. The juxtaposition made Laynie trust them.

"If I'm acting weird, it's because I'm pregnant and I've lost a bunch of babies," she told them within five minutes of reaching their door. "I figure I'd let the elephant out of its cage right away."

"Okaaaaay," said Karen, looking to Jacob. He and Doug, both leery of saying the wrong thing, said nothing at all. "Have you gotten help for that?"

"Lots. But it's almost impossible for me to keep one. My uterus is misshaped. Sort of like a banana. The doctors say I have a—"

"They aren't very hopeful," Jacob jumped in, not wanting to hear the words 3 *percent* ever again. It was a jerk move, and Laynie sneered at him. But she understood that rubbing the number in his face would have soured everything. The Hattens led the way into the kitchen, where they had a pot of glühwein simmering. It had ginger, currants, and black pepper—their own recipe, adapted from one they'd picked up in Munich decades earlier—and they let Laynie have the first taste. She pronounced it good, then said she shouldn't have any more.

"We'll make you some when you're not pregnant," Doug said. Laynie looked ready to cry, and he struggled to recover. "I mean when the baby comes, and you're done breastfeeding too."

Doug looked at Jacob, who raised one eyebrow, and the Hattens saw just how hair-triggered Laynie was about pregnancy. So they talked about other things: the stuff on the walls, life in the Peace Corps in the 1970s, life at Caffeine Paradise, the surprise family in Quebec. After another drink Doug and Karen told Laynie they were from St. Louis and Pittsburgh, respectively, then bashed South Dakota for a solid twenty minutes.

"I feel sad for the men who grow up here," Doug said. "I taught those kids. I love a lot of those kids. But they pretty much get one option—be a hardworking patriot who's just doing his job."

"And whatever you do, don't show emotion!" said Karen. "The men here, they get to up 10, 15 percent of the emotion a human being's capable of handling, and their gauge is in the red. So they deaden themselves to get through life. I saw it in second graders!"

"What about the women here?" Laynie asked.

"She needs more glühwein for that." Doug handed Karen his coffee mug, and she finished it in two giant swigs.

"The ideal South Dakota woman is the farm wife," Karen pronounced. "Capable, physically tough, knows exactly how much of everything you need to get through the winter, wastes absolutely *nothing*. I don't get any respect because I'm all about book learning, which is frivolous to them. Book learning isn't necessary to get through winter."

"I'm trying to pick up as many farm wife points as I can," Laynie said, hoping to derail Karen a bit. The woman was steaming, and not just from the glühwein.

"And you represent art," Karen continued, fixing Laynie with a skewering glare. "Which is even more frivolous and self-indulgent than book learning. Art is something only the idle rich have time to do, so if you make art, you must be one of those rich people who sponge off the real Americans who actually work for a living."

"I didn't coach her to say that," Jacob piped in, and it made Karen ease up.

"I don't want to scare you." She put a hand on Laynie's knee. "I just want you to know the mentality here."

"Didn't your kids grow up here?" Laynie asked her.

"Yes," Doug said. "But they did mission trips to Zimbabwe since they were three. We never asked them to buy in."

"And if you don't buy in," Karen added, "then your kids can't handle staying here and they leave, guaranteed. We've got one in Tucson and one in DC."

"Why do you stay here?" asked Laynie, and the Hattens both laughed.

"Become a schoolteacher in South Dakota," Doug said. "Then ask us how much money you've got when you retire."

They kept up the chatter until Karen announced that she'd had too much glühwein and needed sleep. Laynie, satisfied that Jacob was only a partial pariah, drove home because he'd had too much as well.

"That was a fun evening," she said as she drove past their church. "They're sad, though."

"That's why they drink," Jacob told her. "They're always drinking something foreign. Kir, mojitos, sangria, midori margaritas. Anything to make them feel like they're living somewhere else."

"Is that going to be us? Stuck here in Farm Wife Land?"

For the longest time Jacob wouldn't answer, and Laynie feared that meant yes. But what he said was even more ominous.

"They're sixty-something. We've got to live that long, babe. Got to make sure the pills don't kill us first."

* * *

They talked about their visit to the Hattens right up to the edge of midnight and February. Doug and Karen were both inspiration and cautionary tale—living beautifully from one perspective, living desperately from another. They were as open as anyone around, yet they were perpetual self-exiles in South Dakota and therefore strangers to themselves. Jacob, to Laynie's great surprise, didn't fight when she suggested he was headed for their fate.

"I want to be like them and I don't," Jacob said. "If I've got any roots, they're here now. I just don't want to put them down 'cause I don't want to be a transplanted tree who shrivels and dies."

"Look at Don-o," Laynie told him. "He's from the same place as you, and he's doing fine here."

"You've never heard him bitch about it. Plus, he married a native, and they had a kid here. With a grandpa and grandma and, like, fifteen cousins. Instant roots."

"So, when we have a kid, would that be instant roots for you?"

Jacob liked her positivity—*when*, not *if*. It got him frisky, and they made love with Laynie on top, which she said he'd have to get used to as she got bigger. He didn't object, and afterward they made a deal. Jacob would go grocery shopping with her at Ken's Food Fair in town instead of doing it in Watertown so he could stay anonymous. In exchange she promised to go to an OB/GYN and ask for an early ultrasound. In the morning they found a doctor in Watertown through a friend of Chrissy, and Laynie had to admit that it was a great move. As soon as she made her appointment—for that afternoon, thanks to a cancellation—her movements felt more fluid, and she noticed surfaces around Cocklebur Farm that she could paint as micro-landscapes. The black crackles on the door atop the widow's walk, the weathered grain of the wood on Jacob's Destruction Shack, the dried-up burs themselves, with their pale golden seedpods clinging stubbornly to whatever they touched. She hoped the baby inside her would be that stubborn.

"You've definitely got an embryo with a heartbeat," said Dr. Elise Kermans, whose open face and silvering hair put Laynie at ease. She'd recognized her new patient immediately from her picture with Chad Willhart in the *Watertown Public Opinion*. The ultrasound had to be done transvaginally because it was so early, and Laynie hadn't wanted Jacob in the room for that. Laynie didn't see the baby moving or hear its heartbeat like women got to do in movies, but Dr. Kermans assured her that this would come at twenty weeks or so, when she could do a transabdominal ultrasound.

"Your husband will want to be there for that one," she said.

"Do you think it'll make it that far?" Laynie asked.

Dr. Kermans pursed her lips. "If what you say about your uterus is true—and I'm only saying that because I don't have an MRI in front of me, not because I don't believe you—then you know spontaneous abortion is quite possible. A uterus that's unicornate *and* septate is pretty unforgiving. Its only good quality is having the word *unicorn* in it."

It was the best (and only) malformed uterus joke Laynie had ever heard, and she told Dr. Kermans so. They established a September 10 due date for the baby, whose gender she didn't announce. It would probably come early, she suggested, because the uterus wasn't big enough to last forty weeks.

"Think of all the miscarriages you've had before this as your uterus stretching out bit by bit," said the doctor. "Then one day, if everything goes right, it lets you grow enough of a lining to keep a baby inside the whole term."

"How many do I have to lose before I can keep one?" Laynie asked.

"There's no way to tell. This could be the one, or it could be down the road."

"Or it could be never." Her lips tightened involuntarily like they always did before she snapped at somebody.

"It could be never." Dr. Kermans didn't flinch. "You knew that before you came."

Laynie kept her smile up as Dr. Kermans left the room, but inside she wanted to shout and bang things. There was no reason to get mad at Dr. Kermans, who'd only told her the same obvious truth any doctor would. Laynie wanted a pill, any kind of pill, and knew there had to be a sample of something in one of the exam room drawers or cabinets. She pictured herself scrounging for them and got the hell out of there, finding Jacob in the waiting room immersed in some relentlessly cheerful parenting magazine.

"I don't care how cold it is outside, I want a fucking burger and a fucking ice cream." Laynie felt a receptionist staring from behind but turned and glared her down. "And don't talk to me about *When the baby* this or *When the baby* that. It's *If the baby*. Got it?"

14

The Blood and the Bottle

Laynie reached the twelve-week mark, and Jacob got through his least favorite month, and everything promptly fell apart. On the first Saturday in March, Laynie was foaming up hot chocolates for two local teenage girls who wowed over her Medusa hair when she felt a thump in her belly like a horse kicking a pane of glass. The fragile lining of her womb broke inside her, sending ten thousand shards toward the center of her being in the slowest motion she'd ever imagined. Those shards moved inexorably toward their target: her sense of self-worth, which naively awaited the validation of a successful pregnancy.

She smiled at the girls as they left, scanning the tables at Caffeine Paradise to see who might help her if she passed out. Her miscarriages usually came hard and fast—massive sloughings of her uterine linings, unforgiving announcements that THIS WILL NEVER BE A CHILD!!! A fresh metaphor presented itself: her child was a rock climber, a boy with Jacob's face and her hair, falling off a cliff that turned out to be coagulated blood instead of the solid rock he thought he could depend on. He fell in a slow motion as excruciating as the glass shards, flailing his arms and legs at first but giving up the fight, giving up his chance at life as a scarlet wall of blood cascaded toward his anguished face.

Laynie knew that two regulars, Carrie Ullrich and Denise Spielmeyer, would come running if she shouted from the back room.

So, she stepped away through the swinging louvered doors and collapsed against the fridge with her knees to her chest and her cell phone in hand. Time to call Jacob? No, he'd give her some speech about not caring how many miscarriages they had to live through together. What sentimental bullshit. It would drive her straight back to LA. Instead, she texted Kade that she had a major female problem and couldn't finish her shift. Laynie felt blood seeping through her jeans and made it to the bathroom, but not before a few drops had fallen to the floor.

Inside the bathroom she flushed the toilet almost as soon as she sat down, knowing she might be flushing down a someday-baby with a French name. Kade texted BE RIGHT THERE, and she cried as she pictured him stepping over the blood drops. Then Laynie texted Jacob after all, saying HELP PLEASE and I NEED CLOTHES AND LOTS OF PADS and then, when he didn't respond immediately, I LOST THE BABY.

BE RIGHT OVER, he finally replied. Kade lived in town and showed up first, and Laynie heard him muttering "Shit, oh shit" as he followed the blood trail to the bathroom.

"Are you okay?" he asked.

"Just another miscarriage," Laynie told him, hearing her voice from far away. "Jacob can clean up the floor when he gets here. You don't have to worry about it."

"Are you in pain?" Kade asked through the door.

"Shitloads."

"Then wait a sec."

Footsteps went to the office, and Kade's file drawer opened. Pills? Could it be? Laynie checked to see if she could reach the bathroom door from the toilet just in case he knocked on the door, and that's exactly what he did.

"These'll help," Kade told her.

"Thanks." Laynie slivered open the door, and Kade slipped the bottle through. Its label said HYDROCODONE, and she shook it. A gold mine inside.

"Left over from the dentist last year. Don't take all of 'em at once."

"I won't." Laynie worked up some spit, opened the bottle, popped one and swallowed, and counted out seven pills. She'd have to spread them out because it might take her awhile to find more. Unless Kade went to the dentist a lot. Or Carrie Ullrich or Denise Spielmeyer or those high school girls who loved her hair so much. High school girls could get hold of pretty much anything, couldn't they?

* * *

Laynie ended up stashing the bottle of generic Vikes at Caffeine Paradise because Jacob was picking her up, and she'd never get it past him. If she put them in her pocket or purse, he'd hear their telltale jangle right away. He brought her pads and undies and dark sweatpants and took her to the Sanford Clinic's urgent care around the corner, where they gripped each other's hands in the waiting room and said nothing unless one of the staff spoke to them. When a nurse came to get her, Laynie gestured for Jacob to stay there. He was so choked up that he couldn't even swallow, so he worked up what spit he could and lubed his throat.

It would be nice if he had a pill to swallow, just a little de-stressor. Laynie would be miserable to live with, moping and helpless and angry, and he wouldn't exactly be a ball of positivity himself. Her miscarriage had opened up The Void inside him, and it told him exactly where he could find a stash: in his barn, in the smaller of the rolling toolboxes, third drawer down, on the right, in a plastic baggie wrapped in white electrical tape. Half a dozen Klonopins and nine Xanaxes—enough antianxiety weapons to get him through Laynie's post-miscarriage depression without even touching opiates.

"And what about your suicidal ideation?" asked Daniel beside him, dressed in doctor's whites and looking miraculously cleaned up. Trim beard, short-cropped hair, a posture gleaming with self-esteem. Even the hard Boston accent had softened. "Are you going to pretend you're immune to that too?"

Since when did I ever say I'm immune to anything? thought Jacob, knowing Daniel could hear him.

"You never say it, but you act as if you don't realize the danger you're in."

What's with the clothes? Are you a doctor in the afterlife or something?

"I'm whatever you need me to be to get the point across. Maybe a doctor can keep you from raiding your stash."

My real brother would let me.

"Ah, pills are for pussies!" Daniel's accent returned as his doctor ghost mimed shooting up into the crook of his arm. "Only one way to go if you're serious, Big Bro."

Jacob flipped off the figment, and it burrowed back into the hole in his psyche where it lived. A nurse came by, catching the end of his gesture, and told him that his wife had changed her mind and wanted him in the room after all. He followed her and found Laynie sitting crumpled on another exam table, her skin drained of warmth and her face looking half its size.

"This sucks alone," she said. He put a hand on her thigh and breathed with her, trying to pull the air deeper into her lungs by proxy. The nurse gave Laynie a pill in a little white cup, and she swallowed it, and when they were alone again, she told her husband it was Demerol.

"There's legit times to take stuff like that," Jacob said.

"Where's the line between legit and not legit?"

"I wouldn't call taking a Demerol after a miscarriage falling off the wagon."

"I'll take your word for it." Laynie almost told him about Kade's Vicodin, but why open that can of worms? The two pills in combination wouldn't kill her, especially since the Demerol was only fifty milligrams, but she'd certainly be out of it for a while, which she wanted. Jacob would hold her hand and not expect her to talk, and she'd drift off into an opiate daze feeling loved and supported. It would balance out the last miscarriage she had, when she thought she'd die alone in that crappy motel room.

They waited a long time in the room because Laynie insisted on a female doctor. A woman whose name tag read WENZ, JOAN M.D. came in, and Laynie didn't like her much because she seemed to doubt the severity of the situation. Jacob could understand the doctor because there wasn't much blood, though Laynie explained that she'd lost tons of it at Caffeine Paradise. When Dr. Wenz palpated the left side of Laynie's belly, where her sliver of a uterus was, her patient shrieked and she started taking things seriously. If more blood didn't drain out in the next day or two, she should see Dr. Kermans and get a dilation and curettage to eliminate complications.

"It's the same procedure used for abortions," said Dr. Wenz. "People get scared."

"I've had one before," Laynie told her. "After a miscarriage, I mean."

"Then you know it doesn't diminish your chances of conception later. It just means a longer break before you try to conceive again." She shot Jacob a look that said *Back off demanding sex*, then wrote Laynie a prescription for ten more Demerols. She signed forms on the way out to release her chart to Dr. Kermans. Once she was gone, Laynie held up the prescription and gave Jacob a demented grin. She got that way on opiates sometimes. Gallows humor.

"That's a slippery slope, Lane," he said.

"I think it's more like a banana peel at the edge of a cliff. But would you rather see me in shitloads of pain constantly?"

"You've got to take it like she prescribed it," Jacob said. "No stashing."

"Deal. You can come around every four hours and give it to me in a little white cup, like I'm a mental patient."

She wanted to sob, but nothing came out of her mouth except a laugh that sounded like a growl. *We won't survive this*, Laynie heard herself thinking from far away. *It'll break us. Nobody left standing. Everybody on the floor in tears.*

* * *

To their surprise it didn't break them, even though Laynie ended up going to Watertown for that D&C. She was unnaturally cheerful about it as Jacob drove her, but he chalked it up to her Demerols—which she'd taken exactly as prescribed. Jacob was the one who looked like the world was ending.

"Don't act like they're scraping your baby out," Laynie told him in the prep room. "There's no baby left to scrape. They've got to get the debris out 'cause if there's debris, the next baby in line might have even more trouble sticking."

"Is it okay to sculpt that baby?" Jacob asked. "The one we just lost?"

"Do you mean how it looked when I lost it or what it'd look like if it lived?"

"Not sure yet."

"Sculpt away," Laynie told him, and then they took her to the procedure room. Back in the waiting room Jacob slouched in his chair and thought of a hundred different ways to sculpt their child. The embryo—if it had even lived to twelve weeks and not died in Laynie's womb sooner—would have looked like a sausage with limbs and digits and a gigantic head, but he mostly saw it as a boy raised in the wild, hunting in his loincloth with a short spear.

No, too much like Mowgli from *Jungle Book*. Embarrassingly nonartistic. Despite the fact that his wife was being anesthetized and might never wake up, Jacob felt overjoyed to think about art again. Daniel's death had beaten it out of him, and the miscarriage had beaten it back in. He imagined himself standing at his bench in the barn and molding raw clay with his fingers—the tadpole-ish embryo their child had been at seven weeks, the twelve-week-old fetus that had gone down the toilet at Caffeine Paradise, the twenty-week fetus they'd never get to see. The newborn, the crawler, the toddler, the hunter.

Yes, good to think about art again. Art would keep him off pills. Art would make his posture so perfect and his mind so clear that it would keep Laynie off pills too. After eighty minutes they called him into her recovery room, where her face looked puffy and slack from the anesthetic.

"I'm all scraped out," Laynie said, circling her hand over her belly and whisking it away. "Whoosh!"

"Please don't talk like that." Jacob sat beside her and took that hand so she couldn't do anything else with it.

"How many more times will you stick with me through this? Two? Five?"

"I don't want to have this conversation."

"Just give me a number, Jacob." She never called him that directly unless she was mad or wanted a favor. "It's important for me to know."

"Two hundred forty," he replied, figuring she had twenty years until menopause and dropped twelve eggs a year.

"I'll buy that. I'm not too woozy to know that's a good number to buy."

15

Aftermathing

They had their share of shitty days after the miscarriage. The worst came while February's weather had a March encore, and both of them woke at four thirty in the morning when something the wind tore loose crashed into the bedroom window nearest the bathroom. Even with tons of cardboard on the empty pane and an extra blanket on top of them, it was still too cold to be in the room. They went down to the kitchen to huddle near the stove, but that didn't work because the wind had blown out the pilot lights on both the furnace and the water heater, which Uncle Ed had taken great pains to make nearly impossible with a series of shields and diverters. Even though both machines had emergency shutoffs, Jacob opened some windows to clear any gas before he relit the pilots. They shivered in the kitchen, drinking coffee way too early because at least the coffee maker worked.

"Fuck this place," Jacob said, breathing heavily on his fingertips to warm them.

"Absolutely," Laynie said back. "Fuck this place."

But by and large art kept them out of trouble. Laynie set up a projector she borrowed from Don-o and pointed it at a store-bought canvas, ready to paint once she worked up the mojo. Jacob set up some electric heaters in the barn and worked his clay with sopping wet hands that he had to periodically warm. He'd started with the seven-week embryo, which he called Tadpole, but soon started working on Bighead, the twelve-week fetus who'd died. He didn't like people seeing his works in progress but let Don-o check them out while he was over. It was just the two of them—no wives, no Rico Suave.

"You don't expect praise or approval on these, do you?" Don-o asked.

"Nah, I just want you to know I'm not wasting my time."

"And you show me you're not falling off the wagon after the miscarriage, even though you're thinking about pills half the time."

"Half? No way." Jacob dried his hands on a rag and started covering up his sculptures with plastic. "Fifteen percent maybe."

"Bullshit."

"Okay, twenty."

They went inside to cook an omelet because Laynie had started buying farm fresh eggs from a teenage girl who stopped by Caffeine Paradise every Monday, and they had way too many eggs. Jacob got a text from Lovetrain alerting him to a small shitstorm on SMS, so he let Don-o chop up some veggies and sing in the kitchen while he checked the message boards. Carlos Woodheit in Milwaukee was coming up on the anniversary of his father's murder suicide (wife, brother-in-law, mother-in-law) and wondering why the man didn't kill him too. What had he done to stay alive? Carlos's father had driven his only child to baseball practice, then gone and done his deed. What does it mean to be chosen as the designated survivor? Jacob needed some food before he could wade into that conversation.

"That site's sucking up your life," Don-o said when Jacob came back to the kitchen and told him about Carlos. "Every time you open it up, you're flinging yourself into the danger zone."

"Ah hell, Don-o. *Life* is the danger zone." He took his plate and ate two huge mouthfuls before sitting down. "Don't act like one place is any safer than the next."

Meanwhile, at Caffeine Paradise, Laynie stood behind the counter unnerved by a trio of fortyish hunting-fishing types who kept bitching about Arabs. Apparently, they'd been detoured off their beaten path through Nebraska, and a man behind a gas station counter had talked funny and counted their change funny. They couldn't even hazard a guess as to what kind of Arab he was, and when they made fun of his voice, he sounded more Indian than anything.

Part Lebanese, hello! Laynie wanted to shout at them. *I'm part of your problem!* Jacob had warned her about those kinds of people, hadn't he? She'd been insulated from them because (a) most of them didn't drink lattes, and (b) her entire East SoDakistan experience was a carefully constructed illusion: Cocklebur Farm, Caffeine Paradise, the Donatellis, the Hattens. All inside a bubble.

But what was her alternative? Going all rah-rah about Clark, South Dakota, and running for school board? City council? She'd run into a lot more people like the Arab-bashing hunters that way, and it felt safer to stay in her bubble than to learn how the people around her truly felt. Jacob was right about not telling everybody she was part Lebanese, and Laynie got pissed at him for it. When the hunters left, she had the place to herself, and she checked to make sure that Kade's Vicodins were still at the back of the shelf where the never-used Torani syrups lived: Mojito Mint, Peanut Butter, Shortbread.

She found the bottle and shook it, wondering whether to pop one in honor of the Arab-hating hunters or her unknown Lebanese homies. She did neither but instead cursed her husband for making her see her shiny new home through his jaded eyes. The second she put the bottle back, Kade came in with the niece he wanted to train just in case Laynie missed more time, and she was free to go. She bought corned beef and cabbage at Ken's Food Fair—they were having Famiglia Donatelli over—and drove back to Cocklebur Farm, wondering when the cockleburs would start growing or any damn thing would start growing. She'd never experienced March in any other place than California, and she expected lush plant growth all around her. March in East SoDakistan only offered her a dull, heavy curtain of gray.

Heading south, Laynie saw the inexplicable wooden post on the small part of Mud Lake with the electrical box on it, still surrounded by ice. Every time she drove past it, she imagined taking pictures she could use for micro-landscapes. This time she imagined something else: herself walking on a wire that stretched across the 424 to an imaginary electrical box in the other half of the lake. This version of Laynie Jackman, wearing a flowered hat and a Victorian hoop dress three times wider than her shoulders, was so confident in her steps across the wire that her mind seemed tuned to other things—her favorite cow at home or whether Jacob had fixed the crank on their Model T.

The sight of this alternate self forced her to pull over and get out. By the time she closed her car door, the Victorian Laynie and her high-wire act had moved on. The flesh-and-blood Laynie stepped onto a patch of crunchy, frozen grass that bordered the lake, which had been cleared of snow by wind and sunlight but still offered no promise of growth. Then she stepped gingerly onto the ice, terrified of what Jacob might do if she fell in and drowned. It wouldn't be one life lost but many—her and all his someday-babies. Even if Jacob didn't OD like his brother or pull the trigger of some borrowed gun, he'd be reduced to an emotional vegetable.

Laynie's feet shuffled along the ice, not wanting to press down for fear that she'd step on a crack and go through. But hadn't she seen trucks out on this ice only a week before? Just three days ago, hadn't she seen two men with an ATV drilling holes with power augers? Nonetheless, she walked softly, waiting for a *Craaaaaaaaaaack!* to tell her that she'd gone too far and needed to turn back and run.

She could only stop herself from picturing the lake ice swallowing her up by imagining Jacob's grief in fine detail. When he came to identify her body, would he slam his fist against her ribs so hard it broke them like he'd done with Daniel? Would he call her a *stupid fuck*, or whatever he called his brother? Afterward, he'd blow up the entire world a little bit at a time. Careful not to hurt people, of course, because Jacob didn't believe in hurting people. He'd usher everybody safely out of a building, then blow the living shit out of it.

The ice didn't make a sound, didn't even notice Laynie Jackman's delicate presence. She walked out to the post and saw the wires going from the electrical box down into the water, then slid out her phone and took seventy-eight pictures of the box, the post, and the crunched-up ice around it. She'd start painting the best one right away, even if it meant buying shitty paints and brushes at the Hobby Lobby in Watertown. And she wouldn't take another pill, dammit. She wouldn't take another damn stupid fucking pill.

* * *

"I want to write about the miscarriage on SMS," Jacob told Laynie that night after the Donatellis left. They'd been a perfect distraction, though every time Laynie saw Chrissy breastfeeding Rico Suave, she'd feel a stab in her uterus.

"I don't see why everybody else on your internet thing has to know about it," she said. "Do you tell them everything about me?"

"I won't even mention your name."

"Good. Don't mention this last baby's name either."

"It never had one," Jacob said.

"It had a bunch."

Laynie volunteered to clean up so Jacob could brood in the living room with the computer on his lap. She could feel his angsty vibe all the way across the house and eventually retreated to the widow's walk to smoke an imaginary cigarette in the Carhartt coat the Donatellis had given her that night instead of sympathy flowers. The cigarette helped quell her desire for pills, which occupied 60 percent of her mind. If she'd only saved a single Demerol from Dr. Wenz or snuck one of Kade's Vicodins into her pocket, this would have been a perfect time to pop one. Imaginary cigarettes couldn't send her off to Neverland or Zombieland, but they did the trick of distancing her from the continuous flesh-and-blood crisis called her life. Plus, they kicked in immediately.

"Daddy's got to do what he's got to do," Laynie told the ghost of her first child to reach the fetus stage, which she imagined still floating in her womb. "Hey, if you ever have a brother or sister in there, just say this is where Mommy goes when she gets scared. I don't want them worrying I'll jump."

But Laynie felt about to jump, just for a second. Her head swam, and she trembled at the guardrail, sure she'd tumble down in slow motion. Jacob would sense it and race out to catch her, and the Victorian hoop dress would parachute her into his arms.

"What a nutjob," Laynie told herself with a massive exhale. And it was certifiable, talking to a miscarried fetus like it was still inside her. But didn't they say that pregnancy changed women's brains? She'd read on the news that children's DNA remained with the mother for life—though that probably applied only to mothers who actually give birth. How many more miscarriages would she have to endure, Laynie wondered, to add up to a full forty-week term?

Ugh. The math disgusted her. She flicked her imaginary cigarette off the edge of the railing and, as she followed its arc to the ground, saw her father floating in the air just above where the self that might have jumped would land. Laynie sliced her phone's flashlight through the darkness to look for him but saw only life-sized balloons in his general shape—floating William Jackmans in hideous powder-blue tuxedos, their arms spread wide and their faces pasted with impossibly wide smiles—floating up toward the widow's walk.

"That's not you," she said, laughing at a father balloon that passed close by and jabbing it with an imaginary needle. When it popped, she smelled Dad—smelled the avocados he used to love, mashed up inside their skins and garnished with salt and red chili pepper.

Laynie breathed deep, and the scent raced through her bloodstream, loosening all the muscles that the imaginary nicotine couldn't reach. She felt the scrape of her father's spoon in her femurs, in her fibulas, and knew things would be all right.

Back in the living room, Jacob avoided all intoxicants, both real and imaginary. Instead, he imagined himself wrapped in a blue cloak, something dignified and European that gave everything he said depth and resonance. He created an SMS thread called LOSING AN UNBORN CHILD and started typing.

JACOB_NAS: I've been absent for a while, just lurking around, because my wife and I just lost a baby after twelve weeks of pregnancy, which is when miscarriages are supposed to stop happening. It's been a lousy time, but it's less lousy because we haven't tried drinking or drugging away our sadness. I think it's the first time I haven't done that. Hitting the booze or (more likely for me) the pills has always been my go-to reaction for grief, and NOT doing that feels like turning a corner. But everybody here knows how it feels to turn a corner and end up right back where you were. I'm not fooling myself that I've hit some higher level or anything, but turning corners at least makes you feel like you're getting somewhere.

The weirdest thing about it is that the chance of being a dad got me thinking more about what my father did and how it might pass on. Whenever I thought about my kid—especially if it turned out to be a boy—I could barely get a breath in because it would be able to feel my curse, the same kind of anger inside me that my father had. I felt like I wasn't ready to be a dad because I haven't worked through my shit and that losing this baby let me dodge a bullet. Don't get me wrong, I would've loved this child if it ever came into the world. But it didn't, and now I'm relieved because I don't think I'm ready to be a father. Has anybody else out there—and I know at least a few of you are parents—ever been down this road?

Part 2

* * *

Laynie made Jacob promise not to check the SMS boards until after the mail came in the morning, and that turned out to be a mistake. He drove down and got a giant, battered envelope wrapped in half a dozen layers of tape, with a note from the U.S. Postal Service saying it had been opened for inspection. In the kitchen Jacob knifed through the tape to find his father's NASSEDRING army coat and his mother's crumbling alligator purse inside. A note on Chatwin Motor Lodge stationery from a guy named Dave said the following:

> Jacob, I got your address from the registration card. I don't know if you left these in the room on purpose or not, but if you did I figure you might end up regretting it. Everybody has family and we hate them sometimes but their stuff is important. Don't worry about the postage, just tell your friends about the place. Sorry if I'm just making you get rid of these somewhere else.

Jacob unfolded the army coat and whipped it four times against the kitchen floor, grunting hard. Then he slumped back to the living room, sat on the blue sofa, and opened up his laptop as if he hadn't just brought terrible luck into the house. The first few responses to his message were supportive, helpful, kind. But then Jacob read one from Simeon Gartner that stuck in his craw.

SIMEON: Man, you think you're such a martyr. The murdered mother and the suicide father and the suicide brother and now the dead unborn baby. Boo fucking hoo! That makes you soooooooooooo great just to be able to live and breathe after all the bad shit that happened to you, doesn't it? You've overcome SO much and become SUCH a productive member of human society. Hooray for Jacob, everybody!

Laynie heard him swear and slap down the laptop cover. She came out to the living room with a conciliatory cup of coffee for him even though he looked like he'd throw it at something. He took a sip, handed it back, and showed her Simeon's post.

"Don't take the bait," Laynie told him.

"Everybody hates this guy, Lane. Everybody goes off on him once in a while, and it's my turn now."

Jacob faked a smile, but all he could think about was tearing Simeon Gartner's face off in front of everybody he knew. He stared at the post until the mudroom door closed behind Laynie. She'd be going to her yurt or to the widow's walk, which gave him at least an hour for a flame war. Simeon, he felt sure, was licking his chops.

JACOB_NAS: How about a little respect for the dead, Sim? You could start with your own, which you obviously need to do, and while you're at it maybe learn to respect other people's.

SIMEON: I have plenty of respect for the dead. They rule my goddam life. I just think you're full of shit when you compare a baby that wasn't even BORN yet to your father. Using an unborn baby as an excuse to FINALLY think about what your father MEANT—I mean meant to life on EARTH, not just to YOUR little life—is complete bullshit. You need to think about the meaning of your FATHER'S life, not about some fetus you didn't even know was a boy or a girl. You need to get on your knees and pray to understand your dad, and pray it doesn't happen to you. Nothing else matters. NOTHING!

JACOB_NAS: Does anybody know when Sim got religion? Last time I checked, he was an atheist making fun of anybody who ever went to church.

RONKATZ: No shit. Sounds like a bullshit conversion to me.

SIMEON: I meant "pray" as a figure of speech, dipshits. Anybody who doesn't have his head up his ass can tell there's no god.

ANDYBENT: Cool it down, Sim.

BERRY23: Sim, do you need your ass kicked electronically by all of us at once? We can do that. Some of us have been waiting.

JOYELLE1: I'd be up for that.

SIMEON: Why kick my ass when Jacob N-ASS-edrine is the guy who needs it? Him and his fucking high horse? He acts like he's the only one who ever lived through this shit, and we let him tell us how we should feel just because he started this thing. Shit, even his wife's miscarriage is just an excuse for him to lecture us. Don't you people see the bullshit in that?

FRANKFULL: I've never felt like Jacob told me how to feel. Simmer down, Sim.

SIMEON: Like hell. Maybe if I keep talking, Jacob_Nas(hole) will boot me from the threads. But then I won't have anybody to talk to, and I might start thinking dirty thoughts. Oh, no! I need SMS to keep my head on straight! I'm an addict! I need Jacob!

JACOB_NAS: Let's put it up to a vote, folks? Lovetrain, how long to set up a poll?

LYLEMOTT: about 3 minutes, say the word

JANETC: I think it's rash to banish Simeon for this. We know he's a jerk, but it worries me when I lose track of any of you for too long. He's the last one I want to lose track of.

JACOB_NAS: We're all sick of your pitbull act, Sim. Give it a rest. I'm out of this cesspool.

SIMEON: No you're not. You built this cesspool, and you'll swim in it till you hear my last goddam word.

LYLEMOTT: will you guys quit it? i'm trying to be privately miserable here

JANETC: Take care of yourself, Sim. I'm out too.

A-LEASH-A: Here if you need me.

Jacob started a new thread called THE PURPOSE OF THIS SITE IS NOT FOR SIMEON GARTNER TO VENT HIS RAGE AND FRUS-TRATION, then put up a single post saying "nuf said" and locked it so nobody could add another word.

16

That Baboon Smile

The thread bothered Jacob more than he could admit, and Laynie got desperate to shake him out of the three-day funk that followed. She said she wanted to take an afternoon nap and crawled into bed naked, ready to make love for the first time since the D&C. Jacob joined her—a good sign that he wasn't completely despondent—and although he didn't make any moves himself, he let her coax him hard and straddle him.

"I thought your doctor said don't try making babies for three months," he said.

"I'm not trying to make a baby. I'm fucking my husband."

Being on top let her control the pace, but once Jacob got close to coming, he grabbed her hips and thrust into her, and she remembered the violation of the D&C and the ache that came after it. She remembered what Dr. Kermans said about her uterus getting bigger with each miscarriage and wondered if the waiting period would be a lost opportunity. Then Jacob came, his face twisted up like he must have been thinking of his father or even Simeon Gartner, and Laynie didn't come with him. She rolled off him right away and told him she hurt, and he muttered how he couldn't do anything right today. They slept for an hour, when Laynie got a phone call from DHL saying she had a package—the driver didn't want to try climbing up the hill with all the fresh sleet. She dressed and took

Jacob's truck down and grabbed the paints she'd ordered, then went back to the bedroom to find Jacob just as mopey as he'd been before she seduced him.

"We should go out and eat tonight," she told him.

"What are we celebrating?"

She shrugged. "I just want to celebrate another day of living." Laynie hoped a classic rock reference would make him smile, but it didn't dent his commitment to wallowing. "I think we need to get out of the house more. Hang out with other people."

"Are you going to try to kick me when I'm down and try dragging me to Tammy's Tavern again?" asked Jacob. It was their third argument about Tammy's, which people at the coffee shop said had the best steak in town.

"I wasn't even going to mention it! But it's not good for you to hide from the people you grew up with."

"I'm not hiding. I just don't like them. And it was only four years out of eighteen." He headed for the shower, and the water cut off their conversation. They barely exchanged a glance when she walked past him to take her turn five minutes later. When Laynie stepped out, Jacob wore tan chinos, a button-down shirt, and a pair of dress shoes she didn't even knew he owned.

"What's the occasion?" she asked.

"My wife's forcing me to go to a restaurant owned by a family who treated my brother like shit just to make some abstract point about 'loving where you live.'" He turned from her and looked through his dresser for his tie. "I figure dressing like a lawyer might keep me out of a fight."

"Don't do it if it's *that* hard. Shit, I'm sorry I asked."

"No, you're right." He found the tie with his summertime sleeveless T-shirts. "It's important to face the people who were assholes to you and see if they're still assholes. To believe for a second they've changed, until you realize they're bigger assholes than ever."

Laynie put on a red dress with big yellow octopuses on it, and at five thirty they headed over to Tammy's Tavern, completely overdressed and owning it. Tammy's was east of Clark on the 212, a steakhouse-roadhouse hybrid with an extra parking lot in back so you could sleep off your booze without the neighbors knowing—unless they were parked in back too. It was a squat, square, ugly, brown building with not enough windows. Some of its outside walls looked like a faux–log cabin, while others were simply painted brick. It had been a feed and tack store once upon a time, Jacob said. Just past the front door was a sizable mudroom equipped with multiple shoe scrapers and bristly rugs.

"Is this a place where farm wives go?" Laynie asked him as they scraped sleet off their too-fancy shoes.

"I think a farm wife would show some respect and dress halfway decent. Not like some coastal elite snob."

He checked to be sure she knew he was joking, then decided to get through this ordeal using an old trick of Daniel's: pretend he was so stoned that he couldn't stop smiling. They went inside and stood by the PLEASE WAIT TO BE SEATED sign until a round, angry blonde Jacob's age rumbled over and looked them up and down. Her expression didn't change a single percentage point.

"Been awhile," she told Jacob. Then she glanced at Laynie and said, "I saw you in the paper."

"That's right," said Laynie, too friendly for the situation. "Are you Tammy?"

"No such thing as Tammy," the blonde said. "It just went nice with *tavern*. You want to sit near people or away?"

Jacob said, "Away," and Laynie said, "Near," and the woman ignored Jacob with a smirk. They sat down at a dark wooden booth, in sight of a sixtyish couple who gave them and their clothes the stink eye. On the wall above the couple hung a red sign that said THIS ESTAB-LISHMENT SUPPORTS YOUR RIGHT TO BARE ARMS. It showed a faceless but buxom woman in a halter top holding a pistol in each hand.

"The misspelling is intentional," Jacob said as Laynie examined the sign.

"Duh. Did you sleep with that hostess woman?"

"No. But Daniel did."

"Ahhhh," said Laynie.

"Lucy Norgren, the owner's daughter. See what you dragged me into?"

"I see. Is this the night I have to admit my husband's right and Clark's the most miserable butthole town of all time?"

"It might help. Or this could be the night you start to feel like you belong here, or the night you realize everybody's already against you because of who you're married to."

A younger, slimmer woman with the same face as the first blonde came over to give them menus but also didn't introduce herself. Laynie recognized her from the coffee shop, but the recognition wasn't returned. Jacob ordered them South Dakota Martinis and a plate of chislic without telling Laynie what they were in advance: Bud Light on tap with olives in it, and little chunks of grilled meat eaten with toothpicks and dipped in ranch dressing.

"You wanted to go native," Jacob said, lifting his glass. "Bottoms up."

"I never said that." Laynie clinked anyway. "I just wanted to get you away from thinking about . . . certain things."

"More like *uncertain* things, huh?" Jacob stabbed some meat and washed it down with a giant slug of beer. He wanted to get tipsy and make a fool of himself among people who loathed him—maybe that would make his wife understand how he felt about Clark. Laynie used the chislic toothpick to fish out an olive and scanned the meat and potatoes menu while a fiftyish, stiff-walking man with a CASE IH baseball cap and insulated overalls came over to their table.

"Hey Jake," he said, not reaching out a hand or looking at Laynie. "Nice getup."

"Hey Del," Jacob said back. "You working outside in this weather?"

"Yeah, fixing the same old drainage shit again." He finally looked Laynie's way. "This the lucky lady I keep hearing about?"

"Yep. Got hitched in January."

"Nice to meet you," Del said. "You're our first Californian."

"Second, actually," Jacob replied. "Bridget Domargo's from there too."

"But she was just a baby. And I'm sure there's more coming. Well, good night." He doffed his hat to Laynie, and Jacob shoved more chislic into his mouth to keep it shut.

"So, I'm guessing *Californian* isn't a word you want next to your name here," Laynie said. "Is it better or worse than *Lebanese*?"

"Shh." Jacob's eyes roved around, though he didn't move his head. "It takes a while to learn where you stand in a place like this, and the way people act to your face doesn't always give you the clues you need. They call it Minnesota Nice."

"How long did it take you to figure that out?"

"I'm still taking Minnesota Nice 101," he said. "For, like, the tenth time. Maybe you can study up and pass it the first time, and I can cheat off you."

"Why do you hate them?" asked Laynie. She realized she was biting her lip and about to kick him under the table.

"What? I don't hate—"

"You *hate* them, Jacob. You're not just a guy who doesn't like where he lives—you actually *hate* these people."

"Shhhhhh!" Jacob said again, and that made Laynie feel like she was getting somewhere with him. Jacob took a long breath to compose himself. "They killed my brother. *Started* killing him, I mean. Before I even left, they all circled him and let him know they'd tear him apart. So yeah, I hate these people. I'd get the fuck out if I had an extra penny to my name and somewhere else to go."

Laynie nodded, then took twice as long to compose herself as Jacob had. He slugged down his beer and waited for her pronouncement.

"These people didn't start killing Daniel," she told him. "Your father did, and you know it."

Their steak dinners were fine but unspectacular, and they left before the kind of people who habitually parked in the back lot finished their third drinks. Jacob's phone, which he'd left at home on purpose, had four missed calls and a text from Lovetrain. Simeon Gartner had attacked Frank Fuller, who was freaking out over a murder-suicide in Belgium that closely resembled the one he'd survived. Simeon told Frank to "just deal with it, babyface," so Jacob—even though Laynie asked him to keep off the threads for the night—did his administrator's duty and booted him from SMS for three months. Five minutes later he got a video file over email.

"Hey man," Simeon said. He looked smarter than Jacob thought, not so red in the face and neck as he looked in his crappy profile JPEG. "Trying out my new computer. I love it, don't even have to type. I got that email, and yeah, it sucks being booted, but I deserve it. I'll try not to shit on people from now on. If you take me back, I mean. I might come begging." Then he lifted a coffee mug and said, "Peace to you and everybody," and after that it took him a while to actually stop recording.

That gave Jacob a good, long look at the man. Simeon was strong through the chest and gut, with no flab, and better dressed than anyone would have guessed. He had a white collared shirt on, and from the way the neck fell open, Jacob guessed he'd worn a tie all day. Accountant? Engineer? All people on SMS knew about Simeon was that he lived in Naperville, Illinois, where he did something vaguely managerial for a company that made gigantic spools of wire. He was forty-three, older than almost anybody else on the boards. But he also had one of the most recent murder-suicides among them, so out of pity everybody tolerated his occasional spews of bile. Eight months ago his father, then sixty-five, had shot his mother in an argument over money that Simeon would never explain. Then he'd parked his RV in the middle of the busiest intersection in Naperville and blown his head off with a shotgun.

Jacob played the video again, this time with the sound off. The most telling thing about Simeon was the way he couldn't hold his own eye in the camera when he caught it, by mistake, as he tried to turn it off. He looked straight into it for a moment, but when he saw himself on-screen, his eyes looked away immediately.

I'm like that, Jacob thought. *All of us are like that. Not survivors, just fuckups and losers who got left behind.*

* * *

The next day chugged along normally until it stopped dead at five o'clock, when Lovetrain texted Jacob to TURN ON THE FUCKING NEWS! Jacob was in his butterscotch chair in the near-empty Shrine Room, praying that it might turn into a nursery someday without actually admitting he was praying, and headed down to his computer in the living room. The lead story on all the major news websites featured Simeon Gartner, who'd blown off his hands and most of his face that afternoon while trying to bomb the Midwest headquarters of the Environmental Protection Agency in Chicago's Metcalfe Federal Building.

"Lane?!" he called, but she must have been in her yurt. Jacob couldn't get up to check—his muscles felt dry and brittle, like the plastinated human bodies he'd seen on a science museum website once. He felt raw and skinless. "Lane, I need you!"

His voice quavered in an absolutely recognizable way. The same way Daniel's had quavered over the words *Mom?* and *Dad?* when the Social Services people let the two of them into their Dorchester apartment to gather a few things before becoming temporary wards of the state. The poor damn kid looking for Mom and Dad when he'd been told they were dead fifty times already. Twelve years old, and Daniel already sounded like his entire life had been broken. But he had to keep on living anyway, like a winless football team playing out the season, and he knew it. His voice said so.

"Lane?" Jacob called out one more time. Then he texted her, I NEED YOU. In the pre-bombing photos on the news, Simeon Gartner looked whole and almost wholesome. He wore a blue suit and red tie because he was an executive: the company that made those giant spools of wire had been in his family for seventy years, and a decades-long dispute with the EPA over heavy metal poisoning of groundwater had led to the financial distress that spurred his father to murder-suicide. Simeon had apparently inherited not only his father's company but his rage and grudges as well. He'd smuggled small quantities of plastic explosives past security guards at the Metcalfe over the course of three visits to the EPA that day, then stashed them under a sink in a restroom. He'd mistakenly set them off while assembling his bomb in a toilet stall.

No one else was injured in the blast, which could have been catastrophic had Simeon finished putting his device together. Because the crime took place on federal property, the FBI would investigate it as an act of terrorism. The suspect—though it was ridiculous to call him a suspect with his hands and face blown off—was in critical condition in a Chicago hospital but expected to survive.

SAW IT, he texted Lovetrain, who said he was on his way over. Laynie hurried into the living room to see her devastated husband staring at his computer screen. She sat next to him feeling the fragile energy around him like a sphere of glass so thin that a single breath might shatter it. She caught only the anchorwoman's last words— "no indication of accomplices"—and the word GARTNER beneath the man's picture.

"That's the asshole on SMS," Laynie said. Jacob nodded, and when the clip ended, he switched to another website. As he watched another version of the story, Laynie felt him shrink into himself and into the couch. He'd already retreated into the Jacob who'd just found out his parents were dead. The Jacob who'd broken his dead brother's ribs in anger. She imagined him inside a giant eggshell that she'd have to coax him out of slowly, like a man afraid to be born.

In her mind she took his slimy, yolk-covered arm, but his real arm cleared off the entire coffee table with a single, violent sweep. An empty glass, a Clive Barker novel, the laptop, a stack of bills—Jacob whacked all of them to the floor the way a child clears a board game when he knows he's losing.

"I don't trust myself right now," Jacob said. His voice shook, and his nostrils looked as big as a horse's.

"Should I go away?" Laynie had never been this close before to the fear in Jacob, the violence in him. Now she knew they were the same thing, two life states of the same animal.

"No," he told her. "I don't know. Can you call Don-o? And Lovetrain?"

Laynie nodded, rose from the couch as gently as possible, and retreated to the kitchen with one ear trained on her husband. Part of her was terrified, remembering the way Jacob's mother died and not knowing what would happen if the fragile ball of glass around him broke. Part of her said *You knew what you were getting into*, and that was the more comfortable part to inhabit. Standing in their kitchen wondering what food might calm Jacob down, Laynie felt absolutely and finally married. One hundred percent tied to this person she could never fully comprehend. It was as mysterious as death.

Figgy goat cheese, that was his favorite thing. She put a whole log of it on his second-favorite plate, not wanting to use his most favorite because it might get hurled at something or someone, and she added some crackers even though he liked the cheese plain. Then she remembered to call Don-o and Lovetrain and went out on the back porch so Jacob wouldn't hear her. Don-o had heard the news but didn't know Jacob's connection to the bomber.

"I hope this isn't the big one for Jakey," Don-o said. "What's he like right now?"

"On the couch, staring at the TV."

"Catatonic almost? Then lashing out?"

"Yeah, kinda. He threw stuff on the floor."

"Hang tight," Don-o said. "I'm coming down." Then Lovetrain called her before she could call him.

"Do *not* let Jacob go to SMS or his email right now," he said. "Seriously bad shit. I'm like twenty minutes away. Hang tight."

Hang tight. Both men had said it, but what the hell did it actually mean? She pondered that question abstractly because it was more pleasant than imagining Jacob destroying things and turning on her when there was nothing left in the house to break. Hanging *loose* meant being flexible and receptive to life's many surprising changes. Did hanging *tight*, then, mean being *in*flexible and *un*receptive to them? Or was it an emphatic way of saying *Hang on*, don't let go of whatever you're clinging to or you'll drift away into the stratosphere?

Laynie brought out the figgy goat cheese, but she could tell it wouldn't do a damn thing. Jacob smiled when she handed it to him, probably to reassure her that he wasn't about to strangle her and that she didn't need to carry an eight-inch kitchen knife at all times. Once the cheese was in front of him, he barely poked at it. Simeon's news had opened up a false bottom in his life, revealed to him the chasm between the fantasy of his married happiness and the reality of his broken inner self. In the fantasy he was grounded and approachable and took things in stride. In his actual life he was always as close to despair as his brother had been—he'd simply trained himself to avoid falling off the edge into it. But falling would feel so damn good.

Jacob had his own mental treehouse, like Lovetrain, and falling was the only way he could come down from it.

Simeon's news felt like the start of that falling, and the smart thing to do was let himself go. Make sure that he fell inside his own personal hole of despair before he hurt anybody else, then close the door on the rest of the world until his life ended. Stay in the treehouse absolutely still and barely breathing to make sure the evil man—who was himself, without question—didn't hear him and kill him.

People would come and go. They'd bring plates and take them away. They'd bring little paper cups full of pills and take them away empty. They'd open his mouth from time to time and make him say *Ahhhh* and walk away satisfied that he wasn't dead, though he certainly couldn't be called living, and they'd leave him tuned to his favorite internal radio station—the one with twenty-four-hour static.

"Don't you want the cheese?" Laynie asked, waltzing back into the living room to make sure he didn't open up his computer, which fortunately was still on the floor. Jacob looked at the cheese, but his mouth felt too dry to eat it.

"Thanks," he said. "I don't even want to set foot online right now. I'll get too sucked in."

"That's a very wise idea." Laynie sat on the couch, nestling slightly against him, and milked the moment. Every second he didn't open up the computer was a good one. "Are you thinking about your dad a lot right now?"

"When am I not?" He put a hand on her thigh and let her feed him a piece of cheese, which tasted like milky chalk to him. "They'll shut down SMS over this."

"Maybe that's not such a bad thing."

"Yeah, maybe."

Tires ground against the gravel, and Laynie stiffened at Lovetrain's arrival. Whatever he didn't want Jacob to see would soon be known. They both listened for him, tracking him. Back door, kitchen, funky spot by the stairs. Then he was there, standing in the mouth of the living room, staring at them.

"I feel like I'm in a guerrilla war," he said. "And one of the guys I fought with just went down."

"One man's guerrilla war is another man's terrorism," Jacob said back.

"Terrorism," Lovetrain spat. "What do you bet we end up in jail just 'cause we knew that sick fuck?"

"You didn't *really* know him," Laynie said, but both men raised their eyebrows at her. With Lovetrain around, it was a murder-suicide survivors party, and she knew she'd be disinvited. It didn't take long.

"Jake, there's something you've got to see." Lovetrain stepped toward the couch, looking at Jacob's computer. "From Sim."

"Ah, shit." Jacob turned to Laynie. "Hon, do you mind if I check this out with just Train here?"

"Sure. I'll go out to the widow's walk."

"No." He grabbed her forearm, then realized that was too aggressive and let go. "That's too far away. Please."

Laynie nodded and stood, looking at her forearm. She was less worried about a bruise than some mark of evil that had transferred magically from Simeon Gartner to Jacob, then on to her, and eventually to their not-yet-born children. She saw nothing, not even a red squeeze mark, and went outside to the back porch rocking chair. She kept the door cracked open, knowing there would eventually be a shout. Knowing there would be objects hurled against tables and walls. Inside, Jacob breathed slowly with his diaphragm.

"Open your email," Lovetrain said. "He posted on a delay, or somebody posted it for him."

"I've been afraid of this." Jacob opened his email and found one from Simeon titled A VIDEO MESSAGE FOR SMS. He clicked it open and steeled himself. The video, which had the same background as the one Simeon sent after getting banned, started with him smiling into the camera and straightening his tie.

"How could I forget my wonderful, supportive friends at Survivors of Murder-Suicide? Survivors? You think so? You think you're really *surviving* it, or are you just getting beaten down by it more and more every day, ground down until it squeezes your soul out like a—Like I don't know what. I'm a businessman, not a poet. I'm just saying, people, that you'll never need to be scared of any devil outside you, 'cause the one inside you is big and scary enough. There's a violence gene, you know that? Scientists proved it. And guess what? *You got it!*"

Then he pushed back from his desk and laughed. Lovetrain paused the video with Simeon in mid-guffaw, his teeth showing like a baboon on the attack.

"That's a sick man," Lovetrain said.

"Yeah." Jacob couldn't take his eyes off the still either and had to force himself to hit the PLAY button again. Simeon laughed for almost a solid minute, then turned away from the camera and fell silent. He came back with his eyes wide and his nostrils flared.

"Boo!" he growled. "Well, by now you know what I did, and you're probably praying for me, but if you are, I've got two little words for you: *don'twaste yourtime*. I know where I'm going when my life's over, and it ain't pretty, and I hope you can all work through your personal crap so I never have to see you there. Alicia, I could've loved you if I wasn't so fucked up. Frankie, that joke about the cancan dancer and the tennis balls is still the funniest thing I've ever heard in my life. And Jacob—"

Simeon leaned toward the camera, narrowing his eyes. "The esteemed Jacob Nassedrine, founder of all this bullshit, who helps *soooooooo* many people. I want to say this to you and you alone, you arrogant asshole prick. *Thank you* for teaching me that I'm not alone in my misery, which, looking back on it, was the last thing in the fucking world I needed to know. It was *so* much better being miserable alone, without all the sympathy and understanding. You try *so* hard to make things better, Jacob, but all you do is mess things up. I just wanted to tell you that, man to man, so you'll remember me."

Simeon kissed the screen, then leaned back and blew a dozen more theatrical kisses, calling, "Goodbye, SMS!" He'd figured out how to turn off the camera by then and timed it so the last image in the video was of him flipping the bird.

"Well!" Lovetrain said as Jacob shut the laptop. "At least we know he won't be flipping people off without hands, right?"

"Yeah," said Jacob, smiling. He looked ready to laugh it off, but then a dark cloud passed over him, and his eyes narrowed. In one motion he stood, picked up his laptop, and hurled it like a frisbee through his biggest window. Then he gave Lovetrain a warning glare and threw his coffee table at Ed and Rhonda's TV. Then he picked it up again and threw it through the same window as the computer.

"*That's* how I feel about it, okay?" he shouted. "Anybody asks, *that's* how I feel."

Lovetrain hustled to the kitchen while Jacob destroyed his living room. Laynie had come in from the porch but didn't dare go nearer. Jacob could have thrown them through the window too, and their intestines both shook with physical fear. Then Don-o's truck came racing up the hill, and the man himself soon came running past them.

"Do *not* do this to yourself, Jakey!" he yelled on his way into the living room. Jacob was tearing books and albums from his shelves when Don-o got chest to chest with him, locking his arms around Jacob's back. The same strength that made Don-o such a good hugger made him almost impossible to disentangle from, even as Jacob beat the back of his skull with balled fists. "Don't do this to *us*. Stop, right fucking now."

PART 3

Into the Furious Vortex

17

Echoing

After he stopped crying, Jacob told them where they could find some Seconals—in his barn with his bronze finishing supplies, in a jar marked IRON FLAKES—and they let him take two despite the slippery slope it would hurl him down. The pills knocked him out for an hour, and he woke up seemingly calm, connected enough to the world to vaguely help with the cleanup.

"What a dumbass thing to do," he said as Laynie, Don-o, and Lovetrain swept up his broken glass. The things he'd broken irretrievably sat stacked up by the front door. The laptop, miraculously, still worked, though its hard drive whirred loudly and its display was pinkish. Laynie asked to see the video that sent him over the edge, but Lovetrain refused and left the decision up to Jacob.

"After I've been dead a hundred years," Jacob slurred. "I've got plywood boards cut for these windows, you know. Fit so tight you just have to duct-tape 'em on."

"You've done this before?" Lovetrain asked.

"When my brother was here, yeah. I'll get 'em—they're in the last grain bin."

Laynie startled as he headed for the back door because she imagined him blowing his brains out with a shotgun in that grain bin. That couldn't be since he didn't own a gun, but her thinking it was a bad sign. She followed him, and he didn't protest, and they grabbed flashlights in the mudroom.

"You okay?" she asked him. She was the calming wife, the centering influence. How long would she need to be that? How long could she handle it?

Jacob shrugged. "I'm surviving. I'm such an idiot, though." He went to the second grain bin instead of the third and stopped, forgetting what he wanted. Laynie guided him to the right place, and he saw the three plywood boards right away. The Seconals made his brain so fuzzy that he couldn't get them through the back door, so Laynie did all the maneuvering. The boards fit so perfectly that they didn't even need duct tape. But the living room, like Jacob, would never be the same.

"Gonna need to get some commissions to replace the shit you broke," said Don-o.

"Yeah," said Jacob, flopping onto the couch. "I'll do Simeon with half his face blown off, limited edition. Sell 'em on those true crime TV shows."

He thanked them for cleaning up and drifted back into his stupor. If he held his breath, he swore he could feel the earth turning on its axis. It was a mistake to think of the world as solid because the molten metal inside it sloshed around in slow motion. Couldn't everybody feel the waves of heavy metal crashing against the round walls at the cloistered center of the sphere?

Jacob had lost count of the days since he'd last been high on pills, but he was loving how abstract the Seconals made him, how metaphorical. Visions came and went, like the imaginary Daniel he saw by the front door. He had his usual scraggly beard but wore an old-fashioned baby bonnet, and he sat on the red Radio Flyer wagon they'd fought over when they tried to live together after Ed and Rhonda died. One of them had wanted to keep the wagon as a family memento, and the other said no, Ed and Rhonda bought it at a garage sale and it had no family meaning whatsoever. Jacob didn't even remember who took what side. At one in the morning his phone rang, and Lovetrain urged him to pick up just in case it was the cops. It turned out to be Ed Faston of the Sioux Falls FBI office, who wanted to come over and talk.

"Sure," Jacob told him. "I'm awake but, uh, pretty heavily sedated."

"I'm not taking a statement, Mr. Nassedrine. I'd simply like to gather information."

Faston already knew his address, along with who knows what else. Jacob made massively strong coffee in his French press and waited for his guest in the wrecked living room while Laynie tried to sleep in their bed. Lovetrain took the guest room because he hadn't been sleeping on too many real beds lately, and Don-o got the floor of the empty Shrine Room. Ed Faston's car rumbled up Chambrell Road an hour later and stopped by the front door, which nobody ever did.

"Welcome, Mr. Faston," Jacob told him, sure that the man could sense his Seconal haze. Ed Faston looked just shy of fifty and had a reassuring salt-and-pepper crew cut. Jacob let him in and shook his hand and sat him down on the couch. Right away Faston found a shard of glass, which he set on the window ledge. He surveyed the living room, then Jacob's face.

"I wrecked the room after I got a video message from the 'suspect,'" Jacob told him. "Do we have to call him that, even though he blew his own hands off?"

Faston ignored the question. "Video?" he asked. Jacob didn't want to watch it again but did anyway because he needed to prove to himself that he could see Simeon Gartner's baboon smile and not blame himself for it. Faston watched it twice on the pinkish screen, then started it again.

"Please," Jacob told him with hands outstretched. "I don't think I can hear that again in my life."

"I can forward it to myself, or I can retrieve it from the servers. One saves time, the other doesn't."

"Yeah sure." Jacob vaguely waved his hand. "Forward away."

"This is a purely investigatory conversation," Faston reminded him after closing the laptop. "That means I'm not in a position to say if this might end up in trouble for you, though I doubt it could be criminal. But Gartner has two sisters, and they could bring a civil suit. In your shoes I wouldn't even acknowledge their existence unless they sic lawyers on you, and then you should sic lawyers right back."

Jacob looked down at his hands and was surprised to find them there—he expected only stumps, like Simeon had.

"Simeon's still alive, right?" Jacob asked, and Faston nodded. "Does he know what happened? What he did, I mean?"

"He planned it out, so he knew what he was doing. Whether he knows he's still alive or not is another question."

Jacob liked Faston, a no-bullshit guy who wasn't on a power trip, and told him everything he knew about Simeon. The up-and-down moods, the jokes, the verbal attacks, the site ban, the apologetic video message—which Faston also viewed and forwarded to himself—and the way nobody on SMS really knew what he did for the wire company. Jacob expressed surprise that Simeon hadn't posted a cry for help on the SMS site, but Faston assured him that cries were directed elsewhere. Apparently, he had a more complex relationship with Alicia Cantrell than anyone in SMS knew.

"Don't blame her," Faston said. "She didn't know Gartner was about to go off any more than you knew your father was."

"So you know about my father?"

"We're pretty good at searching the public record." He softened his eyes for a moment. "You might expect some echoes to float up, with this new violence happening."

"Expect?" Jacob waved his arm around the living room.

"There might be more of them. Subtler than this and harder to catch."

That Faston knew his parents' story without having to be told made Jacob queasy at first, then relaxed him so much that he yawned and stretched out on the couch. He answered more questions about Simeon and SMS in general, including many that seemed irrelevant, and Faston casually mentioned that the site had been shut down—temporarily, he said, until things blew over. Jacob said there was no need to ever start it up again since he didn't want to be responsible for copycats who made Simeon a martyr.

"He'll spend the rest of his life in a nuthouse, right?" Jacob asked when Faston finished with his questions.

"Probably. But you should keep track of him in case he ever gets out."

"What's he going to do to me with no hands?" Jacob asked. Faston opened his eyes wide for a second, suggesting endless possibilities. Then he held out a card.

"You should consider counseling," Faston told him. "Or you can call me anytime. White-knuckling and playing the tough guy right now is incredibly stupid."

"I'll try not to be alone."

"You can still be alone with a million people around. That's the tricky thing."

Then Ed Faston thanked him and was gone. He started his white SUV and idled on the gravel awhile, probably calling in a SWAT team or an air strike. When he finally left, Jacob got a coat and hat from the mudroom and crashed on the couch. He slept for two hours until one of the plywood pieces crashed down on the floor with a huge SLAP! and woke him up screaming.

"You motherfucker!" he bellowed at an unseen intruder. His chest felt enormous and drenched in sweat, and his fists were poised to strike as he marched around the first floor, ready to confront the threat. "Come out here and look at me, you fucking piece of shit!"

When he came back to the living room, Jacob saw the board on the floor and knew it was his father he imagined confronting. His father, on the way up the stairs to their third-floor apartment on that December 12. He could stop the asshole now. He could keep his mother alive now.

The first echo. Not very subtle at all. By the time he started crying, everybody else had come downstairs.

"I've got to get out of here," Jacob said. Laynie went to him, opened her arms, and pulled him close.

"Yes, you do," she said. "We all do."

* * *

"Go with him," said Laynie's father as the first hints of dawn warmed their bedroom windows. "Trust him."

She and Jacob lay on their backs holding hands, feeling each other breathe and drifting in and out of sleep. Jacob had finally calmed down from the falling board incident but remained jumpy and shot up at the sound of Lovetrain flushing the toilet down the hall. Laynie felt glad to have Dad around, even though he was acting creepy and poking through Jacob's dresser drawers. His back was to her, but she recognized the splay of his feet, his slight forward lean, the gray of his temples.

First, he pulled out the marble statue he'd given Jacob years ago, though that wasn't possible because it was still in the Shrine Room. Luckily, she hadn't let Jacob put it in the living room like he'd wanted to, or he might have hurled it at her head. When Dad moved on to her drawers, he rummaged more meticulously, examining her underwear like an experienced pervert, and Laynie doubted it was really her father at all.

"Dad?" she wanted to ask the man. But Jacob would freak out, so she glowered at the intruder until his face reddened with shame. As he left the room, Laynie saw the square, dull face of someone who got caught snooping through women's underwear all the time. Definitely not Dad. Did this mean that an impostor, and not actually her father, had told her to go with Jacob? If she did go with him, would she be risking the strangled fate of Grace Nassedrine while he worked through the shit that Paulie and Simeon Gartner dumped on him?

Laynie watched her husband breathe and reassured herself that he was nothing like his father. Okay, maybe not nothing. He could destroy things—including himself—but he wouldn't lay a hand on her. Any damage Jacob inflicted would be psycho-spiritual, an unintentional muting of her brightness as she tiptoed through life in fear of him blowing up. Could she live with it? Wrong question. How *would* she live with it? She squeezed Jacob's hand, and his eyes popped awake.

"Where do you want to go?" she asked him.

"Hot Springs," he answered without hesitation. "To see what Daniel has to say about all this."

"Doesn't he come here anymore?"

"Not since you've been here. That's mostly good, but I need him now."

Jacob closed his eyes, and they hovered at the edge of sleep until Don-o and Lovetrain started moving around. Laynie went downstairs to find them making breakfast and coffee, and she felt grateful for friends who didn't need to ask permission first.

"You guys don't need to stick around," she said. "Don-o, I know you've got to take care of Ricky Ricardo."

"Thanks. Glad you can still make a joke, kinda. How're you doing?"

"We're going to Hot Springs for a while."

"That's where his brother died, right?" asked Lovetrain.

"And where he found me again. So a little evil, a little good."

Don-o's eyes got huge. "Danny didn't just *die* there, he offed—"

"It's not December 12." Laynie cut him off. "That's the only day Jakey could ever do it. We're safe."

Don-o left, and Laynie had a second cup of coffee with Lovetrain to talk about housesitting. He asked to sleep in the guest room because the couch would give him flashbacks of Jacob going berserk. Lovetrain assured her that he'd take good care of the house and confessed that he'd probably spend half his time getting stoned up on the widow's walk, even though Jacob had told him not to many times.

"If he's gone, he'll never catch me smoking. If I jump off, I'll be dead and it won't matter."

"But you won't jump," Laynie said. "It's your new treehouse. You can't leave it."

"You got it, Miss Laynie." Lovetrain winked. "But you're a Mrs., aren't you? I can't call you that."

"How about Laynie J?"

"Okay, Laynie J." Lovetrain's smile told her she'd become something new in his eyes. If not an honorary survivor of murder-suicide, then at least a member of the Fallout Club. Then Don-o's truck raced back up to the house, which couldn't mean anything good, and they held their breaths until he came inside.

"Fuckload of trouble out there," he said. "I saw a news crew pulling up when I left, and now they're setting up down by your arch. Satellite van and everything. I'm not leaving Jakey alone for this."

Laynie nodded and solemnly ascended the stairs. She pictured Jacob losing his shit on a gaggle of reporters, hurling chunks of wood and laptop computers and small marble statues at them. Then she pictured him leaping off the widow's walk, screaming out an endless *Aaaaaaaaaaaaaaaaaaaaaaaaaaaa!* with his arms out wide like a flying squirrel. She stepped on the floorboard that always creaked and knocked on her own bedroom door.

"I see them," Jacob said. When Laynie opened the door, he held up his phone. "I got seven calls while you were downstairs. Did I hear Don-o coming back inside?"

"Yes." She sat on the bed and put a hand on his ankle. Was it a gesture of sympathy or an attempt to hold him in place?

"Good. He can tell 'em to fuck off while I think of what to say. Could you get me a pen and paper?"

"You want to write it in bed?"

"I want to write it in the bathtub, like the dead guy in that French Revolution painting."

"You mean *The Death of Marat* by Jacques-Louis David." Laynie tapped her temple, trying to lighten the mood. "One advantage to marrying an art school grad."

It got a half-smile out of him, and she brought over the notebook she used for writing letters to her dead parents. So what if Jacob read them? Laynie *wanted* him to read them because then he'd know what a mess she was inside, and this would somehow help them both get through the bottleneck that Simeon Gartner had squeezed them into. A bottleneck that might last days, weeks, the rest of their lives. She looked out the window and watched another van with a satellite dish climb up Chambrell Road and stop at the arch.

Don-o looked ready to rip people's arms off as he walked toward the news trucks. Damn, it was good to have him on their side. When this was over, Laynie vowed to help Jacob sculpt a bigger-than-life bronze of Don-o, with a square, bristly jaw and an enormous chest like some Soviet worker-hero from the Stalin era. Then she left Jacob alone with the notebook and climbed up the widow's walk, where she hoped to get a better view of Don-o and the reporters. Lovetrain was already up there, not yet stoned but with a vape pen in his hand.

"It's good Jacob has a friend like that," Lovetrain said. "Somebody who'll go to war for him."

"Yeah, I can't imagine Jacob without Don-o." She closed her eyes at the thought and imagined Jacob's dead eyes staring up at her from the ground below. Helpless, unsupported, dead.

"You know who goes to war for me?" Lovetrain touched her elbow so she'd look at him. "Jacob."

She cried a little, and Lovetrain cried a little himself. Then he suggested that they not actually get stoned but pretend to be, so that the world shimmered with grace. Those were the exact words he used, and when Laynie admired them, he admitted picking them up from the older woman in Watertown whose couch he was sleeping on. She wouldn't have sex with him, but she did let him brush her long black hair and watch her pray. Her silence shook him up so much that he tried to pray himself, and when he couldn't think of anything to say, he cried. The woman, Mona, told him it was the next best thing.

That opened up the floodgates for Lovetrain, and Laynie followed him into weeping. They clutched each other until they were all clutched out, knowing that on one level they'd both lost the Jacob Nassedrine they loved. He'd never be the same after what happened to Simeon—if you sliced his body into a thousand cross sections head to foot, every one of those slices would contain another spot of complete blankness to join the ones that represented Grace, Paulie, and Daniel. Plus spots for at least a couple of embryos too. Laynie climbed down and checked her face in the guest bathroom mirror to make sure she didn't look too awful, then knocked on her bedroom door. Jacob wasn't in the bed, so she tried the bathroom and found him shivering in the empty tub in his underwear.

"You need a towel on your head if you want to be like Marat," she said, taking hers off the rack and wrapping it around his head. He laughed, but it was just a mask.

"Do you want to read it?" Jacob asked, handing over the notebook. "Not bad for a guy with no college, I think."

To all curious about my connection to Simeon Gartner—

I've known Mr. Gartner for approximately a year through
Survivors of Murder-Suicide, a web-based organization I
founded to provide a means of communication and interaction
for those who bear the weight of that particular species of
tragedy. I've never met the man, and know him only through our
conversations online. He is a troubled human being, as are most
people in the organization we both belonged to, and carries more
than his share of anger.

Up to this point I have not known him to be violent, and I was
as surprised as anyone about what happened in Chicago yesterday.
Mr. Gartner never once mentioned the intended victims of
his attack on the SMS site. Because I have no insight into his
motivations, I will not field any questions about him or the purely
online relationship we had. I have nothing more to say and
request privacy for myself and my family in this time of sadness
and shock.

"Sounds fine," Laynie handed back her notebook. "Ten bucks if
you go out and give it to them in your undies."

"Not quite ready for people, hon." Jacob's face got serious.

"I was kidding. Do you want me to go out there?"

"I don't know what I want. You, Don-o, Lovetrain, Chrissy, Ricky."

"I'll go," she told him, planting a kiss on his forehead just below
the towel. Then she ripped Jacob's page out of her notebook and
was off. As she opened the front door, Laynie knew she couldn't
intimidate anyone the way Don-o had. So she sauntered, as languid
as a woman who understood that no individual moment of time,
no matter how violent, should ever take precedence over the sum
total of time. She was a woman who made the effort necessary to
experience the world from the perspective of eternity. She'd show
those reporters exactly what a woman who shimmered with grace

looked like. Grace would tell her what to do and teach her to handle everything.

Laynie saw the reporters before they saw her. When they whirled in her direction and started shooting her with their cameras, her grace failed her, and she felt like she'd stepped into quicksand. She held Jacob's note behind her back, afraid of its contents leaking out prematurely.

"Are you Alania Nassedrine?" called a woman. Sharp. Belligerent. A loud crusader for whatever she felt was right at any given moment. "Can you tell us anything about your husband's relationship with Simeon Gartner?"

Laynie caught Don-o's eye and stopped in her tracks twenty feet from the gaggle without answering the question. Don-o, inexplicably all smiles, strolled over to her.

"Having fun?" she asked him.

"Sure. There's a guy from Chelmsford here, Ray. We're talking Boston."

"What did you say about Jacob?"

"I told them to mind their fucking business, in not so nice a way."

"Then what are they waiting for?"

"Him to crack," Don-o said. "What else?"

She stepped toward the reporters, making sure she had Don-o behind her right shoulder for support. Laynie counted eight of them, plus two bored videographers who sprang to attention. She composed herself while they got their cameras on their shoulders.

"I'm Laynie Jackman, wife of the man you're looking for, and I'm here to read a statement from my husband." Once she read it, they barraged her with questions that she refused to let register. They only stopped when Laynie held up her hand.

"That's all he has to say," she told them. "And our property line actually starts down at the bottom of the road, so you're trespassing right now. Time to leave."

She headed back toward the house, and Don-o went with her, offering his arm. She hooked her own into it, and they walked with locked elbows like boulevardiers in nineteenth-century France.

"How'd I do?" she asked him.

"Fine. Like a queen out there."

"Are they going to leave?"

"Probably not. There's a back way out, but you guys should go first, just in case they see."

"Are you going to do a throw for Jacob before we go?"

"No." Don-o stopped midstride and looked straight through her. "You only do throws when you've got a question. Jakey, he's got no questions at all inside him. Absolutely nothing."

18

Fuck You, Harvey Chancelman

They took the back way out through a makeshift gate in their ex-Hutterite neighbor's fence and snuck onto the 424 heading south. Lovetrain stayed to watch the house, and Don-o drove out the front way, laughing and flipping birds at the reporters as he inched through them with open windows. A brave one came to the front door, but Lovetrain didn't answer the bell. By the time the wind kicked up at dusk, they'd all given up and dispersed.

Laynie took the first leg of the drive to Hot Springs, while Jacob tried to stop the glitch in his mind that kept repeating Simeon's last video. Outside Blunt they pulled off US 14 onto Raccoon Road to switch drivers and give Jacob something else to think about. They buckled up, but instead of driving, he stared at his dashboard and then at her.

"Back in LA," he asked, "did you ever drive around and see people waiting for buses, staring at the world with these dumb looks on their faces? But at the same time they look like they're in this incredibly deep concentration?" He demonstrated for her.

"Sure," Laynie replied, demonstrating right back. "The thousand-yard bus stare."

"Right. It's like they've got five minutes to kill, and part of them says, 'Aha, I've got five minutes to think about *life!*' Then they ask all the big questions, and the universe opens up a crack for them, and they see all the way to the center of things, and then BAM! They understand how all the pieces fit together for this tiny glimmer of a second that barely registers. And then the bus comes, and life goes back to not making sense."

"Is that happening to you right now?"

"Like, every ten minutes. But all I remember is feeling like I missed the glimmer. I can't even picture what it looks like."

Jacob put the truck in gear and kept heading west. He made Laynie promise, for the fourth time, to never ask Lovetrain to play Simeon's final video for her. Then he admitted that he kept imagining his own face taking on Simeon's baboon smile, and Laynie wanted to see what he meant.

"I don't want to do it in real life," he told her. "What if I fall into it forever?"

"How will I know you're falling into it if I never see it?"

Jacob made the face, and to Laynie it looked less like a baboon than a hyena fighting over carrion.

"You were right," he said when his face fell back to normal. "It's good to make in front of somebody."

"I'll tell you if I see it."

"Thanks." Jacob held out his palm, and Laynie set hers onto it. "I remember the first time Uncle Ed took us to Hot Springs, it was like me and Daniel had a place in the world again. We didn't even see the house our first three days in South Dakota—he took us right to Evans Plunge. Nobody knew we were a murderer's kids. We were just human beings, you know? And I lose that sometimes, like my brother did. I keep going back there to find it."

"Well there's your crack in the universe," Laynie told him. "Look through it while you have the chance, I guess."

* * *

Before they left Cocklebur Farm, they'd made a deal with Lovetrain. He'd keep an eye on the news so that Jacob—who'd given Laynie

his cell phone so he could forget the world—wouldn't have to, and
if anything weird happened, Lovetrain would filter it through her.
Just outside Kadoka, at the edge of the Badlands, she got a gang of
texts from Lovetrain saying Jacob should visit CNN.com, preferably
on somebody else's computer so he wouldn't break it.

WHY?? asked Laynie.

BECAUSE HE'S IN IT, Lovetrain said.

The Jackson County Library in Kadoka was a sheet metal quon-
set hut with a storefront tacked on and two metal benches painted
like American flags. Laynie told Jacob exactly what Lovetrain had
said, so he was wrapped in an angry cocoon of silence before he
even stepped inside. Laynie did all the smiling and talking, and as
she walked toward the computers with her permanently damaged
husband, she felt a toxin invading her own skin. Not the short-term
fear of him that she'd felt when he tore up the living room, not a fear
that attacked and disappeared. This was a fear that dug a pit, built a
foundation, and became part of the home she lived in.

She watched Jacob from a few yards away, close enough to rush
over and soothe him if he freaked out but not so close that he couldn't
safely swear under his breath. Jacob expected, from all Lovetrain's
hubbub, that the story would be a headliner. But thankfully he had
to do a search for his own name just to find it.

ALLEGED BOMBER USED MURDER-SUICIDE SITE

Simeon Gartner, suspected in Wednesday's attempted bombing of
the Environmental Protection Agency's district office in Chicago,
was a frequent user of a site developed to increase communication
between survivors of murder-suicide, and may have been influenced
by conversations there. The site, SurvivorsofMurderSuicide.com, was
founded by Jacob Nassedrine, a sculptor from Clark, South Dakota.
Nassedrine, who has no credentials as a psychologist or counselor,
describes the site as providing "a means of communication and

interaction for those who bear the weight of that particular species of tragedy." But according to Dr. Harvey Chancelman of Atlanta, such websites can often do more harm than good.

"*Murder-suicide site*," Jacob growled. "It makes it look like we were training suicide bombers."

"Sites like that can be very therapeutic for people on a surface level," said Chancelman, who specializes in psychological and social rehabilitation in the aftermath of violence. "But without a trained professional guiding conversations, they can simply become conduits for people to vent their violent emotions in ways that, ultimately, only reinforce them."

While it is impossible to determine whether Gartner's participation in this online community played any role in the attempted bombing, Chancelman suggests that Gartner's decision to seek support from it, rather than from a professional, may have been indicative of his unwillingness to change.

SurvivorsofMurderSuicide.com founder Nassedrine claims that Gartner never mentioned the EPA in his conversations on the site, which has been shut down. Investigators have declared the site "of interest," but added that there is no reason as yet to believe it contributed to Gartner's suspected actions. Chancelman cautions victims of violence from relying on such online communities for support. Nassedrine recently commented that "the purpose of this site is not for Simeon Gartner to vent his rage and frustration," and while Chancelman agrees, he also believes that such blunt peer honesty can have a counterproductive effect.

"People who truly want to deal with their grieving don't just get on chatrooms and talk about how they feel," he said. "Simply saying how you feel in front of other people isn't going to make anyone better. Those kinds of forums are a Band-Aid, if anything, and can even exacerbate existing problems."

After that was the same old blow-by-blow that had come out ever since the bombing. Jacob went back to the top of the article and stared at the now standard picture of Simeon, looking businesslike in a suit and tie, and he had no idea how loudly he sighed. He clicked the arrows for more pictures and saw the Metcalfe Federal Building, then the factory of Gartner Wire in Naperville. Then he saw his own face from a museum show in Ketchum, Idaho.

"Not a bad-looking guy," said Laynie, who'd slid over quietly.

"He was a different person. It was two months before his brother died."

Jacob buried his face in his hands but didn't cry. Laynie felt nervous even putting her fingertips on his shoulder, but she *had* to touch him somehow. Had to make sure he knew she was there, so he wouldn't get sucked into the furious vortex of self-hatred and blame that was only a step away. Sucked into the chasm that he could spend the rest of his life falling deeper into, if only he let himself slip and closed his eyes.

That was the thing about those damn cracks in the universe—you could look through them one second and see all the way down to the secret of life, then the next you'd see nothing but emptiness. And once you taste that, it might be all you ever want.

* * *

They rented the same faux–log cabin Laynie had stayed in on December 12 because of its good luck vibe. Jacob confessed that he wanted a pill, and Laynie said nothing, even though she'd packed three of Kade's Vicodins—which she'd cleverly pulled from their hiding place the day before the bombing, as if she'd gotten a psychic alert that something was up—among her pads and tampons. All hell would break loose if Jacob found them, but he wouldn't go looking there.

"Time to be strong, I guess," she told him, though she desperately wanted a pill herself. Laynie imagined a future in which they both gave up on wanting kids and fighting against pills. Why put so much energy into hoping for the impossible and resisting the inevitable? As long as they kept their stashes rotating and never got too deep into one kind of pill, they could spend years as low-level, high-functioning addicts. Decades. A lifetime. Maintaining, keeping afloat, deadening the pain of their roller-coaster emotions. Picking and choosing the kind of high they needed and managing their addictions like short-selling stockbrokers manipulating the market.

They could barely call that surviving, but if they never had kids, what more than survival did they need? Evans Plunge was closed by the time they arrived, and Jacob didn't want to eat a burger at the Vault because he feared their clientele, so they ended up eating a silent and sullen late-night dinner at Taco John's.

"I thought you only went to the Vault on December 12 anyway?" asked Laynie.

"I want to break as many rules as possible to see which ones I really need." Jacob popped a Potato Olé in his mouth and counted his chews to keep from talking. He got up to seventy-two. "You know what? For the first time in my life I can see why Daniel got hooked."

"First time? Really?"

"I mean I can see how *I* could get hooked the way he did. It's like you look in the mirror and think you know what you'll see, but all you get is this blurry smudge."

"Well, that's cheerful." Laynie's attempt at a smile did nothing to change his mood. She didn't feel like bullshitting herself either. She just wanted to be a piece-of-shit pill-popping orphan with him and forget about her 3 percent chance of babies. Fuck that 3 percent—the false hope it offered only made her act like something better than she was, like a self she couldn't maintain.

"We're both seriously depressed people who ought to be in therapy," Jacob said. "And we've both got problems with these." He reached into his pocket and pulled out a tinfoil ball, which he unfolded to reveal two Percocets.

"Put those away," she whispered through her teeth. "People can see."

"One for you and one for me. In case you want to cut the bullshit."

"You're scaring me."

"I'm scaring myself. I'll share what I have with you. I'm not flying solo."

"Understood." Laynie put her hand over his. "Now put it away."

She felt awful for not telling him that she had a little stash of her own, but she could always break it out later if they decided one pill wasn't enough. Could this be their life together? Trying so hard to be straight at Cocklebur Farm and then heading to Hot Springs for an occasional pill-popping vacation? Yes, it could. Laynie could picture it through a cloudy crystal ball.

Back in Jacob's truck, he held out the foil ball, and she unwrapped it. They simultaneously popped a Percocet dry, working up spit together and swallowing together and giving each other the same defeated quarter-smile afterward. It was a defeat, absolutely. An act of cowardice they'd never shared together.

"Fuck you, Harvey Chancelman," Jacob said, raising a fist for Laynie to bump.

"Fuck you to heck." She bumped his first hard, then slumped against his shoulder. "I'm *so* glad I don't have to be perfect all the time. You have no idea."

"Yeah Lane, I think I do."

Jacob drove back to Americas Best Value Inn before the Percs kicked in, and they put their two days' worth of clothes into drawers like they'd be staying for a week. They made sensuously distracted love, but Jacob couldn't come because of the pills—a fact he'd never shared with her because he'd never been on pills around her before. To make up for it, Laynie came three times, and with more abandon than usual because she wasn't so damn uptight about being pure and clean. She wouldn't want to live this way all the time, but how awful could it be every now and then? Some people drank to blow off steam, some smoked a little dope, some popped a few pills. If they were trying to have a baby, they'd be super-clean, of course. But that time wouldn't come for a while, thanks to Simeon Gartner.

"I'm glad you couldn't come," Laynie said. "With my luck, that'd be the one that stuck."

"What a great start to life that'd be," Jacob replied. The Perc had made him looser inside too, and he felt it in his voice. It was more like Daniel's voice, which he desperately wanted to hear. Laynie understood, and she walked with him down to the spot by Fall River where the Nassedrine brothers had gotten stoned for the last time. He had a tarp from the back of the truck that they used like a picnic blanket, and they watched the water flow by, swollen by a hint of late March warmth that melted the snow in the Black Hills. There were patches of snow near them where the sun couldn't reach, and they could look from the snow to the river to the trees to the head-lights coming down Battle Mountain Avenue. They could look at the world and not have to understand it, which relieved them more than they could say.

"This is so dangerous," Laynie said.

"I could get way too used to it." Jacob felt Laynie shiver and wrapped an arm around her shoulder.

"Part of us is dying right now, just from doing this."

"Yeah," Jacob said, letting the syllable stretch. "But we're dying from the second we're born, isn't that what they say?" He saw himself from above, and his body was an energy field, like in a thermal imaging photo. He moved the parts of him that were red and warm toward the cool blue parts of Laynie and enveloped her, surrounded her.

19

Ghosts Weigh In

In the morning Laynie got a call from Maura Bast, who must have had a sensor in her skull that buzzed whenever her dead lover's daughter was on drugs.

"I'm worried about you," she said. Maura was at the tennis club. Loud serves sounded in the background. Jacob went for coffee, and Laynie told Maura about the family in Quebec, the latest miscarriage, and the Simeon crisis, and it felt good to let herself admit to being overwhelmed. She couldn't quite tell the truth about the pills, though. Laynie asked how the house was, since Dad's will stipulated that Maura could live in it—provided she wasn't in another long-term relationship—until a preselected team of medical and financial professionals declared Laynie stable enough to inherit it.

"Still standing," Maura said. "Are you ready to come back?"

"Not yet. This is a good place to work things out. Plus, you know how long it takes me."

The conversation meandered pleasantly before ending on an upward note, and Laynie felt she'd given Maura a solid false front. Jacob returned bearing coffee, and she floated the idea of moving back to LA together someday.

"In *that* house?" Jacob asked. "With your dead parents hanging around?"

"How's that any different from Daniel? Plus, my mom never lived there."

"Touché." Jacob couldn't picture himself back in LA—he was too fragile now, too self-questioning, and maybe always would be. LA crushed people who carried even an ounce of excess doubt, and to be honest, he'd never had anyone there except for Nolan Tinsley (dead), his Smeltville cohort (scattered), and Laynie (moved to South Dakota). They got over-caffeinated and went to Evans Plunge to squat in the lukewarm water, trying to figure out how long they needed to stay away from Clark and what, if anything, would be different once they went back.

"You're sure there wasn't anything else in the news about Sim?" Jacob asked. He'd been keeping his promise and not checking the news, not poking through Laynie's purse for his phone.

"I forgot to tell you," said Laynie. "Sim's pleading not guilty."

"Who the fuck else could've done it?" Jacob looked ready to break his world all over again, but in the water he had nothing to destroy. And he had to keep his cool because if he got kicked out again, he might not be able to come back on December 12. There was no telling what kind of hell would break loose if he screwed up his deathiversary ritual.

Jacob slapped the water hard with his arms outstretched like wings, then went under with his eyes open and looked around for Daniel. He'd be slouching around as usual, head in the clouds and thumb up his ass, but Jacob needed him desperately because he understood what it was like to be dead. That's what Simeon Gartner should've been, dead. Blown to pieces with the bomb he made himself and now claimed he was *Not guilty* of setting off. The fact that Simeon was still alive and Daniel wasn't irked Jacob so much that his body shook, and when he came up for air, he looked to Laynie for comfort and found nothing. She simply wasn't there. No sign of her at the surface, no sign of her underwater.

"Lane?" he said, and then he shouted it loud enough for the crowd of morning regulars to notice. Jacob felt like his wife had been stripped from the universe, and his heart boomed twice inside him without seeming to pump any blood. He was stagnant inside, his position in the world unchangeable: the lost boy stuck on the back porch of a third-floor apartment in Boston, knowing that his father had tried to hang himself there and wondering if he himself would die if he jumped from it. Stuck in his contemplation of no-thing-ness, in his own treehouse, in the secret cloister where he wasn't certain he wanted to exist at all.

"Lane??" Jacob called again, and his voice quavered. More people looked at him, even the lifeguard on duty, and he thought for sure she'd decided *Fuck this life* and willed her lungs to stop pulling in air. He went under again and scanned for her dead body but saw nothing nearby except the legs of a grandmother and a toddler. The one person that still connected him to the universe was gone from it. Chased out of time, like Jacob wanted to be. It felt like he had a second heart now, tucked under his right collarbone, but it was the size of a rabbit's and beat two hundred times a minute.

"Laynie!" he shouted when he came up, half-enraged and half-pleading. She approached him from behind, having circled around to keep out of his view.

"Boo!" she said when he turned, giving Jacob her best smile in hopes of jollying them both out of his malaise. He blanched like he'd seen the wrong kind of ghost and grabbed her by the shoulders.

"Don't you *ever* do that to me again," he said, his voice shaking.

Laynie felt his hands against her. They were large, and her shoulders were small, and his thumbs pressed too close to her throat. She knew Grace and Paulie's story, and she panicked, thinking of the army coat and the alligator purse and wondering what evil karma they'd thrown into Jacob's life when they returned to Cocklebur Farm.

She stepped back in the water and shoved his hands away, then felt with her fingertips where his thumbs had been. Then she covered up her throat entirely, and it was her turn to shake, her turn to feel fear. She was alone in this hostile, nowhere place, trapped with a man who could hurt her. Who *had* hurt her. The warm water turned ice cold for Laynie and her lips blubbered, and she had to get out.

"I'm so sorry," Jacob said, crying now and holding his hands out toward her retreating face, the way he'd held his hands out toward the anagama doppelgänger of her that he'd sculpted, so long ago, before he ever met her.

* * *

Laynie took the truck back to Americas Best Value Inn, left Jacob's phone, and hauled her bag across town to the Stay USA. He moped around Evans Plunge all day, and people gave him wide berth because they couldn't tell if he was about to yell at them or cry. Laynie drove up to Rapid City to shop for things she didn't need but bought nothing. It would be useless to accumulate anything now, she thought, because she might not be sticking around. Her husband had put his hand on her throat, after all. What kind of woman sticks around after that?

Though was it really his hand, and was it really her throat? She was overreacting. That didn't mean she had no right to be scared of him, which she was for the first time ever. Fear was reasonable with all his violent baggage spilling out because of Simeon motherfucking Gartner. Over the phone at bedtime they agreed that what happened at Evans Plunge could never be their final scene. But they both knew a fade to black when they saw one.

"Please don't run away for four years this time," Jacob said. "I don't think I'd make it. I'd rot from inside out."

"Me too. We never should've taken those pills."

"Awful idea. I can't lose you, Lane. I feel like I'm driving on the wrong side of the road, asleep at the wheel."

They blubbered over the phone and said they loved each other and promised to meet at Mornin' Sunshine Coffee at eight the next morning. Laynie flopped on her bed, focusing so much energy on refusing to take Kade's Vikes that she couldn't think of anything else on Earth. She stayed up most of the night, accompanied by a silent version of Mom doing her makeup at a gaudy white table with poorly angled mirrors. With her bald head she looked like a 1920s German drag queen cabaret singer—she must still have been doing chemo in the afterlife. Her face looked mannish, twice as thick as it had actually been, and she tried on one wig after another to try masking it. But it never worked, and she never turned to speak to Laynie. Didn't have a word to say, apparently, to help with her daughter's plight.

Or *was* she helping by staying silent? Was she doing her daughter the biggest favor possible by keeping her mind off the Vicodin stash? Jacob, back at the faux–log cabin, also had assistance from the dead in getting through the night. If you could call it that.

"You stupid fuck," said his father, who peeked every two minutes through the window blinds as if waiting for somebody to come claim the gambling money he owed. "Of all the shit you could've done, you half-strangle her. What the hell?"

"I barely touched her."

"Tell it to the cops."

"She's not going to the cops, Dad." Jacob felt he had to be careful not to mumble those words too loudly, though there was nobody on the other side of his walls to overhear him. "If she went to the cops, they'd already be here."

"Logic's on Big Bro's side, Daddy-o," piped in Daniel, who was mostly letting Paulie and Jacob hash it out while he did crossword puzzles in the corner. As in real life, he only did crossword puzzles when he most needed to avoid reality.

"I'm not talking to you," Paulie told his youngest. "You're not part of the conversation, so why stick your face into it?"

"Because you're a cruel and emotionally stunted man who didn't deserve us," Daniel said. "There, do I sound as smart as your golden boy Jacob now?"

"Some golden boy," snorted Paulie. On and on it went like that—the same kind of hostile back-and-forth muttering that Jacob knew he'd have to endure all day and night in the afterlife. Dad and Daniel did their jobs. They'd kept him up until morning, when he could at least face his demons in the light and know what the hell he was shooting at.

* * *

"I'm still wearing my ring," Laynie told him first thing at Mornin' Sunshine. "I want you to notice that." She flashed it at him, and he flashed his own back.

"It sounds like there should be an *even though* in there somewhere," Jacob said.

"Even though I need to step away from you. Or I need you to step away from me, I'm not sure which."

"I should be the one to step." Jacob heard the hopelessness in his own voice and muted it. He had to act positive *even though* his wife might never trust him again. "I can stay out here for a few days. Daniel had friends here."

"That's what worries me." Laynie popped an imaginary pill into her gaping mouth and gulped it down theatrically, bulging out her eyes as if the pill got stuck in her throat. "If they're his friends, they probably aren't that wholesome."

"Who said anything about wholesome?"

"You sound like a man about to go on a binge."

"And you sound like a woman who's trying to pretend she isn't." He sat up straighter, feeling the tide of the conversation shift his way. "I can smell it on you, just like you can smell it on me. Don't you think our marriage would be better if we didn't bullshit each other?"

"Yes. How long do you need for your binge?" Laynie asked. "A week? Two?"

"Ten days is the longest I ever go. I'll call you if I'm coming home before that."

"Deal." She raced straight up to the edge of tears and looked over, then retreated. "Promise me I won't get a phone call and have to drive out here to identify a body."

"I promise." Jacob's left hand went to hers, and he made sure she could see their rings together.

"I'm scared for you." She kept a straight face when she said it, then blubbered.

"I'm scared for me too. Just don't forget to be scared for yourself, okay?"

20

The Deeper End

Jacob called the highest-class drug buddy of Daniel's that he knew—
Cliff Burchill, whose brother was a state senator—and asked if he
knew of a place to crash for a few days. Cliff knew exactly what Jacob
meant, since he had a makeshift room atop his garage that Daniel
had used with some regularity for just such occasions. It had a toilet and a sink and bare drywall, plus cable TV and almost the same
mountain view as Cliff's million-dollar house on Lois Lane outside
of Hill City, an hour north of Hot Springs and quietly removed from
Mount Rushmore traffic.

Cliff's place functioned like a college party house without the
pretense of classes and degrees. He didn't pretend to be anything but
a lush and a user, but he kept tight control over who came in. People
who fought, couldn't control their intoxicants, or refused to let others
have a good time were axed after a single strike. Anyone who seemed
liable to overdose accidentally or bring low-quality drugs into the
house never got invited at all. The house was big enough for Cliff to
bring in bands and for people to sleep over without being piled on
top of each other, and his Sunday morning brunches—often prepared
by a Jamaican caterer friend—were legendary. Cliff's family had
made their pile in real estate, but in the 1990s he'd gotten involved
in Chinese plastic manufacturing. He'd always had a soft spot for

Daniel, and it bled over to Jacob, who'd been over to the big house four times to party down, play guitar with his brother, and get laid.

"It's a natural fit at a perfect time," Cliff told Jacob over the phone. "I've been thinking about Danny. Found a rabbit's foot of his behind a couch."

"The purple one?"

"Yeah. Have you been looking for it?"

"It's the last one he had except the yellow one he gave me," Jacob said. He didn't mention that he'd left the yellow one in a truck stop bathroom in Pennsylvania.

"Well, now you'll have two. If Danny's brother needs a place to cut loose, I'm all for that."

"Thanks, man. Only thing is, my wife took my truck and drove back East River."

"Your *wife!?*" Cliff said. "Holy shit, we got some catching up to do."

They arranged a pickup that evening at Evans Plunge, though it would be Cliff's friend Roy Sweet ferrying Jacob north on US 385. He checked out of the log cabin motel and soaked himself in the pool, telling his brother's ghost about the found rabbit's foot but not even getting a grunt from him in response. Not even Jacob's memories of good times at Cliff's house got Daniel talking. At four o'clock Sweet Roy—as he was universally known in Cliff's crowd—pulled into the Evans Plunge parking lot in a white Chevy SUV that made Jacob think of Ed Faston's. He had the same understanding look as Ed too, the same graying, fortysomething temples. He'd been Cliff's buddy since grade school, and he'd weathered well for a man who'd been riding the party train for three decades because he knew when to hop on and hop off. Sweet had an off button, a system to warn him of danger ahead, that Daniel never found. Jacob wasn't sure he had one either, but now was the time to find out.

"Glad you're alive, Jake," the man said, stepping out of the Chevy. He looked as supremely tanned and tight in the face as a marathoner.

In his blue blazer with gold buttons, he seemed on his way from a yacht to a boardroom.

"Good to see you, Sweet," said Jacob as they briefly hugged. He liked the fact that men in Cliff's crowd hugged, since he had almost nobody to hug in Clark except Don-o. Though in Cliff's world, hugs came so cheap they were meaningless.

"Hear you got married and all." Sweet Roy opened the back door for Jacob, who found a letter-sized envelope waiting for him.

"Yeah, and now she's got my truck. You might need a couple beers to get that story out of me."

"Well, no beers in this vehicle. Cliff left you a little something, though."

Inside the envelope was Daniel's purple rabbit's foot, which Jacob immediately affixed to his keyring. There were also two white tablets: a football-shaped ten-milligram Percocet and a rectangular two-milligram Xanax. He caught Sweet's eye in the rearview mirror and worked up enough spit to down both pills.

"Do these mean I have to tell my wife story?" Jacob asked.

"Tell as much as you want, Jake. If you get sleepy, just pull the middle seat belt all the way open and you can lay right down."

Jacob talked, mostly about his brother but also about Laynie and Simeon Gartner, and he said some things he didn't remember after the pills kicked in. He liked confessing to Sweet Roy, who knew everything that went on at Cliff's house. He was the majordomo, the guy who disinvited people and gave them warnings. Like Santa Claus, he saw you sleeping and awake. Jacob stretched out on the back seat and felt his body slosh around as the SUV navigated the turns, rises, and falls of the highway, and when it finally stopped at Cliff's house, he felt like a rock star on his way to a rehab center. Though he was after a different kind of rehab—throwing off the shackles of quasi-sainthood to flirt with darkness.

Cliff was in the middle of a business conversation when Sweet ushered Jacob into the big house, and the boss man waved from behind his fishbowl office window. The office was on the second floor and let Cliff see most of his domain—the open kitchen, the party floor, even a sliver of the indoor-outdoor pool deck downstairs.

"To the Rat's Nest, then," said Sweet, who carried Jacob's small duffel bag through the kitchen and out a side door toward a detached garage. Jacob had never been to the room above it, but he'd heard about it from Daniel.

"I didn't know it had a name," Jacob said.

"Your brother's the one who named it." When they reached the garage, Sweet Roy handed Jacob his duffel at the foot of the steps. He clearly didn't go up there—his warning system wouldn't allow it. "He called Cliff's office the Crow's Nest, so he figured this was the Rat's Nest."

"He was up here a lot, huh?"

"Enough to have a plaque. Don't turn out that way too, all right? One's enough for a family."

"Our parents are dead, Sweet. We can't embarrass 'em anymore."

"Doesn't mean they don't care." Roy put a hand on Jacob's shoulder. "You should know Danny was here for five days right before he died. I don't know if he was making up his mind or not, but . . ." He trailed off.

"But it's the facts," Jacob said.

"Yeah, it's the facts. I don't know if that changes what you think you're doing here, but I guess you'll be the first to know. Do yourself a favor and make sure I'm the second."

* * *

"I spend most of my time now negotiating bribes for access," explained Cliff—resplendent in his $200 silk Hawaiian shirt, his $300 Greek sandals, and his prematurely white Colonel Sanders beard—over venison stew with cornbread in the kitchen at sundown. "Say you want to mold three million toy soldiers and all the cheap plastic factories are *officially* booked up for months ahead. Years. So, you call me, and I call my folks in Yiwu to negotiate a fair price for interrupting their existing schedule and getting your product in line. What do you spend your time doing these days, Jake? Still sculpting?"

"Nothing worth shit since Daniel died. I got married, though."

"Tell us all about the lucky lady," Sweet said, and Jacob laid out all his and Laynie's cards. Their dead loved ones, their miscarriages, their mutual fear that the other would be next to die, their mutual pill problems. Jacob blurted out the Simeon story in jagged pieces, and it only fell together when Cliff searched on his phone for the CNN article Jacob was in. Then he told them his thumbs had been at her throat, though barely for a second, and they grimaced because they knew his family history from Daniel. It wasn't a real act of violence, he reassured them—even Laynie knew that. Just a reminder that he was capable of one, and it was enough to run her off.

"And here you are in the Rat's Nest," said Cliff, pushing his plate aside to make room for a blue plastic fishing tackle box. "Looking to bottom out and rebound."

"Something like that." The box, which Cliff turned toward Jacob, was a portable pharmacy. Jacob poked a curious finger at some blue and red Tuinal capsules, which must have come from overseas because they weren't made in America anymore.

"Take one Tooey, and that's it for you," said Sweet. "Bad in combos. Ruin all your fun."

"And you've got to have fun if you want to rebound," added Cliff. "No fun, and you might as well stay bottomed out. I ought to put that on a fuckin' T-shirt, right?"

Jacob let Sweet and Cliff guide him through the evening's indulgence, which remained marvelously smooth and controlled. He could get a PhD from these two in managing drug addiction. They calculated every high and took just enough—half an OxyContin instead of one, one chunk of hash instead of two, two shots of fancy bourbon instead of four—to remain exquisitely buzzed for exactly as long as they wanted to. One of Cliff's girlfriends showed up and sang a beautiful, husky a cappella "All Along the Watchtower" when they moved to the party floor. She sang Van Morrison's "Cyprus Avenue" while Jacob accompanied her on an acoustic guitar. Then they did "Can't Find My Way Home" by Blind Faith, even though Jacob couldn't sing along because the lyrics choked him up. Another half-dozen people came over, and Sweet found Jacob an electric guitar that Daniel had played back in the day, a wood body 1979 Martin, and after that it would take a hurricane to keep Jacob from playing music.

Jacob knew he was at Cliff's to go through the same bottleneck that Daniel had gone through before dying. The same dark night of the soul, self-inflicted but nonetheless as real as anything he'd experienced. Instead of dying at the end of it, Jacob was going to get reborn and sail up up up into a new life, into a new self that wouldn't ever need pills again. He was going to rebound like nobody's business, send himself bouncing so high on the joy of life itself that no chemical high could ever touch it.

In the meantime, though, he'd ride the party train as long as its wheels clicked smoothly against the tracks. Cliff's girlfriend brought Jacob a bourbon and ginger ale and gave him a puff of hash, and he played a version of Neil Young's "Southern Man" that had people falling on the floor and howling. At one in the morning he took a break and overheard somebody bad-mouthing Daniel.

"—sounds like that guy who used to play here," a man said to a couple of women two tiers out of his league. He looked like a Houston oil business wannabe. Starched yellow shirt, a tan as fake as Sweet's was natural, cowboy boots made from some endangered animal. "Real scraggly, kind of a loser."

"I know who you're talking about," Jacob said, stepping toward the man and smiling. "Dirty blond hair, never shaved, about this tall?" He put a finger to his forehead.

"Yeah, he was always slouching around talking to himself. I think he was into the heavy shit. Loser, like I said."

"What's your name?" Jacob asked, sticking out his hand.

"Vinnie." The man took it, but Jacob didn't let it go.

"I'm Jacob. That loser's my dead brother, Daniel, so watch what you say about him." He clamped the hand tighter.

"I'm sorry, man. Let go of me, okay?"

"You think one little sorry's enough?"

Jacob kept squeezing Vinnie's hand until he got down on his knees. Then one of the women touched his shoulder and said, "Isn't that enough?" and he let the hand go, turning his back without even looking Vinnie in the face. Two minutes later Cliff found him alone in the bathroom hallway.

"Don't worry about it," Cliff said, wrapping an arm around Jacob's shoulder. "Vinnie's a pain in the ass to everybody, but you shut him up good tonight. You're a fuckin' folk hero. Here." Cliff dropped a two-milligram Valium into his palm. "Lightweight stuff, but it's all you'll need to get some sleep. Tomorrow I want you to do something for me."

* * *

Back at 1 Chambrell Road, Laynie zipped through Kade's stash faster than she intended and needed to scrounge for more pills. She knew from their time together in LA that Jacob liked to hide his stashes, so she channeled his vibe and posture and existential panic in an effort to find them. She stood in one place and made her breath shallow as she contemplated life's meaninglessness and her own complete failure to cohere. It might not have been Jacob's exact vibe, but it must have been harmonically compatible, or they never would've gotten married. Not that the marriage was guaranteed to last, of course. The thought of it ending helped her to sink more deeply into the chaos and hopelessness that she and her husband shared, and it made her fingers fidgety. She wanted something small for those fingers to pick up, something that would make her inherent lostness feel like a normal state of being that she shouldn't bother fighting.

Laynie went from room to room like this, waiting for hidden pills to call to her. For a moment she saw herself as a water diviner, holding a forked stick in front of her, but she didn't know exactly how to use it, and the image dissolved. In the guest bathroom she got a particularly strong feeling, and the medicine cabinet thrummed with potential. It was full of over-the-counter medications, some of which dated back to Ed and Rhonda and had expired ten years ago. Laynie felt she had no right to throw these quasi-relics away— they might outlast her in the house if her marriage kept falling to shit. Nonetheless, she lined them up on the toilet tank, looking for opiates and sedatives hidden among them. A faded box of Imodium sounded promising from the way it shook, but she found only a few stray Zyrtecs inside.

Once she'd emptied the whole medicine cabinet, Laynie gave its edges a tug and felt a give. Little shims of wood kept it lined up with its supporting two-by-fours, and she went down to the mudroom to fetch a screwdriver so she could pry them out. While standing in front of the old, dilapidated chest of drawers, she had another divining rod moment and started digging through the various tools and household implements that crammed up each one. In the bottom drawer she nicked her hands on screws and hooks before finding a bottle in the right back corner with two Percs, five Vikes, and a yellow capsule she had to look up on her phone. It was Nembutal, which she'd heard of but never had.

Genius. She popped the yellow pill and almost forgot the screwdriver, then marched upstairs to gouge loose the shims. Laynie stacked them on the floor in the position she'd found them, laughing at herself for thinking she could rebuild them exactly with a strange new drug in her system. Once the shims were out, the cabinet moved easily. Laynie pulled at it to test its weight, then yanked it out of the wall with more strength than she thought she had.

The edge of the glass came within a quarter inch of crashing against the porcelain sink, but she managed to keep it whole and set it on the floor. Inside the space carved out for it, duct-taped to the sheet rock, she found a little pink plastic zip-top plastic bag like the ones jewelry stores used for spare backs to earrings. When she pulled off the duct tape, Laynie found the bag stapled to the drywall. She held the bag against the wall while she carefully pried loose the staple with the screwdriver.

What would happen if she dropped that bag? It would probably fall until it hit another stash point. She had to figure out where on the first floor it would fall because she might find more bags there. In the pink one were four Tylenol 3s with codeine, three Valiums, two Percocets, and one Seconal.

A perfect little vacation in a tiny pink bag, hidden in plain sight the whole time she'd been at the house. She was a genius, and she would survive.

21

Inquisitions

"Don't think we've never seen this before," Chrissy told Laynie on Sunday morning, when she and Don-o brought Ricky over for a self-invited brunch. They provided the frittata and salad. "We've seen Jacob *exactly* like this before."

"Like what?" Laynie needed to protest this interrogation just a little. The Donatellis were her best friends, sure, but they'd barely known her a season. They hadn't earned the right to be brutally honest with her yet.

"You know what we're talking about," said Don-o. "Playing doctor. Prescribing yourself the goodies."

"Are you sure that's not Jacob you're picking up on your radar?" Laynie asked.

"I'm pretty sure he's doing it too." Don-o disgustedly speared a piece of frittata. "When he heads West River, it's always party time."

"Will my inquisition go better if I admit I'm taking pills?" asked Laynie.

"Yes," replied Chrissy, switching Richard from knee to knee. "But you don't have to say those exact words."

"I want to." Laynie put down her knife and fork and looked at her friends across the kitchen table. She sat up straight, her posture as perfect as Mom always wanted, then put her hand to her heart and intoned, "I'm taking pills!" like some dying matriarch. Chrissy and Don-o looked at each other, their lips involuntarily curling.

"Are you high right now?" Chrissy asked.

"I popped last night, but only a doctor could say if it's still in my system." This was a lie because she'd taken a bright red Darvocet—found among Jacob's bronze finishing gear—only four hours earlier. It was past its half-life, sure, but still making her unpredictable.

"When Jakey gets like this we give him a little rope," Don-o told her. "Not enough to hang himself with."

"Rope's an awful metaphor with his family history," Laynie said back.

"But it fits." Don-o put his elbows on the table. "The longer your binge goes, the more frequent the check-ins get. It's what you call an inversely proportional ratio."

"It sounds like you're my probation officers."

"And that's how it feels," Chrissy told her. "Which sucks. I'm sick of it with Jacob, and now he's brought home somebody else we need to spy on."

She retreated to the living room to feed her son, leaving her husband to stare through Laynie. His stare worked—it was useless to try hiding any secrets from Don-o because her biggest one was already out. *Addict.* No matter what else she might end up as—artist, mother, barista—she was still *addict* underneath them all.

"I wanted to get clean, and I thought I was getting there," Laynie told Don-o. "We both were. Then I lost the baby, then Simeon Gartner happened. I needed a break."

Don-o rolled his eyes. "Jakey says the same shit. 'I just need a vacation from myself, man!' It's delusional crap."

"But can't you see it's *necessary* delusional crap for some people?"

"No. What you're really addicted to—no, what your *husband* is addicted to, 'cause I'm just guessing for you—is the delusion that you can take a vacation from yourself. There's no vacation. Every second counts. If you guys ever get lucky enough to be parents, you'd better learn that. Or heaven help you, your kids'll be a mess."

Laynie watched him push back his chair and stand in what felt like slow motion. With her timing thrown off, she stood up too quickly, and when the blood rushed to her head, she put a steadying hand on the kitchen table.

"You *are* high right now," Don-o said.

"Do you plan on giving Jacob the same lecture too?" asked Laynie.

"I want to do it face to face, but I don't feel like driving out there."

"But if it was December 12, you would, right?"

"Next December 12 I think I'll tape him to a chair." Don-o blew a soft whistle toward Chrissy in the living room, their rising four-note love call to each other. This time it meant *Let's get the hell out of here,* and Chrissy blew it back. "He's squeezed everything he could out of that damn day. Dead parents, dead brother."

"Plus me. The light to balance out the dark." Laynie curtseyed, something she hadn't done since grade school.

"Yeah." An involuntary smile broke through Don-o's stone face. "Let's hope you actually turn out that way someday."

* * *

"So your wife's in the same boat as you?" Cliff asked that afternoon. Last night's party had lasted until dawn, and the Jamaican brunch had come and gone. They were in his garage looking at a red 1968 Mustang convertible that Cliff had sideswiped against a tree and wanted Jacob to assess and/or fix.

"Ghosts and pills. Yeah, about the same boat." Jacob squatted down to look at the passenger side fender and door, which would need replacing. "Only difference is, my boat's got the violence gene."

"What are you gonna do? You're too smart to let yourself go like Danny did."

"Am I?"

"Come on, Jake. I'm the Danny of my family. If it wasn't for Chinese plastic, I'd be on the street or dead."

"You're way overestimating how much I have my shit together."

"I see a lot a people in *our* boat," Cliff said, "and you're in better shape than most. You've got control of yourself 97 percent of the time, and the other 3 you're a wild card. Some people would kill for 50-50."

"I see it different." Jacob patted the Mustang's fender and stood up. "I'm living in a totally meaningless world 100 percent of the time, and for 97 of that I'm pretending I'm not. For the other 3 I can't pretend anymore."

"Then you see reality, and the pills help you deal." Cliff scoffed. "That's bullshit to keep your addiction going. Look, Jake. I don't want to hear you left my place and offed yourself like Danny did."

"Do I look like a guy who wants to off himself?"

"Not yet. But you look like a guy who wants to go on a deeper binge than he can handle." For a moment Cliff looked like a high school principal. "I think you should back off the candy."

"You mean starting right now?" asked Jacob.

"Tighten up the binge. You had a great night, one more ought to do it." He jutted his chin at the Rat's Nest. "Your brother belonged up there, but you don't."

"Are you sure that's not just wishful thinking?"

"I'm not sure," Cliff said. "But it's what I want to believe."

Jacob agreed to make this his last night and started planning his exit. He'd look online for a fender and door to make sure Cliff didn't get ripped off, but for now he could smooth it out if he had a compressor and a suction puller.

"That's what I'm talking about." Cliff gave Jacob a quick, big-brotherly pinch on the shoulder. "The Jacob Nas I believe in is competent and wise."

"How about the Jacob Nas who's staying in your Rat's Nest?"

"He's anybody's guess."

Jacob drove the Mustang to Rapid City to get the tools he needed. He checked in with a junkyard to look for a fender and door, and the guy there said the fender alone would cost eight hundred bucks—if he could find one. While in town he shopped for used wheels and found a red 2002 Ford Explorer and put some money down on it. Then Jacob went back to Cliff's to throw himself into the Mustang job, believing that work—the honest, red-blooded American kind of work, not the sissy bullshit art that had torn him from the bosom of acceptance at Clark Junior-Senior High School—would be his salvation. Maybe Clark had seen him with perfect clarity. He should've stayed a welder, stayed contextualized there, because once he stepped out of their world, he had none to step back into.

The art world? Fuck that too. He'd barely earned his current gallery in Sioux Falls a penny, and in the art world you either earn people money or you get forgotten. The scattered pieces of his work that had ended up in little museums would languish for decades in storerooms until some snotty Ivy League curatorial intern pulled them out, looking for career-making gold, and saw his name. A quick web search would reveal that Jacob Nassedrine's artistic net value was zero, and the intern would shove his work back into the closet.

He had plenty of time for thinking because he had to be supremely patient with the suction puller. Old cars had much thicker skins than today's, and Jacob had to inch his way from the outer edges of the damage toward its center. He fantasized about writing a book called *The Tao of Automotive Restoration*, which resembled *Zen and the Art of Motorcycle Maintenance*—about the extent of his Zen studies. Each of the sixty-four *I Ching* hexagrams would correspond to some aspect of fixing up old cars, and—by metaphorical extension—to the rebirth of the self when you reach the end of your rope.

Hexagram #20, *Kuan*, or *Contemplation*, would teach the reader how internal doubt or conflict creates self-opposition—sort of like the mess that happens when you don't think your restoration through from start to finish and end up having to redo your work. Hexagram #42, *I*, or *Increase*, admonishes us not to be greedy when the getting is good but to remain humble and appreciate the ebb and flow of our fortunes. Jacob related this to a restorer's temptation to get more work done in a day than was reasonable.

"Bull-sheeeeeeeeeeeet!" called Daniel from the tiny back seat of the Mustang. "Everything that comes out of your mouth right now is bullshit, Big Bro. Some of the stuff you're putting *in* your mouth too."

"So, my brother who OD'd is giving me a hard time for taking drugs. Funny."

"I took *actual* drugs," Daniel said. "Not medicine that's pretending to be drugs. I knew I was dying that night. You could die from stupidity without even knowing what a stupid fuck you are."

* * *

That night a bassist who could sing and a drummer with a terrific electronic kit came up to Cliff's house, and the impromptu trio played the classics. Hendrix, Clapton, Pink Floyd for a change of pace, a botched but inspired version of the Velvet Underground's "White Light / White Heat." After each set Jacob asked Cliff for a little something—half a Xanax, a shot of bourbon, some hash or grass—and was sent to Sweet Roy to fetch his allotment. Jacob wanted to follow their example, measuring out his high perfectly and sailing along on it. It was a new Jacob, someone who could enjoy intoxicants without whining *Oh no! I'm an addict!* every time he stepped off the sainthood train.

Everything went great for the first three sets. A busty blonde moved to his sinuous sounds and pointed her cleavage straight at him, which gave his guitar an extra jolt even though he was a proper married man. But then the drummer wanted to slow things down and suggested "Heading for the Light," which was the last song Jacob had played with Daniel and the only song—though he hadn't known this until then—that he never wanted to play again in his life.

He did it anyway, wanting to show God / fate / the universe that he was a trooper who wouldn't cut and run at the first sign of trouble. But he couldn't restart his voice after the first chorus, and the bassist had to finish singing for him. His electric guitar refused to re-create the jangly feel of the Traveling Wilburys' acoustic original, and at the end, when the drummer and bassist expected him to jump onto the final chord, he broke into a bluesy solo that neither of them could make sense of. They stepped away from their instruments and let him wail away, and Jacob was almost ready to stop when he heard his brother's last words.

You know what I love about my Big Bro? My Big Bro never gives up. For nothing.

According to reports the next morning, he was about to smash the 1979 Martin when the bassist stopped him. Jacob searched for the busty blonde hoping to hurl himself into her for the night, though he knew he'd never actually do that. Instead, he ran into a Joan Baez lookalike in a yellow straw hat and a guy in a tux who counted out a handful of round white pills.

"Spare one of those?" Jacob asked.

"Sure. Great show up there."

He clapped the guy on the shoulder, made sure Cliff and Sweet hadn't seen him, and checked out the pill in a bathroom to make sure it wouldn't fuck him up in unexpected ways. Jacob wanted to be fucked up in exactly the ways he expected, just a little more than usual. Okay, a lot more than usual. He wanted to get his body right over the cliff's edge between life and death so he could wave down to his brother, but not so far that he'd fall over that edge himself and join Daniel in the land of suicides who relived their deaths every day. He didn't want it to be Fentanyl or some crazy Russian shit like krokodil that ate your skin. With the C2 on one side and nothing on the other, it looked harmless enough, and he popped it in his mouth. But then he pictured himself dying in Cliff's bathroom, imagined the disappointed look on Cliff's face when *another* stupid fuck of a Nassedrine died on him—this time without even the decency to get off his damn property first.

So, he kept the pill in his cheek and looked it up on his phone. It was a clonazepam (thus the *C*), a generic of the sedative and anti-convulsant Klonopin, at the biggest possible dose of two milligrams (thus the *2*). Jacob swallowed it and splashed water on his face and headed out. The first thing he saw was an empty glass and bottle of mescal with a huge shot left, which he downed. Then Cliff, who hadn't seen any of his sneaky indulgences, offered Jacob a pipe filled with fresh hash chunks.

"Looking for a nightcap?" Cliff asked him.

"Yeah. How'd you know?"

"The way you played that last song, I figure you're done for the night." He handed Jacob a lighter. "Just bring that pipe down in the morning, okay?"

Jacob promised he would and climbed up to the Rat's Nest, surprised to find a couple of college-age kids on the verge of fucking at the top of the steps. He said something unkind, and they scattered, and he punched a wall as soon as he got inside, hitting a stud. He flopped onto the bed and rubbed his hand a moment, willing the clonazepam and the mescal to take the pain away from his knuckles. Then he asked the hash to do the same, and it finally did the trick.

"Look at you, pussy," said Daniel, materializing in the opposite corner wearing their father's NASSEDRING army coat. He looked skinny and cold as hell. "You're like one of those pretty-boy actors who take a bad combo and end up dead."

"What I took's not making me dead." Jacob heard the slur in his voice and hoped he was right. "Nothing heavy enough."

"If you want to come over to my side, do it like a man. Don't roll the dice like a pussy."

"I never said I want to come over to your side, Runt."

"You don't have to say it, dipshit." Daniel dropped something on the floor—his needle, Jacob knew—and snatched it back up. "Every time you breathe, I can smell it on you."

* * *

On Monday morning Laynie got way too high—she took half a Percocet before remembering she'd already taken a Vicodin—and sat shivering on the blue living room couch staring at the damage her husband had wrought. Holes in the wall that he'd punched. Broken furniture still piled up by the door, with a bunch more no doubt in the bushes outside. Those damn sheets of plywood, cutting off all but a few slivers of light. Laynie had two blankets around her, one for the early April cold and one for the torpor that the drugs caused, and she stared at the spot on the wall where the TV used to be.

On that wall her mind projected a soap opera of a marriage falling apart because of pills: the spectral stares and dull movements of the doomed couple were accompanied by violin music that somehow managed to be sentimental and jagged at once. They stood on either side of a finely lacquered wooden column, both barely touching it as if they questioned its actual existence—and questioned their own, of course. You could hardly call yourself a pill popper if you didn't question your own existence. The actress playing Laynie was Suzanne Pleshette from *The Bob Newhart Show*, her hair vaguely Afro-like and with a bright flowered blouse adorning her trim torso. The man playing Jacob was Michael Landon from *Little House on the Prairie*, with a red-striped shirt and suspenders and his grimy white hat in one hand.

Why on earth would she play this scene out with actors from TV shows from before she was born? Her parents would've watched those shows, but she'd only seen internet snippets of them. The *Little House on the Prairie* reference made sense for Jacob, since he'd grown up on the prairie, sort of. But why was she the wife of a psychologist?

Laynie closed her eyes to better imagine the scene at the column, which unfolded like a cross between an avant-garde play and a documentary about two animals about to fuck or fight. Suzanne Pleshette and Michael Landon turned in slow motion around the column, never letting their fingers lift from it and never quite catching each other's eyes. They looked past each other, merely occupying the same space without actually being together.

Which is really how her marriage had been since Simeon exploded, right? Though now, of course, they weren't even in the same house or even the same time zone. It would stay that way until they opened their own branch of Pill Poppers Anonymous and got down on the floor, pounding the last of their stash into dust and finally showing a little passion. Well, check that—Jacob had shown plenty of passion in ripping apart the living room. But neither of them had shown any passion whatsoever in confronting their pill problems.

Laynie wanted Suzanne Pleshette and Michael Landon to get down on that floor and pound away at their addiction problem, and that's exactly what they did. They looked like primordial apes on their knees, the sides of their fists pounding the floor in startling unison against their common enemy. The whole floor turned out to be littered with tablets and capsules, and anywhere their fists hit, they could destroy something. Only then could they look at each other's eyes, which were so furious and red that they couldn't be lit up by any other force than self-loathing.

The banging from Laynie's fantasy segued into knocking in real life, and she called "Hello!" even though she didn't believe anyone was there. She would've heard the tires. The knocking came again, very real, and at the front door Laynie found a tall, mustached, sixtyish man in jeans, mud boots, and an ancient lined denim jacket. A white truck as grimy as Michael Landon's hat idled behind him.

"Sorry to bother you, miss," said a watered-down Marlboro Man voice.

"It's okay, I wasn't doing anything." Laynie smiled back at him like Bob Newhart's wife might. Gentle. Understanding of his troubles and sure she didn't have any of her own.

"I'm looking for a guy up here who does bodywork. My grandson wrecked up a truck of mine pretty good."

"Could it be Ed Nassedrine?"

"I don't know the name. Just heard somebody up this hill did bodywork."

Laynie studied the man, calculating the many ways their conversation could end. She didn't feel physically threatened, and in fact the man looked scared of her. If he was used to farm wives, she must have looked like a harlot from another planet in her—

She realized she had two blankets over her shoulders. She didn't look like a harlot at all, more like a crazy bag lady. Laynie softened her eyes like TV people do when they're about to give bad news.

"I'm sorry—Ed Nassedrine died a couple years ago. I'm his great-nephew's wife."

"Oh. Does your husband do bodywork?"

"I don't think so." Laynie watched his eyes furrow in distrust. How could a woman not know if her husband did bodywork? "We're newlyweds. I'm not from here, and I don't know his life here very well."

"Oh, okay then." The man started backing off the porch just as Laynie noticed how cute his *Oh* was. That little dovelike coo was the cutest thing about South Dakota. "Where you from?" he asked her.

"Los Angeles." She wanted him to say *Oh* again, but he didn't.

"Well, you made it through winter, looks like." He gestured toward the blankets. "Mosquito season's near as hard."

Then he was gone, and Laynie watched him wave, and when she got back to the couch, Suzanne Pleshette and Michael Landon were both passed out on the floor. They'd changed their minds about destroying the pills and decided to lick them up instead. The dust of crushed tablets whitened their hanging-out tongues.

Laynie was out on the widow's walk, properly clothed and decidedly not on drugs, when a red Ford Explorer came up Chambrell Road just before sundown. It was an appropriate place for her to be, given that Jacob had been (metaphorically) drifting at sea and was potentially (almost certainly) lost. Was another stranger coming to visit, ready to ask if Jacob repaired farm equipment or hypnotized sheep? When the Explorer parked unsettlingly close to the Dodge, she knew it was him. He looked inside her little green Honda as if expecting to find her sleeping inside.

"Yoo-hoo!" she called down, trying and failing to make the same cute *Oh* sound as her Marlboro Man–lite visitor. Jacob shook his head, slid open the barn door, and closed it with barely a click. She heard him sigh twice as he mounted the spiral staircase. He didn't have to shoulder the door because Laynie pulled it open for him. She leaned against the railing, and he stood opposite her. Hardly a romantic reunion.

"Hello, husband," Laynie said.

"Hello, wife." He showed his ring, and she showed hers.

"I want to ask you a very honest question, and if we have any hope, you'll give me a very honest answer."

"Fire away," Jacob told her.

"Do you have a stash?"

"Yes." When Jacob looked down at the Explorer, Laynie knew it was in there. That morning he'd bought a grab bag from the kid at Cliff's who'd given him the Klonopin. "You?"

"Yes."

"Where'd you get it?"

"Not saying," she said.

"That's because you found my stash here." Jacob gave her the fakest smile she'd ever seen on anybody. Which said a lot, considering that she'd grown up in LA.

"Stashes. You're very creative about that, you know."

"I pride myself on being creative." He leaned back against the edge of the widow's walk, and Laynie flinched at the thought of him falling over. "So, what other rules do you have, wife?"

"I never said I had rules."

"But you do. You've got your planning face on. Do we have to tell each other when we're popping?"

"That sounds like a good idea."

"Do we have to tell each other *what* we're popping?"

"Yeah," Laynie said. "Show it in the palm. No cheating and no bullshitting."

Jacob nodded and held out his hand for her to shake. Laynie shook it extra hard and tried to pull back, but he wouldn't let go until he kissed her knuckles. Then she kissed his knuckles, and the deal was made.

22

The Bottleneck

"Nembie for a Nembie," Laynie said in the kitchen the next afternoon, after Jacob had finally called to get glass for the living room windows. She showed it on her palm, as their rules demanded.

"Totally unfair," he told her, bouncing a Nembutal in his own palm. "I weigh, like, eighty pounds more than you."

"You don't get extra just because of a genetic accident. Deal or no deal?"

He nodded, they both popped, and they went their separate ways to let the Nembutal kick in. Once they felt its dull, thuggish embrace, they hung around in the living room imagining new ways to arrange it. Pretending the living room was a studio apartment in San Francisco, with no more space than what they saw before them, killed an hour. They killed another by talking about replacing the blue couch, which had too many bad memories lurking in its fabric for Jacob's taste. They killed a third hour talking about the art they imagined making when they got clean and were reborn again, phoenixes free from their pesky, pathetic little addictions.

Their faces felt like dough from the Nembies and could be molded into any expression, but their muscles didn't bother. At some point Simeon Gartner's name came up, and Jacob confessed that he still did the baboon smile when she wasn't looking. Laynie cajoled him into making it while she watched, but his face barely changed.

"Sometime when we're not pilled up," he told her. "Promise."

"When's that going to be?"

"Ten days, max."

"So, you're starting a new clock?" Laynie asked. "You're not count-ing your days West River?"

"I don't know. Are you counting yours when I was gone?"

It was too early for sleep, so they went through the kitchen cup-boards looking for food to eat or throw away. Laynie found an ancient bag of Zatarain's Crab Boil, which had been sent to Ed Nassedrine as a joke by a Louisiana navy buddy. It was at least thirty years old by Jacob's calculations, and he declared it a family relic.

"Then we have to go for a drive with it," Laynie insisted, clutching it to her heart.

They compromised and poured it into Jacob's most decrepit cooking pot, boiling it up like a witches' stew with other things they found in the cupboards. Marshmallows hard enough to give you a concussion. Cornbread mix, which Daniel used to love eating when he was high. Several packets of a spice that Laynie, who had an excellent nose, couldn't even identify. A tiny box of Cheerios that declared itself best if used by September 2002. Packets of licorice tea. Menthol cough drops.

They stirred their witches' stew most dramatically. Laynie jumped up and kissed Jacob and said she loved him, and he would have said it back had he not seen Daniel's unmistakable slouched figure stumbling past the window. His Nembutal felt doubly oppressive, not quite done with him.

"What?" Laynie asked.

"Just saw my brother out there."

Laynie went to the window and looked out. Yes, something was there, and it had the same vibe that Jacob always ascribed to Daniel: dejected, defeated, waiting for the game to be up. It was made of darkness and moved like smoke. It dissipated and passed out of her vision.

"What if I see him too?" Laynie said.

"Trouble. But if he starts talking to you, talk back. He's your brother-in-law. Bad shit'll happen if you ignore him."

* * *

That night Jacob dreamed of his anagama, which he'd built into the highest hill on Cocklebur Farm when he first came back but hadn't used since two weeks before Daniel died. First thing in the morning he drove over a truckload of wood and stacked it by the firepit at the hill's base. Anagamas work by capturing the smoke and ash as it rises up from the pit to the chimney, randomly glazing the clay set inside. Jacob's setup wouldn't cut muster in Japan—some wouldn't even call it a proper kiln—but they were too uptight over there anyway. In LA he'd met Japanese anagama guys who'd come to America because their grandfathers weren't famous enough for them to be taken seriously.

So, Jacob did his own thing, building his anagama his way. Once he had the wood stacked, he climbed up to pull off the curved sheet metal cover to the chamber where the clay would fire, then swept the space free of debris. From the barn he took the six bisque-fired Japanese-style masks that he'd previously declared unfit for the anagama but now understood enough to fire.

The set, intended to be a family, consisted of three men and three women. Once he placed them in the chamber, Jacob recognized Laynie's expression in the females. Not the Laynie he'd met in Hot Springs but the one who'd been stoned on pills the night before. A blank look, invulnerable because it had given up hope. Weird—he'd sculpted them months before Laynie came back to him, yet captured her essence in clay once again. The male faces now looked like an amalgam of himself and his brother. A Daniel who'd never killed himself and a Jacob who slunk through life trying to escape notice. They were defeated, self-sabotaging faces that would eke their way to the hour of their deaths. Laynie came out to the anagama hill and climbed up it to look down at the masks in their chamber.

"That's my face," she said, quoting a line from their more hopeful past. "Yours too."

Jacob shrugged and covered the chamber. Laynie climbed the hill up to the brick chimney and looked out over the grain bins while Jacob arranged wood in the firepit. She climbed down and pulled a square of tinfoil out of her jeans pocket. Inside were two OxyContins, which she placed on her palm.

"I didn't know if it's against your rules to do a firing when you're high," she asked.

"I don't have half the rules you think I do." He picked a pill and popped it.

"No, but you've got twice as many rules as *you* think you do."

Laynie popped her pill, and they talked, finally, about what happened in Hot Springs. She knew he hadn't intended to strangle her, but she was incredibly afraid of him then and hadn't gotten fully unafraid yet. Jacob hadn't gotten unafraid of himself either. It was a simple, complete clearing of the air, and they both felt good for five minutes until they realized they'd popped Oxys with nothing in their stomachs.

After breakfast they made love, hoping Jacob could come before the opiate kicked in, but they'd spent too long at breakfast, and he couldn't. Nonetheless, they felt like a successful married couple, finally able to navigate each other's ups and downs. Too bad it was all fake, all pill-induced bullshit. If they admitted it was pill-induced bullshit, did that make it any less so? And when bullshit falls away, is it necessarily truth you find underneath, instead of more bullshit all the way to the core?

"I think our lives are built on bullshit," Laynie pronounced.

"Like pretending we're not addicts, you mean?"

Laynie nodded as she got dressed. "What if we stopped pretending and admitted it?"

"We'd probably pop more," Jacob said with a laugh. "The only thing that keeps me popping all the time is thinking how special I am for quitting binges after ten days. If that goes out the window, who knows how fucked I'd be."

They got dressed and went to the kitchen, where they made super-strong French press coffee because they both loved a caffeine buzz on top of their opiate haze. Then they went back out to the anagama on what Jacob said was a perfect day for a burn: 40° with no real wind. Jacob arranged the firewood and told Laynie he wanted her to start the fire.

"Wouldn't that be bad luck?" she asked. "Since I'm not a sculptor?"

"This ain't the Samurai days, lady." Jacob sounded very Marlboro Man–esque, and Laynie wondered how their marriage would go if he sank into that part of himself. It lurked inside him, not far from the surface. You don't grow up in the middle of nowhere, learning to weld when you're fifteen, and not have a little Marlboro Man in you. Jacob grew more sexily taciturn as he set up the tinder and kindling so that a single match would get the whole three-day fire going.

"Here," he said, handing that match to Laynie. Then he gave her the box it came in. She struck the match, and once it caught, they prayed—the word was definitely apt—for the fire to cleanse them, to burn away whatever wasn't essential in their lives and let them make one more last stand to become fully human. Even halfway human would do. Prayed to make this their final binge and let their only addictions be life and each other. And their love for a baby. Of course, a baby. The fire got hot and smoky, and within two minutes Laynie had to pull off the hood of her Carhartt.

"I was thinking about what you said about talking to your brother," she told him. "I've already said some stuff to him, while you were gone. I asked him to take it easy on you when you were in Hot Springs. Not tempt you to the dark side too much."

"He didn't listen."

"I told him not to keep you hostage. The dead shouldn't keep—"

"Seriously?" Jacob scoffed. "You're more a hostage to dead people than anybody I've ever met."

"Are we going to have a fight over who's more of a hostage to dead people?" Laynie sat on the ground with her chin on her knees, no longer caring how hot the anagama's fire made her. Jacob wondered if they were breaking up again, if he'd said or done the *exact* wrong thing like he'd done on their first wedding night back in LA or even at Evans Plunge the week before. He reached for her hand, and she took it in a grim, apelike gesture of reconciliation.

"Something's got to change," Laynie said, "or we'll be the same people after all this as we were before."

"After all what?"

"Everything!" Laynie waved her arms in all directions. "Me coming here, us getting married, the miscarriage, the fucking pills. If we don't change, it means I've put all my eggs in a basket with a broken bottom. And you have too."

* * *

Jacob had forgotten to check the weather before starting the anagama and ended up feeling stupid. Early spring in South Dakota was a crapshoot, and like many people who didn't genuinely want to live there, he expected warmth to come simply because the calendar suggested it. By the second morning of his firing, the sky had turned charcoal gray. Wind, mostly from the north but occasionally in stray gusts from the east, flung the chairs off the master bedroom deck again and sent them tumbling across the property.

The window guy, who'd finally come, said the wind was too rough to work in. An old bird's nest had blown into the living room during the hour while he had the plywood down, and Laynie wanted to keep it. Jacob complained about the possibility of lice and ticks, which made no sense whatsoever because winter had barely passed, so she put it in her neglected studio. The quasi-yurt looked mostly like it did before Simeon Gartner happened: Don-o's projector now pointed at an empty four-foot plastic square that sat on an easel Jacob had thrown together for her, waiting for her to paint an enlarged image of the Mud Lake electrical box on it. Laynie plugged in her phone and turned on the projector, but nothing happened—her power supply needed a recharge. When she hauled it into the mudroom to plug it in, she found Jacob bundling up: thermal undies, cross-country ski pants, the inevitable Carhartt coat with a gray GoreTex raincoat over it, a red balaclava, gloves with liners.

"Are you sleeping out there?" Laynie asked him.

"Gotta make something to guard the fire. Too much wind, and snow's coming."

"Can't you stop the fire and start it again when the snow's gone?"

Jacob grunted like she'd suggested something both inane and sacrilegious, then headed out into the wind. For someone who loathed South Dakota, he belonged here more than he knew. He was the kind of man who, a century ago, would have tied a rope around his waist to go feed the cows in a blizzard. She couldn't do that, though at least she'd tug the rope every once in a while to make sure he wasn't dead.

Und vut vould you do if he wass dead? asked her father's voice. Yes, unmistakably his, though it sounded like a Germanic James Bond villain's. It terrified Laynie because she only *heard* the voice, didn't *feel* it like she had when he first died, and this meant that Dad had passed over into the next stage of death. He was as dead as Mom now. Laynie decided not to take a pill, since it would lead her into darkness and dismay, and instead drove up to Caffeine Paradise to try getting some shifts. Kade's niece was at the counter, and she didn't remember Laynie at all. She promised to leave Kade a message, though.

Boom! Just like that Laynie felt removed from the collective memory of Clark, South Dakota. Her imaginary standing as Jacob's wife had disappeared the night they went to Tammy's Tavern, and her imaginary standing as the woman who'd been photographed in the arms of a local football hero had disappeared too. When she left Caffeine Paradise, the weather outside had changed as drastically as the weather in her mind. She drove around Clark looking for HELP WANTED signs that didn't exist and then drove home, kissing goodbye her dream of befriending the locals and saying, "Come on over, we'll cook you something!" She'd never actually done that, true, but she wanted the possibility now because she felt it slipping away. Laynie believed she was the kind of person who might do such a thing once she settled in and made Jacob more pliable, and she cursed Simeon fucking Gartner for blowing up her dreams.

That was the moment everything started unraveling, and Laynie wished Jacob would go see a damn shrink about his massive payload of Simeon guilt before it smothered them both. Since they were legally hitched, that meant he was on the insurance coverage her father had arranged for her, which came with great mental health benefits. He couldn't claim poverty and say they didn't have money for a shrink—that FBI guy offered him some for free, after all. If they needed money, would Maura Bast liberate some cash to keep the future father of William Jackman's grandchildren out of the nuthouse? Or would she let their loser asses twist in the extra-strength South Dakota wind?

What *was* the day Simeon lost his shit, anyway? Laynie couldn't remember and didn't have the stomach to look it up. Would it come to have as much significance to Jacob as December 12? If it became even a tenth as important as the family deathiversary, there would be *two* days when Jacob might lose his own shit in spectacular fashion. It would be awful for both of them and any child they made—as if any self-respecting embryo would willingly plant itself inside her wonky, melodramatic womb.

Laynie terrified herself by thinking that everything bad between her and Jacob would start happening on Simeon Day instead of Deathiversary Day. Her next miscarriage, a stillbirth, the death of a child who actually managed to get born but came out horribly wrong. She wasn't paying attention when the 424 curved around Antelope Lake—way past the house, which she'd completely missed—and she almost hit a big UPS truck head on. Laynie pulled a U-turn, and as she drove up Chambrell Road, she saw Jacob sledgehammering a tree stake into the ground near the anagama hill. She bundled up to go help him, and he didn't ask where she'd gone.

"Hold this," he said when she showed up, tipping a tall green tree stake in her direction. She held it in place as Jacob whacked it into the ground, which was fortunately wet and yielding. Not quite soft enough for the farmers to start plowing but enough so they could start planning to. Next Jacob positioned three six-by-three-foot pieces of sheet metal against the stakes, and she held them while he drilled big holes in them and fastened them to the stakes with baling wire. The resulting windbreak they'd built bent loudly but would keep snow off the fire. Then Jacob went to his woodpile, pulled two logs out from under the tarp, and handed them to Laynie. She put them in the pit where she thought they belonged, and he got down on his knees to blow the flame back up to a small roar.

"How many Farm Wife points did I just earn?" she asked when he stood and put his arm around her.

"Fifteen thousand. But you can't be a *true* farm wife unless you were born on one."

"So, my points don't count, you're saying?"

"Oh no. They count."

Laynie replayed Jacob's *Oh no* multiple times, listening for the sweet little Northlands coo she'd heard from the man who came asking about bodywork. It wasn't there and never would be, but she loved him anyway, and they held hands tight—so brutally tight that it felt like their pill jag was done and they'd made themselves clean through the miracle of sweat and smoke.

* * *

By three in the afternoon Jacob's good mood was obliterated because the wind had changed direction, rendering the windbreak moot and killing the anagama fire. The masks had been in there only thirty hours—far less than the seventy-two he wanted.

"You can always start the fire again," Laynie suggested when he came in to tell her the bad news.

"The woman who taught me anagama was from Japan, okay? They have specific ways of doing things. Like with green tea and calligraphy."

"But you already said the Japanese were too uptight about it."

Jacob almost flipped her the bird but instead suggested they pop. Now that the anagama fire was dead, he felt no reason to be a saint. She got a Valium from her stash, which of course had been stolen from Jacob, and he took a Xanax from the stash he'd gotten West River. This way they could safely distance themselves from America's opiate crisis, claiming superiority to hillbilly heroin addicts. They went their separate ways again, waiting for their anxiety meds to kick in even though they didn't do so as dramatically as opiates would, and Laynie found herself drawn to the spare bedroom. She hovered in the hallway until she heard the mudroom door closing—Jacob on his way to the barn—and stepped into the guest room to find Daniel Nassedrine sitting on the bed in a blue hoodie and gray sweatpants. He stared at his running shoes, which looked brand-new, and glanced up just long enough to acknowledge Laynie's presence.

"Why'd you leave this place?" she asked him. "When you and Jacob lived here?"

"When you want to be dead," Daniel explained, "it's hard to be around somebody who doesn't. My Big Bro doesn't *really* have a death wish—he just wishes he had one 'cause of me. That could cause problems for you, sis. Lots of mixed signals."

"You're a lot more coherent than I thought. For a junkie, I mean."

"I'm a figment of your imagination who tells you what you need to hear," Daniel's ghost said. "I'm as coherent or incoherent as you're willing to accept. Hey, better get ready. He's pissed."

Just then the back door slammed, and Jacob swore. Laynie took her sweet time getting downstairs, giving Jacob a chance to calm down. Once he settled down at the kitchen table, her Valium had kicked in and she could handle anything. She sat across from him and smiled, trying her best to make her face say *It's okay, husband. I'm here, I'm not leaving.*

"Did you try to get the fire going again?" she asked him.

"Yeah," he grumbled. "Didn't work. Fuck this place, you know? Seriously, fuck this place and everything about it."

"Absolutely," Laynie said, slowly nodding her head. "Fuck this place and the horse it rode in on."

23

False Phoenixes

Four days later the pills ran out, and they started fresh with the kind of renewal they both loved. *Free from pills!* they wanted to sing from every rooftop in Clark. *Free at last!* But they had enough sense to know that they'd simply reached the end of their stash, and circumstances demanded either a lie of renewal or a calculated strategy for getting hold of more pills. They'd lost access to Medge's supply because the second-string caregiver, angry that Jacob had skipped town without telling her, had demanded back the house key.

The next binge always waited around the corner for each of them, and now that they'd binged as a couple, it waited for them as a couple too. As individuals, they'd always loved their sham resurgence after a binge. Hadn't Laynie forced herself into one merely to feel happy when she declared her love for Jacob and moved into Smeltville? Their mutual sham resurgence had triple the force, since it was not only Laynie Jackman and Jacob Nassedrine falsely rising up from the flames but their marriage as well.

They did all their usual things: eating more vegetables, not drinking alcohol on consecutive days, stretching that wasn't quite yoga and breathing that wasn't quite meditation. They ran back to art, telling themselves and each other that it offered them everything pills could. Laynie charged her battery pack, changed the photo of the electrical box sticking out of the frozen lake that pointed at her canvas, and actually started a micro-landscape for the first time since Dad died. Jacob refired the faces in the anagama twice more, flashing them with roaring fires for five hours each time and throwing random things into the flame to see what they did. Iron powder, baking soda, banana peels, newspaper. While the faces cooled, he worked on his embryo and fetus, Tadpole and Bighead. Both looked more real to him with rough, imperfect surfaces, so he didn't try smoothing out the clay.

They had a right to call themselves artists again, and it made them feel sexy. They made love in Laynie's yurt, *en plein air* by the anagama hill, and up on the widow's walk—which they agreed would either bring bad luck or dispel it. They found motivation to sweep out and disinfect the kitchen cupboards they'd cleared in search of pills to destroy, found motivation to sift through the mudroom junk drawers. They found the strength to crush the surprise stash they found in the second drawer, hidden in a prescription bottle full of five-amp and ten-amp car fuses.

They also found the patience to get out more, to confront the beast of Jacob's disdain for South Dakota that dampened Laynie's potential happiness. They went to De Smet to see how Laura Ingalls Wilder lived and bought a fridge magnet. They went to Tammy's Tavern twice in one week and even tried Doug's Place right in the middle of Clark, which had great hot wings but was run by a guy who'd been one of Daniel's most adamant tormentors. Jacob went straight to the bar, where Doug worked, and curtly nodded his head.

"Evening, Doug," he said, speaking to the man for the first time in almost fifteen years.

"Sorry to hear about your brother, Jacob. It ended too soon."

That was it for conversation, but it represented an enormous step toward the forgiveness and reconciliation Jacob needed to live here at least halfway happily. He required an armistice, a general amnesty, and he had to start it by laying down his own weapon of resentment.

"I've got to change," the New Jacob told his wife over wings and mini-burgers. "Can't be scared of running into people who pissed me off half a lifetime ago."

"I 100 percent agree," replied the New Laynie. They decided to skip booze and dessert because they wanted their bodies clean, and that night's lovemaking officially started their next BabyQuest adventure. They ate vegetables for a post-sex snack and took probiotics, then made love again in the morning and ate fruits and multivitamins. They ordered red clover tea online, since it was supposed to help with sperm quality, then went to their respective studios, vowing to work all day and only come out to eat.

At five Jacob told Laynie they were due up at Chez Donatelli by seven. He showered off his layer of clay grime, feeling watched by their commingled family dead who'd gathered outside the master bathroom door. Daniel stood talking conspiratorially with Laynie's mother, while her father played poker with Paulie and Aunt Rhonda. Uncle Ed pushed Grace in a wheelchair—she must have just had chemo. Where was Daniel? Boycotting them all, Jacob figured.

Then it was Laynie's turn to shower, and she skipped washing her hair to save time. She saw only one ghost: Daniel, who calmly poked his head into the bathroom. He was decent and didn't try to sneak a peak at her naked body through the frosted glass shower door. He simply wanted to make sure she was alive. Being a good Big Bro to her, the way Jacob had been one to him.

* * *

"I want you to do a throw with me and not waste any time," Jacob told Don-o when they came in. Don-o fetched a set of extra-special coins and they went to the barn, where Jacob threw the requisite six times and got two identical trigrams: a broken line followed by two solid ones.

"You lucky dog," Don-o said, plucking up the coins. "You ready for a little action with your honey tonight?"

"Always. Why?"

"This one's all over the map. It's got a lot of names, but I kid you not, the most popular one is . . ." He leaned in and made his voice sultry. "*Gentle Penetration.*"

"Get outta here!" Jacob whacked Don-o's shoulder.

"Go check out the books in the living room. You can barely get two people to call it the same thing, but half the translations have the word *penetration* in it." Don-o tried to keep a straight face. "Does that word have any meaning in your personal life?"

"Bite me, man." Jacob's smile got even bigger than his friend's.

"So you're screwing freely now that you're done with your binges, huh?"

Jacob's lungs stopped in midbreath. Don-o and Chrissy could predict the dawn and dusk of his binges as well as he could, and denial would be ridiculous.

"We're done with pills," Jacob said. "Hopefully for good."

"It sucks having two people to watch out for, but it's easier if your binges are in sync." Don-o squinted one eye. "Are you getting help this time or still doing your white-knuckle bullshit?"

Jacob made a fist and looked at his knuckles. "Still white. People kicked their habits before there were shrinks and twelve-step programs, you know? Hey, what'd the rest of that hexagram say?"

"All sorts of shit. It's the trigram for wind, doubled, so basically you've got two winds *penetrating* each other. Confucius says, 'The grass bends when the wind blows on it,' which is sort of like 'Go with the flow.' Basically, lose your ego and submit yourself to life."

Jacob nodded and showed Don-o some pictures on his phone—the anagama faces, the rough-hewn models for Tadpole and Bighead—and thanked God / fate / the universe for a friend like this. Don-o put up with Jacob's bullshit, but he also bounced back instantly from being covered in it. He simply washed it off and started fresh.

"I'm glad you're my shoulder to cry on," Jacob told him, giving

Don-o a real hug for the first time since before the Simeon incident. "I wish I could be that guy for you."

"Nah, my cousin Rex does that. He's the shoulder I puke on."

"Do you puke on him about me?" Jacob pulled out of the hug to see Don-o's face.

"Sure. No crime telling you."

Meanwhile in the house, Chrissy was more surgical and less effusive with Laynie. It made sense because they didn't know each other like the two men did, and they didn't have the *I Ching* to help them talk about Laynie's problems. They sat at the dining room table, rarely used and cluttered with bills. Rico Suave played with blocks on a blanket between the kitchen and living room.

"It isn't a matter of not trusting you two," Chrissy said. "If both people in a marriage have an addiction problem, they should probably get help from people who know how to deal with them instead of getting help from each other."

"So, you think we should go to rehab?"

"It's not like you've both got careers holding you down. I don't know how you are for money, but Jacob's house is paid for. He could take a mortgage out, then you could check into rehab and get clean enough to *stay* clean."

"What makes you think we won't do that on our own this time?"

Chrissy grunted and shook her head. "Because I've seen Jacob go through more cycles than anybody alive. Give me a calendar, and I can chart it out to the day."

* * *

They didn't go to rehab, or even make a call about it, because they believed they had enough steam to get over the hump and roll down into the Land of Clean all by themselves. They were climbing up a mountain in rarified air, two Little Engines That Could, and on the other side of it was the magical green valley where they didn't have to pop pills anymore. Where they didn't have to confront their own sense of meaninglessness because they'd accepted it or transcended it or something like that. By one alchemical process or another, the meaninglessness of their lives would cease to matter to them. They'd shake it off their shoulders like a skin that had never quite been fully shed.

Their fundamental meaninglessness couldn't be helped, after all, since it came with the territory of being human. It might even come, they theorized, from the root of life itself—though they doubted aloud whether God / fate / the universe would have created something without meaning. But the *potential* to be meaningless resided in all things, exactly like the potential for absolute unity.

"I don't think we're born meaningless," Laynie said as they picnicked at the top of the anagama hill, where they could see for miles with the day's clear weather. "The problem is we're too bothered by not knowing what our meaning is to actually look for it. By *we* I mean *us*. You and me."

"Being meaningless doesn't bother me," said Jacob. "It's other people being dead. Don't you think about people dying as soon as you meet them?"

"Sure. Don-o, Chrissy, Richie, Lovetrain. Even my OB/GYN! You seriously didn't know this about me?"

"Of course I knew. I just don't know how much it plays on your mental TV or if I'm always the one who dies on you."

"You're always in the trailers." Laynie put on a deep male voice. "'Coming soon, the existential thriller *Jacob Is Dead*. How will Laynie Jackman survive?'"

Jacob laughed and hoped Laynie wouldn't ask him how often he thought of *her* being dead. It might become a competition, with the one who thought most about their dead spouse clearly loving the other more. He didn't think about Laynie dying very often, but when he did, the Swiss cheese holes inside him all grew bigger until they turned into one giant hole that took up all but the corners of the slice. Would Laynie feel bad that her imaginary death didn't merit its own unique hole or gratified that it had been the final blow to his psyche and precipitated his final dissolution? No way to know without asking her.

* * *

Their metaphysical bent continued into the evening because Lovetrain—who'd been avoiding Jacob since the Simeon incident—invited himself over for dinner with a girl named Rain. They'd been friends back in middle school and ran into each other online a few weeks back, and she'd driven all the way from Portland to see him. Laynie and Jacob both sensed his opportunity to stop couch surfing and graduate to a real relationship, so they enthusiastically agreed to have them over. Rain was a nurse and highly employable, though they wondered how her pink-and-purple hair would go over in South Dakota. She was thicker around than Lovetrain everywhere and wore a thin black choker with fake rubies on it. He wore an oversized jacket and a skinny 1980s tie, and he smelled like he hadn't figured out how to use cologne.

"I'm probably the only person you'll ever meet who was there when Lyle got his nickname," Rain said as they gathered in the living room, which finally had windows but still looked bombed-out because Jacob hadn't patched up the walls. The others drank wine, but Rain didn't because—well, she just didn't. "It was a sixth grade dance, and Mrs. Hebner came in looking a little more stoned than usual, and when it was her turn to deejay, she put on a certain song from the seventies, and Lyle here was the only one to dance to it. We were all like, 'What the heck is this stuff?' But he went out there and boogied his tail off alone, and he didn't care if we were starting at him. He just kept right on going until the song was over, and then he took a bow." She leaned over on the blue couch and kissed his cheek. "That's my Lovetrain."

Until then they'd seemed like a sketchy, fly-by-night couple. But that kiss, and Lovetrain's blush in response, showed they had potential. Jacob and Laynie headed into the kitchen, ostensibly to get more wine and cheese, but they kissed and groped by the fridge the way they figured Rain and Lovetrain were doing on the couch. Then they headed back to the living room and caught Lovetrain wiping tears from Rain's cheek.

"Oh, I'm a mess," she said. "But I can talk to you people, right? I mean, you've been through all sorts of shit. Lyle told me."

"Sure." Laynie nodded. She looked at Jacob until he nodded too.

"I'm crying because the hardest thing—and I know your parents are all dead and everything, and Jacob, I know your baby brother's gone. The hardest thing about really *being* with somebody is that I had a kid when I was eighteen, and I put him up for adoption. Part of me is always with him, and I'm scared I'll never be able to give myself to this guy here—" She nudged Lovetrain's elbow and tousled his hair. "Who I spent ten years of my life thinking about in the back of my mind, and who's here holding my hand when nobody else back home will. Because Rain's a hot mess who can't stop crying over her poor adopted baby. Because Rain can't just *Get over it* like they want her to."

Then Rain choked up and stopped talking except to apologize, though everybody else said she shouldn't. She and her beau stayed past midnight, and she volunteered to drive home, playing the role of sober nurse. But as they waved goodbye, Lovetrain looked like the stabilizing influence, the one who kept them moored.

"It's hard to picture him being the anchor of anything," Jacob said. "But damn if he's not doing it."

"Come here," Laynie told him, pulling him to the couch. She wanted to make love on the spot where Rain and Lovetrain had spent most of the evening, hoping their pheromones might give her good reproductive luck. She felt vaguely pornographic dry humping

Jacob on the cursed blue sofa and fantasizing that she could absorb another woman's fertility through her nostrils, but that's exactly what she found herself doing. She felt sure she'd get pregnant for keeps this time because the fecund, ample scent of Rain permeated her. When she couldn't stand not having Jacob inside her, she pulled her jeans down and leaned over the couch so Jacob could come inside her from behind and launch his spermies as deep as they could go.

It was primal, the way Jacob shouted. Like something from the days before *Homo sapiens* started parceling up the world with names and numerical values so people could get more, more, more. He entered The Void and fell freely through it, enjoying the fall because he knew the bottom was cushioned with feathers and flowers that smelled just like his wife. Then, when language and mathematics lugged him back to consciousness, words quickly followed.

"Your period was due five days ago," he told Laynie. "You better check."

24

Retreats

Laynie tossed all night alone on the blue couch, terrified. If she had a baby inside her, it would have been conceived in Hot Springs when she was on Percocet and done its most important early growth during her binge. She'd finally have an embryo stick, but it would be deformed, physically and mentally, by the stupid pills she and Jacob couldn't shake. A baby born an addict. A baby destined to share its Uncle Daniel's fate before it even breathed.

Morning urine worked best for pregnancy testing, so Laynie held out on the couch until sunrise and did her test in the downstairs bathroom at five in the morning. That way she'd have at least a sliver of time to keep the news—the desolation or the relief—to herself. The test came up positive, its twin red stripes laughing at her, taunting her, and Laynie considered stomping it but decided that showing Jacob would be easier than using words. She went upstairs and woke him up, holding the magic wand in his face.

"You don't look so happy about it," he said.

"There's somebody living inside me who knows nothing but a mother on drugs. I'm terrified. This happened in Hot Springs."

"But I didn't even come."

"Well, one pesky sperm must've done a jailbreak." Laynie went over to her side of the bed, crawled in, slammed the wand down on her nightstand, and collapsed. "I've never hoped this before, but I don't—"

"You don't want to stay pregnant?" Jacob rolled over to face her.

"No. I was going to say, I don't want a baby who's an addict before it's born."

"There's no guarantee it's—"

"There's no guarantee of *anything*," Laynie said. "I'm so sick of myself I can't even look at you. I can't even be near you."

"What are you saying?" Jacob sat up, plenty awake now. "Are you leaving?"

Laynie hadn't been thinking that, but it made sense. The fallout of this pregnancy would be entirely predictable. She'd blame him for knocking her up when they decided to be careful because of the pills, then she'd blame herself for taking pills in the first place. Then she'd have another miscarriage and be so relieved about it that Jacob would accuse her of not really wanting a child. Or if the baby stubbornly got born okay, she'd live in constant fear that it was fated to become an addict.

What an awful way to raise a baby! If it didn't destroy their marriage, it would slowly dissolve it, like a nail in a Coke bottle of self-doubt. The more Laynie thought about it, the more logical leaving sounded. Not ditching Jacob permanently, just giving herself a little retreat—without pills this time!—so the possibility of a deformed baby didn't put too much pressure on them.

"I need some time." Laynie didn't know what she was going to say until she heard her own words. "Don't tear up the house again."

"What?" He grabbed her arm. "You're seriously leaving?"

"Jacob," she said as firmly as she could manage. "Don't grab my arm, or my neck, or anything else."

He let go, curled up into a ball, and wept as Laynie climbed out of bed and gathered some clothes. She found that taking leave of a dead person paled in comparison to taking leave of a living one because the dead stayed mute and kept their complaints to themselves. The living held leaving against you—maybe forever, even if you came back.

"If you're coming back," Jacob said, his voice mucusy and trembling, "then prove it to me."

"I will." Laynie leaned over him and kissed his forehead, and her own tears dropped onto his face. It made everything worse for both of them. Jacob took her hands with supreme gentleness and let them go the second she started easing away, and then he moaned. As Laynie slipped out the back door, she knew he wouldn't destroy the house because he'd implode this time rather than explode. Collapse into himself, become a hermit crab on a beach that couldn't find a new shell and got bleached and shrunken by the sun. Instead of growing into a bigger shell, it would shrink into a smaller one, something less than its former self, with less life force and less hope.

Jacob stayed in bed for a few more minutes, listening to Laynie make coffee downstairs. When tires crunched the gravel, he stood up to watch from the window as her Honda rolled beneath his Cocklebur Farm arch and down Chambrell Road. Its light disappeared and reappeared and turned south by the mailbox. He figured Laynie would wander around for a few days, hopefully not getting raped and killed and eaten by satanic savages, and then she'd wander back. Would their marriage always be like that? Some instant storm or cataclysm blowing them up, then some equally powerful but vastly slower-moving magnetism bringing them back together?

It would take time to get used to. Maybe his whole life. Jacob walked down to the kitchen for food and found a note at his table spot that said HERE'S YOUR PROOF. On it were the saxophone mouthpiece, the green lizard brooch, and the strip of photo booth pictures from Santa Monica pier.

Yeah, she'd be back. She just needed to hide out—that was her way, and he had to be patient. Jacob convinced himself of this until he felt composed, but he felt The Void just around the corner. The panic of his mind told him where a stash of pills were—in his barn, too deep in the piles of heavy junk for Laynie to have reached in her search. It was good to know where they were, but he wouldn't take them. He'd be good. Perfect this time. A damn saint.

* * *

Decisive people take decisive action, Jacob heard a man's voice repeat over the course of a dreary gray April day when the sun decided to call in sick and the wind tried to take over its job. He couldn't place the voice's owner. Daniel, covering up his accent in yet another attempt to tease his brother into suicide? Bill Jackman, wanting him to do something melodramatic to bring Laynie back? No, the voice came from some TV actor on an ancient show that Ed and Rhonda watched in reruns. Peter Falk or Telly Savalas as some sagacious, night-prowling detective who understood the brutal nature of man. He acted as decisively as he could manage and called his wife.

"Jacob," said her voice mail greeting. "I'm driving home because there's people I need to see there. I'll text you when I stop for the night because I don't want you worrying too much."

"How about not making me worry at all?" he shouted as he hung up, feeling a smashing frenzy coming on. But no, he'd be civilized. He decided to focus his energies on the Destruction Shack, and for a solid hour under a dirty mercury sky he hurled lacrosse balls at it. For another fifteen minutes he crawled around looking for a lost ball, equating it with his lost wife, and he finally found it halfway down the hill in a patch of cocklebur that had been pummeled into softness by winter's wetness. The burrs were soft enough to squash, though the tips of the spines could still prick his skin. It was a stubborn plant, as stubborn as he'd have to be if he wanted to climb out of his outhouse pit of a life. The same pit he could swear he'd just crawled out of days ago. The same pit his brother slipped into—or flung himself into—and died in.

Decisive people take decisive action, sure. But you decided to fail just as much as you decided to succeed, and failing was a hell of a lot easier. Jacob replaced the lost ball and the lacrosse stick exactly where they lived in the outhouse, not wanting to upset the balance of the universe by leaving anything out of place. He picked last year's burrs off his sweatpants, wondering if Laynie would be back in time to see his next crop of cocklebur in June. Then he went to the barn, where he decisively pulled all the tarps off of his foundry gear. He made sure the McEnglevan Speedy-Melt B30 was in working order, checked to see if he had enough wax to fill his molds and enough bronze ingots to do a pour. Once everything was in place, he took the wraps off of Tadpole and Bighead and officially started the process of turning them into bronze.

"Ain't wastin' time no more!" he sang to them in a crotchety old man's voice. Jacob could feel himself sprinkling them with plaster to start the molding process. He wanted to flick the plaster off his fingertips, breathing life into the clay so the clay could breathe life into the wax and the wax could breathe life into the bronze. But it was too soon. As he put Tadpole and Bighead in his drying box—about the size of a phone booth, with box fans on all four sides and above—his heart thumped with creation. The Jacob he wanted to be was coming back, the decisive Jacob who had enough balls to make something out of nothing. As soon as he turned the fans on, he called Don-o.

"I'm back on the horse," Jacob told him. "Doing bronze. Come see my barn."

Don-o agreed but didn't announce a time because he had to deliver Rico Suave to Chrissy for a post-work date with her mom friends. Jacob went back to preparing his work space, checking his mold materials: the Smooth-On silicone rubber, which came in two buckets that he'd have to mix together and use within an hour. Brushes for the first two layers, a spatula for anything beyond that, plus a spray can of release agent for when the rubber cured. Jacob set up temporary plywood walls around his workbench and heaters to make sure the air would be warm enough for the rubber to set. Preparation was everything, and he was a master of it.

"Just like old times, huh?" said Don-o as he slipped through the barn door.

"Yup." Jacob set the can of release agent where he wanted it and laid out the brushes in the order he'd use them. He wanted Don-o to see how calm he was, how together.

"You're gonna need stuff to keep you busy with Laynie gone."

"Huh?" Jacob stopped in midmotion and forgot what he was reaching for.

"She called me. Asked me to keep an eye on you." Don-o crossed his arms. "Said it was going to be a dangerous time for you. Gee, I wonder what the fuck that means."

"You know what the fuck it means. Stop pussyfooting around." Jacob picked up the can of release agent and smacked it back down. "She ran off 'cause I knocked her up by mistake when we were on pills, and she's scared of having a baby with eight heads."

"Do you blame her?"

"No!" Jacob shouted at Don-o the way he wanted to shout at Laynie that morning.

"It's good to hear some anger in your voice. So I know you give a shit."

"What's with the arms and the face?" Jacob imitated Don-o's body language. "You look like you're trying to be Mussolini or something."

"Be real with me, Jacob. Your wife called me 'cause she thought you'd start another binge."

"Well, I'm not." Jacob swept his arms around, gesturing at his work. "Better things to do. Like I'm sure you have better things to do than spy on me."

Don-o stepped closer, grabbing hold of Jacob's eyes with his own. "I just want to see what they look like now," he said, "so I can compare them when I make my random checkups."

"Random checkups?" Jacob mock-saluted him. "Yes sir, officer."

"I'm doing this for your wife. You don't want me doing it for *you*, I can see that."

"Want to do a throw for me?" Jacob had never pushed Don-o away so hard, not even after Daniel's suicide. "Tell me all about the great big questions guiding my life?"

"You're in a shitty, dangerous place, my friend. I've seen those eyes before, and so have you. We both know what's next."

Don-o left, slamming the barn door closed on its slider. His truck whipped a U-turn outside, and Jacob listened as it rumbled away. Everything was quiet except for the racket of the box fans.

"Just you and me now, Big Bro," said Daniel.

"You fuck off too." Jacob said it aloud and counted to a hundred to calm himself, but with each number The Void gnawed harder at his insides. He shuffled to the trunk where he kept his thickest sticks of red sprue wax—an inch around and two feet long, big enough to make the drainage systems on a life-sized bronze. He carefully removed them until he found a box labeled WAX WIRES that contained a mystery tin foil ball of pills that he didn't even want to look at now.

No use. Now wasn't the time. He set them silently on his workbench, knowing they'd be there when he needed them, and went inside to get food.

* * *

It felt weird for Laynie to be on the road without any possessions of the dead to give away. She looked forlornly at gas stations and rest stops where she might leave something, at mom-and-pop motels too deep into nowhere for the chains to go. But she had nothing to give away in memory of anyone, and the only thing she truly had to memorialize was her own naïveté. She was a part-time, low-level addict who'd married another one of her own kind, and she had no right to expect a life without melodrama. Even if neither of them opened Pandora's box again, it would loom over their lives. Every moment a voice would whisper *Do we open it now? Do we open it now?*

The day would come, Laynie believed, when they could render to Pandora what belonged to Pandora—isolate the roots of their addictions and rip them out, even if it meant tearing out viable parts of themselves. This was not that day, but she felt it would be soon. She had no pills left except for the Advil and Aleve she bought to keep her back from screaming, and when she got to LA, she'd be under the watchful eye of Maura Bast. Then, through rehab or white-knuckling or some act of God / fate / the universe, she'd wash herself clean somehow and drive back to South Dakota and make one final, *final* last stand with Jacob. He'd have to fight his way to the Land of Clean himself if he wanted her to stay, and if he slid his way to the Land of Death instead, she'd have no choice but to let him wither.

Who could deny the elegance of her plan? Laynie's uterus, perhaps sensing her resolve, refused to cooperate and forced her off of Interstate 80 just past Omaha with a familiar, slipping feeling. She tucked in a pad to guard against the oncoming onslaught of blood, and she'd already bled through it by the time she checked in at Jan's Inn & Suites twelve minutes later.

She didn't want to celebrate the fact that a potentially monstrous embryo was flushing itself out of her system, a potentially brain-damaged and addicted human soul. But she did allow herself a breath of relief and almost called Jacob to say he could stop worrying about the baby because there was no more baby. Jan's Inn & Suites had a pool that was closed and a turtle kids could climb on, but nothing else to do. Laynie turned on the TV and piled all the towels underneath her just in case she fell asleep and bled a lot more. There were cooking shows and ocean-side real estate shows and a movie about a suicidal teenage girl who falls in love with a colorful tropical fish and becomes relentlessly happy. It was so hideously saccharine that Laynie couldn't watch for more than a minute at a time, but she couldn't get away from it for more than three minutes at a time either. Because she was that girl, desperately needing something that would make her happiness as relentless as her sadness.

Where was *her* magical fish? By all rights it should have been Jacob, but he was even more damaged than she was. He needed a magical fish at least as much as she did, and people only got to be each other's magical fish in fairy tales. In reality marriage means helping your partner survive when they realize that their magical fish is impossible.

That damn fish! She'd be thinking about it forever. Laynie caught the end of the movie, and it was way too predictable: the crazy girl met a boy and made friends, and high school became a haven where her uniqueness could flower. This infuriated her because it was so unimaginative, so beneath its potential. The girl could have ditched everything to become a champion yodeler or slipped into the Indonesian jungle to catalog dying languages. Something ambitious, meaningful! Laynie drove around the motel's neighborhood, and everything was about trucks, trucks, trucks—places to fix them, to learn to drive them, to wash them. She stopped at the Sapp Brothers truck stop on Sapp Brothers Drive and ate chicken fried chicken, which she'd never had before and loved the sound of, and she kept her ring hand conspicuous so that nobody would confuse her with a lot lizard. Then, after she washed the too-greasy food down with a second cup of decaf, she wrote a letter to her father—something she seemed capable of only when on the road.

TO: William Jackman, Hotêlier Extraordinaire
FROM: Laynie-Pie

Dear Dad—

Today I accomplished a number of things, which I list here in no particular order.

1) Ate chicken-fried chicken.

2) Left my husband because I was pregnant with a baby who was conceived when we were both on pills.

3) Nearly bled all over my car when I started having a miscarriage on the highway.

4) Got incensed at a stupid movie that treated suicidal thoughts like something you can cure with a stupid fucking fish and a boyfriend.

5) Considered getting a hysterectomy so I'll never have to deal with the bullshit of miscarriage again. The OB/GYN who told me about my funky uterus, who mentioned it as a last resort way back when, could slice and dice me and get rid of the problem. What do you think?

She stopped there because anything beyond contemplating a hysterectomy would have to be monumental, like *Attempted suicide and failed*, which Laynie didn't believe she was actually thinking about. But she must have been because Jacob's brother crawled by in her imagination, searching on his hands and knees for drugs on the truck stop floor.

I know that my marriage isn't over because I just saw Jacob's dead brother, which I' m sure any psychologist would find disturbing. I find it disturbing myself, but I'm used to it by now. I slept in Daniel's bed for a while, you know. My skin cells have sunk down into the same place where my dead brother-in-law's skin cells used to go.

Do I sound morbid? Absolutely! Do I mean to worry you? Absolutely not! Do you have a right to be worried about me? One thousand percent! I think you've been worried about me since the day you let me buy that saxophone mouthpiece, which I understand the significance of finally, *finally*, after all these years.

It was your "What the hell, her mother's dying, let her buy what she wants!" moment. A letting go, a ceremonial renunciation.

Jacob would say this moment was a silent recognition of The Void, which is what he calls the force that makes him want to take pills. He's read a little Zen (just a tiny bit, to be honest), which is why he gets away with things like that. But I'll say this much for him: the man knows as well as anyone alive that The Void is the only path to understanding. He knows that people like us have to let ourselves fall into The Void in order to keep from becoming non-beings, no-things. He knows that human beings are divided into the ones that ask AM I ALIVE? vs. the ones who shout I'M ALIVE!!! and anybody who can't see that this is an ENORMOUS difference in perspective will never understand me or my husband.

Screw them if they don't want to see The Void. Screw them if they want to fill their lives with the beautifully packaged bullshit of mundane success and half-baked happiness and magical fish that make you stop wanting to kill yourself. I love Jacob because he threw that bullshit away. He's tough because he stares at The Void all day and can handle the fear that he might throw himself into it, but I want to be even tougher than that. I want HIM to be even tougher than that. I want us to be the kind of people who can look The Void in the face and not worry about throwing ourselves into it at all.

Isn't that what you're afraid of? That I'll see the truth and just jump—throw myself off the edge of it like ~~mom~~ Mom threw those coins into the Grand Canyon out of thanks for me? Isn't that fear why you won't come visit me now?

A loving, human animal in pain and confusion,

25

Infinities Between

With Laynie gone, Don-o pissed at him, Lovetrain immersed in Rain, and the Hattens off to Zimbabwe, Jacob found himself alone with his sculptures, his pills, and his dead brother. He got a surprise call to look in on Medge for a few days—his temporary sketchiness had been forgiven once word about Simeon Gartner got around—and he used the opportunity to build his stash, though he limited his pilfering out of guilt. After a sleepless night caused by Laynie failing to text him that she'd safely reached a mom-and-pop motel, he popped a stolen Valium and launched into the binge that Don-o had so reliably predicted.

Just a mini-binge, Jacob promised himself. He'd make sure everything was out of his system when he poured Tadpole and Bighead, and the excruciating slowness of the molding process worked in his favor. The Smooth-On silicone rubber took eight hours to cure, and he needed four or five layers of it. Shortcuts would prove disastrous, so he developed a rhythm: mix the Smooth-On, brush on a layer of rubber, set an alarm for eight hours, pop a pill, putz around the house, daydream of freedom from and/or complete surrender to pills, fall asleep, turn off the alarm, start all over again.

Freedom from pills was ridiculous to imagine when Jacob had them in his system. The Land of Clean, which he imagined as an endless field of sunflowers that he rode through on an old-fashioned

273

bike with a giant front wheel, laughed as it receded from him. Jacob
didn't trust himself to get there the hard way, through rehab and/or
self-discipline, and figured he'd have to trick himself somehow—lock
himself out of the Land of Pills in a way his mind couldn't even trace.
Daniel's ghost dropped by while the first coat of Smooth-On cured,
but only to call Jacob a pussy and disappear. Laynie's ghost, or some
long-distance emanation of her, took on Daniel's role at the house
and stumbled around sullenly, observing Jacob and judging him.

"This is unacceptable," the Laynie ghost would say, without indi-
cating what specific thing bothered her. Or, "Will you please get
your shit together and grow a spine?" It didn't sound like her at all,
though maybe this is what his long-term cowardice and addiction
would turn her into. Jacob's father had something to say about that.

"Better give her a talking-to, or she'll stay like this," Paulie told
his son. "You'll be pussy-whipped in no time."

"Talk like that again and I'll burn your fucking army coat, and
you'll have nothing left in the world," Jacob said. "How's that sound?"

Paulie didn't answer. Jacob's alarm went off, and he tested the
molds, which were dry to the touch, then mixed and brushed on
another layer of Smooth-On. After he cleaned up in the barn sink,
thunder sounded outside—bizarre for April. He wanted it to be a
sign that Simeon Gartner had died in Illinois, so he wouldn't have
to worry about a handless, half-faced man trying to ruin his life, but
the internet refused to let him off the hook. Simeon could still get
inside his mind, still get him to blow up buildings, still get him to
blow up himself. Jacob took one of Medge's Demerols, and it was all
okay for a while, though even he wasn't stupid enough to pretend
it would last.

* * *

Two time zones away, in Glendale, Laynie changed the bedsheets
in the apartment above her father's garage where she used to stay

when she didn't have a place to live. In that sense it was a high-class version of the Rat's Nest at Cliff Burchill's house and of the guest room at 1 Chambrell Road. All of them way stations, places of repair or further dissolution. Was it possible to live one's entire life in way stations, on your way from one identity to another?

If this question had risen from the spaces between Laynie's innards, where it lived, and up to her tongue, she would have spoken it and answered *Yes*. Instead, it remained in her depths, a hidden knowledge that nonetheless drove her. On her first night in Glendale she told Maura Bast everything: the miscarriage at Caffeine Paradise, Jacob's meltdown over Simeon Gartner, their mutual binge, the possibly deformed baby that she'd miscarried on the road. The sequence of events made complete sense when reported from a distance, like a rough patch in a strong, enduring marriage. But in order for her and Jacob to have that kind of marriage, something needed to change enormously—or an enormous number of things needed to change infinitesimally.

"I feel like the gap between who I am and who I want to be isn't that big," Laynie told Maura as they sat in Dad's study drinking fancy brandy from his favorite snifters. His big brown leather chair dwarfed her as much as the butterscotch one in Jacob's Shrine Room. "But every single cell in me has to want to make the move. Just a little shift, but I can't decide if it's half a degree to the right or half a degree to the left."

"It might help to stop putting so much junk into your cells," said Maura as she stood, impossibly statuesque, to pour them a splash more brandy. "Bodies get uncooperative when they're abused. Minds too. You abuse yourself more than anybody I know."

"And I'm not even a real drug addict. A real one would tell me to get serious and quit fooling myself."

"Change the order," Maura said. "Quit fooling yourself first, then get serious."

The conversation got even more honest once they transitioned from drugs to reproduction. After giving up the pro tennis chase at thirty-one, Maura had gotten married (which Laynie knew) to a man who had a vasectomy without telling her (which Laynie didn't know) and thus lost thirteen childbearing years. She and Laynie's father never used contraceptives, but she'd never gotten pregnant even once. One fertility doctor suggested that her intense athletic training—which on three occasions had stopped her periods entirely for months at a time—might have thrown her entire reproductive system out of whack.

"Though it's an incredibly resilient system," Maura said in a man's voice, putting a finger under her nose like a mustache. She sounded like Walter Cronkite. "Capable of withstanding tremendous injury and insult and still functioning as intended."

"What did you say back?" Laynie liked this version of Maura and wanted to keep her around. Needed her desperately, in fact.

"I told him I used to wish I didn't have a uterus, back in the tennis days. And maybe I was being punished for thinking that."

"What'd he say back?"

Maura dropped the imitation. "He said a uterus can't keep track of wishes. Only a mind can."

That night above the garage, drunk on Dad's brandy, Laynie thought about Maura's predicament. A womb that didn't want babies in it, then decided it did, then lost thirteen years to a deceitful husband. Ouch! Laynie never told Maura about her hysterectomy fantasies, but in the morning she called the office of Dr. Marisa Ramey, the OB/GYN who had originally diagnosed her uterine problems. That doctor had left the state, but one named Robert Schantz had an opening on Friday afternoon. She didn't mind a man because she wouldn't be getting examined. It would be a consultation only, an exploration of an idea. Merely speculation, without the speculum.

When the time came, Laynie put on an olive pantsuit that she only used for interviews. She didn't want to look hysterical while asking about a hysterectomy but put-together and sure of herself. She cut a deal with the office manager to pay by check without billing insurance, told her story to a nurse in an exam room—including the automotive miscarriage but omitting references to controlled substances—and waited for Dr. Schantz to knock on the door. With his glasses and supremely bushy white sideburns, he looked like the science fiction writer Isaac Asimov, whose face graced several books in Dad's library. He looked much meatier in the shoulders than his line of work required.

"Come to my office if we're just going to talk." He pointed down the hall. "Better light."

Laynie followed him to a room with a big walnut desk that had her file on it. Stacks of file boxes lined the walls, which were oddly devoid of pictures and diplomas.

"You're my third-to-last patient ever," the doctor said, "so I can be honest with you. I'll be living on a houseboat in Lisbon by the time you deliver."

"Deliver?" Laynie felt a momentary vertigo. What did this man know that she didn't? "Did you read the notes from your nurse?"

"I did. I think a hysterectomy is radical and unnecessary, and retiring helps me say that more easily. I'd hate to see children lose their chance at life because you're frustrated."

Laynie nodded and wondered if Dr. Schantz was some kind of evangelical pro-lifer, with the way he talked about unconceived children like they already had an identity. She expected scorn and judgment for wanting her own womb taken out, but Dr. Schantz's face showed her only understanding. How many other women had come to him like this, at the ends of their ropes?

"I think *desperate* is a more appropriate word than *frustrated*," Laynie told him.

"Desperation rarely results in pregnancy. How long have you been married?"

"Four months. I've had two miscarriages since then, and one of them had to be scraped out."

"And before that?"

"It depends on if you count late periods or only full—blowouts, I guess."

"If you count!" Dr. Schantz slid her file away so he could put his elbows on the desk and his chin on the backs of his folded hands. *"If you count!"*

Laynie wanted to smack him with the folder. "I'm sorry, I don't understand."

"I don't want to get too New Agey here, but if you look at life as if it's micromanaged by some tit-for-tat, bean-counting God who's keeping *count* of everything you do wrong, then it's hard to let yourself do anything right."

"I don't think God's a bean counter."

"Are you sure? Because it sounds like you've got a million beans on one side of the table for all the things you've done wrong, *including* your miscarriages, and a few left on the other side for the things you still like about yourself. And you're scared you'll lose all your bets and run out of beans."

"I'm down to my last two or three," Laynie said. She couldn't stand how right Dr. Schantz was about her but wanted him to keep on talking.

"Well, you're not gambling, you're just living. And if there's some kind of God, which I'm not totally convinced of myself, don't you think he, she, or it is too busy loving life to count beans?"

Laynie steered the conversation back to reality. "What do you think of Dr. Ramey's estimate on my chances of carrying a pregnancy to term?" she asked.

"Three percent, and Dr. Rahman agreed with her. But it's a useless number." He shook his head so vigorously that his sideburns wobbled. "It's easy to cling to a number like that so you can keep your hopes down. It's a self-protection mechanism."

"Do you have a better number for me to cling to?" Laynie didn't realize until she spoke that she was leaning across the doctor's desk, her face barely a foot from his.

"Fifty percent," he told her. "Every fertilized egg that implants is either going to grow to term or it's not. It's much simpler math and harder to torture yourself with. You've got two hundred million years of mammalian evolution on your side. Don't quit on it, and it won't quit on you."

Laynie stifled a laugh until she bid Dr. Schantz good luck in Lisbon, but once she left the office, the laugh leaped out of her and filled the hallway. How many times had Jacob said 50 *percent*, and now she had a doctor telling her the same thing? He'd never let her forget it if he knew. She kept seeing a new smile on Jacob's face, a *See, I told you so!* smile that loosened up her own cheeks. It unwound some spastic facial muscle that kept her stuck in mourning—a muscle that was connected to her misshapen womb and made it so tense it rejected everything that sought a home in it.

Once out on the street, she walked down North Brand Boulevard toward the Galleria and all its promises of shopping therapy. Laynie wouldn't need that today because Dr. Schantz had given her a good, bracing slap in the face, the kind he'd probably given to a thousand babies' rumps. Didn't old-school doctors slap babies to get them breathing, or was that only on TV? He'd given her a dose of reality that was the opposite of gloomy but was frightening in its positivity. Saying 50-50 instead of 3 *percent* would strip away her self-protective fears and her self-torture over all those miscarriages, past or future. A lost baby was a lost baby, and the next time around she'd either lose the baby or she wouldn't, ad infinitum until she had no more eggs left to drop. A mammalian process. Something she had to trust. Two hundred million years.

Yes, it made sense. Perfect, delirious sense. Laynie barely noticed the world she moved through until the smell of a Peruvian restaurant pulled her back to her senses. Then the air of Glendale felt impossibly thick, as if she had to claw her way through it. As if she were busting through a thick, gelatinous membrane to those early mammalian times.

A few doors farther down sat an empty store with its walls stripped down to two-by-fours and all sorts of construction equipment inside, and as she passed it, Laynie saw a man sitting on the dirty, black-and-white checkered floor. He wore a white toga and looked like a cross between Gandhi and John F. Kennedy, and on either side of him were sacks and sacks of dried beans. In front of him he counted them out—two on this side, two on that side—and when Laynie caught his eye, he winked at her so slowly that she couldn't miss it, then gave her a faint but unmistakable ghost of a smile.

That was it! The bean-counter God who she'd thought had been micromanaging her life, telling her with one wink that she was utterly full of shit! Bean counting was her way of fooling herself, her false conception of life, her failed self-protection from emotional pain that caused her so much *more* pain. Only by exposing herself to pain would she get beneath the bean counting and the micromanagement and into something like an actual self that could move forward in the world.

Laynie stopped dead in her tracks, making a man in a tan suit and a ridiculous black bowler hat stumble around her, then went back to the empty store. No Gandhi or JFK, no piles of beans. Only a short, dark Central American–looking man moving sacks of concrete or plaster. As she stood there, she felt something click in her lower back where the horse riding injury had happened so long ago, and her spine straightened and her lungs filled as if she had extra space in them she always forgot to use. Her feet stayed glued to the sidewalk, and she kept staring through the store window until the man turned and half-smiled at her.

It was the same smile that the imaginary Gandhi / JFK / God had given her but without the wink. She smiled back while all her cells changed their orientation half a degree to the left and hit the RESET button of her life on Earth.

26

Zombie Time

After the last layer of Smooth-On cured, Jacob started on the plaster jacket to stiffen the molds so he could pour in the hot wax. It was another hurry-up-and-wait process: mixing a small batch of plaster, covering the rubber first by sprinkling it on with his fingertips and then brushing it on, and leaving it to dry. Repeat, repeat, repeat. He didn't have to be as uptight about the plaster drying as he did about the rubber curing, so he used his drying box to cut down on the wait time. He could also do the plastering while high, which added extra pleasure as he neared the end of his pilfered stash.

Jacob needed all his wits about him when it came time to build the red wax positive, however, so he jumped off the party train and only dug into the stash at bedtime. When the molds were ready, he took out Rhonda's old electric frying pans to melt the wax that he'd pour into the molds. He set the first pan for 220° and the second for 200°. If he timed everything right, he'd be able to lower them to 180° for the second melt so the wax would cool evenly through the layers.

The melt went well, and he poured the red wax into the plaster molds without a hitch. Lost wax casting was ridiculously painstaking—a huge pain in the ass, actually. But Jacob loved using the same process as Rodin, Bellini, Henry Moore, and all those dead Greek and Roman master sculptors who didn't leave their names on a single thing they made. When he pulled off the molds to work directly with the positives—a near–carbon copy of the original clay models—Jacob was downright sober. He took out his wax chasing tools, which looked a lot like dentist's equipment, and adjusted the surfaces of Tadpole and Bighead until they felt right. He wanted them to look rough and sticky except for their heads, which he smoothed out meticulously in the wax.

"I'm gonna change your name to Mr. Clean, with a skull like that," Jacob told Bighead. A boy, he felt sure it would have been. Once he finished chasing the wax, Jacob built the sprue systems: branchlike wax structures that would, once he covered everything with the big plaster investment mold and melted out the wax, leave channels for the hot bronze to flow into evenly. This made for a piece that had the same thickness all around. When Jacob finished the sprues, Tadpole and Mr. Clean both looked like they had a dozen oversized intravenous tubes keeping them alive.

"Think we could've kept *you* alive?" he asked Mr. Clean. Then, with nobody around to see him cry, he wept for the babies who'd been lost and for the Jacob Nassedrine who he'd never be able to call Mr. Clean. The self that would keep on fucking up and falling off the wagon even when he was sixty. Eighty, if he lived that long. Maybe that ought to be his next set of sculptures—busts of himself through the ages, becoming weaker in the flesh and spirit. The final one would be a fist-sized clump of bronze with half a mouth and half an eye.

That reminded him too much of Simeon Gartner, so he put the thought out of his mind. Once the sprues were done, Jacob added a pouring cup and vents to make sure hot air could escape when he poured the bronze. Then he used chicken wire and tarpaper to make frames for the investment molds, which were squat cylinders the size of a pony keg of beer that had to get super-dry in order to take the molten bronze without cracking. He mixed up plaster and sand and water and poured some into the bottom of the cylinders to let it dry there, which ensured that the structure would hold and not leak when he eventually poured the rest of the mix in. While the bottom layers dried, he cleaned the wax positives with Goo Gone and a pair of nylon stockings to make sure they wouldn't get air bubbles when he put them in the plaster.

Finally, he brushed on some shellac. By then the base of the investment molds were dry enough, and he mixed up new plaster and sand. Jacob submerged Tadpole and Mr. Clean upside down into in their receptive cylinders smoothly, then turned each gently to work out any air bubbles. He wanted to sing Aerosmith's "Back in the Saddle" because he felt like the old Jacob Nassedrine was back, the one who had what it took to get as famous as Nolan Tinsley. But when he opened his mouth, the plaintive, elongated chorus of a Neil Young song came out:

Why do I?
Why do I keep fucking up?

It didn't make sense to him. He wasn't fucking up at all but getting his life back together. Why that song, in that moment, when he wanted to tell the world he was becoming the real Jacob Nassedrine again, instead of the shadow he'd let himself turn into?

* * *

It would take a couple days for the investment molds to dry, and after that he'd put them in the kiln upside down to melt out all the wax and gauge how much bronze he'd have to melt. Medge's regular caregivers had returned, so Jacob found himself with time to kill and no pills to kill it with except for the surprise waiting in the box labeled WAX WIRES. He opened it ceremonially and found four burnt orange tablets that looked like M&Ms. It was actually Thorazine, a

1950s-era antipsychotic and the granddaddy of mind control drugs. At one hundred milligrams, the second-highest dose available, these babies were enough to knock a bigger man than Jacob on his ass.

"Not a bad find," said Daniel, peering over his Big Bro's shoulder as Jacob lined up the pills on his kitchen table. Thorazine was one of the few pills Daniel respected because he'd been on it once at a hospital after an angry nervous breakdown. Jacob, who'd been in LA then, had missed all the fun. "But not exactly a recreational drug."

"I'll get my recreation how I feel like," Jacob told him. Since all he had to do was wait for plaster to dry, Jacob could afford to get laid out flat. What the hell else was there to do, neaten up the house for a wife who might never come back? His only worry was that Laynie might finally decide to call him exactly when the Thorazine hit. In that case he'd either let the phone ring through or pick up and let his slurred voice reveal his stupid truth. Jacob took a deep breath, smelling plaster residue on his hands, and popped his first-ever Thorazine.

Stupid. He'd probably kill himself by accident, the way Daniel warned him he might. He didn't feel anything for ten minutes, though he stared at the three remaining pills on the table as if they could enter his bloodstream through his eyes. When Jacob stood up, he got such a head rush that he had to lie down on the kitchen floor, and as his head settled, his dream of becoming a father drained out of him like an expired self-delusion. What right did he, an idiot who'd taken an antipsychotic drug for fun, have to think he was prepared to be a father?

After the Thorazine kicked in fully, Jacob pictured a boy about four years old with his face and Laynie's thick, wild hair. At that age it had to be the one she'd lost after burning the license. The child saw those M&Ms on the table and popped them all, crunching down.

No! Jacob wanted to shout, and he wanted to leap up and dig the pills out of his son's mouth. But he couldn't move because his limbs felt like they weighed eight thousand pounds each. He imagined that he was lifting his right arm slowly toward the pills in a titanic effort to hide them from the boy, but that arm hadn't even lifted from his kitchen floor. He felt like a granite mountain with a river flowing around him, changing his shape over thousands of years.

"Getting any recreation yet?" Daniel asked him.

Just giving myself time to think. Jacob spoke with his inner voice, using the channel only Daniel could receive.

"You'll get it. This shit turns you into a zombie. Is that what you want?"

I don't know what I want.

"Ah, bullshit. You know what you want, you just don't have the balls to do it."

I have the balls.

"No, Jake-o-Rama." Daniel sounded like the older one now, the survivor. "If you had any balls, you would've come over to my side a long time ago. Don't be like some teenage idiot who thinks he can jump from one moving car to another trying to prove he's got balls, then ends up getting his head crushed. Don't die from fucking up."

The Thorazine experience was emphatically not a high, but it lasted eight hours that Jacob could have been sleeping. He spent most of it on his kitchen floor, freezing sometimes, overheating others, and occasionally locking his jaw so tight that he felt his molars might shatter. For the first two hours the next morning, he felt groggy and didn't know what day it was, but time and two cups of coffee sharpened him up. As he leaned against the kitchen counter drinking it, Jacob looked down at the spot on the floor where'd he'd had his zombie time. How would it feel to be the child of a man like that? Jacob had seen his father passed out drunk before, but that was different. Paulie got incredibly animated and then maudlin, and then he just crashed. Jacob had been like a corpse that forgot it was dead, and his imaginary son had seen him. What would a little kid think of him there on the floor? Daddy's sick. Daddy's in trouble. Daddy's dead. The boy grew to eight and then twelve, and he had questions.

"Why do you keep doing that, Dad?" His name was Emery, for no reason at all. He sounded just like his dead uncle Daniel, even though he'd never been to Boston in his life. "I was right in your face, and you didn't hear me. It's like you were in a coma."

"I've got a lot of demons, kid," said Jacob, though he knew this was a lie. He had only one demon, and it was himself.

"There's got to be more productive ways to face your demons, capisce?"

Emery must have picked up *capisce* from Don-o, and that got Jacob chuckling. He shuffled to the barn to check on the cylinders, but they were still too wet to bake—they sounded wrong when he thunked them. Another day to wait. Back in the kitchen he let the Thorazines stare through him. He could take all three and probably die, which was one way out of his problems. But he hated his brother for chickening out like that, and his father before him, and with Laynie gone, there was nobody to find him the way he found Daniel. He could be decomposing for weeks. So, Jacob did the logical thing and popped only a single Thorazine, which he found less heavy than the first. He didn't quite pass out but fell into a state of stumbling around and staring at walls. In the kitchen, in the living room, in the funky space by the stairs.

But going up those stairs? Too much effort, plus the fear of falling. Jacob eventually braved the bottom stair to contemplate a grease mark that looked like a face when he tilted his head one way but like a humpbacked bear when he tilted it the other. He started to appreciate Thorazine because it sort of made him trip in extremely slow motion. The three times he'd done acid with Daniel, he felt himself careening, like an Olympic slalom ski racer with a blindfold on. But the Thorazine slowed him down to a delicious, glacial crawl. He remembered seeing the Galapagos tortoises at Reptile Gardens south of Rapid City, where Ed brought him and Daniel after their first visit to Evans Plunge. Those tortoises crawled through life so slowly they could live to be two hundred years old. How long could he live if he figured out how to crawl through life as slowly as they did?

Thorazine slowed him down plenty, but it couldn't be the answer for long. The face on the wall started looking angrier, and the bear disappeared, so Jacob retreated from the stairs. It was sunny outside and not too windy, so he shuffled to the barn to check the investment molds without knowing how long it had been since he'd checked them last. On the way he saw Daniel's ghost moving just as slowly with his weird heroin gait. Not quite a shuffle but still hesitant, deliberate, uncertain. They crossed paths and didn't even wave to each other. Then Jacob heard a truck rumbling up Chambrell Road—Laynie or Don-o probably, ready to catch him high and give up on him for good—and he moved as fast as the Thorazine let him.

It turned out to be Braden Iverson, one of the few kids from Clark who'd been decent to him in high school, and they'd done welding projects together sophomore year. Braden even came to the funerals for Ed and Rhonda, and though he never sought Jacob out, he was always cordial when they ran into each other. He pulled all the way up to the barn and stepped out, waving, but his face fell when he saw Jacob's.

"You okay?" Braden asked. "Jake, you look like a ghost."

"I've seen a couple lately." Jacob walked up and shook Braden's hand and, without planning to, gave him a half-hug. Braden was his height but bigger around—a bit of a lummox actually—and Jacob rested his head against his friend's shoulder a moment. Yes, friend. He needed one, and Braden showed up.

"Serious," the man said, stepping back from the hug. "What's wrong?"

"Wife problems."

"Wife?" Braden cocked his head.

"Yeah, got hitched in January. But I ran her off, I guess."

"Sorry to hear that. Hey, I was just stopping by to see if I could borrow your TIG and an argon tank."

"No problem. Grab a couple rods while you're at it. You remember where it's at?"

"Sure do. Right side, over in the corner." He made directions with his hands. "You okay, Jake?"

"Drank too much last night. Hungover."

"It's four in the afternoon." Braden put his hands in his pockets.

"Is it?" Jacob shrugged, glad he'd killed half the day already. "Good to see you, Bray. Wish I was in better spirits, you know?"

"I know the feeling," Braden said. "Thanks for the welding stuff. I only need it for a couple days."

"Hang onto it awhile," Jacob told him, waving as he headed back toward the house. Only when he got through the mudroom door did he remember that he'd gone out to check the investment molds. Oh well. They could wait until Braden left. An indeterminate amount of time later, Braden waved at Jacob through the kitchen window as he drove off, his eyes sure they'd seen something fishy but his mind unsure of exactly what.

"Close call," said Daniel's ghost from the kitchen table, but that was all. Jacob looked at the two remaining Thorazines and thought of taking another so he could open up a new channel between him and his brother that he *knew* was waiting for him to discover it. A wavelength where they could talk—not just chatter and bicker but really *talk* about life and death and all things in between. But no. Still not time yet.

* * *

The second pill wore off while Jacob slept from eight at night until ten in the morning, and when he pronounced himself fully awake, he flushed the last two Thorazines down the toilet. It wasn't recreational at all, like Daniel said. More like punishment, a gauntlet in which he was both the victim running through and the gang of perpetrators beating that runner with sticks. But he was done with his punishment now, and after today his life would be different. He would be more himself, less afraid of his own fragilities. Free from his own stupidity because he'd be done with pills for good. Not a saint who always had to fight off temptation but a man who could ignore The Void within him permanently.

Out in the barn the investment molds were finally dry enough to burn out the wax. That meant he was one step closer to the pour, one step closer to truly being a bronze man again, and unless something went wrong with his equipment or he lost his nerve, the pour would happen today. Jacob ripped off the tarpaper wrappings and struggled to get the molds upside-down in his kiln because the Thorazine hangover made him uncoordinated and slightly weak, but he got them in and put heavy pans underneath them to collect the melted wax. He set the kiln at 1,400° to burn the wax out quickly, calculated how much bronze he needed, then uncovered the Speedy-Melt and put forty half-inch cubes of Belmont Special H silicon bronze alloy #4939 into his crucible. He loved how smooth Special H looked melting down, but it wasn't time to start the melt yet because Special H liked getting poured as soon as it got hot enough. It didn't like to hang out and wait.

Jacob took his time with everything, half because it had been awhile since he'd done a pour and half because he wanted to savor the freedom he felt. He'd flushed those last two Thorazines down like they were the last two pills he'd touch in his life. He'd said goodbye to them in style, finishing his career as a pill popper with one that Daniel respected, which meant Daniel had to stop calling him a lightweight pussy. When the wax stopped dripping, he turned the kiln down and opened the door a crack to let the molds cool down enough to touch. Next came breakfast and coffee, a shower to make sure he didn't have the Thorazine crawling around anywhere on his skin, and the assembly of his accoutrements for the pour.

Most important among these would be the contraption he'd designed to let him pour solo from his large crucible, which he'd normally need a partner for. Jacob had built a heavy-duty tripod, equipped with wheels and a weighted pulley, to hold the other end of his lifting tongs while he pulled the crucible out of the furnace and set it on a platform of firebrick. He could then swap out the lifting tongs for the pouring shank, wheel the whole thing up to the investment mold, and pour the bronze without human help.

Jacob had spent three days building this device back when Daniel was living at Cocklebur Farm and they were desperate to avoid each other. He'd tested it twenty times with water before actually using bronze and knew it worked perfectly. The contraption had an ever-changing nickname, much like Richard Donatelli and the city of Watertown, and this time Jacob named it Jean-Michel in honor of his Quebec family. He composed an imaginary letter to Denis Nasreddine in Thetford Mines, promising to come up next Christmas and bring a surprise.

A pregnant wife, Denis would think. But it would be a sculpture, a bust of some mutual Nasreddine ancestor Jacob had picked from the sheaf of photos. He set out all the gear he'd need: face shield, thick canvas overalls, leather apron, and aluminized shirt and spats to cover his shins and boots. The knuckles of his spare foundry gloves—he couldn't find his brand-new ones—looked ratty, but they'd do in a pinch. He fired up the propane and switched on the furnace, which would take twenty-five minutes to get the bronze up to the 2,000° mark.

Then it was time to sit back and watch the Speedy-Melt work its magic. Jacob thought about what patinas to use and imagined a rough, greenish, ancient-looking one for Tadpole. As for Mr. Clean, he had no idea yet. Lots of wax on the head, for sure. Jacob turned the kiln all the way off, put his kiln gloves on, and inched the investment molds off their rack. He felt their heat as he finessed them onto his cart, then rolled them over to the little sandbox where he'd do the pour.

"Okay," Jacob told his never-born child, about to be given a double life in bronze. "You'll feel real hot for awhile, but you'll cool down. Life's like that sometimes."

He tossed a mental coin and decided to pour Mr. Clean first. When his pyrometer said the bronze had reached 2,005° Fahrenheit, Jacob turned off the furnace and donned his safety gear. The mechanical Jean-Michel held tight to the lifting tongs, ably helping him lift the crucible out of the furnace and onto the firebrick platform with ease. But as he swapped out the lifting tongs for the pouring shank, Jacob realized that he'd forgotten one small but crucial step in the pouring process: skimming the least pure metal off the surface of the crucible the way you skim cream from a pail of fresh milk.

In fixing this error, he made a dumb rookie mistake. If your skimmers aren't warmed up first, they can make the bronze splatter, and this is exactly what happened. As he dipped his first skimmer in, a glob of molten bronze leaped out of the crucible and landed on the glove that covered his right hand. Jacob swore at himself and thought nothing of it, but then the molten bronze worked its way through hairline cracks in the leather and came into contact with the knuckles of his right pinky and ring finger.

Jacob screamed like nothing he'd ever heard or imagined. He tried to pull off the glove, but the metal, leather, and flesh had already congealed into a single mass. He grabbed his fire extinguisher and blasted it at his hand to stop the burning sensation—which had been a bad decision, the doctors told him later, though they never explained why. It stopped the pain for a moment, or at least changed the nature of that pain long enough for him to call 911, then Ryan Donatelli.

"I'm hurt, Don-o," Jacob told the voice mail. He tried to clench and unclench his right hand to keep it moving, even though he could barely feel it. "Oh God, I'm hurt. Ambulance coming. It wasn't drugs, I swear to you. I promise it wasn't drugs."

CODA

Float On Down the River Lethe

27

Django

Jacob went by ambulance to an emergency room in Watertown and then to a burn unit in Sioux Falls, where nobody had seen an injury quite like his. Before Don-o and Chrissy could get there, he saw a hand reconstruction specialist named Dr. Nancy Mulliter, who didn't feed him bullshit.

"We can do a lot with grafts to cover up the surface," she told him, "but the tendons and ligaments around the knuckles are so damaged that you'll never have the same grip or flexibility again. The nerves too. Do you lift things for a living?"

"I'm a sculptor," Jacob said. "Or I *was* one. I did this pouring bronze."

Her eyebrows furrowed. Bad sign. "You'll need help with that from now on."

"When do you start cutting me?"

"We'll put you under in about twenty minutes. Sooner is better in your case."

They wouldn't let Jacob look at his own hand as they wheeled him to an operating room, and when the anesthesiologist put him under, he tried to think of Laynie just in case he died. Instead, he thought of Bill Jackman and thanked him for the health insurance, without which Jacob would have to sell the house to pay for his stupid mistake. Don-o and Chrissy were there when he came out of surgery.

"Looks like you finally bottomed out," Chrissy said.

"First Vince Van Gogh cut off his ear, then Jacob Nas poured molten bronze on his hand." Don-o pinch-rubbed the spot between Jacob's neck and shoulder. "The great ones, they always sacrifice their bodies."

"Anybody call Laynie?" Jacob asked.

"That's your job." Don-o nudged Jacob's phone closer to him on the bedside table. "Just in case you're wondering—yes, you turned off your furnace and kiln before you left the barn. The place didn't blow up."

Jacob tried reaching for his phone with his right hand, which was strapped down at the forearm. "Shit, I'll have to do everything left-handed now."

"You could be the Django Reinhardt of bronze," Don-o told him.

"That's the first thing I thought when I felt the metal go through my glove," Jacob said. "Ah hell, now I've got a lifetime of Django Reinhardt jokes from Don-o."

"A lifetime," Chrissy said. "I like the sound of that word. 'Cause for a while, we weren't sure you cared about having a lifetime at all."

* * *

Laynie was playing tennis with Maura Bast when Jacob's call came, proud of herself for winning a point that Maura didn't hand her. After that they planned to meet with Dad's lawyer, and in the evening they'd have some of his friends over for a picnic dinner. It felt like her last day in LA even before Jacob told her what happened.

"How bad is it?" she asked him.

"Real bad. Like, months of rehab bad. Things I'll never be able to do again bad."

"Were you on something?"

"No. I took something the day before, but I was clean when it happened."

"The day before isn't clean!" Laynie's livid tone made Maura stop dead on the other side of the court.

"Say what you want, Lane. I forgot to warm my skimmer and I got splattered, and I was wearing shitty old gloves."

"What can't you do anymore?"

"Get an ounce of sympathy from my wife, I guess," said Jacob. "Look, I'm telling you a fact. You decide when to come back or *if* to come back."

"Do you seriously think I'm not coming back if my husband's hand is ruined?" Laynie hated how shrill she sounded. "Of course I'm coming back."

She hung up and looked around for Maura, who could tell their match was over and had started packing up her gear. Laynie told her what had happened on the way to Dad's house, crying when she pictured Jacob's hand as a black, shriveled claw against her skin.

"It's a good thing we're going to see Peter," Maura told her. "Hand rehab costs a lot of time and money." She stuck her right wrist in front of Laynie's face, showing off a frown-shaped scar at its base. They talked with the lawyer about the money and the house, about whether or not Laynie was ready to start proving her suitability for inheritance with drug testing. She mentioned Jacob's hand injury, and Peter said the will stipulated that money could be released for medical purposes, which relaxed Laynie so much that she fell into a kind of waking coma and felt her body drifting out of the room.

The money. The house. She'd trade them both to see Dad again. He didn't even have to be alive—she could meet him outside of time for coffee and donuts and ask him what it was like to be dead, and that would help her figure out how to be alive. What was wrong with her that she didn't believe she could know one without the other? Everybody else seemed able to live without knowing what death was, but she'd been stuck on the question for half her life.

"Excuse me," Peter asked, calling her to attention. "Is there anything else you and your husband need?"

"Just the safety net for now, thanks. We'll get by."

When they got home, Laynie packed up and brooded and tried talking to the Gandhi / JFK / God she'd seen in the shop window, but he was busy counting beans again. Didn't wink at her, didn't even glance her way. She pictured herself taking care of Jacob like a nurse would, feeding him soup and wiping his ass, but things couldn't be that dire. Could they? She pictured various prosthetic hands, from a 1950s-style metal pincher hook to one so fleshlike that she couldn't tell Jacob's bad hand from his good one as they caressed her naked back.

SEND ME A PICTURE OF IT, she texted him, but he said CAN'T, IT'S BANDAGED. Laynie sent him a kiss emoji, and he sent back an inexplicable monkey emoji that made her think he was drugged up in the hospital. A slippery slope that might lead him to being drugged up once he left, too. Though ruining his own hand ought to finally beat some sense into him. She pictured the bad hand, bony and demonic, struggling with a cigarette lighter and burning down that beautiful house at the top of their hill to make sure he'd never find a pill hidden inside it again. Maybe then they'd move back to LA, where there would be better doctors for Jacob's hand. What if some hack in South Dakota ruined it and he really did need a prosthetic? Laynie finished packing, put the suitcase in her Honda's trunk, and joined Maura in the kitchen to prep for the guests.

"Keep me busy, please," she said. "My mind is being ridiculous."

The picnic dinner went fine. People she'd met at Dad's parties but didn't know by name mingled with Maura's friends, all of them strangers. The closest person to Laynie's age was Maura's niece, a snobby volleyball star at UCLA who looked just like her aunt, only blonder and taller. It was clearly a transitional party, a segue from the place being Bill's house to being Maura's house. Laynie drifted away, though the party kept following her until she secluded herself in her high-class Rat's Nest. She kept the lights off so nobody would follow her there and called Jacob.

"I just want to know if I'm going to feel anything different when you touch me while we're having sex," she asked him right away.

"Well, that's a fine hello."

"I'm serious. Can your hand feel my skin? Is it going to feel dead against me?"

"The only thing that'll be different is if I'm standing up and you're hanging off my hips, grab my *left* hand if you think you're falling."

"Ha. I know this is weird," Laynie said, "but I'm not going to believe your hand isn't a claw until I see it."

"Just like you're not going to believe I'm off pills until you see it, right?"

"What were you on the day before?"

"Thorazine," Jacob told her.

"Seriously? Isn't that what they give psychos who take five cops to hold them down?"

"Exactly." The silence on the line weighed as much as a bronze monument to the man Jacob used to be. He was doubly damaged now—in psychological ways no one could see and in a physical way everyone could.

"How do I know this isn't just one more 'going clean' story that ends in another binge?"

Jacob let out the heaviest sigh Laynie had ever heard. "All I've got to do when I want a pill is look at the back of my fucking hand, Lane. It'll scare me straight every time."

* * *

Laynie took her time driving home to 1 Chambrell Road because she didn't have anything more than over-the-counter pills to ease her back pain, and she didn't even want to drive under their paltry influence. She got out every two hours to stretch and stopped at a few of the spots that had led her to Jacob: the Wagon Wheel Motor Lodge outside Vegas; the rest stop in Littlefield, Arizona; the bubble chairs in Glenwood Springs. She didn't have the guts to cut through Wyoming and visit Evans Plunge because Daniel's ghost might be there, and he'd talk trash about Jacob. Laynie considered writing another letter to her father but forced herself not to by looking at the back of her right hand and imagining, for at least the thousandth time, what Jacob's injury looked like.

PICTURE PLEASE, she texted him while pumping gas, because the bandages were supposedly coming off that morning. SUSPENSE KILLING ME. Laynie knew he didn't like jokes about death, so she added METAPHORICALLY. The photo that came back wasn't as hideous as she feared, but it looked like someone had smashed Jacob's two outside knuckles with a mallet. That whole side of his hand was diminished, and when she pictured him working with clay, he couldn't even tear off a chunk of it. Laynie blew up the picture on her phone and saw a discolored skin graft over his knuckles and fingers, with all sorts of pale stitches crisscrossing its edges.

CAN'T EVEN SQUEEZE THIS THING, said Jacob's next text, which showed a light-yellow ball of putty in his palm. It took a while for Laynie to realize this was a video. His right pinkie and ring finger curled slowly over the putty, but that was all it could do. NOT SLOW MOTION, said his next text. She wanted to tell him she believed in him, but that would sound corny, so instead she told him SENDING YOU PERSISTENCE. Once the gas tank filled, she pulled into a parking spot, bought herself an ice cream, and called Chrissy.

"How's Jacob doing?" she asked.

"Better than I thought," Chrissy told her. "The hand doesn't look horrible unless you stare at it. And unless he's trying to grab something, you can't really tell it's injured."

"Did they give him painkillers when he left the hospital?"

"The doctor wrote him a prescription, but he tore it up right in front of her. Ryan was there."

"Do you think he'll stay clean?"

Chrissy took a while to think over her answer. "As long as I've known him, he's been scared of fucking up," she finally said.

"But now he has," Laynie said. "Royally."

"Exactly. Now he's got a scar he can see, on top of all the ones inside that he can't see. It's different this time. He's beat-up, and he's smaller than before, but he's here. He's still him."

28

Tabula Rasa

It was almost midnight on the third Thursday in April when Laynie passed under the COCKLEBUR FARM sign, and she didn't even notice that spring had finally come to South Dakota. She hadn't come home out of married obligation to Jacob, or because he was the only one who could understand her and complete her, but because she wanted to finish what she'd started: the process of sharing her life with him, giving herself to a union larger than herself that had its own life and breath, its own inhalations and exhalations.

Jacob's purple Dodge wasn't there, only the red Explorer that Laynie figured would be hers now. They'd need money for his medical bills, and she'd gladly sell her Honda if it meant him having two useful hands. As she walked through the mudroom, she wanted to ditch forever her constant frantic careening between self-loathing and grudging self-acceptance. She wanted to slow down and dispel the demon of aloneness, which had been chasing her since the moment she understood—down in her cells, down beneath words—her mother's impending death. The demon of aloneness that reactivated with every subsequent death because running away from it defined her being, her incessant leave-taking, her harum-scarum course through life.

As Laynie stepped into the kitchen, she saw her Three Sacred Things and laughed. Jacob keeping them right where she'd left them was as much a sign of trust as her leaving them in the first place. There would be awful times with Jacob, she knew. If she had another miscarriage, he'd feel the pain of her uterus in his damaged hand, and they'd both want pills, both turn to each other for the strength to resist them. There would be moments when his right hand wouldn't do what he wanted it to, and his mind would demand a pill to drown out his own futility.

That desire wouldn't go away—once an addict, always an addict, no matter how deep or shallow your addiction was—but they didn't have to heed it. Before things finally broke for them, they'd given in because The Void screamed inside them and they simply wanted to shut that screaming off. Now, Laynie felt certain, they'd been humbled in exactly the way they needed to be humbled and wouldn't be freaked out by the screaming. They'd hear it, sure, like sailors of old heard the sirens. But if they had enough rope to hang themselves with, they also had enough rope to tie each other to the mast until the sirens grew hoarse and gave up.

Laynie went upstairs and checked in on the spare bedroom and decided to sleep there again for at least the night, maybe longer. She fetched the spare sheets and made the bed fresh, deciding she'd be the last person to sleep on this mattress before they dumped it for a new one with less bad history. She woke to the sound of Jacob's truck door but dropped her head back to the pillow, pretending sleep. Jacob tiptoed into the house, smiling when he saw Laynie's car keys on the kitchen table. When he passed the guest bedroom, he saw the lump on the bed and blew a kiss to his wife, who blew one back, and then went to bed early.

There would be plenty of time to talk in the morning. Plenty of mornings, he knew, if he stopped worrying so much about fucking up and simply lived.

* * *

At seven the next morning Laynie woke to the rumble of a tractor outside the guest bedroom window. It was their ex-Hutterite

neighbor, announcing the true arrival of spring by plowing his fields.
She thought she'd woken up first but found Jacob in the barn already,
with the Speedy-Melt already fired up. The investment molds for Tadpole and Mr. Clean sat in his kiln getting warm enough to accept the
bronze. He wore his canvas overalls and leather apron, his aluminized
shirt and spats and his face shield. His new foundry gloves—which
he'd left, inexplicably, behind a long-defunct heating oil tank in the
basement—covered his good hand and his bad one. The air around
the furnace shimmered with heat like Smeltville had when Laynie
first walked into it, back when their love was full of possibilities that
hadn't been lost yet.

"Were you always going to finish the pour today?" Laynie asked,
"or did you decide to do it when I showed up?"

"B," Jacob said, and it felt like the only sound she might get out
of him for hours.

"Did you warm your skimmer?"

He pointed his bad hand at a round, palm-sized piece of metal
next to the furnace that had holes all over its surface and a two-foot
handle. It looked to Laynie like a flyswatter or lollipop—too small
and insignificant to cause injury. She fixed her eyes on his hand, and
Jacob left it hanging in the air as she walked over to it.

"Can I?" she asked him, already pulling on the glove's fingers.
Laynie slid it off and ran her fingertips over the bad knuckles. It
looked even more caved in than it had in the picture he'd sent, more
diminished in power. He'd probably have to squeeze balls of putty for
the rest of his life so the damaged muscles wouldn't atrophy. Laynie
turned his hand to look at it from another angle, and Jacob winced.

"Sorry," she said. "I'll get used to being gentle with it."

"Probably before I do," Jacob told her. She kissed the indentation
between his ruined knuckles, and he kissed her hand on the same
spot. They'd done this before, their bodies knew, but their minds
didn't remember when. Laynie inspected the graft, which looked

paler than the rest of his hand and felt papery, like it didn't have quite enough blood rushing through it.

"Where did they take the skin from?"

"My right ass cheek. The surgeon liked my left cheek better, but she didn't want to cheat the world."

"Oh, stop." Laynie chided him with a small whack on the rump that turned, though they weren't sure how, into an embrace. Not some gigantic display of passion but a simple folding into one another. An act of reverence for their marriage, which was bigger than they were and which they'd both given up something to create. Not token things either but immense psychic structures that used to hold them together and keep them bolted in place. Without those structures they risked floating off into a no-thing-ness as inviting as the oblivion of pills. Their reward for letting go of those structures was something like life.

"When are you moving back into the bedroom?" Jacob asked. "Do I have to rip open the walls to prove there aren't any pills in there?"

"I thought about burning the place down to get rid of the pills."

"I've thought about that a hundred times. Speaking of fire."

Jacob slipped his right glove back on, flicked down his face shield, turned off the furnace, and uncovered it. The bronze inside glowed, and using his left hand, he skimmed the impurities off the top and stuck the skimmer headfirst into the sandbox. He wheeled his cart to the kiln, pulled out the investment molds, wheeled them over to the sandpit, and set them in place for the pour.

"You're way too close," he told Laynie, who backed up halfway to the barn door.

"Did you wait for me to get here so I can call an ambulance just in case?"

"I waited 'cause you're my good luck charm. C'mon, don't jinx me with talking."

She watched as Jacob, moving more methodically than she'd ever seen, used his mechanical tripod helper to pour the molten bronze from the crucible into the waiting molds—first Mr. Clean, then Tadpole. When the bronze reached the top of Tadpole's pouring cup, he rolled the crucible back to the firebricks and let it sit there. He double-checked that the furnace and kiln were both off, then removed his safety clothing by his workbench.

"How long before you can knock the plaster off?" Laynie asked.

"An hour probably. But I won't be here in an hour."

"Oh?" She waited for Jacob to come over and kiss her, but instead he folded the clothes and stacked them neatly on their shelf.

"I'm going to Hot Springs to get rid of some ghosts," he said.

"I'm tired of ghosts."

"I know. That's why you should come with me."

"I just drove for four days." Laynie stretched her back theatrically.

"I know. Give me one more day. Please."

"What's in it for me?" she asked, though of course she'd say yes.

"Me not asking you to move back into our bedroom till you're ready. Deal?"

They left after breakfast, and Laynie slept on the way, massaging her aching back with a lacrosse ball she'd borrowed from the outhouse bucket. They tried not to talk much, both knowing that they had to learn internal silence if they wanted to stay in the Land of Clean. The answer to their problems lay not in some new kind of thinking but in using silence to shrink The Void inside them that their dead loved ones had left behind. Their small addictions had not only expanded their respective Voids but eaten tiny parts of themselves they once considered solid. Extra words nibbled at the edges of those Voids, threatening to collapse their borders and turn into an emptiness so vast they could never patch or fill it.

Jacob drove all the way to Hot Springs and cut his engine outside the Fall River County Sheriff's Office. Then he reached for his mother's alligator purse, which sat on the floor by Laynie's feet. "Do you want to watch me do this?" he asked her.

"I think you should be your own good luck charm on this one," she told him, climbing out for a stretch as Jacob headed inside.

"I need to turn in some evidence," he told the woman at the front desk. She stared at the alligator purse, puzzled. She led him to a windowless room with a metal table, and two minutes later a limping, sixtyish man came in and introduced himself as Chuck Fettis.

"Remember an OD?" Jacob asked him. "A year and a half ago, in December?"

"That hippie kid?"

"He was my brother. I've been hanging on to this."

Jacob set Daniel's syringe on the table and let Officer Fettis stare at it.

"What the hell am I supposed to do with that?" the cop said.

"Keep me from throwing it in the river and letting some kid find it. My brother's dead, and I don't want it. It should be where he died. Daniel Nassedrine, that was his name."

Jacob pushed the syringe across the table and left without a further word, not bothering to take the alligator purse. He wiped sweat from his brow and hopped back into the truck, and Laynie did the same. Bonnie and Clyde must have felt this way when they first started robbing people, she thought. Absolutely free to do what they wanted and be who they wanted.

"Did you lay your burden down?" Laynie asked Jacob.

"Yep. Laid it right down."

His next stop was WillieJax Pawn & Consignment, where he got $100 for Daniel's cherry-red Fender Telecaster. He asked Laynie to drive up to Rapid City while he called the hotline for Women Escaping a Violent Environment, which didn't list a physical address— completely understandable, given its function. Jacob said he wanted to make a $100 donation in his mother's name and arranged to meet one of WEVE's volunteers at the Working Against Violence, Inc., office on Quincy Street.

"Somebody can use these clothes too," he told the woman who met him, handing her Daniel's death clothes and the NASSEDRING coat in a neat bundle. He couldn't look at her for long because she bore emotional scars he recognized from his own mirror. Had she been on SMS maybe? One of those silent lurkers who joined but never spoke?

"What did you say your mother's name was?" the woman asked him, and he wrote it down on a slip of paper for her because his throat wouldn't let him speak it. His right hand cramped up before he finished her name. Then he went back to the truck and cried, curled up in a ball in the passenger seat. When they got home at almost midnight, Jacob marched straight to the barn and grabbed a sledgehammer and knocked the plaster off the investment molds. Inside were Tadpole and Mr. Clean, looking nothing like an embryo or a fetus at all. Looking like something that had once been much larger but had lived through a fire and shrunk. Just as he and Laynie had lived through a fire and shrunk—become diminished versions of what they might have been.

But they could grow back, that was the great thing. As long as they didn't try growing back into exactly what they'd been before the fire in their lives, they could grow back into something more true than they'd ever dared to hope for.

* * *

It took Laynie five days to move into the big bedroom, longer than last time. She wanted them to develop a new rapport first, build around this new species of silence that didn't ache to be filled with self-doubt, self-recrimination, self-anything. To create a way of being together that didn't invite the dead to feast on the energies of the living, which they admitted they'd been doing almost constantly in their desperation to keep the dead alive. It was possible to keep them alive indefinitely, as they'd been doing for years. But the dead required so much energy that they were bound to deplete the living.

The invited dead fed on the emotional lifeblood of their living hosts, who offered it freely whether the dead wanted to keep living or not. Most dead people, like those Laynie and Jacob loved, wanted to stay dead instead of being perpetually offered the energies of the living, who made themselves near-ghosts in their attempt to keep the dead barely breathing. But how could the dead turn down that kind of love? In the silence they'd discovered out of necessity, the last remaining Nassedrines faced their deepest addiction: making the dead live again. The pills were an echo of that, a derivative of that. Once they buried the dead, the pills would follow.

On the fifth day, before Laynie moved back into the bedroom, they followed their ex-Hutterite neighbor's lead and turned over ground where Aunt Rhonda had once planted a garden. Laynie planned an even bigger one that she'd be able to see out her studio window, and she marched Jacob toward the spot where she wanted to plant. His bad right hand sat in her good left one, and he didn't flinch because she'd learned exactly how to hold it. When she stopped and showed him the spot, he just laughed.

"If you break up the ground here," Jacob told her, "you'll have cocklebur creeping all the way to the house. That stuff loves broken ground. This ridge is like a castle wall, keeping it out."

"So maybe not until we find a way to sell cocklebur," Laynie said. She looked down the hill at the huge swath of yellowed weeds, some knee-high and others smushed against the ground by the long weight of now-melted snow. Some green shoots emerged from the ground, though Jacob said they wouldn't really start coming up until June.

"Do you think I'll be pregnant by the time they come up?" Laynie asked.

"I'm not betting money," Jacob replied. "Not playing percentages either."

"It's 50-50 now. No other percentages to play."

She took his hand again, and they walked to the top of the anagama hill to watch the neighbor plowing the corner of his land nearest the 424. As wind whisked away the dust from behind the tractor, Laynie wanted to forsake her micro-landscapes and paint what was vast—acres of broken soil, fields of cocklebur, even the clouds she felt were so clichéd. She felt it as a small detonation inside her, the same way she felt an egg dropping some months, and knew that making art and making children both came from the same stubborn root. Two hundred million years of mammalian evolution on one branch of it, fifty thousand years of humans trying to understand the world on the other.

"I should spend more time outside," Laynie said.

"I didn't spend much time outside my first winter here either," Jacob told her. "But we've got a good month now before the mosquitoes start trying to kill us."

Jacob wanted to get back to work on his bronzes, and Laynie retreated to her grain bin. She connected her phone to Don-o's projector and pointed it at the canvas, trying out various super-enlarged images of the rusted electrical box. Nothing looked good—nothing looked like the work of a new self. It was all the same old stuff Laynie Jackman painted, and she didn't want it anymore. The internal detonation hit her again, and she imagined paintings of the sky leaning against the walls of her quasi-yurt. Dozens of them! Would it be so terrible to paint the sky? Such an awful betrayal of her artistic principles?

Laynie didn't know for sure, so she remained in limbo and painted nothing. She simply occupied her space. When Jacob finished whatever he was doing to Tadpole and Mr. Clean, she watched him walk slowly from barn to house, looking at his ruined knuckles and squeezing his right hand shut with a pained look on his face. It must have been even harder than he expected, working with that hand. Laynie gave him a moment to settle and followed him inside, then glided up the stairs and into the master bedroom. She climbed up on his hips to make love and was incredibly careful with his right hand, not asking it to bear an ounce of her weight.

"Does this mean you're moving in?" he asked her as they slipped into the shower together.

"Yeah, pretty much." She used his inflection when she said it, which made them feel more married.

"I want to do a drive," Jacob said, kissing her ring.

"For who?" she asked him.

"Not *for* who, *to* who. I want to go to Quebec, and I don't want to wait for Christmas."

"Oh." It made absolute sense to Laynie. "Of course. Tomorrow?"

He nodded, and she noticed gray at his temples—two small streaks, more prevalent on the left side, that she hadn't noticed before. She hadn't seen them starting to come in, and that bothered Laynie because seeing them was her spousal right. Then again, she hadn't been around for the accident. They'd probably started graying as soon as the bronze hit his skin, reminding him that he had finite time to do an infinite job on Earth.

29

Things They Couldn't Know

They took four days to drive to Thetford Mines, an asbestos mining town of twenty-five thousand that a Canadian magazine had voted as the worst place to live in the country because of the pollution. Upon arrival, Jacob and Laynie vehemently disagreed. Their slow drive had allowed Denis Nasreddine to contact more of the family, which was flung throughout Quebec and didn't usually gather outside of Christmas. Denis lived on rue Labbé, dangerously close to Pâtisserie St-Noël, a bakery and pastry shop where he'd instructed Jacob and Laynie to meet him after his teaching day finished. He was a formal-looking, fortysomething man with a starched white shirt and every jet-black hair in place, and he stood a full head shorter than Jacob.

"Petit-cousin," he said, embracing the American lightly but not kissing him on the cheek as Jacob had feared. Jacob said the same words back, and Denis's smile at his halfway decent pronunciation whisked the tension out of the moment. He ordered them the semi-official pastry of Quebec: the Jos Louis, featuring round, thin slices of velvet cake alternating with layers of cream and covered with chocolate frosting. They already knew Denis couldn't put them up because all his flooring was being replaced, but today he couldn't even let them into the house. He'd made a reservation for them at Auberge la Bonne Mine, a bed and breakfast slightly out of town where they could stay for two nights until a wedding party took the entire place over.

"And then you do couch floating," Denis said. "Less noise in my house, then, but too much still."

Jacob explained why they wanted to come up before Christmas. The miscarriages, the haunting memories of their recent dead, the hand injury. They needed a different connection to the world. They didn't mention addiction. Denis, ever the genealogist, asked Jacob questions about his parents and brother and eventually pulled a spiral-bound hardcover Strathmore artist's sketchbook—the same kind Laynie used—out of a leather satchel to note his answers. The family tree, he told them, would change. His formality fell away and his hands came to life when he drew new branches for it. They swooped across the page, connecting names and circling question marks next to dates.

"Are you an artist?" Laynie asked him.

"Not like you two. Yes, I spied on you with the internet. My art is this . . . drawing of people over time. To bring them into one place when all times are together. I do this for my family and for love of history."

"And for yourself?" Laynie's interest grew the more she saw his hands at work.

Denis shrugged. "It helps me understand the world. And you? Laynie is your birth name?"

She spelled *Alania* out for Denis, and his face became an exclamation point.

"Ah! We have an *Aleyna* in the book, first cousin of my grandmother. A Lebanese name. The family name comes from there."

"I had a Lebanese great-grandmother!"

"Her name? Do you know?"

"Marina."

"She is a saint. Not your great-grandmother. I'm sorry, I don't know her—maybe she was. But the Marina of her name is a Byzantine saint, ninth century, so your great-grandmother probably was a Maronite Christian. Some of us also are."

"And the rest?" Jacob asked.

"Some Muslims, some nothing. My parents were Maronite, and I'm a little bit believing but afraid of church."

"I hear you," Jacob leaned across the table. "So, if the Nassedrines split off from the Nasreddines when we went south into Maine, I'm part Lebanese too."

"Yes. The first ones came from Beirut in 1889. So, four generations back. When you have children, they are—" Denis did some quick calculation, then threw up his hands. "Part Lebanese. I'm not good with math. So—" He flipped a new page in the notebook. "*Jacob et Alania*. The French way is easier on my mouth. May I call you Alania?"

When she nodded, Denis started a new page in the notebook with their names at the top. She startled when he drew the decisive downward line that would lead to their eventual offspring.

ALANIA (née JACKMAN) ——┬—— JACOB NASSEDRINE

There wasn't a question mark at the end of the line, only a blank space leading to an inevitable new human that would require a date and a name. An eventuality, not a possibility. They made plans for dinner—poutine at Fromagerie la Bourgade, no room for argument—and Denis went to his house to check on the progress of his remodeling. Jacob and Laynie, who insisted on being called Alania for the duration of their stay in Quebec, headed to Auberge la Bonne Mine and made love as soon as they got to their room. He rocked behind her as she gazed through sheer curtains at a white wedding gazebo, and after Jacob came, she insisted on doing a headstand on the bed to help one valiant sperm find its way to an egg. Alania didn't care if it was an old wives' tale disproved by science.

"This is the place," she told Jacob, who leaned back against the headboard and stared at her upside-down face. "This is where it happens, I know it. We had to get out of the country, where our old bullshit can't find us."

"Hate to break it to you," Jacob said, "but your bullshit always tracks you down."

"But it's got to go through customs and everything, so we've got a little grace period. Two days, maybe three."

"I hope so, A-la-ni-a."

"Try it with three syllables, not four. *A-lan-ya.*"

"Yes, *A-lan-ya.*" Jacob had to admit it sounded good that way. Felt perfect in his mouth.

"Good. Now faster. *Alanya.*"

"*Alanya. Alanya. Alanya.*" He kissed her belly. "Good enough?"

"Yes. Now get that baby name generator of yours going. This is the place, I'm telling you. Asbestos mines and all."

* * *

They spent four days in Quebec, driving around to the places Denis sent them and meeting distant relatives, and for those who didn't know English, he'd prepared a letter in French explaining who they were. Jacob's highlight was a visit to a farm near Parc National de Frontenac, where a trio of boys used the last remaining patch of ice from their backyard hockey rink to launch pucks at an outhouse.

"Must be genetic," he told Alania, and when he explained to the boys what he did with lacrosse balls back in South Dakota, they insisted on teaching him how to take a slapshot. There were hockey players in the family, the boys told him. One even made the NHL, and another played in the first ever game of the now-defunct Lebanese national hockey team.

Alania's highlight was the tour of Lebanese restaurants in Montreal. She stuffed herself, reasoning that (a) she'd never get this kind of food back home, and (b) if she fed their maybe-baby enough Lebanese food, which it was genetically predestined to like, then it might cling to her uterine lining in pursuit of more. She decided that when they got back to Cocklebur Farm, she'd invite the Donatellis and the Hattens and Lovetrain and Rain over for a Lebanese feast of lamb meatballs, tabouli, a rice and lentil stew, and maamoul—date cookies covered in powdered sugar that she'd bought a mold for and couldn't wait to bake.

They couldn't know, as they left Quebec behind until the following Christmas, that Alania would go back to her birth name permanently and take on Jacob's surname despite her earlier insistence on keeping her own. It wasn't acquiescing to the patriarchy, she told herself. Laynie Jackman simply couldn't stay pregnant, but Alania Nassedrine might. Why not give her a chance?

They couldn't know that Alania would fail to have a miscarriage six days after her period was due. Or nineteen days. Or thirty-three days. Nor could they know that she'd get through the entire first trimester before visiting Dr. Kermans—an act of restraint that Laynie Jackman would have been incapable of but that Alania Nassedrine took in stride like the earthy woman she longed to keep becoming.

They couldn't know that Jacob would, damaged right hand and all, finally finish waxing Tadpole and Mr. Clean on the day of his wife's twenty-week ultrasound, which revealed serious problems with their child's feet. It wasn't quite clubfoot, Dr. Kermans said, but the child had a genetic defect that caused several of the bones in his forefeet to fuse together. They curled decidedly inward, and correcting that would require several complex surgeries by specialists in Minneapolis spread out over at least four years.

They couldn't know that William Jackman's house—and indeed nearly every penny he amassed in his lifetime—would be poured into their child's surgeries. Or that those surgeries would force Jacob, who needed more health insurance for his family than his father-in-law's policy provided, to take a full-time job at a production foundry in Huron and eventually supervise the production of molded bronze machine parts, cherubs, Rodin knock-offs, Jesuses, and Buddhas.

They couldn't know that Jacob would never get famous, never become the art star he wanted to become as a teenager, but instead would give up his ambitions and only make bronzes on weekends for people he loved. They couldn't know that Alania would forsake her micro-landscapes to paint the clouds she once derided and eventually develop a satisfying regional career. Nor could they know that Don-o would be the one to break through and sell his work to museums in New York and Europe.

They couldn't know that Laynie, the Californian who already had a home, would find one in South Dakota. Or that Jacob, the Bostonian who desperately needed a home, would never let South Dakota be his. Though he'd learn, once he became a father there, to hate it less.

They couldn't know that their son, prematurely birthed by Caesarean on the third Saturday in February with a thick head of Alania-esque hair, would be called William Daniel Nassedrine in honor of his dead grandfather and dead uncle, or know that he'd earn the odd nickname of Gilly. Laynie couldn't stand Willie, Jacob couldn't stand Will, and neither of them could stand Billy or just plain Bill. But Guillaume was French for William, and Gilly sounded short and unique.

They couldn't know the kind of hell they'd be stuck in once Gilly reached eight months and started trying to crawl, which caused him to scream almost constantly because of the pins in his feet. It would almost break their marriage, break their own nerves, break the spirit of their child.

They couldn't know that to fight back against his early foot problems, Gilly would grow up to become a halfway decent runner and take particular joy in hurdling—though he'd never set any state records like his uncle Daniel. They couldn't know he'd get so obsessed with the yo-yo, which he fell in love with after Richard Donatelli gave him a fancy purple one for his seventh birthday, that Jacob would build him a heated shed with sixteen-foot-high ceilings so he could practice his moves year-round. By the time he turned seventeen, Gilly Nassedrine would visit thirty states and eight countries to participate in yo-yo tournaments, eleven of which he would win outright. Every time he left home to travel with his fellow yo-yo geeks, Jacob and Alania would get as nervous as any parents in the world.

"He better not die on us," Alania would say when they dropped him off at the airport for a trip to Japan, because she always said that when he left.

"If he does, I'll kick his ass," Jacob would say, because that was his parting line.

They couldn't know that during this particular trip, Gilly would impregnate a girl from Portland named Bianca Patenaude, or that they'd have a granddaughter named Monica by the time their son finished high school. Gilly would use the money he earned from yo-yo competitions, as well as from coaching yo-yo on the side, to pay for childcare while he and Bianca went to Oregon State the next fall.

"He's one determined motherfucker," Jacob would tell Don-o as they sat back on the wraparound porch at Cocklebur Farm, watching a bright-red sunset through meshy gray clouds. "I'll give him that much."

"How that guy jumped out of *your* nuts, I'll never figure out," Don-o would reply. "He's a prince, Gramps."

"Ah, bite me," Jacob would laugh, ensuring that Don-o called him Gramps at every opportunity thereafter.

They couldn't know that Alania would never get pregnant again after Gilly—no brothers or sisters for him, no more miscarriages, no periods at all. Dr. Kermans called it "premature ovarian insufficiency" instead of "early menopause," but the result was the same. Her reproductive system had limped and dragged itself along for years, produced an international yo-yo champion, and shut itself down.

They couldn't know a single one of these things by Christmastime, when they headed back to Quebec for a proper Nasreddine/Nassedrine family reunion—though they did know that Alania's pregnant belly would make her the star of the gathering. They couldn't glimpse even a slice of their future as they stopped at the Nordik Spa-Nature just north of Ottawa to sit together in properly hot water, which they'd never done together before. It was an expensive and hedonistic treat, but they didn't know about their onerous future medical bills yet. When they got to their chosen hot tub, Jacob whipped off his bathrobe and hopped right in, but Alania tested the water with her feet first. She knew pregnant women weren't supposed to be in too long anyway.

"Holy shit," Jacob said when Alania took the robe off and stepped in beside him. His eyes widened in mock fear of her belly.

"Is that any way to talk to your wife?"

"When she looks as big as a house, yeah."

Alania splashed him and sat, then put his right hand where the baby's head was. Jacob plunged his face in, put his mouth to that spot, and hummed a few bars of a song he didn't know the name of. Something minor key. Something that made him think of decadent Europe a century ago, between the world wars. Why on earth was he thinking about world wars now, in a hot tub with the love of his life, with their longed-for baby on its way? When Jacob surfaced, Alania took his right hand and pulled it close to her face. It didn't look too bad anymore—like somebody had removed parts of it with a tiny melon scoop—but it was weak, old-mannish, non-Jacoblike.

"How does it feel?" she asked him.

"Like it's probably always going to feel." Jacob took his hand back from her and squeezed down on the baby's head with all his fingers, trying especially hard with the bad ones. "Got any baby name ideas?"

"Definitely not William," Alania said.

"And definitely not Daniel," Jacob replied.

But years later, after Gilly's surgeries were done, they would both confess that they'd decided, right then and there in the hot tub at the Nordik Spa-Nature, to give their child the names of the two dead men who'd brought them together. Who else would be strong enough to carry those names but a child who'd been so hard to bring into the world, who'd only come after being called a thousand times?

"Deal," Alania said. "No naming him after dead people."

"Deal." To seal the agreement, Jacob held up his right hand for a high-five. Alania pulled hers back just before their palms struck, laughed at the near miss, and interlaced her fingers with his. Jacob squeezed, and she squeezed back, and it hurt like hell, and he let it.

THE END

IN THE FLYOVER FICTION SERIES

Ordinary Genius
Thomas Fox Averill

Jackalope Dreams
Mary Clearman Blew

Ruby Dreams of Janis Joplin: A Novel
Mary Clearman Blew

*It's Not Going to Kill You,
and Other Stories*
Erin Flanagan

The Usual Mistakes, and Other Stories
Erin Flanagan

Reconsidering Happiness: A Novel
Sherrie Flick

Glory Days
Melissa Fraterrigo

Twelfth and Race
Eric Goodman

The Floor of the Sky
Pamela Carter Joern

In Reach
Pamela Carter Joern

The Plain Sense of Things
Pamela Carter Joern

Stolen Horses
Dan O'Brien

Haven's Wake
Ladette Randolph

Because a Fire Was in My Head
Lynn Stegner

Bohemian Girl
Terese Svoboda

Tin God
Terese Svoboda

Another Burning Kingdom
Robert Vivian

Lamb Bright Saviors
Robert Vivian

The Mover of Bones
Robert Vivian

Water and Abandon
Robert Vivian

The Sacred White Turkey
Frances Washburn

Skin
Kellie Wells

The Leave-Takers: A Novel
Steven Wingate

Of Fathers and Fire: A Novel
Steven Wingate

To order or obtain more information on these or other University of Nebraska Press titles, visit nebraskapress.unl.edu.

CPSIA information can be obtained
at www.ICGtesting.com
Printed in the USA
LVHW030250210121
677006LV00004B/303

9 781496 225023